STRONG SUSPICIONS

A SOPHIE STRONG MYSTERY

AMY RENSHAW

Library of Congress Control Number: 2021916487

ISBN 978-1-7373533-1-7 (paperback)

ISBN 978-1-7373-533-0-0 (ebook)

To receive special offers, bonus content, and updates on new releases,
sign up for my newsletter at amyrenshawauthor.com

1

May 1, 1912, Milwaukee, Wisconsin

Sophie inched open the elegant ballroom door and peeked inside, not wanting to draw attention away from the speakers on the stage. Mrs. Hilda Rock stood at the lectern on the left, an intimidating figure with her commanding height and grim expression. She wore her black dress like armor, as if in mourning for the days of yesteryear. Atop a tightly wound knot of red-brown hair sat a monstrous hat, massive ostrich feathers swooping across the brim and along one side.

"It would be unseemly for women to have the vote thrust upon them," she declared, her powerful voice resonating with superiority. "The gentler sex is not prepared for involvement in politics, nor is it necessary for us to become so."

At the lectern on the right, Mrs. Clara Elliot stood just as tall, but with a more refined and regal bearing. Her dove gray cashmere dress was serious, but not foreboding, conveying her inherent comfort with understated wealth. She wore a gold "Votes for Women" pin circled with purple amethysts—

the suffrage colors. Her golden hair was lightly streaked with silver, but her face was mostly unlined, though she was nearly forty. Her modest but elegant hat sported a small spray of artificial leaves and berries. The last time Sophie and her Aunt Lucy had dined with Clara, she'd asserted that no one who valued God's creatures could condone their destruction for the frivolous purpose of adorning ladies' hats. Sophie agreed. The immense creations were heavy, too. Sophie preferred to leave her own dark brown curls unadorned when she could get away with it. Tonight she wore a straw hat with an upturned brim, a sprig of purple velvet pansies nestled at one side.

"Suffrage would disrupt the sanctity and unity of the family," Mrs. Rock declared. "We would inevitably see antagonism between the sexes and discord between husband and wife."

A light patter of applause from some ladies in the audience followed this statement. Sophie took advantage of the noise to open the door wider and slip inside. She spotted Aunt Lucy in the rear row of chairs, her ample back and shoulders recognizable in a lavender shawl she'd knitted herself. She always wore it to events like tonight's debate, saying it helped her feel protected from the slings and arrows of the propaganda from the Antis, as the opponents of suffrage were called. A second wrap was draped over the empty chair next to Aunt Lucy, reserving it. Sophie scurried over and sat down. Aunt Lucy gave her arm an affectionate squeeze.

"How is it going?" Sophie whispered.

Aunt Lucy rolled her eyes. "The usual. Hilda Rock is spouting nonsense and Clara is biting her tongue. It's Clara's turn soon." She glanced at Sophie. "You're late. Is everything all right?"

"The school board meeting went long, and Mr. Vincent

cornered me as I was leaving. I had to listen politely for a while before I could extricate myself."

"Fascinating, I'm sure." Sophie grinned, then turned her attention back to the stage. She pulled her notebook and pencil out of her bag.

"Are you reporting on this for the paper?" Aunt Lucy asked.

"I'll give it a try. Mr. Barnaby probably won't want to publish it, though. You know how he feels about the cause."

Lucy clucked her tongue.

Onstage, Hilda Rock jabbed a thick, accusatory finger at the faces of those seated in the front rows.

"Make no mistake," she declared. "Suffrage is not the simple act of casting a vote upon occasion. How could women vote intelligently except by attending primaries, and nominating conventions, and using all *manner* of other means to build their knowledge of the candidates?"

Aunt Lucy huffed. "Good heavens. She makes it sound as if we're talking about Biblical knowledge."

Sophie nudged her aunt with an elbow, biting back a smile. Though Sophie was unmarried at twenty-two, Lucy made no attempt to shield her from the realities of life. Aunt Lucy had never married either, but Sophie suspected untold romantic adventures enriched her past.

"Imagine a mother canvassing for votes, supporting men other than her husband, and submitting to the low practices of politics. What will become of the children who grow up unsupervised, while Father makes speeches for his candidate, and Mother associates with the opposition?"

Some women nodded their heads as they listened. Others shook their heads—disagreeing with the speaker, Sophie hoped—and murmured to their companions.

"A woman's place is in the home. That is our sphere of influence. Removing women from the influential position we hold as the moral guides of our husbands and children and throwing us into the brawling sewage of politics can only degrade and weaken family ties."

Sophie jotted down some key phrases. Mrs. Rock tightened her lips into a sour pucker, then went on. "And what of the working women, the suffragists say, who have no man to provide for them? Well, surely they already bear more pressing cares than they can manage. Why should we add to this the weighty responsibility of educating oneself about the political realm? What do women know about national defense, banking, railroads, and a world of things with which men have wrestled for years and still not perfected?"

Hilda leaned forward with a smug smile. "The majority of refined, educated ladies do not *want* the vote. We are wiser than that. Do not be swayed by the lonely, self-absorbed man-haters who support suffrage." At this, Sophie thought she saw Clara clench her jaw.

Sophie inhaled a deep, calming breath, then forced her shoulders to relax as she exhaled. She'd heard all the Antis' arguments before, of course, but sitting still and listening to them after a long day at work was another matter.

Aunt Lucy patted her hand. "Don't worry, Clara will put her in her place."

Lucy and Clara Elliot had been inseparable throughout Sophie's youth. Clara said Lucy had pushed her into suffrage work, but Clara had a talent for oratory. She seemed to relish using her public speaking gift and her considerable wealth to promote women's rights.

Hilda Rock's voice rose as she spiraled into her grand finale. "We are already equal, albeit in different spheres from men. To participate in politics would be to imitate men and lose one's feminine powers. Imagine if women voted to legalize—" she leaned forward and stage whispered "—*family limitation methods.*" She paused for emphasis, glaring at her audience from under heavy brows. "The human race would be destroyed."

In ringing tones, she declared, "The noblest function of woman, as ordained by Our Lord, is to bear and rear children." Hilda bowed her head slightly and fell silent. There was another smattering of light applause.

Sophie clapped her hands softly in her lap and whispered to Aunt Lucy, "I'm just applauding that she's stopped speaking."

Aunt Lucy snorted a laugh. Sophie directed a wave of positive thought toward Clara and prayed that her words would persuade any doubters.

Clara looked around at the audience with a serene smile. "Thank you for coming out tonight and allowing us to share our thoughts with you. I appreciate your time and kind attention."

She stood behind her lectern with calm dignity, her shoulders straight, her voice assured. If she had notes, she didn't refer to them.

"Arguments opposed to giving women the vote are both out of date and out of place," she began. "They may have been justifiable two or three centuries ago, when women were restricted to weaving tapestries and looking after children, but not in the modern era. Today, women take an active part in public affairs. Why, our own Belle Case LaFollette is a highly regarded lawyer, writer, and orator. As she often says, suffrage is a simple matter of common sense."

Sophie saw Hilda's eyes narrow to menacing slits.

Clara continued, "Over seven million women in this country are engaged in earning their own living. To widen our sphere of influence can only enrich our nation. It is good for the wife, it is good for the mother, and it is good for the family."

Her look was sincere as she met the gaze of audience

members around the room. "Women are American citizens. We pay taxes and obey the laws, and we must have a voice in creating those laws. Currently, we are governed without our consent. The opposition to the enfranchisement of women is not an argument; it is a masculine prejudice."

Aunt Lucy nudged Sophie. "I came up with that line."

"Good one," Sophie whispered.

"My colleague, Mrs. Rock, has painted a foreboding picture indeed of equal rights for the sexes." She gestured to Hilda gracefully, as if referring to a confused child. Mrs. Rock glared back at her.

"In contrast to the destruction that Mrs. Rock foresees, allow me to suggest a more realistic view. A better understanding and a closer comradeship form between husband and wife when they have public as well as private interests in common. I know this was the case when my dear husband David was alive. For I assure you," she said, smiling and leaning forward, "though I am a suffragist, I am not a man-hater."

Members of the crowd chuckled.

"David was a judge in this city. We often talked about political issues. These conversations did not cause strife between us. Quite the contrary; in fact, they brought us closer. We were not blessed with children, but we had the good fortune to join family meals with friends. Children are educated in citizenship when they hear public affairs being discussed by Father and Mother around the family board. How can mothers teach their children to be capable citizens when they have no knowledge of politics themselves?"

Sophie jotted these lines as fast as she could, a proud smile on her lips.

"The government is not something that is isolated from feminine interests," said Clara. "Government concerns itself with matters that touch intimately our homes, happiness, and prosperity. Roads and schools clearly concern women. Women do ninety percent of the buying in our country. When the costs of cloth and sugar increase, it is women who must plan and pinch to make ends meet. And I assure you, if they won't meet, it is the women and mothers who sacrifice and go without."

Sophie noticed several women nodding their heads. How many of their own desires and dreams had been abandoned to improve the lives of children and husbands?

Clara went on with several minutes of well-reasoned arguments.

Then she said, "Each of us has a right to make the best of his or her own life. If a woman has the same power as a man to decide moral issues in the ordinary concerns of life, she must have the full right to express her judgment on the laws regulating society. Again, thank you for your time and consideration. God bless you."

Sophie and Aunt Lucy sprang to their feet with enthusiastic applause, as did many others. A resounding whistle soared out from somewhere in the crowd. Then women began to file toward the exit. A few men were among them, heads bowed as they seemed to listen with respect to their companions' opinions.

Aunt Lucy exchanged pleasantries with friends who passed them as she waited for a break in the slow-moving stream. Finally, she moved forward, pulling Sophie's hand. "Let's go out the side door and catch up with Clara."

They weaved through rows of chairs and knots of audience members who had paused to chat with neighbors. Escaping the ballroom, they hurried down a long, plushly carpeted hallway, emerging into a parlor with a welcoming fire in the hearth.

Mrs. Rock and Clara stood at the center of the parlor, a curious group of onlookers circling them.

"How dare you!" Mrs. Rock spit out.

"Oh, dear," muttered Aunt Lucy. "Here we go."

"Please, Hilda, spare me your outrage," said Clara. "Clearly the brewers in our city support your opposition efforts, since they fear that women will vote for Prohibition. Their power, as you well know, is considerable."

The restraint she had shown onstage had obviously worn thin.

"That's preposterous. I have never collaborated with the brewing industry," Mrs. Rock said.

Clara smiled sweetly and arched her eyebrows. "Call it women's intuition," she said.

The surrounding ladies tittered.

Mrs. Rock's face flushed. "You have never been womanly, Clara Elliot," she said. "Always pushing yourself forward, like a man. It's not natural."

Clara took a breath before answering. "Who made you the arbiter of what is natural and womanly, Hilda? You are certainly no role model of virtue."

"Well, you're nothing more than a-a fortune hunter. You're obviously happy to be a wealthy widow."

A pained expression flashed across Clara's face, and Sophie saw her clench her fists.

Hilda pressed her lips into a tight line. "No doubt you drove your husband to an early grave with your unnatural behavior."

Sophie sucked in a breath. The Elliots had been devoted to each other, despite their twenty-year age difference.

Clara's face became a mask of fury. "You shrew. Keep your filthy accusations to yourself."

She lunged at Hilda and gave her a shove. A startled Hilda stumbled backward, her arms windmilling awkwardly. For an awful moment, Sophie thought she might fall on her posterior, but then a companion caught her arm and she regained her balance.

Aunt Lucy rushed forward, grabbing Clara's arm before she struck the other woman again. "Don't stoop to her level, Clara. Let's go home."

Hilda Rock scowled at Clara, her face a deep scarlet.

Aunt Lucy shot Sophie a "help me" look, and Sophie moved swiftly to Clara's other side. "Is the car out front, Mrs. Elliot?" Sophie asked.

Clara was breathing fast, but Sophie saw her attempts to marshal her self-control as they walked together toward the door. Sophie glanced back at the observers who milled about in the parlor. It was a small group, but large enough to ensure that news of the ladies' spat would spread around the city, like an electric current sizzling through wire.

From the corner of her eye, Sophie saw Hilda pat her imposing hat and smooth her dress, while matronly admirers clucked over her.

"Such a vicious temper," Hilda said in a loud voice. "Not womanly at all."

Clara froze, clenching her fists again. "I'd like to throttle that—that—wretch," she muttered.

Sophie and Aunt Lucy managed to jostle their friend out the door. Clara's chauffeur, Dante Allegro, stood next to the black Cadillac. He whipped open the door as soon as she was in sight. Clara stepped onto the running board and slid into the back seat, pulling Aunt Lucy in at her side. Sophie dashed to the other side of the car and joined them. It was a new electric model, so Dante only had to push the start button instead of operating the crank. The car moved away from the curb. A clattering carriage pulled by two horses followed the automobile. What few cars there were shared the streets with the horse-drawn conveyances that many people still favored.

"Don't say a word," Clara hissed to Aunt Lucy. Lucy just patted her hand.

Sophie looked out the window and watched Milwaukee's downtown buildings slip by.

"I WANTED to take the high road," said Clara. Aunt Lucy snorted. They were seated in front of the fireplace in Clara's comfortable library after a tense car ride.

"Truly, Lucy, I tried. But that woman—" Clara closed her eyes briefly and shook her head. "It is in the past now and can't be helped. How much damage did I do?"

Aunt Lucy opened her mouth to reply, but Clara held up a finger, silencing her. "Sophie, what is your assessment?"

Sophie glanced from Clara to her aunt and back again. "There weren't many people nearby when it happened. Maybe six or eight ladies."

"But gossip…" Aunt Lucy began.

"They'll gossip, of course," Sophie said. "But only a few will be eyewitnesses. We can call any remarks they make exaggerations."

"Which they will do anyway," said Aunt Lucy. "And Hilda will chime in with her own ridiculous version."

Sophie said, "I'll write up the debate for the paper, and I'll say something like… um… you continued the discussion informally in the parlor. If I minimize the drama, it might help."

Ellen, Clara's housekeeper, entered carrying a tray with a teapot, cups, and cookies, which she placed on the coffee table. The Elliots had employed a large staff and entertained often when Mr. Elliot was alive, but now Clara preferred a quieter lifestyle. Only Ellen, Dante, and Louise, the cook, remained.

"May I get you anything else, Mrs. Elliot?" Ellen asked.

"No, that's fine, Ellen. But have you seen Agnes? I expected her to attend the debate."

"Your sister went out about a half hour before you arrived home."

Clara's brow furrowed. "All right. Thank you." She pinched the bridge of her nose.

"What has Agnes been up to lately?" Aunt Lucy reached for the teapot.

Clara looked up, her eyes troubled. "I'm not sure. My sister loves to be mysterious."

Lucy nodded and handed a cup of tea to her friend. "Well, we can be thankful she wasn't around to see your... uh... interaction with Hilda, or you'd never hear the end of it."

"That's the truth."

Sophie nibbled on one of the mouthwatering butter cookies. Clara and her older sister, Agnes Thompson, had lived together since Sophie's childhood. Sophie doubted she'd seen Agnes smile in all of those years. Clara claimed that Agnes had been a comfort when Mr. Elliot passed away, but Sophie had a hard time imagining it.

"Well, Lucy, I suppose the chips will fall where they may. What's next on our agenda?"

"We're mailing out letters about the November referendum. They will go to five hundred women around the state, and to the legislators, of course. Then we need to find more volunteers for the boat trips this summer."

Sophie's eyebrows lifted. "Boat trips? That sounds fun."

"The idea is getting a lot of attention," Clara said. "Families flock to the riverbanks in the summer. They may as well listen to a suffrage speech while they eat their pie. Of course, Agnes thinks we're foolhardy and sure to drown."

"Once we have the full slate of volunteers, we can finalize the plans," said Aunt Lucy.

"I'd better start persuading Mr. Barnaby now to let me cover it for the paper," said Sophie. "When will you go?"

"I believe in mid-July. That's when we can be sure of the best weather," said Clara.

The front door opened, then slammed shut with such force that the walls shook. Sophie jumped and spilled some tea in her lap.

Clara leaped to her feet. "Agnes, is that you?" She hurried to the library door and flung it open. But Agnes stomped past her sister without a glance in her direction.

"Agnes!"

"I can't talk now, Clara," she called over her shoulder, stomping up the stairs.

Sophie mopped up the tea on her skirt with a napkin. She hoped it wouldn't stain.

Clara turned. "I'm sorry for her rudeness. You know how she can be."

"Think nothing of it, dear," said Aunt Lucy. But her brow was knit with concern.

Clara plucked two cookies from the plate and then dropped into her chair like a rag doll. "Good heavens, what next?"

2

———

Lively music drifted through the door of Mrs. O'Day's boarding house as Sophie slid her key into the lock. She smiled, warmth washing over her and driving concern about the suffrage debate from her head. She pushed the door open, hung her cloak on a hook, and entered the parlor.

Ruth, Sophie's roommate, stood near the fireplace, eyes closed, her bow flying across the strings of her violin. Oliver, Ruth's fiancé, tapped the foot of one lanky leg in time to the music and smiled fondly. Edna and Margaret, who shared the room next to Sophie and Ruth's, laughed as they danced in a reckless circle around the braided rug. Mrs. O'Day sat in her customary wingback chair and clapped her plump hands to the rhythm, her knitting forgotten in her lap. Sophie eased into the chair next to Oliver, sat back, and let the music carry her away.

Ruth played "The Grizzly Bear" and "Apple Jack Rag" before the dancers collapsed with exhausted exclamations. Glancing at Oliver affectionately, Ruth ended her medley with "Let Me Call You Sweetheart."

Sophie joined in the applause, and Ruth bowed from the

waist with a professional air. She placed her treasured instrument carefully in the case at her feet and snapped the lid shut.

"Well, if that doesn't deserve some refreshment, I don't know what does," Mrs. O'Day said, getting up. "I'll be back in a wink."

Ruth joined Oliver, and as he reached over to clasp her hand, she gave him a sweet smile. Then she leaned forward and said, "You're late getting back, Sophie. Is everything all right at the paper?"

"Just fine," she said. "I went back to Mrs. Elliot's after the debate. I'll tell you all about it later." She didn't want to reveal the evening's events to the entire party, since they didn't put Clara or the suffragists in the best light.

Wondering about the time, Sophie's gaze instinctively went to the broken ornate wooden clock on the mantel, its hands fixed at ten-ten. It had been carved by Mrs. O'Day's late husband, and she trusted it to no one else for repair. Sophie then glanced at the wristwatch Aunt Lucy had given her for graduation. She sighed with relief that it was just past eight; she had an early morning start.

"We got some good news today," said Ruth. "Oliver was selected to be Dr. Horace's assistant next fall. It will be wonderful for his career."

"It *could* be helpful, if I can keep up with him and not make any colossal blunders," Oliver said. "And it will be a tremendous amount of work."

"As if you've ever let down a professor," Ruth said. "You'll be marvelous."

They were both dedicated medical students, their ambition fueling long nights spent over textbooks that Sophie didn't comprehend. As the only woman in her class at Milwaukee Medical College, Ruth had to endure condescending smirks from students and professors alike, even though her grades eclipsed those of her peers.

Mrs. O'Day returned carrying a tray with a pitcher of apple cider and her well-loved shortbread. She set it on the coffee table, and Margaret poured for everyone. Sophie took a long drink of the tangy beverage. She sent up a silent prayer of thanks that she'd found these friends. She was still getting to know Margaret and Edna, who had moved in last fall, but they seemed amiable. Ruth had immediately become a fast friend when they'd met at the boarding house two years earlier.

Sophie recalled the desperation of that summer day after graduation, when she had dragged herself up the now-familiar steps of the house. She'd visited at least twelve boarding houses that day, only to find that the rooms were either already rented or run-down and filthy. She'd begun to wonder if a decent room was too expensive, and she'd be forced to head back to Chippewa Falls to live with her father instead of launching her career in Milwaukee. Aunt Lucy had offered to let Sophie continue living with her, but Sophie felt determined to be on her own. Ruth had been exiting the house after viewing their room and deciding she couldn't afford the rent, and she had literally collided with Sophie in the doorway. In the apologies and laughter that followed, they both realized they were in need of lodging and decided on impulse to throw in their lot together.

Sophie heard the light tap of footsteps on the stairs, and the scent of gardenia perfume wafted toward them. Ruth grimaced at Sophie, who rolled her eyes in response. With the aplomb of a princess, Vivian Bell descended the stairs, her pale fingers trailing lightly along the banister. She wore a diaphanous dress of sky blue, with a neckline that swooped just shy of indecency. Her hat sported a wide, upturned brim with white and blue stripes, an eye-catching bow at one side.

Sophie tamped down a surge of envy. Vivian often showed off her fashionable hats and accessories, presumably purchased with her wages from the millinery department at Gimbels.

When she reached the ground floor, Vivian paused and looked around with wide eyes.

"Why hello, ladies," she drawled. "And Mr. Rosenthal. What are the bluestockings up to this evening? A musical gathering, is it?"

"Hello, Vivian," said Ruth. Sophie gave Vivian a half-hearted nod as she sipped her cider.

Vivian drifted toward the sideboard table near the stairs and flipped through the mail that Mrs. O'Day had piled on a tray.

She picked up a small envelope. "Sophie, is this a love letter for you?" She eyed Sophie under fluttering lashes. "Oh, wait—it's for me. My mistake. Well, you don't have time for beaux with your busy *career*, do you?"

She whisked the envelope into her beaded purse. Vivian made no secret of the fact that her goal was to snag a wealthy husband as soon as possible, at which point she would gladly end her employment.

"I'm very happy with my career, thank you, Vivian," Sophie said.

"Oh, of *course* you are."

The door knocker sounded, and Vivian opened the door to greet her escort, a dashing young man in an expensive-looking suit. They murmured to each other, then he held her cloak as she slipped her arms into the sleeves, his hands resting for just a moment on her shoulders. She smiled up at him coyly, then fluttered her fingers at the group in the parlor.

"Well, ta-ta, everyone!" She didn't wait around to hear if anyone answered.

They didn't.

Edna narrowed her eyes at the closed door. "That girl is too full of herself. I'd like to take her down a peg or two."

"Oh, Vivian puts on airs, but she's just a lost lamb," Mrs. O'Day clucked, picking up her knitting.

Sophie disagreed with this assessment, but Mrs. O'Day seemed incapable of criticizing anyone, least of all the young ladies who shared her home.

Oliver drained his cup and stood. "Well, Ruth, I've got that exam tomorrow morning, and if I leave now, I can squeeze in some more studying." He picked up his hat from the side table and plopped it atop his wiry black curls.

"I'll walk you out," said Ruth. "Then I must put my nose to the grindstone as well."

Oliver tipped his hat. "Thank you for the sustenance, Mrs. O'Day. Delicious as always. Good evening, ladies."

Ruth took his empty cup and placed it with her own on the tray, then led him to the door. There, she ducked out to the porch—for a quiet word and a kiss, Sophie suspected. Ruth had been engaged to Oliver for as long as Sophie had known her. She wore a simple gold ring with a small sapphire to signify their intention. Both had resolved to finish medical school before they wed, planning to open their own practice one day and work side by side into their dotage.

Ruth returned and collected her violin case. "I'm going up, Sophie. Good night, everyone."

"I'll come with you," said Sophie. "I'm bushed."

She trailed Ruth up the stairs, which were illuminated by an oil-powered sconce at the top landing. To the right of their bedroom door, Ruth had hung a small mezuzah containing a tiny piece of parchment with holy words from the Torah. Ruth tapped the symbol with her finger before entering. Sophie followed Ruth's lead, feeling a sense of security in performing the act, even though she knew little about Ruth's faith.

Their room was small but inviting, both twin beds topped with homemade quilts in shades of blue and green, stitched by Ruth's *bubbe*. They shared the battered wooden desk and bureau. In the corner next to Ruth's bed, two milk crates served as cases for her huge medical books. An oil lamp sat on a narrow table between the beds. Mrs. O'Day had installed electric lighting in the downstairs parlor, but hadn't bothered with it on the second floor, since oil lamps worked just as easily. Ruth struck a match and held it to the wick, then replaced the glass chimney on the lamp as the room filled with warm, golden light.

Sophie opened the bureau drawer and pulled out the cotton nightdress and the wool socks she wore to bed. Even in May, the nights got chilly. They had a small oil heater, but to conserve fuel, they left it unlit whenever they could. Sophie exchanged her thin stockings for the thick socks, then unpinned her unruly mahogany curls and let them fall to her shoulders. Looking in the mirror, which was foggy with age, she tugged a wood-handled hairbrush through the locks, falling far short of the hundred strokes Vivian claimed were essential before bed. Then she braided her hair loosely and tied the end with a scrap of frayed ribbon. Ruth was already absorbed in her studying, so Sophie picked up her toiletries and went down the hall to the bathroom, bringing her stockings and handkerchief to wash out in the sink.

In the bathroom, she dabbed some soap on her skirt where she'd spilled the tea, pleased that it was almost invisible. After washing her face and brushing her teeth, she returned to the room and draped the damp stockings and handkerchief over the mirror to dry. She opened the closet door and stood behind it for privacy as she shrugged out of her jacket, skirt, and shirtwaist, unbuttoned her corset, and pulled on her nightdress. The lace trim on her cuff flapped against her palm where it had torn away. She kept meaning to stitch it, but there was never a moment empty enough that sewing seemed the best way to fill it. After hanging her clothes in the closet, she padded over to bed, and covered a yawn with the back of her hand. She wound the alarm clock, checked that it was set for six, and snuggled beneath the covers.

"Good night, Ruthie. Don't stay up too late."

"Good night, *zeeskeit*," Ruth replied.

Sophie wasn't sure of the exact translation of the Yiddish term, but the affection in Ruth's voice conveyed its gentle meaning.

She closed her eyes and soon nodded off to sleep.

WHEN SOPHIE WOKE the next morning, she breathed in deeply and let her mind roam over the day ahead. Before she could sink back into sleep, she thrust her right leg out into the crisp air and threw off her quilt. Ruth had already gone downstairs, silent as a breeze, leaving her bed neatly made.

Sophie plucked fresh bloomers and stockings out of the bureau, then hurriedly dressed. She pulled her curls into a knot at her nape. Lastly, she put on her wristwatch and tucked her notebook and pencils into her bag, put a clean handkerchief in her pocket, stepped into her sturdy-heeled black shoes, and went out the door, tapping Ruth's mezuzah as she left.

In the kitchen, Mrs. O'Day was busy scrambling eggs, humming a tune from the night before. As she'd expected, Ruth was at the table, engrossed in a forbidding anatomy textbook. Sophie picked up a cup and poured some coffee from the pot warming on a corner of the stove. She sat down opposite her roommate, spilling a bit of coffee when she noticed the book was open to a ghastly drawing of a human form, the flesh missing to reveal bones, muscles, and other details that didn't bear thinking about. Sophie plucked a knitted napkin from the basket on the table and mopped up the spill. Not wanting to interrupt her friend's train of thought, she sipped and waited.

When Ruth looked up, her eyes shone with customary brightness, despite the early hour.

Sophie nodded solemnly. "Good morning, Dr. Lewenberg."

"What dreams may come," quoted Ruth. "I hope it's not seamstress Lewenberg or schoolteacher Lewenberg by this time next year."

Her modesty was laced with anxiety, but Sophie knew better than to be concerned about her friend.

"Indeed," she said. "I heard that the medical college is eager to dismiss the 'A' students without graduating them, so as not to make current physicians feel inferior."

Ruth laughed. Mrs. O'Day placed plates of eggs and evenly browned toast in front of them. "Are we still going to the eleven o'clock matinee at the Butterfly on Sunday?" Sophie asked, scooping up some eggs. Their cherished weekend pastime was to take in a show at the marvelous Butterfly Theater on Wisconsin Avenue, named after its dramatic façade shaped with thousands of light bulbs.

"I'll try, if I can squeeze in enough studying," Ruth hedged.

"None of that now," said Sophie. "That was last week's excuse. We owe it to the hardworking musicians and actors to support their art."

Ruth's expression softened. "You're right," she said. "I'll go."

"That's the spirit."

They reminisced about some of their favorite perfor-mances and decided the best had been the great Italian baritone they'd heard last summer. Too soon, Sophie's watch read seven-thirty, so she swigged the rest of her coffee with an undignified gulp and grabbed a final remnant of toast. She put her empty plate in the sink.

"I'm off to keep our fair metropolis stocked with soup recipes and sewing tips," she said.

Mrs. O'Day looked up from the stove with a smile. "You have a lovely day, and don't let those boys give you any trouble. We'll be out at the polls before you know it."

"I have a good feeling about the November referendum," Sophie said. Recalling the upcoming bid for women's suffrage in Wisconsin brought back the debate of the night before. Sophie began turning around phrases for her article in her head.

Outside, the sunshine and fresh air invigorated her as she started for the *Herald* office. She felt a twinge of guilt at her light heart, at a time when so many mourned loved ones lost on the *Titanic* just a few weeks ago. Sophie had read the accounts that poured into the office that day with a mixture of horror, sadness, outrage, and envy of the journalists who covered the disaster. The Milwaukee survivors had become local celebrities, and Sophie had devoured their stories—all written by men, of course. One day, she'd write breaking news stories that rivaled anything her male colleagues could manage. The enticing vision of a front-page story with her byline propelled her the ten blocks to the *Herald* building.

3

At her desk in the corner of the newsroom, Sophie fed a pristine sheet of white paper into her Remington type-writer. She flipped notebook pages, then mused about how to summarize Mrs. Rock's ridiculous arguments as she drummed her fingertips on the keys. And how to minimize the conflict that had capped off the evening? She began to type, the scene flickering in her mind's eye like a motion picture.

Now and then another reporter would stride past her desk, giving her a nod if he bothered to glance her way. In the year Sophie had been at the *Herald*, she'd grown accustomed to being the only woman in the room. Most of the men ignored her, and none took her seriously. They seemed to think her career was a hobby to fill the time until she could capture a husband. But she assumed they considered that outcome improbable, given her unfeminine pursuits. Mr. Barnaby, the city editor, gave the impression that her position was a necessary evil, to satisfy the whims of the paper's female readership.

"Strong!" P.J. Barnaby bellowed.

Sophie jumped up in mid-sentence and grabbed her notebook, her stomach tightening as she walked to his office. She stepped past him, and he banged the door closed, then dropped into his weathered desk chair and frowned at her over the tops of smudged eyeglasses.

Sophie sat down and cleared her throat. "Is everything all right, Mr. Barnaby?"

"Heck no, Strong. The world is going to Hades in a handbasket. But that's nothing new."

Sophie's stomach unclenched slightly.

Mr. Barnaby rummaged through the mounds of papers on his desk.

"These brewery families. It's not enough to just make their beer, sell it, and go home. They have to create a spectacle." He extracted a thick, satiny card from the morass and held it out to her. "We've been summoned by Mrs. Thelma Wolff to pay homage to her annual Spring Gala on Saturday night. We cover it every year, and every year she complains. This time she insists we get the woman's angle."

Sophie sensed Mrs. Wolff's commanding presence in the invitation's weight alone, elegantly embossed with sweeping gold letters. She looked up. "It will be at..."

"Wolff Mansion. *Castle* is a better word for that place."

The mansion was as legendary as its occupants, with over thirty rooms, a dozen bathrooms, and sprawling grounds. Sophie had walked past it, but she never dreamed she'd get to step over the threshold. Her stomach dropped in a rush of nerves.

"Go over on Friday to take a gander at the wonders she has planned. On Saturday, blend in with the bigwigs. Keep Mrs. Wolff happy, and write it up like she tells you to."

She nodded. "I'll do my best."

"Do better than that. Delight her. Make her fall in love with our paper. Now beat it."

"Thank you, Mr. Barnaby."

Despite the caveats, Sophie felt a surge of anticipation. This could be a huge opportunity. If Mrs. Wolff liked her work, Sophie might be invited to more events—and eventually she'd discover some *actual* news.

She dropped the invitation on her desk, then went to the office library and tugged open a heavy drawer marked "W." Flipping back to "Wolff," she found thick files bulging with clippings, organized by subject. Every week brought a new story about the family, their brewery, their incredible amusement park, or one of their many other ventures.

Sophie discovered a stack of articles about the Spring Gala and skimmed a few. She saw why Thelma Wolff considered them unsatisfactory. They were dry and businesslike, with none of the flowery descriptions of gowns, décor, and entertainment that Sophie gritted her teeth and wrote about on the ladies' page. Covering the gala wasn't hard news, like a labor strike or a house fire, but it could lead to more exciting assignments. She imagined herself entering Wolff Mansion for the event.

A hot flush of panic swept through her. What could she possibly wear? Did she dare risk Vivian's mockery by asking for advice, or to borrow a dress? The idea made her cringe. Lost in thought, she turned to go and smacked into Benjamin Turner.

"Oh!"

"Whoa, good morning, Miss Strong," he said, grasping her forearm with a supercilious chuckle.

She blushed as she pulled her arm away from his. "Please excuse me, Mr. Turner."

His dark eyes glinted with amusement as he nodded at the file in her hand. "It's best to stay alert, even when visions of ball gowns are dancing in your head."

"Just doing some research," she said. "For an assignment."

"I have a book on interviewing that I can loan you, if you like. They probably didn't teach you that at finishing school."

"You know very well I went to—" She caught his sardonic grin. "Oh, never mind." She pushed past him and headed for the exit.

"Watch that temper, Miss Strong. It's not professional."

"Just carry on with your research, Mr. Turner. Come to me if you need any help with the big words."

She congratulated herself as she returned to her desk. She often didn't think of a snappy comeback for Benjamin Turner until hours after the exchange.

ON FRIDAY AFTERNOON, Sophie left the *Herald* office and took a streetcar up Grand Avenue to Wolff Mansion. She walked along the steep drive, taking in the home's opulence while fighting off flutters of nervousness. She'd been instructed to use the side entrance, but she eyed the elaborately carved front door and considered ringing the bell—would Mrs. Wolff ever know? Surely a servant would answer. But Mr. Barnaby would be furious if she angered Mrs. Wolff before writing a word. She sighed and followed the path around the house. A short stairway led to a plain wooden door at the lower level, and she knocked.

"Come in!" shouted a female voice. "I don't have time to be answering doors."

Sophie entered and found herself enveloped in the delectable scents of cinnamon, sugar, and vanilla. A woman turned from the giant stove, holding a large tray of tarts in two oven-mitted hands. She set it on the huge wooden work-table, then went back to the oven and brought out another tray. Nearby, younger women kneaded dough and mixed batter with practiced strokes while eyeing Sophie with curiosity. Sophie's mouth watered, even though she'd eaten an egg salad sandwich at lunch.

"And who might you be?" asked the cook. "I don't give free samples, if that's what you're thinking." Her tone was gruff, but her eyes sparkled.

Sophie smiled. "It smells delicious."

"Well, that kind of flattery will get you a cookie, but nothing more." She reached into a jar and pulled out a pink-frosted sugar cookie.

"Thank you." Sophie took a bite, marveling as it melted into chewy goodness. "I'm amazed at what some women can accomplish in the kitchen, while the rest of us are a hazard to humanity."

"Well, my mother taught me, and her mother taught her. But you're not here for a baking lesson, I'm sure."

"I'm Sophie Strong, from the *Milwaukee Herald*," she said. "I'm here to see Mrs. Wolff about the party tomorrow night."

Another woman bustled in, wearing a plain black dress, keys rattling on the chatelaine at her waist.

"It's a *gala*," she corrected. "You don't want to be calling it a party. I'm Mrs. Harding, the housekeeper. I'll take you up."

Without waiting for a response, she strode out of the kitchen.

Gobbling the last bite, Sophie hurried after her up the stairs. They emerged into a dining chamber with a huge, gleaming table, surrounded by at least two dozen richly upholstered chairs. Mrs. Harding swept through the room, across the tall-ceilinged foyer, and into a sumptuously furnished parlor that glowed in ivory, rose, and gold. The housekeeper indicated a chair.

"Wait here," she said. "I'll have a maid fetch Mrs. Wolff."

Assuming that locating the lady of the house could take some time, Sophie walked around the perimeter of the room, gazing at the enormous windows, vases of white and pink roses, and a gleaming grand piano. A life-sized oil painting above the fireplace showed a tall, well-built man with salt and pepper hair standing behind a delicately beautiful woman who sat perfectly straight, her chin tilted, with just a hint of a smug smile. Sophie recognized Ruben and Thelma Wolff from photos and sketches in the paper.

She heard delicate but rapid footsteps crossing the foyer and quickly took a seat. Thelma Wolff glided in amid a cloud of sandalwood fragrance.

"Miss Strong, thank you for coming," she said graciously, as if she'd given Sophie a choice.

Sophie stood up and resisted the urge to curtsy. "How do you do, Mrs. Wolff?" She held out her hand to shake, but Mrs. Wolff seemed not to notice and lowered herself gracefully into a chair opposite Sophie's. Sophie sat again, unsure what to do with her hands.

"I am very well and *very* busy," Mrs. Wolff said. "There is so much to do, and I must oversee every detail. I decided to take the time to orient you today, though. Everyone will be costumed tomorrow night, of course."

"Co-costumed," said Sophie, trying not to make it sound like a question. Somehow she'd missed that on the invitation.

"You will of course wear a costume, so you don't stand out among the guests. I want the event covered in the paper, but I don't want my friends to feel they're being *spied* upon." She rose to her feet. "Come along, I'll show you the ballroom."

Sophie followed, her mind reeling as she wondered where in the world she might locate a costume that would enable her to blend in with millionaires.

The ballroom buzzed with maids dusting furniture and polishing glass panes set in a long row of French doors that led out to a large patio. Mrs. Wolff described her plans for an ornate decorating scheme meant to evoke the gardens at the Palace of Versailles, though she intended to dress as Queen Elizabeth of England.

"The musicians will perform there," she said, pointing to a raised platform covered with a Persian carpet. She bustled over to a grand piano even larger than the one in the parlor and picked up a sheaf of papers. "This is a list of some of the more well-known pieces they will play, in case you don't recognize them when you hear them."

The comment was meant as an offhand insult, but since Sophie's musical education was sparse, she didn't take offense.

Mrs. Wolff handed her a detailed menu and a long guest list. "You will be familiar with many of the names, I am sure," said Mrs. Wolff. Sophie took the hint that if she wasn't, she should do some research. Mrs. Wolff explained that the evening would begin at seven o'clock, with music provided by a six-piece band, several hours of dancing, and a light supper at eleven.

"I believe that is all you will need," said Mrs. Wolff. "Please be prompt tomorrow night, and be observant, without being intrusive."

"Thelma!" a masculine voice bellowed down the hall.

Mrs. Wolff gave a sharp intake of breath and closed her eyes for a moment. Then she composed her mouth into a placid smile and turned toward the intimidating form of Mr. Ruben Wolff, who now filled the doorway. His hair was swept back with glistening pomade, and he wore a neatly trimmed mustache. The expertly tailored suit conformed to every bodily plane and radiated wealth.

Mrs. Wolff said smoothly, "My dear, this is Miss Strong

from the *Milwaukee Herald*. She will be writing about the Spring Gala."

He looked at her like he'd just noticed Sophie for the first time. "Miss Strong, it's a pleasure to meet you," he said, giving her a polite nod. Then he turned back to his wife. "Davis tells me our costumes have changed again for tomorrow night, but I told him he must be mistaken."

"Yes, I changed them. I had no choice. Captain and Mrs. Pabst are coming as Napoleon and Josephine."

"And what did you decide on, without the benefit of my opinion?"

"Queen Elizabeth and William Cecil. They were the simplest solution, since of course we want to be royalty. I assumed you would have no objection."

Mr. Wolff's shoulders relaxed. Sophie wondered what he had worried his wife might say.

Mrs. Wolff turned to Sophie. "This is the one time I approve of gossiping maids—they're helpful in avoiding duplicate costume disasters. Now you have four of the costumes you'll want to be aware of tomorrow night. I'll have a maid show you out."

"No need for that. I'm going out myself." Mr. Wolff swept one arm out to guide Sophie through the doorway. "Right this way, Miss Strong."

"Thank you for your time, Mrs. Wolff," Sophie said.

Mrs. Wolff nodded regally; Sophie thought she would easily fill Queen Bess's shoes.

As she and Mr. Wolff progressed down the long front hallway, Sophie racked her brain for an interesting question to ask.

"Are you looking forward to the Spring Gala, sir?" was all she could manage.

Mr. Wolff grunted. "Oh, you know, we have to do these

things now and then. It's wise to remind everyone we're alive and kicking over here."

"I expect many of your business associates will attend."

"Yes, they'll all be here. Suppliers, competitors, customers, hangers-on. Got a few deals in the works that we might hash out over cigars." He looked thoughtful. "It should be an interesting evening."

Mr. Wolff paused at the hall table to pick up a few envelopes. He shuffled through them and tossed them back.

He gestured to a pair of antique beer steins standing guard nearby. "Those were my grandfather's, you know. My father brought them from Germany all those years ago. Amazing he managed not to break them on the ocean voyage."

"Quite impressive," said Sophie. She cleared her throat. "Have you had any unionizing at your brewery?" she asked, grateful she'd thought of a timely question. Workers around the country formed unions in every industry, pressuring employers for safe conditions, reasonable hours, and fair wages.

"Now that's a big subject for a young lady," he said.

They came to a stop at the front door. The butler handed Mr. Wolff his hat and held his coat while the great man shrugged it on. Then he opened the door. A driver waited expectantly next to a shining black Rolls Royce.

Mr. Wolff turned to Sophie and tapped his hat brim. "We have no trouble of any kind, Miss Strong. Least of all with unions," he said. "Good day to you."

He walked away and got into the car before she could ask anything more.

Sophie made her way back to the street. As the auto roared past, and she glimpsed Mr. Wolff in the backseat, reading a newspaper. She wondered which one it was. Then she headed for the office, where she could jot down the details to remember for her story. Her nerves jangled. She desperately wanted the approval of both Thelma Wolff and Mr. Barnaby.

By the time Sophie remembered her dilemma—what costume to wear—The *Herald* building was in her sight. There was nothing in her closet that she could transform into something suitable. She had no idea where to start, or even what costume might be appropriate for her role. Distracted, she stepped into the street, but a blaring horn jerked her to attention and cut through her reverie. A Model T swerved around her.

Her heart pounding, Sophie realized there was an obvious answer to her problem. She turned the corner and headed down Jefferson Street toward the only person who could help her—and would delight in doing so.

CLARA ELLIOT'S bedroom was a soothing refuge decorated in soft shades of blue. A four-poster bed topped with luxurious azure bedding stood at the center.

"Thank you so much for helping me, Mrs. Elliot," Sophie said.

"It's my pleasure, my dear." Clara whisked open a door and beckoned Sophie to enter.

The outsized dressing room held two long rows of gowns in every conceivable fabric and style, wreathed in the aromas of lavender and cedar. Sophie took in the layers of silk, taffeta, velvet, and cashmere in shades that ranged from deepest indigo to palest gold. Brass hangers were adorned with roses just as elegant as the clothes they held. Sophie gazed with wide eyes, feeling like a peasant in her serviceable blue cotton and sturdy shoes.

"It's shameful, really," said Clara. "The money that's gone

into this wardrobe could feed an orphanage for a year. But I try to make amends. For now, we may as well use it. Let's see... the costume pieces are at the back."

She pushed aside a series of hanging gowns, then showed Sophie a skirt of midnight blue tulle that glittered with silver beads sewn in star patterns.

"I was starlight in this one. That was a night to remember." She moved it along. "A bit too dramatic for you this time. Hmmm. Mary, Queen of Scots? Too serious. The Queen of Hearts? What was I thinking? Oh, here we are. This is perfect."

She pulled out a gown of pale-green silk with a taffeta overskirt embroidered with tiny pink and yellow flowers. The bodice was a deeper green, its modest neckline trimmed in gold.

"Springtime," Clara announced. "Fresh, sweet, not too flamboyant. You can wear flowers in your hair, and there's a matching green silk mask."

"Oh, Mrs. Elliot, it's beautiful. But maybe there's something simpler. I'd be afraid to ruin it."

"Oh, pish!" Clara insisted. "You may as well enjoy it." She held the shimmering skirt out as she eyed Sophie. "Let's see... I'm taller than you, but Ellen can do a few quick alterations."

"But what if you want to wear it later?"

"Heavens, I won't be dressing as springtime again," said Clara. "But you're just the right age. Try it on, and I'll ring for Ellen."

Sophie was still struggling with the tiny buttons at her back when Ellen breezed in with a sewing basket. She did up the buttons, then appraised Sophie's curves. She pulled at fabric here, stabbed in some pins there, and then pronounced, "That will do nicely."

Sophie barely recognized her reflection in the tall, oval

mirror. A few unruly dark curls had escaped their knot and were framing her face. The smooth fabric caressed her limbs and draped in gentle waves at her neck. Ellen held the pinned sections away from Sophie's skin as she shimmied out of the gown. Then Ellen bustled out of the room. Sophie felt like Cinderella after midnight as she pulled on her regular clothes.

She found Clara by the window, gazing fondly at a framed photograph. "This was a ball we hosted here. Those were good times."

Sophie smiled at the image of a younger Clara sparkling on the arm of her husband, who gazed down at her lovingly.

Clara put down the photo and clapped her hands together. "Ellen is an absolute genius with her needle and thread. Come back tomorrow afternoon and we'll get you fixed up. Then Dante can drive you over to the Wolffs'."

"You're like a fairy godmother," Sophie said. "I'll return the dress on Sunday morning."

"Oh, there's no hurry," said Clara.

"I don't trust myself to keep it any longer than that."

Clara smiled. "Well, if you insist, maybe you could stop by the suffrage office on your way and pick up the correspondence I left on my desk. You'll save me a trip."

"I'll be happy to," said Sophie.

"I have a pair of pearl earrings that will look lovely with that outfit. Come with me and I'll show you."

Clara sailed out of the dressing room and Sophie followed, smiling with delicious anticipation at the evening to come.

4

———————

The lustrous silk and taffeta skirt swished around her legs as Sophie mounted the steps to the front door of Wolff Mansion. She presented her invitation to the tight-lipped butler. He glanced down his long nose at it, flicked his eyes to her, then gave a solemn nod.

After depositing Mrs. Elliot's shimmering wrap with a maid, Sophie followed the lilting sounds of stringed instruments and the line of guests drifting toward the ballroom. Just beyond an arch of greenery and flowers that wreathed the doorway stood Thelma Wolff, resplendent as Queen Elizabeth, nodding decorously at each guest she greeted. Her braided red-gold wig was topped with a jeweled crown. She wore a white silk gown embroidered with golden blooms, a gem glinting at each center. A frill of delicate lace adorned her neckline, and the same lace edged her handkerchief and fan. Though a pearl-studded mask covered her face, Thelma was a beauty, even at an age that Sophie guessed was around forty.

Thelma had said Mr. Wolff would dress as the queen's trusted advisor William Cecil, but the man at her side wore

34

the long blue coat, white breeches, and white waistcoat of a Revolutionary War soldier. Sophie glanced around for Mr. Wolff. As she drew closer, she recognized the sharp, dark eyes and angled jawline of Ruben Wolff behind a blue satin mask. His tricorn hat sat atop a brown wig gathered in a queue at the base of his neck. Sophie wondered what had caused his change of costume. She reached the front of the line and met the cool blue eyes of Mrs. Wolff.

"Good evening, Miss Strong," Thelma said. "As you can see, Mr. Wolff has circumvented my carefully planned presentation, in favor of playing soldier. One of *many* in attendance."

Ruben smiled and shrugged. "I didn't care to be the queen's lackey. And look at this fine weapon." He pulled a pistol from a holster at his waist.

Sophie's eyes widened as he waved the barrel casually in her direction; then she realized it was only realistically painted wood.

"Ruben, put that away before you frighten the guests."

Thelma's eyes flicked past Sophie to the next couple in line. Sophie did her best to emulate the curtsy she'd seen from other women, but she lost her balance and staggered clumsily, catching herself just in time to avoid tumbling to the floor. As she shook hands with Mr. Wolff, she thought she saw charitable good humor in his smile.

In the ballroom, Sophie encountered a dazzling feast of sound and color. Enormous bouquets of roses poured out of waist-high vases, alternating in white and crimson. Small tables around the edges of the room held silver candlesticks, the flickering light bathing the room in an ethereal glow. Couples glided across the floor in time to the music, most with costumes from vastly different worlds, giving the pairs a dreamlike quality. There was Cleopatra with Robin Hood; a pirate with Marie Antoinette; Mephistopheles with an innocent-looking shepherdess. Scents of cologne and powder mixed with the floral bouquet and a faint tinge of perspiration.

Sophie wondered what thoughts swam behind the elegantly masked eyes. If she could find fresh words to describe the scene and its wealthy participants, she might win Thelma Wolff's approval, and perhaps an entrée into other events. Unfortunately, the term most prominent in her mind was *ostentatious*. It irritated her to witness two hundred guests in extravagant costumes, dripping with jewels. Much of the city's population struggled to fill their plates each day, even when employed by the magnates in attendance tonight.

She shook her head, trying to dislodge the thought. Aunt Lucy always urged putting oneself in others' shoes, so she would attempt to set her opinions aside and take on the mindset of an heiress.

She noticed a cluster of older ladies seated at the end of the room, farthest from the musicians, their costumes faded and tired, as if they'd been pulled from an attic after years of neglect. There she could be inconspicuous while she got her bearings. Sophie took a deep breath and wove her way through the guests crowded at the sides of the dance floor. The music paused for a moment, and the laughter, conversation, and the tinkling of glasses seemed unusually loud. Then the music resumed, and the party sounds receded once more.

A Spanish toreador blocked Sophie's path suddenly, his red velvet jacket bedecked with swirls of golden thread and tiny beads. He wore a golden sash around his waist, black breeches trimmed in gold, and a magnificent red cape. A black velvet hat rested on jet-black hair that Sophie suspected was a wig, and a matching mask revealed only dancing brown eyes. He bowed at the waist, then held out an expectant hand in Sophie's direction.

She smiled and shook her head. "Thank you, sir, I'm flattered, but I'm not—"

Before she could finish the sentence, he pulled her toward him and spun onto the dancefloor. He led with a strong, athletic finesse, and as they melted into the crowd of dancers, she followed instinctively. Not for the first time, she was grateful for the dance lessons Aunt Lucy had forced on her as a teenager. She considered twisting out of the Spaniard's grasp and stalking off, but that seemed indecorous. Besides, casually mentioning the experience in conversation would be a fun way to make Vivian jealous some evening at the boarding house.

Still, the Spaniard appeared so pleased with himself she felt obliged to protest.

"Really, sir, that was most ungentlemanly."

His lips twisted into a wry smile. "You looked so serious I decided you needed a bit of fun. Just enjoy the dance." His voice had an accent she couldn't place. Was it part of his act?

She swallowed, feeling warmth in her stomach as his muscular shoulder shifted under her left hand.

"It is customary to be granted permission before whisking a woman onto the dance floor," she said.

He just laughed softly. She fixed her gaze on the gold buttons adorning his chest. He was an excellent dancer, and she found herself relaxing and letting the music wash over her. She imagined being a guest at the party instead of a reporter, invited for an evening of leisure and flirtation. She glanced up and caught him watching her intently.

He leaned closer and whispered in her ear, "See, it's not so terrible."

She shivered at the tickle of his breath on her neck.

For the next few minutes, her feet moved in effortless rhythm. Then the music ended, and she stood at the older ladies' chairs she had been heading for before she was swept away. She slipped into one of the chairs at the rear and met his eyes, struggling to keep a smile from her lips. The mysterious Spaniard winked mischievously, bowed again, then turned and sauntered off, his cape swinging behind him. Her eyes followed of their own accord.

As the next dance began, Sophie discreetly pulled a tiny notepad and pencil from her bag and rested it in her lap among the folds of pale-green fabric. She surreptitiously jotted her thoughts. If the guests saw her taking notes, they would be on their guard, and she wanted to capture the authentic atmosphere. Graceful young ladies in breathtaking concoctions of silk, beads, and lace seemed to float across the floor in a haze of smug privilege.

After watching several dances, Sophie stood and edged her way between groups of guests. Recalling her earlier perusal of the guest list, she managed to spot the mayor, a congressman, and the owner of a posh hotel, despite their costumes. Servants circulated with silver trays bearing small plates of delicacies, and Sophie's mouth watered. She'd missed Mrs. O'Day's dinner. She longed to grab a plate and head outside to eat in the cool breeze, but she didn't dare.

"Wolff Park rakes in a pretty penny, don't you doubt it," she heard a gentleman proclaim. He was dressed as a knight, with a sword at his hip, but his generous belly and beefy face suggested he wouldn't make a good showing in battle.

"He's giving away popcorn by the bushel, and the hordes can get into the place for only a nickel," said the man next to him, who wore a nobleman's costume. "Not to mention what he paid for all those rides."

The other man chuckled. "It's genius. He's got hundreds of customers thronging the place every weekend, all of them seeing his name everywhere, and there's nothing to drink but his own products. I'll wager he's been in the black for the last five years."

"Well, that's a good point. He's building some new attraction, too."

"Always got irons in the fire, our Ruben does. And if this Prohibition nonsense ever comes to pass, he's got a guaranteed income and thousands of loyal customers. Not as much to be made in lemonade as in beer, but it's better than nothing."

"As long as we keep the ladies away from the polls, we're safe from Prohibition," the other man said. "No man is going to vote against his right to have a drink now and then."

"Too true. My daughter started rumbling about suffrage a while ago. Took back her dress allowance and locked her in her room for a few days, and that was the last I heard of it."

His friend chuckled. "By the by, have you seen Ruben? I want to get his opinion about the latest union kerfuffle at our shop, before we're all too soused to talk sensibly."

The other man shook his head as he pulled out a pocket watch. "It's after ten, so you'd best shake a leg," he said. "The liquor is flowing freely."

The men nodded amiably and parted ways.

Unions and the threat of Prohibition were common topics in the paper, though Sophie rarely got to include them on the women's page. It would be difficult to wedge business affairs into her article about the Spring Gala, but she wanted to stay alert for leads. She'd discover a front-page story eventually that would render her name worthy of mention as its author.

Sophie gazed around the dance floor, spotting the mysterious Spaniard as he glided past with a stylishly costumed young lady in his arms. Under the arched entrance to a hallway, she caught sight of Mrs. Wolff. A man in blue leaned toward her, his lips moving urgently, though she kept her eyes fixed on her guests. He reached for her, but she jerked away from him, her mouth twisted in contempt. His head was turned away, so Sophie couldn't see his face clearly. Could it be Mr. Wolff? Thelma Wolff eyed the dancers and pressed a handkerchief to the side of her nose. The gentleman grabbed her arm and leaned closer, but she responded with a withering glare. He released her, and she disappeared down the hallway. The man bent down, his black hat ducking below the crowd and out of Sophie's sight. She couldn't help but wonder if the Wolff home was a peaceful one. She thought perhaps not.

Sophie turned her attention to the band on the elevated stage. She recognized "Blue Danube" by Strauss, followed by the modern "You're a Classy Lassie." She tapped her foot to the tune, but stayed well behind the guests that ringed the dance floor to avoid being distracted by another invitation— or compulsion—to dance. Snatches of gossip floated through the air as ladies and gentlemen of all ages skewered their peers for being too haughty or meek, too beautiful or plain, too foolish or serious. It seemed an impossible task to avoid the critical eyes and wagging tongues of Milwaukee's elite, and no behavior was too minor to escape notice.

After she'd made another leisurely circuit of the room, Sophie thought she saw a dark-blue coat that could belong to Mr. Wolff. Dancers kept sweeping into her line of vision, so she couldn't be sure. He seemed to be staring at someone on the opposite side of the room with an expression that looked confused, almost afraid—starkly out of character for what she knew of Ruben Wolff. Was it he who had argued with Mrs. Wolff before, and had the exchange unsettled him? The man downed his drink, then slammed the empty glass onto a nearby table. A couple blocked Sophie's view of him again. When they passed by, the man had disappeared.

Sophie ducked behind a pillar and let her back slouch against its cool surface as she flipped through her notepad. She'd written several costume descriptions and her general impressions of the crowd, but the words seemed stale. Her feet ached in the unfamiliar shoes, and the endless noise was giving her a headache. Sophie pushed aside the lace at her wrist to peek at her wristwatch, surprised to discover it was nearly eleven. Supper would be served soon. She decided she'd earned a bit of fresh air.

When she slipped out the French door, Sophie was grateful to find the sounds of the party muffled by the heavy panes of glass. A sprawling, brick-paved terrace stretched out behind the house. She gazed up at the stars and took a deep, cooling breath. Her shoulders eased as her eyes drifted over the lush shrubs and flowers, sheltered by the graceful arms of tree boughs. She thought of the scraggly backyard at the boarding house, with Mrs. O'Day's carefully tended patch of vegetables in one corner. There was nothing so utilitarian as a potato or carrot growing here.

Sophie pattered down the wide steps and followed the pebble-lined path. The sweet scent of freshly trimmed grass blended with a heavier fragrance of roses and peonies. From somewhere up ahead she heard a smack, then a muffled cry and frantic struggling.

"Hello?" she called out, moving toward the sounds. "Is everything all right?"

There was a sudden stillness, then another cry. Sophie hurried her steps. She startled as a young man pushed past her without a word. Sophie wanted to stop him, but she was drawn to the desperate sobbing.

Rounding a bend in the path, she found a red-haired maid huddled on the grass near a tree trunk, weeping into her hands. Her black uniform was torn at the shoulder, revealing a pale and shaking upper arm. Sophie rushed over and the girl stiffened. She couldn't have been more than sixteen.

"Are you all right?" Sophie asked.

"Oh!" the maid gasped and looked up, then her face flushed. Sophie noticed that her lip was bleeding. "I-I'm sorry, miss, don't mind me." She swiped away her tears.

"May I help?"

The girl shook her head fiercely. "It's m-my fault. I should —" She touched her sore lip.

"Did that man attack you?"

She nodded. "Mr. Davis has always been kind, but tonight h-he'd been drinking. He grabbed me, and—" She broke off, her eyes filling again.

"It's not your fault," Sophie assured her. She reached out to help the girl to her feet.

"But I agreed to walk with him. He came in while I was putting out supper in the dining room. He said we may as well get some air while the Wolffs weren't looking."

"It's *still* not your fault."

The maid let out a shaky sigh, then fingered the torn sleeve of her dress. "Mrs. Harding will be furious. I could lose my job. Especially if Mr. Davis—"

"Just tell Mrs. Harding that I ran into you and tripped, and I grabbed your dress by accident," Sophie said. "That's believable. Is this Mr. Davis one of the servants?"

The girl nodded. "Mr. Wolff's valet. And his chauffeur, too."

With a soft smile, Sophie handed the girl a wrinkled handkerchief from her bag. "It's an unfortunate truth that we girls need to be prepared to fight off groping hands."

"Y-yes, I know. But I thought he cared for me. Then he got so angry. I tried to get away—"

Sophie rummaged in her bag and pulled out a safety pin. "Here, let me help." She reached for the torn fabric and pinned it in place, tucking the pin out of sight.

"Thank you, miss."

"I'm Sophie. I'm a reporter—not a guest."

"My name's Brigid," the maid said, wiping her nose. "You're a newspaper girl? It must be grand to come to parties like this for your job."

"Well, it's my first one," Sophie admitted. "I'm not sure

I'll ever be invited to another one." She rubbed the girl's arms. "You're going to be okay, Brigid. Try to put it out of your mind if possible, for tonight. Tomorrow you can think up a scheme for revenge."

Brigid brushed away a tear. "I will." She smoothed her rumpled skirt, pulled her apron into place, and gave Sophie a fragile smile. "Thank you, miss."

She took a few steps toward the house, then looked back. "Are you coming inside? You shouldn't be out here alone either, if you don't mind me saying."

"I'll be right there."

Brigid hurried off, and Sophie followed more leisurely. The garden that had once appeared inviting now took on a sinister gloom. Sophie wondered how many other girls had wrestled with unwanted attention among its shrubbery. But the silence soothed her after the bustle of the party, and her head still ached.

Then the crash of shattering glass echoed through the night.

Sophie froze for a moment, unable to believe what she'd heard. She ran back to the house. The terrace was still deserted. She dashed up the steps and went inside.

The music had stopped, leaving the ballroom quiet. A silver tray lay on the floor, shattered glass glistening in an arc around it. The maid who had presumably held it wept softly. All eyes were trained on three burly figures who wore hideous monster masks. Sophie tiptoed as close as she dared, her view partially blocked by guests.

"You waste money on parties while our kids go hungry!" shouted one.

"We demand fair pay!" growled another, waving a pistol at the crowd.

Sophie was certain the weapon, unlike Mr. Wolff's wooden prop, was functional.

The third monster pulled a bottle from his coat pocket, and Sophie recognized the dark green label of Wolff Lager. The man tipped it upside down, then produced a lighter, flicked it to life, and touched the flame to a tail of cloth poking from the bottle's mouth. Sophie shrank back in horror as he stretched his arm and hurled the flaming bottle into the crowd. With startled shrieks, the people jumped away from it, and it clattered to a stop at the feet of a man who looked down at it in confusion.

He swerved unsteadily as he went to pick it up, nearly toppling over. Through the press of bodies Sophie couldn't see much, except for part of a blue coat. She craned her neck and got a clear view of the man's shaking hand. She heard a strangled cry before the man careened out the French doors with the lit bottle. He hurled the bottle deep into the garden. The explosion blasted in her ears and vibrated the floor beneath her feet. Chaos broke out as women screamed, some fainted, and men shouted orders. A cluster of men ran outside.

In the struggle to keep her footing among the frantic shoving, Sophie saw the monsters pull rags from their pockets, set them on fire, and toss them onto tables. There was more shrieking and confusion as the flames caught the tablecloths. A group of men rushed toward the monsters in a threatening manner, but the one holding the gun waved them off as he and his cohorts fled out the front door.

Sophie peered around the room, barely able to comprehend the utter destruction of the wonderland that had existed mere moments before. Chairs were overturned as guests rushed past, trying to collect their loved ones and exit without being trampled. Men tore off their jackets and slapped them on the burning tables to smother the flames. Sophie turned and ran back to the garden, suddenly worried that someone had been injured in the explosion.

Following the men's shouts, she hurried down a path between rows of leafy trees. Her toe struck something. She looked down and yelped at the severed head gazing up at her. She stopped and forced herself to breathe; it was only part of a broken statue. She noticed water seeping toward her feet. She rounded a hedge and saw the charred remains of a fountain. Wisps of smoke drifted from the rubble, and the tang of gasoline stung her nose. The figure that had once stood triumphantly among flowing water was now a mangled lump, except for a stone hand that reached out helplessly from the wreckage. Men trampled about the area, stomping out sparks. Sophie took in the damage, relieved to see that no one appeared to be hurt.

Someone grasped her upper arm roughly. She turned to see the glittering eyes of the Spaniard.

"What are you doing out here?" he demanded, the strange accent gone. "Don't you know it's dangerous?"

She pulled her arm away. "My whereabouts are none of your concern."

He shook his head in disgust. "Stupid girl."

"I beg your pardon!"

"There are potential murderers on the loose, and you're wandering around like a nosy schoolgirl."

The word "murderers" jarred her, but she said calmly, "I'm a reporter. It's my job."

"Yes, I know."

"Who *are* you?" She reached for the black mask that shielded his face, but he pulled away.

"Well, come on, your *job* is inside. There's nothing more to see out here." He took her arm again and tried to guide her back toward the path.

She jerked away from him and studied his eyes again. Were they faintly familiar?

There was no time to stop and consider it. He was right:

an incredible story was unfolding inside. Throwing another angry glare in his direction, she hurried back to the house.

Roses were strewn across the floor and trampled. Servants rushed around, attempting to assist frantic guests. Men held weeping women in various stages of distress. Sophie reasoned that Mr. and Mrs. Wolff had to be at the center of it all, but she was unable to see them from where she stood. She pushed her way through the crowd, bits of broken glass crunching beneath her feet. Snatches of conversation reached her as she moved about.

"Really, did the Wolffs have no one alert at the door?"

"Must have been one of those damned unions," a man growled. "Said something about money."

"My beautiful costume!" someone said.

Sophie passed a court jester who stood on a chair, calling out a woman's name.

"I'm here, Stanley!" came the shrill response from across the room.

Sophie's empathy warred with her reporter's instinct. Ambition won out. She approached two young women huddled against a wall, craning their necks and peering into the melee as if looking for a rescuer.

"Did you see what happened?" Sophie asked the taller of the two.

The smaller girl answered. "It was horrible. A crowd of thieves just stormed in and started shouting and demanding money and jewels."

"How many were there?"

"Oh, a dozen at least," claimed the girl. "I think someone was shot."

Before Sophie could ask another question, the taller girl said, "Look, there's Father!" She pulled her sister's arm, and they scurried off.

Sophie looked for her next source, seeking out single

partygoers or women in pairs who seemed confused. She noticed the Spaniard escorting a distraught young woman across the room. He glanced at Sophie, but she turned away and walked up to a servant who was gathering the charred remains of a tablecloth.

"Did you see if anyone was hurt?" she asked.

He shook his head. "Not that I could see. The tablecloths are trash now, and the tables will need refinishing, but it could be worse." He rushed off with his ruined bundle of linen.

Sophie approached an older lady standing alone. "Did you hear what they said?" she asked. But she was met only with a dismissive glare.

She moved on to a young gentleman who stood at a table, fortifying himself with a glass of beer. "What were the intruders shouting?" she asked him.

"Told everyone to hand over their billfolds and jewels," he claimed. "Say, do you need some help? Where's your escort?" He eyed her with interest.

Sophie pointed to an unknown gentleman heading in her direction.

"Ah, there he is," she said, waving to the stranger. The man took another swig of beer and plunged into the crowd.

Within twenty minutes, the ballroom was nearly empty, and Sophie had heard several versions of the tale. The group of intruders varied from two to twelve, and their intentions ranged from burglary to kidnapping and everything in between.

Honestly, Sophie thought, readers blamed reporters for inaccurate stories, but who could possibly sort out the truth in such a motley mess of claims? She began to question her own memory of the events. Sophie ducked behind a pillar and jotted some notes. Then she took a deep breath and headed for the exit.

Emerging from the ballroom, she spotted Mr. Wolff in the foyer, giving fierce orders to a servant. She had to look twice to be sure it was him. He'd taken off his mask, but now he wore a white shirt with a wide ruffled collar, black knee breeches, and a maroon velvet coat with gold buttons. She moved in his direction, wondering if he'd give her a quote for her story.

Mrs. Wolff emerged from a shadowy corridor, patting her enormous wig. She reached her husband just as Sophie drew near and listened.

"You changed your costume in the midst of all this? What were you thinking?" she said to him.

"You were the one who was so upset about my soldier costume, so I decided to put on the getup you chose. When I heard the commotion, I came down as soon as I was decent. Damn lot of buttons on this thing, you know."

"Oh, I'm sure you had help with the buttons, Ruben."

"Don't start, Thelma."

This was met with stony silence. Then Mr. Wolff said, "I'll inspect the damage."

He strode into the ballroom.

Mrs. Wolff's eyes followed him, glittering with malice. She gave another order to the staff and wearily ascended the plushly carpeted stairs.

Sophie found her wrap among the few pieces left behind in the guests' haste to depart. She put it around her shoulders. Even the butler had deserted his post, so she opened the door and let herself out. She'd just reached Grand Avenue and was scanning the street for a hansom cab when two police cars passed by.

The police weren't fond of journalists, so she was happy to leave before they arrived. She reasoned that she wasn't missing out on any crucial details. She was sure the intruders were long gone, anyway. She walked a few blocks before finally flagging down a cab.

"Miss? You're not alone out here, are you?" the driver called to her.

Sophie sighed. A man wouldn't have been questioned, of course. But a woman was expected to be escorted at all times.

"I got separated from my parents," she told him. "But our home isn't far." She held up a dollar bill to show that she could pay his fare.

"Where to, then?"

She gave him the boarding house address and climbed into the carriage. When she sat down, her aching feet cried out with relief. She closed her eyes and replayed the evening's events in her head, mentally composing paragraphs as the cab clattered down the street.

5

———

On Sunday morning, Sophie strode up the sidewalk to the Majestic Building at her usual brisk pace, though her head felt fuzzy from the night before. She'd been exhausted after the Spring Gala, but still had difficulty falling asleep as dramatic images of the evening flashed through her mind. Ruth had left a note telling Sophie she was going to the library and would meet her at the Butterfly for the noon matinee. The time had been underlined twice. Sophie kicked herself for forgetting Mrs. Elliot's request to stop by the suffrage office for her correspondence. She'd barely have time to pick up the letters, return Mrs. Elliot's gown, and get to the theater before noon.

Grand Avenue was nearly deserted, and the peal of distant church bells echoed through the air. Businesses dominated this section of town, their windows dark, since it was illegal for most to be open on Sunday—though it wasn't the Sabbath for every faith, as Ruth had informed her. Luckily, theaters were exempt from the restriction. Jostling the awkward garment bag with Mrs. Elliot's costume over one arm, her purse dangling from her wrist, Sophie pushed the key Aunt Lucy had given her into the lock. To her surprise, the door popped open before she could turn it. It must not have latched properly, she thought.

Sophie entered and closed the door, making sure the latch clicked in place. The photography studio and barber shop on the first floor of the building were both dark. She walked up the stairs, feeling a dull ache in her legs from dashing around Wolff Mansion the night before. The Butterfly Theater's cushioned seats would be a welcome relief. Maybe Ruth wouldn't notice if Sophie drifted off for the tiniest nap while the lights were low.

At the top of the steps, the insurance man's office was closed and dark. There were a couple of other doors beyond his, but she'd never bothered to find out what went on behind them. She rounded the corner and noticed a ribbon of light under Mr. Pitman's door—the young lawyer who'd moved in a few months earlier. Did he always work on weekends? He didn't seem busy enough to warrant extra hours. Sophie stifled a yawn, nearly stepping on a piece of cloth that blended into the tawny wooden floor. It appeared to be a handkerchief that wouldn't likely be missed, but she picked it up and tucked it into her pocket anyway. She'd add it to the motley collection of lost and found objects that her practical aunt kept in the suffrage office.

The hallway was dim, but as Sophie approached, she spotted an oddly shaped package in front of the suffrage office door. As she drew closer, she frowned. It looked like a sack of some kind—could it be mail? Or laundry? Both seemed improbable. Sophie took another step, then stopped in her tracks, her breath catching in her throat. Her heart thumped madly as she tried to make sense of what she saw.

The crumpled heap of fabric was a dress. Horror crept into her veins as she took in the two booted feet emerging from the hem, toes pointed awkwardly in opposite directions.

This was a person... a woman had collapsed at the door, her head drooping against her chest. Aunt Lucy? Mrs. Elliot? The garment bag and her purse slipped from Sophie's grasp. She ran over and dropped to her knees at the woman's side.

"A-are you all right?"

She realized the absurdity of her question. As she took in the sprawled form, it occurred to her that the woman was too tall and broad to be Aunt Lucy or Mrs. Elliot. Relief rippled through her chest, followed by shame. Even an unknown lady deserved urgent assistance.

"Ma'am?" she croaked. Sophie reached for the woman's hand. Though they both wore gloves, it felt cool and still. She tapped her pale cheek with shaking fingers. Also cold.

Only then did she see the dark, foreboding stain across the woman's chest and the appalling hole torn in the fabric of her gown. Sophie's throat constricted, and she forgot to breathe. It couldn't be... She hesitantly lifted the broad brim of the feathered hat up from the woman's face. The brassy auburn hair looked familiar. Though barely recognizable in her stillness, her mouth slack and silent, it was Hilda Rock.

"Mrs. Rock!" She pressed her fingers to the woman's neck, hoping to feel a pulse. Nothing.

Sophie's eyes returned to the woman's chest. The torn fabric was smudged with black. It must be a gunshot wound, she reasoned. She fought against the nausea that rose in her throat.

Sophie reached above Hilda's head to the doorknob and pulled herself to her feet, careful not to disturb the body. She forced herself to take a deep breath and stand perfectly still. It wasn't her first discovery of a dead body, but the first had been so long ago; she resolutely blocked it from her mind.

She took in every detail of the scene with a reporter's eye, ignoring her hammering heart. Hilda Rock wore a light wool, navy-blue traveling dress, the jacket trimly tailored, with a row of gold buttons down the front. Her boots were sturdy. Had she been planning a trip? Sophie could see no purse or luggage nearby. Had she been robbed? Allowing her eyes to drift over Hilda's form, avoiding the terrifying stain on the woman's chest, Sophie caught the glint of a watch fob pin dangling from her lapel. If it was a robbery, wouldn't a thief have grabbed it? She peered closer and saw that the glass face was shattered, the hands frozen at five after eleven. She swallowed, wondering if Mrs. Rock had taken a breath after that moment.

Sophie heard the distant *thunk* of something hitting the floor. She jerked her head up, and sweat broke out across her back. Had the killer returned to remove the evidence? She had to get help. She had to find the police. There was no telephone in the suffrage office, and even if there had been, she couldn't imagine stepping over the lifeless body of Hilda Rock to enter and use it.

Turning, she stumbled back down the hallway.

"Help…" As if in a dream, she could barely make herself speak. "Help!" she tried again, lifting her voice a little louder.

She tried to open Mr. Pitman's door, but it didn't budge. She knocked fiercely. "Mr. Pitman? Are you there?" Silence.

Sophie ran to the stairs. Then she heard another *thunk*. A chill crawled down her spine. This one was closer. But next came a plaintive meow as Anthony, the stray cat that often wandered the building, pranced around the corner. When he saw Sophie, he mewled again and scurried to her side, rubbing against her calf.

"Crazy cat," she muttered. She grabbed the banister and hurried down the stairs.

The street was still empty, the bright spring sunshine incongruous with the frightful scene she had just left. She rushed down the sidewalk, scanning dark windows, hoping for an open shop or a friendly face.

At last she caught sight of a policeman in a navy coat and tall hat, walking in the other direction across the street from her.

"Officer?" she called. He didn't turn, so she took a breath and shouted, "Officer!"

The policeman turned. Seeing Sophie's frantic wave, he ran to her. His large, firm hand circled her upper arm, as if he expected her to swoon.

"Miss? Do you need help?"

She pointed to the office building, now a block away. "There's a woman back there... on the second floor... I-I think she's dead." The word sounded obscene as Sophie allowed herself to think it for the first time.

The officer took a whistle from his pocket and blew three short, shrill blasts. "Show me," he said. "If you don't think you'll faint."

She jerked her arm from his grasp. "I'm not going to faint." For some reason she felt insulted, though she had to admit it was a perfectly reasonable concern.

He pulled a revolver from his coat pocket. Sophie eyed it warily, and they rushed back to the building. He went in first and mounted the stairs slowly, with Sophie following. When they reached the top, she said, "Around the corner," her voice quavering. The officer stepped forward cautiously.

Another officer ran in the door, his pale, freckled face alert under the tall cap.

"Police!" he called.

"Up here," said the first officer.

The second man jogged up the steps. Sophie pointed, and he rounded the corner. She heard the quiet rumble of their voices. Her heartbeat had begun to slow. She took some deep, steadying breaths and glanced uneasily around the hallway at the locked doors. Could the killer still be hiding somewhere?

Killer. The word echoed in her head. She remembered Mrs. Rock's terrible stillness and cold skin. She could have been dead for hours. Surely the killer was long gone. Still, Sophie moved to the end of the hallway, feeling more secure with the two officers in sight.

The first one caught her movement. "Do you know if there's a telephone in this building?"

"Mr. Pitman has one, but his door is locked."

"There's a call box a couple of blocks west," said the second officer.

"Get the coroner," said the first man. "Then call the station. Ask them to send someone to take over Fraser's beat so I can deal with this."

The younger officer clumped down the stairs and out the door. The first officer pulled out a notebook and jotted notes with a small pencil.

It occurred to Sophie this was a story—a real, scandalous, criminal news story. And she was a reporter. She had a job to do. She'd expected to feel excitement when she finally got the chance to write truly shocking news. But all she felt was dread. A life had been snuffed out in the very building where her aunt and her friends spent hours working. She swallowed hard and reached for her purse, but realized she'd dropped it earlier in her haste. She walked a few steps down the hall to where it lay next to the garment bag. She bent to pick up both items.

"Stop!" The officer's deep voice startled her. "That could be evidence."

She held his gaze as she picked up her purse and the bag. His eyebrows shot upward.

"They're mine," she said. "I must have dropped them when I went to find you." She set the garment bag neatly on a bench next to Mr. Pitman's office. Then she tugged open her purse drawstring and pulled out her own notebook and pencil. From some deep reservoir, she gathered her courage. She drew her shoulders back, lifted her chin, and walked toward the man, stopping at Mrs. Rock's booted feet. "I'm Sophie Strong of the *Milwaukee Herald*," she told him.

He groaned, rolling his eyes. "A lady reporter." He shook his head. "I should have known. Don't touch anything."

"Your name, officer?"

"It's Detective Zimmer."

She sized him up. He was tall, with sandy brown hair and deep blue eyes. He had to be under thirty, she guessed. Her brows furrowed as she took in his uniform. He didn't look like a detective. He wore a standard uniform, like the low-ranking officers she spoke to in the rare instances she was allowed to cover petty crimes involving women. She was sure she hadn't met him before.

"Yes, I'm dressed as a beat cop. I lost a bet. But you've got this backward, sweetheart. I'll ask the questions. What are you doing in a deserted building with a dead woman on a Sunday morning?"

"Do you know who she is?" Sophie asked.

"She's not carrying any identification. If she had a purse, it's long gone."

"I'll tell you her name if you agree to help me with my story," Sophie challenged.

His jaw flexed, as if he was gritting his teeth. "What are you doing here?" He glanced at the office door, where "Wisconsin Woman Suffrage Association" was painted in black letters on the glass. "Are you a suffragist?"

Sophie just shrugged innocently and gave him a wide-eyed smile.

He glared. "You know, I could take you downtown to the station for questioning."

"Really? That sounds like an interesting angle for the paper."

He clenched his right hand into a fist. Then he let out a breath. "I'll tell you what I can for your story. Now who is she?"

Sophie felt a ping of satisfaction. She was getting the hang of this reporting job. "Mrs. Hilda Rock."

"Friend of yours? Or enemy?"

Sophie shook her head. "She's a well-known speaker."

"So she's a suffragist, too."

"Actually, she speaks *against* suffrage."

"So you shot her?"

"If I had, would I have run for the police?" Sophie asked.

"So you just decided to pop by the suffrage office to see if there were any corpses around that you could write about?"

"I'm here to pick up some papers from the office. Oh, drat —what time is it?" She checked her wristwatch and saw it was eleven-thirty. Her plan to meet Ruth had slipped her mind.

Detective Zimmer consulted a pocket watch, apparently not expecting her to have a timepiece of her own. "It's eleven-thirty. Riley should be back any minute."

Sophie closed her eyes. "Well, at least this time it's not my fault."

"You have somewhere to be?" he asked.

"It doesn't matter."

"So you stopped by to pick something up at the office. How did you know Mrs. Rock?"

"She's well known in some circles," said Sophie. "She speaks widely."

Zimmer rubbed his chin. "And now she's dead in front of the suffrage office."

"What's your next step in the investigation, Detective? I'll need to report this for the *Herald*."

Zimmer gave her a dismissive glance. "No comment."

A couple of wooden chairs were tucked away in an alcove

down the hall. Zimmer went over and grabbed one in each strong hand. He set them down facing each other, near Mrs. Rock's still body.

"Have a seat, Miss Strong," he said.

Sophie sat, realizing that her legs had become a bit unsteady. Detective Zimmer shifted his chair so he could see the corpse and both ends of the hallway. "Start at the beginning. Tell me why you're here." His eyes darted periodically around the scene.

She explained her errand again. She gave her address at the boarding house. Reluctantly, she provided the names and addresses of Aunt Lucy, Mrs. Clara Elliot, and Miss Agnes Thompson. No, she didn't know any of the other women who came to the office. No, she didn't work with them.

"My hands are full with my job," she told him. "Though I support women's suffrage, of course."

"Of course," he said sardonically. "So Mrs. Elliot asked you to stop by the office. And you happen to have a key for the building. Do you often run errands for Mrs. Elliot?"

"No, but she's a family friend. I was planning to return a dress I borrowed."

"But you had a key..." he prompted.

"Yes, my aunt gave it to me. But when I started to unlock the door, it popped open. It hadn't been closed properly. As if —well, as if someone left in a hurry."

"But you went in anyway? Alone?"

"I didn't think anything of it. I wasn't afraid. I've been here lots of times."

"To visit Mrs. Elliot?"

"Or my aunt. They're close friends."

"So, if Mrs. Rock speaks against women getting the vote, I imagine you and your aunt and her friends don't like her much."

Sophie wasn't about to admit that they all loathed Hilda Rock. "She's entitled to her opinion."

"When did you last see Mrs. Rock? Alive, that is."

She didn't want to implicate Mrs. Elliot by describing the events at the debate. She considered inventing an answer. Hilda Rock was visible around town. She might have spotted her while shopping, or—

"Miss Strong?"

"Umm, there was a debate. On Wednesday evening. She and Mrs. Elliot debated suffrage at the Woman's Club."

"Did anything unusual happen at this debate?"

Sophie recalled the angry exchange between Mrs. Rock and Mrs. Elliot. He was bound to find out about it, but it wouldn't be from her. "The women voiced their opinions about the issue." It wasn't technically a lie.

"Can you think of anyone who would have wanted to harm to Mrs. Rock? Other than you and your friends?"

She frowned. "My aunt and I, and our friends, do not agree with Mrs. Rock, but that's not the same as wanting to hurt her. Political disagreements don't lead to murder—at least not among ladies."

"Is that so? Well, do you know anyone else who's got a grudge toward Mrs. Rock?"

Sophie imagined there were plenty of people who were put off by the woman's haughty manner. But could that have motivated the murder?

"Miss Strong?"

"She's not... she wasn't a pleasant woman. But no, I don't know who would want to kill her." Sophie's mind raced as she tried to think of who it could have been. A thief? Was that why her purse was missing? But why would a thief leave her watch behind? And what had she been doing in the office building on a Saturday night?

"What about her family? Do you know where I could find her husband?"

"She was a widow. I haven't heard about any family members."

Detective Zimmer tucked away his notebook and pencil. "You seem like a curious young lady."

"I've learned it's best to keep my eyes open," she told him.

"Well, leave *this* matter to the police. If you must report it, stick to the facts and keep it short. None of that yellow journalism you newspaper girls are known for."

Sophie bristled. "I don't write sensational stories. I'm a professional."

"All right, if you say so." He sounded unconvinced. "Just stay out of the way. It's dangerous to go poking your nose into a murder." He stood, signaling the end of their discussion, and Sophie did the same.

"I'll write my report for tomorrow's edition. If I have questions, where can I reach you?"

He frowned. "As I just said, keep it brief. Any details you offer could tip off the killer and hamper our investigation."

She waited, watching him expectantly.

He sighed. "I'm at the Central Station on Oneida and Broadway. But I'm usually out on cases. I'm a busy man."

Sophie smiled sweetly. "That's why I *so* appreciate your promise to help me." She tucked her notebook into her purse. "Do you need anything else from me?"

"You may be asked to come down to the station to make a report," he told her. "Someone will get in touch with you if that's necessary."

"Then I'll take my leave, Detective Zimmer. Thank you for your kind assistance." Sophie held out a hand to shake his. He looked down at her extended fingers and gave them a half-hearted squeeze.

"You take care, Miss Strong."

Sophie held her head high and walked toward the stairs, willing her wobbly knees to keep her upright. Before she turned the corner, she glanced back down the hall to see Detective Zimmer watching her and frowning.

6

Sophie opened the door to her little room, tapping the mezuzah as she entered. The show at the Butterfly had already started, but Ruth would surely forgive her for missing their date when she learned of the day's events. On the table between the two beds stood a mason jar from which three daisies smiled up at her hopefully. Sophie sank onto the mattress, tugged off her shoes, and collapsed onto the pillow.

She closed her eyes, hoping to quiet the dull pounding behind them. But the image of Hilda Rock's lifeless body slumped against the suffrage office door swam into view. She struggled to replace it with something peaceful: the smooth surface of Lake Michigan stretching out to the horizon on an overcast day or the wind whispering through leaves in a canopy of tree branches. But after a few seconds, the gruesome sight intruded. She blinked her eyes open and gazed up at the white ceiling with its familiar trails of tiny cracks.

She knew she should have raced to the newspaper office to write up her account of the murder while it was fresh in her mind—not to mention the Spring Gala—but she couldn't face it just yet. She'd grab a quick nap and then go in. Her eyes drifted closed.

"Sophie?" Someone knocked softly on the door.

It seemed like only an instant had passed since she'd closed her eyes.

"Yes?"

"There's a carriage here for you, Sophie."

She was surprised to hear it was the hesitant voice of Mrs. O'Day, who rarely came upstairs.

"A carriage? Are you sure it's for me?"

"I'm sure. You have a visitor." Sophie heard her descend the stairs.

She couldn't imagine who would call on her, especially in a carriage. With a tired sigh, she dragged herself upright and pulled her shoes back on, then ran her fingers over her dark brown curls, tucking straggling wisps into place as best she could. Then she went downstairs, curiosity simmering in her mind.

In the entryway by the front door, among the ladies' coats and umbrellas, a man stood stiffly erect in a crisp, black wool coat and matching cap.

"Hello?" she said. "I'm Sophie Strong."

The man gave a solemn nod. "Yes, Miss Strong. Mrs. Wolff is waiting for you."

"Mrs. Wolff? We don't have an appointment. Is she outside?"

"She's at Wolff Mansion, miss," the man said, looking incredulous at the very idea that Thelma Wolff would venture out of her realm to call on a mere mortal.

Sophie was stunned by the woman's arrogant assumption that she would be available at her beck and call. Still, she had no intention of refusing.

"Just a moment," she said. As she turned to dash back upstairs, she saw the man's expression was pained, as if he were uncomfortable at the thought of leaving Thelma Wolff waiting for more than an instant.

She collected her bag with the ever-present notebook and pencil, and glanced at her reflection in the mirror over the bureau. She still looked slightly disheveled, but she shrugged. It wasn't her fault that she didn't look her best when responding to an impromptu summons on a Sunday afternoon.

In front of the boarding house stood the magnificent carriage, an elegant "W" surrounded by golden swirls on its side, led by a pair of stomping black horses. The man held open the carriage door and offered one gloved hand. Sophie rested her fingers on his and ascended.

As the door snapped shut, she settled onto the velvet seat and breathed in the rarefied air of unimaginable wealth. The interior of the carriage was spotless, with thick maroon damask curtains covering the windows. So secure were the walls that she could barely hear the clatter outside as the vehicle progressed through the streets. She rested her head on the back of the seat and wondered what Mrs. Wolff could want with her now.

After a few minutes Sophie pulled aside a curtain, seeing Wolff Mansion loom into view. They slowed to a stop under the portico in front of the main entrance. The driver helped Sophie step out. The butler eyed Sophie from the open front door, looking just as displeased as he had the night before. He silently led her to Mrs. Wolff's private parlor, where the great lady awaited her arrival.

"Miss Strong, good afternoon." Sophie opened her mouth to reply, but Mrs. Wolff had no time for pleasantries. "I wish to discuss the Spring Gala."

"Yes, ma'am."

Mrs. Wolff gestured to a chair with one graceful hand, and Sophie took a seat.

"There were some unfortunate incidents last night which are best forgotten," said Mrs. Wolff. She spoke in clipped, tightly controlled sentences, as if she could barely contain her rage at the disruption of her carefully planned party.

"You're speaking of the labor protesters, the fires, and the explosion, I presume?"

"The trespassers and the vandalism, yes," said Mrs. Wolff firmly. "None of this will be included in your report."

Amidst the drama of finding a murder victim, Sophie hadn't given much thought to how she would handle the fiasco that the Spring Gala had become. "Mrs. Wolff, I—"

"Assuredly you understand that your role is to provide appropriate press coverage of the event. Mr. Wolff and I wish to avoid calling attention to these... *criminals*. It will only encourage them to take their nonsense further."

Sophie remembered the men's shouted complaints. She bristled at the idea that feeding their children could be considered nonsense, though she didn't abide the destruction they had caused. She knew she shouldn't argue with such a powerful woman, but she couldn't help herself.

"Mrs. Wolff, you had two hundred guests here. Surely you understand that it can't be kept quiet."

Mrs. Wolff pursed her lips into a bitter knot. "People will gossip, I suppose. But the official account of the evening *must* remain dignified." She paused, casting her glance around the opulent room. "Events in our home, regarding our family, are recorded for historical significance, Miss Strong. There is more at stake here than a vulgar story."

Sophie felt heat flood her face. "Vulgar? Accurately recording the event is hardly vulgar." Even as she said it, her brain screamed at her not to argue with Mrs. Wolff, but she was incensed.

Thelma eyed Sophie with distaste, her pale eyes icy. She let a weighty silence stretch between them before she spoke.

"Miss Strong," she said, her voice low and authoritative. "If you are inclined to disregard my simple request, I will see that you are dismissed from your position. Indeed, my influence will prevent you from ever being employed as a journalist again. I suggest that you consider carefully where your duty lies."

Sophie clenched her teeth as the threat echoed in her ears.

Mrs. Wolff stood. "Good day, Miss Strong."

Choking down the furious retorts that sprang to her lips, Sophie stood and nodded politely. "Mrs. Wolff."

Sophie left the room and walked briskly down the marble-tiled hallway, struggling to remain calm. She knew the Wolffs were powerful. She had been warned that her report must be flattering. Still, she kept hearing the words of the intruder who was desperate enough to antagonize one of the most influential men in the state—and maybe the country: "You waste money on parties while our kids go hungry!"

Sophie came to a halt. She had somehow sailed past the hallway that led to the foyer, and now she found herself in an unfamiliar part of the mansion. She turned, biting her lip. Long corridors seemed to stretch endlessly before her. As she studied her surroundings, considering what to do next, a frame on the wall just beyond one of the doorways caught her eye. It looked like a framed newspaper. She looked about, and seeing no one coming, she indulged her inquisitiveness and darted into a room lined with book-shelves.

Near the doorway hung a beautifully carved wooden and gilt frame. Beneath the gleaming glass, printed on silk, was the front page of the women's charity edition of the *Herald* from 1895. Aunt Lucy and Mrs. Elliot had fond memories of working on this paper in their youth. At a time when female journalists were almost unheard of, a passel of ladies had taken over the *Herald* offices for a day and created this special edition to raise money for local causes.

What was it doing in the Wolffs' library? Of course, many people of influence had purchased a silk copy to support the effort, even at its hundred-dollar price, but something about its placement in the library suggested a special interest.

She scanned the columns, looking for clues.

"Women Own It All," proclaimed one headline. Below it, an advertisement for Pozzoni's Complexion Powder reminded female readers of their responsibility to look their best. Then Sophie spotted a line that made her gasp.

"Mrs. Thelma Wolff, who worked as one of the editors, commented, 'There has been a great deal hard work, much amusement, and an overflowing of enthusiasm.'"

Sophie read it again. She couldn't imagine the reserved Mrs. Wolff as part of the eager cadre of women who stormed the *Herald* office on that long-ago day. There were no names attributed to most of the articles, but she quickly scanned the page for more details. She gasped again when she saw a reference to Mrs. Hilda Rock as the contributor of a somber account of school news.

They had all worked as journalists for a day. Why had Aunt Lucy never mentioned that Thelma Wolff and Hilda Rock had joined them?

Sophie wished she could read the whole edition. Maybe she'd borrow a copy from the *Herald*'s morgue—the basement where the complete archives were kept. She wondered if Aunt Lucy and Clara had written about suffrage that long ago. The topic of suffrage was conspicuously absent from the framed front page.

Still deep in thought, Sophie jumped when she heard a man clear his throat nearby. Thinking the butler must have found her and could direct her to the front door, she turned. To her horror, Sophie found herself face to face with Ruben

Wolff. She felt her face grow hot as embarrassment crept over her.

He stared at her blankly for a moment, then broke into his customary easy smile.

"Well, hello, Miss... Is it Stark? Forgive me, you're the journalist, are you not?"

"Yes, sir, I'm Sophie Strong. I'm sorry to disturb you. I just left Mrs. Wolff, and I—"

He chuckled. "Lost your way, have you? Happens all the time." He glanced at the wall hanging. "I see you've found one of Mrs. Wolff's prized possessions. Hard to believe she traipsed around the city as a reporter, isn't it?"

"Yes, it is."

"I am leaving now, so I can show you the way to the door. I just came in to collect some papers." He strode over to a table by the window, picked up a thick leather portfolio, and began paging through the contents.

"I—that is—thank you, sir."

Sophie glanced around the room and noticed that one of the chairs had a decidedly feminine lap blanket draped over the back and an open book resting face down on the cushion. Did Mrs. Wolff spend time in the library as well? Sophie longed to walk over and see what she had been reading, but she didn't want Mr. Wolff to catch her snooping.

He snapped his portfolio shut and moved toward the door. "Shall we?"

As they walked down the corridor together, Sophie racked her brain for something to ask him—as any journalist worth her salt would do when alone with a celebrity—but her mind was blank. This was a golden opportunity, and she was letting it slip through her fingers.

Finally she said, "Your Spring Gala was quite memorable, sir."

"It was indeed. We won't forget that one any time soon."

"I hope you'll be able to repair the damaged fountain in your lovely garden."

He waved a hand, as if an explosion on the grounds was no great cause for concern. "Oh, that won't be a problem. Not much harm done, thank goodness."

Sophie furrowed her brow, remembering the broken plaster and the stone head that had rolled into her path. The damage had seemed significant to her, but maybe Mr. Wolff measured such things differently.

"Have there been other protests at your brewery by labor activists?"

They had reached the foyer, and when Mr. Wolff turned to face her, his smile had vanished.

"Not at all, Miss Strong. My employees are a happy lot."

She looked into his dark-brown eyes and noticed the firm set of his jaw. Gone was the jovial man she'd seen just a moment before. Sophie could see traces of the ruthless ambition that must have been required for him to amass a fortune.

"That's lovely," she said, forcing lightness into her tone. "Maybe I'll interview some of them one day. Our readers would love to know what it's like to work for such a successful company. Many women are employed in your bottling plant, are they not?"

Mr. Wolff studied her for a moment, then his face relaxed back into a smile.

"The ladies do have the necessary skills to succeed at the bottling plant, that's true. But they are there to work, Miss Strong. With as much product as Wolff Brewery produces, I'm sure you understand that they have no time to speak with reporters."

Before she could persuade him, a cold voice from behind them cut her off.

"Miss Strong, I am surprised to see you still here," said Thelma. "Our business has concluded."

Then she turned to her husband. "Ruben, may I speak with you before you go?"

It was phrased as a request, but she spun around and walked down the hall without waiting for his answer.

"Certainly, my dear," Mr. Wolff called after her. He gave Sophie a nod. "Good day, Miss Strong."

"Thank you, sir. Good day to you."

The butler whisked Sophie out the door and closed it resolutely behind her.

Sophie glanced around for the carriage, but it was nowhere in sight. The comfortable ride must have been a one-way luxury. She walked down the steps, then slowly traversed the long driveway. Her headache had subsided, replaced by a swirling jumble of thoughts.

Did Mrs. Wolff truly think she could keep the events of last night out of the public eye?

Sophie's earlier exhaustion had vanished. With the words of Mr. and Mrs. Wolff echoing in her head, she headed down Grand Avenue. The darkened storefronts and offices passed by in a blur as she made the two-mile trek to the *Herald* office.

Though it was a Sunday evening, Sophie wasn't alone in the reporters' room. A few of her colleagues were scattered about the office, exchanging jocular barbs and hesitantly pecking at their typewriters. She fed a crisp white page into her Remington and had just rested her fingers on the keys when Benjamin Turner breezed past from the direction of the office library.

"Working on Sunday, Miss Strong? Nothing too troubling, I hope."

"All in a day's work, Mr. Turner."

Though she kept her voice airy, the sight of Hilda Rock's body flooded her mind again, followed by snippets of her conversation with the irritating Detective Zimmer.

Sophie stared at the blank page. Maybe it would help her to deal with the memory if she got down the story of the murder. It would just be a short item, since there were few known facts. And, she recalled grimly, Detective Zimmer had warned her to keep it brief. She forced her fingers to type out the details.

When she'd finished, she reread the two paragraphs. It stabbed her heart to think that the life and death of a woman—even a woman as aggravating as Mrs. Rock—could be reduced to such a simple account. She wound the knob at the side of the machine, pulled out the page, and put it face down on her desk. She rested her hand on it for a moment as she sent up a silent prayer for the soul of Hilda Rock. Perhaps Mr. Barnaby would allow her to write an obituary, and she could dredge up some positive things to say about Mrs. Rock. Sophie had heard she'd been involved in some worthy causes before becoming an Anti.

Sophie rolled a new sheet into the typewriter and turned her attention to the Wolffs' Spring Gala. Should she write the true story with all of its drama, risking the ire of the Wolffs and subsequent unemployment? Her stomach fluttered at the thought, but lines of type began to march through her mind. She imagined her name on the front page in a blaze of notoriety. This was quickly followed by a vision of herself huddled on a street corner, homeless and starving, with a small bundle of ratty belongings at her feet.

The prudent thing would be to write the story Mrs. Wolff requested. Surely Sophie would have another chance to cover such exciting news, when it wouldn't cost her job. And that's what Mr. Barnaby had instructed her to do. But yet... he couldn't have known how chaotically the evening would end.

She chewed her lip, staring at the blank page and warring with herself. Then she began to type.

AN HOUR LATER, Sophie rolled her final page out of the typewriter. She'd written a flattering account of the grandiose Spring Gala, as requested. But then, unable to restrain herself, she'd also included the protesters' astonishing intrusion and some of the chaos that followed. The Wolffs had been painted as blameless and generous hosts set upon by vandals, pushing aside her suspicion that the intruders had been motivated by legitimate injustice. She scraped back her chair and stood, stretching to relieve a cramp in her neck.

Benjamin Turner typed with even, practiced strokes as she walked past his desk, though she felt his eyes on her back. Mr. Barnaby's office door was open, and she went in. She looked around the cluttered room that spoke of his love for the "newspaper game," as he called it. Clippings of some of his favorite stories were tacked to the wall. Typewritten sheets peppered with his familiar red pencil marks were scattered across the desktop. A metal tray overflowed with copy for the Monday edition.

Her heart pounding, she dropped her story on top, praying it wouldn't be the last one she'd write.

7

The next morning, Sophie eyed Mr. Barnaby's office from her desk, waiting for him to summon her with his customary bellow. Surely he'd have something to say about the murder or the Spring Gala story. But through the window she saw his head bent over his desk, scribbling notes with his red pencil and periodically calling for a copy boy to deliver pages to the composing room for typesetting. She longed to know what he thought of her work and if she should write an obituary for Mrs. Rock, but he looked so harried she didn't have the nerve to interrupt him.

The presses would roll at three o'clock that afternoon. With no requests for revisions, Sophie typed up notices about parties, weddings, and other society events for Tuesday's edition.

Later, she was glad for some fresh air when she left to attend a meeting of the Women's Christian Temperance Union. She stopped at the hospital to get an update on renovations that were underway, only to learn that a delay in a shipment of Italian granite had stalled them. As she hurried back to the *Herald* office, she heard shouts coming from the alley behind the building. It sounded like the newsies had a rowdy game going while they waited for their evening papers. Maybe they were pitching pennies or playing marbles. But then came the *clang* of a trash can toppling over and a frantic scrabble of feet across the pavement. The tone of the shouting turned tense.

She quickened her steps, then peered into the dim, narrow alley.

"Oof!"

She heard the exclamation just as a wiry young body fell into her path, flopping across the sidewalk like a tossed rag. She nearly tripped over him, but reached for the brick wall and caught her balance in time. The boy scrambled to his feet, wiping blood from his nose and throwing up his fists. He took a step back into the alley, but Sophie seized the collar of his dirty jacket and held him in place.

"That's enough!" she growled in her best attempt at an authoritative tone. She glared at the group of boys, who grumbled in protest. "Do you want me to call the cops?"

Just then, a window of the basement print room was flung open. The boys shoved toward it, waving coins in grubby fists. A man's ink-stained hands began taking the money and thrusting stacks of freshly printed newspapers through the window. As each newsie grabbed the copies he'd paid for, he took off down the alley, the scuffle forgotten.

The boy she held jerked away from Sophie, giving her a disgusted glance. She realized with a start that it was Sam, who sometimes greeted her cheerfully as she entered or left the building. Today he looked even more raggedy than usual. He ran to join the noisy crowd of boys, pulling coins from his pocket.

Sophie was about to move on when she noticed something odd about the jacket he wore. Though it hung nearly to his knees, it looked torn along the bottom, as if excess material had been ripped away. Several spots were blackened, and there was a large hole behind one shoulder. It was a rag, but something about it tugged at her memory.

Sam grabbed his stack of papers and headed down the alley, away from Sophie.

"Wait!" she called. "Sam!"

He ignored her, not bothering to look back. She quickly moved into the alley to catch up with him, careful not to brush her sleeves against the dirty walls of the buildings. She grasped the back of his coat again.

"Get off!" he yelled, swiping at her hand, but she held fast.

He glared at her. "What do you want? A thank you? I'll just have to finish that fight later."

"I just want to talk to you."

"I ain't got time to talk. If you can't see with your own eyes, I got papers to sell."

"But you're bleeding—"

He brushed a hand over his upper lip to wipe away the trickle of red, and she saw that his knuckles were raw and scraped.

"It ain't the first time," he said. "Let me be."

"Let me buy you something to eat. And you can clean yourself up a bit. It won't take long." The words slipped out before she'd even made up her mind about the offer.

Sophie heard his stomach rumble at the mention of food. Judging from his gaunt ribs, he didn't get much nourishment.

"I can't leave my beat. I'll lose my customers."

"Come back when you're done," she said. "Can you meet me at Louie's around six?"

The cafe a few doors down from the *Herald* office was a familiar haunt for reporters and typists.

"All right, it's your coin, Miss Strong," he said, rolling his eyes.

She watched him dash off, the bulging canvas sack of papers tucked under one arm. Then she entered the office, the tang of fresh ink and hot newsprint filling her nostrils. She picked up a copy of the new edition from the rack in the lobby and waved at the secretary who controlled visitors' access to the upper floors from his desk.

Sophie leaned one shoulder against the cool wall and flipped through the pages. She was gratified to find her brief account of Mrs. Rock's untimely death at the bottom of page one. Murders were fairly rare, even in a city as large as Milwaukee, so it warranted a modest front-page spot—without her name, of course, but Mr. Barnaby knew its origin. Like most papers, the *Herald* projected an impartial image, and few stories were attributed to their authors.

She flipped the pages quickly, ignoring the ink that rubbed off on her fingers. On page thirteen, she caught her breath, rapidly scanning the story. She gritted her teeth and read it more carefully, her heart pounding harder with each line. Then she slapped the pages closed and stomped up the marble-walled staircase to the second floor.

Sophie went to her desk and took off her coat. Mr. Barnaby's office door was closed. She tapped her pencil on her desktop as she waited. Even as she fumed, a corner of Sophie's mind was relieved to focus on something other than the untimely demise of Hilda Rock.

Benjamin Turner emerged from Mr. Barnaby's office, looking customarily smug. Sophie grabbed her newspaper and knocked on the frame of the open door.

Mr. Barnaby didn't look up. "Yes?"

"May I have a moment, Chief?" She was pleased that her voice didn't waver, even though her stomach felt tense and her heart continued its rapid rhythm.

He looked up. "Strong? What is it?"

She entered and shut the door behind her. "I noticed my story was drastically edited."

He drew his brows together and frowned. "Your story? What do you mean?"

"The one about the Wolffs' Spring Gala."

"The party? I took out a few adjectives. We don't have space to wax nostalgic about ladies' dresses."

Sophie tried to keep her voice calm. "I'm not referring to a few adjectives. What about my description of how intruders broke up the party and set fire to the place?"

Mr. Barnaby's eyes grew wide. "Have a seat, Miss Strong."

His uncharacteristic use of the title "Miss" gave her a flicker of anxiety. She sat.

"Now, what in the Sam Hill are you talking about? And keep in mind that I'm a busy man."

His voice was low and controlled, but she saw tension in his jaw.

Sophie swallowed. "Three intruders barged into the Spring Gala. They set fire to the tables and threw a home-made bomb. The night ended in chaos."

"Well, if that's the case, this is the first I've heard of it. I printed the story that was in my box this morning. As I said, I took out a few adjectives."

"What? How is that possible? I wrote it yesterday after-noon and left it on your desk."

"Maybe you turned in an earlier draft of your story by mistake." He whipped off his glasses and pointed one earpiece in her direction. "I'll remind you, however, that I am the city editor at this paper, and I'll print what I think is best."

Sophie met his gaze steadily. It was her word against his. She was sure she'd typed only one version, but she *had* been upset. Could she have made a mistake? The actual typewritten copy had likely been destroyed by now, or lay buried under piles of discarded pages in the composing room.

"It was a *scoop*, Mr. Barnaby. Mrs. Wolff wanted me to suppress the story, but—"

"You thought you knew better, is that it?"

"Well, I—"

"Listen, Strong. There are things going on in this city that you don't understand. I told you what kind of story to write, and Mrs. Wolff did the same. That is your job. Journalism isn't a game. This is serious business."

Sophie flushed. "The truth is serious business too."

"There are many ways to tell the truth, Miss Strong. You are fortunate to have a job at this paper. Hell, you're lucky I don't fire you this minute. Go back to your desk. Write about Women's Club meetings, and recipes, and fashion shows. Leave investigative reporting to experienced men who are better suited to the task."

Dots swam in front of Sophie's eyes. For an instant, she saw her work not as the start of a brilliant career, but as busywork to keep her readers focused on homemaking. She forced the image out of her mind. That may be how P.J. Barnaby viewed her, but she refused to let it discourage her.

She straightened her shoulders and lifted her chin. "And if I don't?"

"There are plenty of girls who would be happy to take your place. Get out of my office."

His voice was cold as he waved one hand toward the door and lowered his eyes to the papers on his desk.

Sophie stood, her legs shaky beneath her, and somehow made it back to her desk, not seeing or hearing the surrounding bustle. She sat down and took deep, even breaths. This wasn't the end of her journalism career. She hadn't been fired. She'd reported a murder, however briefly and anonymously. She would find another chance to write a *real* story. Something that didn't involve tyrants like the Wolffs. If she dogged Detective Zimmer enough, she could be the first to report the solution to the crime.

At that thought, her stomach churned. She was viewing Mrs. Rock's death only as a way to advance professionally; had she lost all human feeling?

She tried to push the notion out of her head and reached for the correspondence piled on her desk. On the top envelope, she recognized the familiar handwriting of a nurse who regularly sent in health advice. Sophie slit the envelope open with one finger, wincing as the thick paper sliced her flesh.

THAT EVENING, Sophie sat at the rear corner table in Louie's with her notebook, pencil, and a cup of black coffee. She had intended to drum up new story ideas while she waited for Sam, but her mind kept drifting back to her bizarre missing story. What could have happened? She tried to replay her every move of the day before, but some of it was foggy. Then she found herself pondering who could have shot Hilda Rock. She ticked off possibilities: lunatic, thief, disgruntled servant, angry relative, offended neighbor...

She sighed. Sophie knew Mrs. Rock was abrasive and loud, but she didn't have any clues about her personal life or who might have wanted to kill her. She wondered what the police had discovered so far.

She was on her third cup of coffee when the bell on the door jangled. Sam entered, and Nellie, the owner's wife, eyed him suspiciously from behind the counter where she was slicing a cherry pie. When Sophie waved him over to her table, she seemed to relax. The other patrons didn't look up from plates of meatloaf or hash.

"Hi, Sam. How was your afternoon?"

He shrugged. "Same as always, I guess."

Nellie came over. "What'll it be?"

Sophie looked at the battered young face across from her. "A bowl of chicken soup for me," she said.

"Me too," said Sam. "And coffee, please."

"How about meatloaf and mashed potatoes for my friend?" Sophie suggested. Sam's eyes widened, but he didn't argue. "And two glasses of water, please."

"Comin' right up." Nellie turned on her heel to deliver the order to her husband.

"What do you want to buy me grub for?" the boy asked in a suspicious tone. "You flush with coin or something?"

Sophie chuckled. "Hardly. Just nosy, I guess."

Nellie plunked their water glasses on the slightly sticky table, along with a cup of coffee for Sam, and she topped off the cooling liquid in Sophie's well-used mug.

Sophie pulled a clean handkerchief from her purse and handed it to Sam. "Here. You're still a bit bloodied up."

He looked like he wanted to protest, but he took the handkerchief, dipped it in the water, and rubbed at his face. Afterward, he looked marginally better. He tried to hand back the handkerchief, but she shook her head.

"Keep it. I have more."

He shoved it in his pocket without a word, then took a gulp of steaming coffee.

Sophie sipped her own coffee and looked at him. He couldn't be more than thirteen, she thought, with roughly chopped brown hair and a face that appeared somehow delicate despite its perpetual scowl. A tan pullover shirt that had seen better days and few washings covered his chest.

Her gaze moved again to the coat.

"That's an interesting coat you're wearing." Sam looked around the room, not responding, so she pressed on. "I'm wondering where you got it."

His eyes darted back to her. "I found it, fair and square. That's what the fight was about. Archer thinks he can take anything he wants, just because he's older and bigger than the rest of us."

"You're pretty slim. Think you can hold on to it?"

"I have so far," Sam said, jutting his chin out.

Sophie nodded. "I figured you found it, and it looks warm. I noticed it because it's similar to one I saw recently."

"Oh yeah? Well, nobody's missing it, cause when I found it, it was on fire."

He held up one arm, and she spotted a charred hole under it.

"It was on fire? And you put it out?"

"Well, of course I put it out, or I wouldn't be wearing it, would I?"

"Where was the fire? I didn't hear about it."

Sam rolled his eyes. "It wasn't a house that burned down. Just a little fire in a trash barrel. Down the alley from that big office building—the Majestic."

Sophie's heart thumped. Could it be related to the murder somehow?

Nellie arrived with their food. Sam picked up a fork and dug in eagerly. His manners were better than Sophie had expected, but he still ate with surprising speed, as if he feared the food could be whisked away at any moment. She started on her soup.

"Seems kind of dumb to set a good coat on fire," she said. "Who would do that?"

"Beats me. Looked like some rich fella," the boy said. "Didn't wait around for the whole thing to burn, though. Soon as he left, I grabbed the jacket and stomped on it."

"You didn't get burned?"

"Not much."

"It looks like you cut off the bottom of the coat. Was it pretty long?"

"Yeah. It was long. Why are you so interested?"

Sophie wondered about that herself. It was hard to be sure in its dilapidated state, but somehow it looked like a costume from the Spring Gala.

"There was... um... some trouble at this meeting the other day, where I saw a coat like that. When did you find it, anyway?"

Sam just shrugged, intent on his food. "The other night. Saturday, I guess. Late."

"I think that coat might help me figure out what happened that night."

"I can fight you too," he said with a grin. "You'd be easier to beat than Archer."

He scooped up a generous forkful of meatloaf and mashed potatoes.

She smiled. "I don't want to fight you for it. I wondered if I could buy it from you."

"Yeah? Well it ain't for sale. If I'm gonna fight for it, I'm gonna wear it. Otherwise guys will think I lost. They'll gang up on me even more if they figure I'm easy to beat."

"Sounds exhausting."

Sam sighed. He looked up at Sophie with weary brown eyes framed by long lashes.

"No time to be exhausted," he said. "I got a little brother to feed."

"What about your parents?"

"Yeah. What about 'em?"

Sophie nodded. "I know. They can't always be counted on. Does your brother sell papers too?"

"Naw. Does a few odd jobs sometimes. But he's been sick for a while."

"Let me know if I can help. My roommate is a doctor. Well, she's studying to be a doctor."

Sam snorted. "Whoever heard of a lady doctor?"

"There aren't many of them. She's the only woman in her class at the medical school. But she won't be the first. Not even the first one in Wisconsin."

"If you say so. Most ladies I see are mothers or spinsters."

She raised her eyebrows. "Some have jobs, you know. You must see a lot of shopgirls while you're selling papers."

"I guess." He tore at a slice of bread, sopped up the remaining gravy on his plate, and stuffed it into his mouth. "Hey, thanks for the grub, but I gotta get going."

He took a second piece of bread, wrapped it around a scrap of meatloaf, covered it with a clean section of the handkerchief, and shoved it in his pocket. Sophie guessed it was for his brother.

"Thank you for talking with me," she said.

"Any time." He gave her a disarming grin, and she wished he were heading off for a cozy evening with loving parents instead of what she assumed was a cold hovel with only his ill brother for company.

"So long, Miss Strong."

"It's Sophie."

"Okay, *Sophie*. See you later, *Sophie*." He chuckled and headed for the door.

She put some coins for the meal on the table and picked up her bag. Then she thought of something else. "Sam, wait!"

He kept walking, so she followed him outside. "Sam!"

He stopped and eyed her expectantly.

"I'm sorry; I know you have to go. Do you have any of the material left? The part that you cut off the jacket?"

He rolled his eyes. "No, I do not. Gotta go." He turned

and ran down the street. She hoped he felt energized by the hearty meal.

Her heart constricted as she watched him rush off, imagining the long hours of shouting and selling each day just so he could buy a meager supper for himself and his brother. They should both be in school. She wished she could help, but she could barely keep her own roof over her head.

With a sigh, she turned and headed back down the street toward home, looking forward to Mrs. O'Day's roaring fire and a chat with her housemates. She'd ponder mysteries of Hilda Rock and the Spring Gala Fiasco tomorrow.

8

———

On Tuesday, Sophie used a complimentary ticket sent to the paper to attend a mid-afternoon concert at the Wisconsin Conservatory of Music. Then she interviewed one of the instructors about the value of music lessons for children. She allowed herself the luxury of a pleasant walk back to the office, soaking up the spring sunshine. Along the way, she passed a new cafe on Third Street. She ducked in for a slice of carrot cake and a cup of coffee served up by the proud owner, who was happy to give her a quick interview. She told him she'd find room for a little nugget about his cafe on the women's page in the next couple of days. Thus fortified, she returned to the office, where the familiar scents of ink, paper, cigarette smoke, and stale coffee were oddly comforting.

It was late afternoon, and the place was fairly empty, though she noticed Benjamin Turner pecking at his type-writer keys. Mr. Barnaby wasn't in his office, and Sophie was relieved to avoid another encounter after the clash of the day before. She pulled out her notebook and scanned her notes about the concert. Deciding to add a few details about the history of the conservatory, she pushed back her chair and went into the office library to check the file.

As usual, the drawer she wanted was at the bottom of the cabinet. She kneeled on the floor and pulled open the heavy wooden drawer, then began flipping through folders that bulged with years of clippings. As ever, her curiosity was piqued by the topics she passed on the way to *Conservatory of Music—Carroll College, Chicago & North Western Railway, City Hall.* She could spend hours exploring Milwaukee's tumultuous past. Forcing herself to stay focused on her goal, she extracted the conservatory's file and got to her feet.

She was startled to see Benjamin Turner standing at the end of the row of cabinets, watching her.

"Mr. Turner, you surprised me. I didn't hear you come in."

"Good afternoon, Miss Strong."

He made no move to open a filing cabinet or scour a bookshelf.

"Are you looking for something?" she asked.

"You, actually."

"I beg your pardon?"

"Look, I saw you talking with the chief yesterday. He looked pretty mad."

Sophie felt her cheeks flush. "I don't see how that's any concern of yours," she said. "If you've come to gloat—"

"No, it's not that." He fell silent again.

"Mr. Turner, if you have something to say, please say it, so we can both get on with our work." She couldn't quite read his expression.

"I switched your story."

Her heart thumped in her chest. "You did *what?*"

"I switched your story. After you left on Sunday. I typed up a version without the brouhaha at the end."

"But why—how did you—you changed my story? Are you crazy?" Her face grew hotter.

He rubbed a hand over his jaw. "It's not a good idea to cross people like the Wolffs. I doubt the Chief would have printed it, but still."

"It's none of *your* business what I write! Why did you even read it? Since when does my work interest you?"

"I knew something was up."

"But how? The Wolffs were determined to keep it quiet. Do you have an informant?"

"Something like that."

"Mr. Turner, you're speaking in riddles. I don't have time to decipher them. In the future, I'll thank you to keep your hands off of my work. I'll do the same for you."

She held the file tightly against her chest, as if to protect herself, and moved for the door.

"I was there," he said.

She halted and turned around. "You were *where*?"

"At the Spring Gala."

Sophie was stunned into silence. She tried to imagine how Benjamin Turner could have managed to get into the party. Had he been lurking in the garden? Disguised as a servant?

He hadn't been a guest, surely. One of the intruders?

She eyed him suspiciously. "That's impossible."

It was his turn to look offended.

"You underestimate me," he said loftily. Then his tone softened. "I'm working on a big story, and Wolff is part of it. I was researching that night. I didn't want to arouse Wolff's suspicion."

"What do you mean? What kind of story?"

"I can't tell you that."

She was silent for a moment, trying to make sense of what he was saying. If he was investigating the Wolffs, she might have noticed details that he didn't. But she trusted him even less than before, after what he'd done.

"I don't know what you're up to, Benjamin Turner, but stay out of my business." She stalked to the door. As she exited, she glanced back and caught him watching her, an unreadable expression on his face.

"You're a graceful dancer, Miss Strong," he said with a wry smile.

He turned on his heel and left by the other door at the opposite end of the room.

Sophie froze, her thoughts racing. She had danced with one person at the Spring Gala—an unknown man dressed as a Spaniard. It couldn't have been Benjamin Turner. Could it? She tried to recall an image of the costumed man. He had been dark and about the same height as Mr. Turner.

She shook her head, resolving to put Benjamin Turner and his ridiculous claims out of her mind. She flipped through the file on the conservatory, finding the facts she sought in a clipping about its last anniversary celebration. Back at her desk, her fingers flew across the keys as she typed the story, unsure if her sentences were even logical.

She glanced at Mr. Turner's desk, trying to dislodge the niggling curiosity about his claim to be working on an important story. It didn't matter if he was telling the truth, or if he had been the Spaniard. She'd be neither collaborating with Benjamin Turner nor dancing with him again.

But what was his big story? She'd love to steal it right from under his nose. Could the Wolffs be up to something illegal?

When she finished the concert story, she typed up a paragraph about the cafe with the delicious cake. Then she took both pieces to Mr. Barnaby's office. Though Mr. Turner wasn't around, she dropped her stories on the top of the stack in the basket with a flourish of her arm. Still incensed that Mr. Turner had interfered with her work—no matter what excuse he offered—she refused to be discouraged by him.

Sophie was gathering her things at her desk when she heard running footsteps in the hall.

"Miss Strong! You here?"

She looked up to see a boy burst through the door, his cap askew. "Sam?"

The empty canvas bag flapped against his torso, and he gripped a folded piece of paper in one grubby hand. "Miss Strong, I've got a message for ya."

"A message? From whom?"

"Dunno. A bicycle messenger gave it to me. Said he was too busy to come find you."

Sophie unfolded the paper and immediately recognized Clara Elliot's elegant penmanship.

At police station. Please come. C.

Police? Mrs. Elliot? The two were wildly incongruous.

"Thank you, Sam," she said. "I have to run."

She rummaged in her purse and pulled out two pennies for his tip. She tugged on her gloves, pinned her hat in place, not minding that it was slightly awry, and dashed out the door.

9

The atmosphere of the central police station on North Broadway was thick with the odor of unwashed bodies, cigarette smoke, and fear. Sophie had been before to write about pickpockets or vagrants arrested on Milwaukee's streets. But this was the first time she'd personally known someone who was being questioned. The knots in her stomach tightened. Surely they wouldn't arrest a lady as distinguished and wealthy as Mrs. Elliot—would they?

Sophie walked up to the large desk that stood on a platform just inside the door and waited while the officer on duty barked into a candlestick-shaped telephone. He replaced the earpiece in its cradle and slammed the instrument down with a grimace.

"I'm Sophie Strong of the *Milwaukee Herald*. I'm here to see Mrs. Clara Elliot," she told him. She had no intention of writing a story about Mrs. Elliott's experience with the police, but she hoped the paper's name would open doors.

The officer gave her a hard look. "Mrs. Elliot is being questioned. Wait over there."

He jerked his head toward a grimy wooden bench along

the wall, currently inhabited by a man in rags with matted hair who stared at the dirty floor. She could smell the alcohol on him from where she stood.

"She requested my presence during the interview. Which room is she in?"

She moved toward the hallway that led to the interior of the station, though in truth she had no idea how to find her way around. She'd never ventured past the lobby before.

"Nothing doing, miss. Over there." He pointed to the bench again.

"Detective Zimmer is expecting me," she insisted. "Which room?"

He sighed. "Miss, that's not how this works. You can talk to your friend after the detective is through."

"He won't be happy to be kept waiting," Sophie fibbed. "I'll find them myself."

She took a few steps into the hallway, but a rotund, baby-faced officer blocked her progress.

Spotting him, the desk officer called, "Rudolph, go ask Detective Zimmer what he wants us to do with Miss Strong here."

"Yes, sir."

Officer Rudolph jostled back down the hall. Sophie watched him, hoping to see which room he entered, but he turned a corner and was out of sight. Not wanting to join the foul-smelling man on the bench, she flattened herself against the wall and tried to look unobtrusive. She pulled out her notebook and leafed through the pages for something to do with her hands.

The main entrance burst open and two officers came in. Each officer wrestled with a separate handcuffed and protesting man.

"I didn't do it," one shouted. "You got the wrong guy."

The officer shoved him toward the desk. "Shut up, Malloy. I heard it all before."

At Sophie's right, Officer Rudolph reappeared in the doorway.

"Come with me, Miss Strong."

Sophie followed the younger man, hoping he really was taking her to Mrs. Elliot and not planning to lock her in a dismal interview room to keep her quiet—or worse, a jail cell. He led her past a wide-open room full of cluttered desks staffed by harried policemen, some speaking to people who were tearful, sullen, belligerent, or a combination of the three. Sophie and Officer Rudolph turned down another narrow corridor, over cracked floor tiles and past dirt-smudged walls, then stopped at a battered wooden door scarred with gouges along the bottom, as if it had seen a good share of angry kicks. He gave it two sharp raps and opened it, then waved Sophie inside.

A surge of relief washed over her when she saw Mrs. Elliot seated at the table with Detective Zimmer. She looked tired and terribly out of place, but not much worse for wear.

Detective Zimmer glanced up. "Take a seat, Miss Strong."

She slipped into the chair next to Mrs. Elliot and gave her hand a quick squeeze under the table.

Zimmer frowned at Sophie, his brows drawn into a tight line. "As I'm sure you know, Miss Strong, detectives aren't in the habit of inviting visitors to an interrogation. But Mrs. Elliott apparently has some *influence* with Chief Johnson."

Mrs. Elliott turned to Sophie. "I've known him since we were children."

"Yes, it's very touching to reunite with an old friend," Zimmer snapped, glowering at both of them. "But that will only get you so far. The chief doesn't let murderers go free."

Sophie cleared her throat. "If you recall, Mrs. Elliott was nowhere near the crime scene, Detective Zimmer."

"So she claims, Miss Strong. And if *you* recall, the murdered corpse of Hilda Rock was propped against the door of the Wisconsin Women's Suffrage Association."

Sophie kept her expression neutral as she met Zimmer's gaze. "That has nothing to do with Mrs. Elliott."

"Don't be obtuse, Miss Strong. Mrs. Elliot spends many hours at that office, and Hilda Rock was a vociferous opponent of suffrage. I have since learned that Mrs. Elliott carried on a heated debate with Mrs. Rock mere days ago. In fact, it was so contentious that Mrs. Elliot shoved Mrs. Rock."

Sophie glanced at Mrs. Elliot and saw her wince, then returned her gaze to Zimmer.

"Mrs. Rock did not make a formal complaint, if I recall," she said.

Zimmer pulled a handkerchief from a pocket and covered his fingers with it as he lifted a thick white card from the file folder. Its edges looked worn.

"Does this look familiar to you?" he asked.

Mrs. Elliot's brows furrowed as she recognized her own name printed on the card. "Why, I haven't used those cards in... it must be two years or more."

"You don't use calling cards anymore?"

"Of course I *use* them. But I had new ones made." She reached into her purse and felt around, then frowned. "I keep them in a silver case. I believe it's on my desk at home. Would you like me to go home and retrieve it?"

"That won't be necessary. Why the new cards?"

Mrs. Elliot cleared her throat. "It seems silly now, but I was shopping with a friend, and we came upon a print shop that was displaying more ornate cards. Many of them were quite colorful. My friend ordered some, and the gentleman who owned the shop was so young and eager, I felt drawn in somehow."

"So why would someone have this old one?"

"I haven't any idea," said Mrs. Elliott. "It's odd that anyone would keep it for so long."

Zimmer let a silence stretch out. Then leaning forward, he glared at Mrs. Elliott and said, "Did you ever pay a social call on Mrs. Rock, a person who notoriously opposes women's suffrage?"

"No—that is, not recently."

"When did you last visit her?"

"Many years ago. Fifteen, at least. She wasn't always opposed to suffrage. At one point she was part of the movement."

Zimmer's eyes narrowed. "You're saying she switched sides?"

"That's right."

"And when did this change of heart occur?"

"I believe it was after she married. Her husband was a brewer."

"Why would she do such a thing? Suddenly decide that women shouldn't have the vote after all?"

"I haven't a clue. It was a shock to all of us—her friends and acquaintances, that is."

Sophie was stunned. Hilda Rock had worked in *favor* of suffrage? With Aunt Lucy and Clara Elliot? No one had ever mentioned any of this.

"We found this card in Hilda Rock's pocket," Zimmer said, his eyes fixed on Mrs. Elliot. "At the murder scene."

Mrs. Elliot met his gaze blankly.

Sophie spoke up. "Detective, are you suggesting that Mrs. Elliot killed Mrs. Rock, and then left her calling card behind? That's preposterous."

Detective Zimmer ignored her, staring intently at Clara Elliot.

"What happened on Saturday night at the suffrage office,

Mrs. Elliot? I'm going to find out, so you might as well tell me."

Clara's voice remained calm. "As I explained, I have no idea. I was at home. I had no reason to be at the suffrage office at such an hour. In fact, I wasn't there at all on Saturday."

"Who were you with? Can anyone vouch for you?"

"My sister Agnes was home."

"You spent time together?"

"It—it's possible. I'm not certain."

Detective Zimmer sighed. "Who else lives in the home? Do you have servants?"

Mrs. Elliot looked uncomfortable. "Well, yes, of course. There's the cook, the housekeeper, and the chauffeur."

Zimmer produced a piece of paper from the folder and took a pen from his shirt pocket. "Write their names for me here, please. And your sister's—Agnes, you said?"

Clara nodded and picked up the pen. Detective Zimmer scraped his chair away from the table and stood. "I'll be back."

He left the room, slamming the door behind him. Sophie heard the click of a key being turned in the lock. She swallowed hard. The room suddenly felt cramped, the air stifling.

"Thank you for coming, Sophie," Clara said. "I suppose I should have called my lawyer, but I was so surprised to be here, I couldn't think straight. I just remembered you'd met this detective."

"I'm willing to help if I can," Sophie said.

Clara wrote the names of her sister and her household staff with sweeping, graceful strokes, then rested the pen on the paper.

She rubbed her forehead. "I don't believe this is happening."

"Do you want to call your lawyer now?" Sophie asked.

Clara shook her head. "Surely we're about done here."

Unable to restrain her inquiries, Sophie asked, "You were friends with Hilda Rock? And she worked *for* suffrage before she campaigned against it? Why have I never heard of this?"

Clara sighed and turned to Sophie. She looked much older than she had when they'd gleefully combed through her closet together, looking at frothy dresses.

"Lucy and I have a history with Hilda, you might say. And yes, she switched sides in the suffrage debate."

"Why doesn't anyone talk about it?"

"It isn't relevant. It was seventeen years ago. I suppose men think Hilda came to her senses. And Lucy and I... I guess we felt betrayed at first. But there's been so much vitriol since then. I can barely remember the girl Hilda used to be, when we were working together. She's changed—she *had* changed, that is. I keep forgetting she's dead."

"Well, for heaven's sake, don't tell Detective Zimmer that you felt betrayed," said Sophie.

Clara gripped Sophie's wrist. "I did not kill her, Sophie. I would never do such a thing."

Sophie looked into her earnest blue eyes. "I know you didn't. But is there anything else you haven't told me? I don't want to get caught off guard again."

Clara cast her eyes downward, and her face clouded.

"What is it?" Sophie asked. "There's something else, isn't there?"

"It's Agnes—" Clara began. But her words were cut off by the return of Detective Zimmer. He banged the door shut, making both women jump.

He returned to his chair, tossed his folder on the table, and looked at Clara, brows drawn together. "You haven't told me much, Mrs. Elliot."

"As I explained, Detective, I know nothing about Mrs. Rock's death."

He opened the folder and tapped the calling card with one fingernail. "And yet, this card troubles me. As does your contentious history with Mrs. Rock."

Clara looked at him, her mouth set in a tight, silent line.

Detective Zimmer held her gaze for a long moment, then sighed. "Unfortunately, I don't have enough evidence to arrest you. *Yet.*"

Sophie heard Clara expel an unsteady breath.

"I will visit your home very soon, Mrs. Elliot, to question your sister and your staff. There's more to this story than you're telling me."

"Detective, I assure you, I have told you everything I know."

"Yes, so you've said. But with all due respect, I find it hard to believe you." He stood. "An officer will show you out."

In two strides, he was at the door again. "Rudolph!" he yelled.

Sophie and Clara got to their feet. The young officer appeared in the doorway and Zimmer waved his hand in the ladies' direction in a silent command. Sophie and Clara filed past Detective Zimmer and traced their steps through the hubbub of the station and onto the city street.

10

———————

In her library, Clara stared with dull eyes into the flames of the crackling fire. After a moment, Sophie cleared her throat.

"Mrs. Elliot? Back at the station, you were saying something about your sister."

Clara looked up. "Oh, do call me Clara. We're old friends, and you're a grown woman now."

"I'll try," said Sophie with a smile. "But it's a lifelong habit."

Clara nodded. "I'm worried about Agnes. She's been acting strangely."

"How so?"

The housekeeper, Ellen, entered with the tea tray, and Clara waited until she'd gone before continuing.

"Agnes has been coming home late at night. Ten or eleven o'clock. It isn't like her. She rarely has social engagements."

"Does she have a new friend? Maybe a gentleman friend?"

Clara frowned, looking dubious. "I guess it's possible. Of course, she doesn't tell me anything. She seems distracted. I'm worried she may be ill."

"What was she doing on Saturday night, when Mrs. Rock was killed?"

Clara looked up sharply. "I don't know."

"But at the police station, you said—"

"I know, I know. I wasn't sure what else to say. But I've been racking my brain, and I am not certain that I saw Agnes at all that night."

Sophie bit her lip. "Let's take it step by step. What do you remember?"

Clara sighed. "I was a little melancholy, to tell you the truth. I was thinking about you at the Spring Gala, and how David and I used to go to so many wonderful events. I looked through my old diary. I even got out some love letters I'd saved." She smiled.

"You were here in the library?"

"Yes. I heard the door open and close at some point—I'm not sure exactly when. I was getting sleepy, and I didn't want to rouse myself to see if it was Agnes or one of the servants."

"Do you think she could have..." Sophie let the question hang in the air.

Clara shook her head vehemently. "No, she couldn't have. She's always been a bit odd, of course. We're not really close. But murder? Impossible."

"Okay. So you and Agnes didn't see each other that night, but that wasn't unusual. There's no crime against that. And there's no crime against coming and going at odd hours, either. It doesn't mean she's a murderer. To start with, where would she get a gun?"

Clara gasped, her eyes wide.

"What is it?" Sophie asked.

"My goodness, I had forgotten all about it. David had a gun."

"Is it still here somewhere? Where did he keep it?"

Clara tapped her lip. "I know I saw it, when I was going

through his things, a couple of years after he died. I always meant to do something with it, maybe ask Dante to sell it. I just never got around to it." She snapped her fingers. "It's in a drawer, in his dressing room."

They hurried upstairs to Clara's bedroom. When they'd explored Clara's miraculous closet on Friday, Sophie hadn't noticed the door on the other side of the room. Now Clara opened it to reveal a gentleman's dressing room, just as spacious as her own. There was a large bureau topped by a wide mirror, and a few suits still hung on hangers.

Clara gestured to them sheepishly. "I gave away most of his things, but there were some—" She broke off. "It's funny how many memories can be associated with an ordinary suit of clothes."

She went to the bureau and tugged open the bottom drawer. Inside, Sophie spotted a brown and blue tartan scarf, some books, and a silver shaving cup and brush. Clara pushed them out of the way and pulled out a black leather case. The brass lock on the front flipped open easily.

"I should have kept it locked, I know," Clara said. "I just never thought..."

She lifted the lid and stared at the contents, speechless. The interior of the box, covered in green wool baize, was divided into sections. Sophie saw a handful of bullets, a powder flask embossed with an eagle and stars, two small round tins of caps, a cleaning rod, and other items she couldn't name. But at the center, the revolver-shaped space sat glaringly empty.

"I FEEL LIKE SUCH A FOOL," said Clara.

They'd scoured the room for the weapon and come up

with nothing. Now, in the dining room, her soup sat untouched in front of her.

"I should have locked it up. Or gotten rid of it. I just—it was hard to go through with David's things, let alone part with them."

"It proves nothing," insisted Sophie. "About the murder, I mean. When was the last time you saw the gun?"

Clara looked up at the ceiling, her brow furrowed. "Let's see... maybe five or six years ago? David died in '04. And a couple of years went by before I felt up to sorting through his things."

"A lot can happen in five years," said Sophie. "Anyone could have taken it. Maybe a servant, or a workman who came to fix something."

"Oh, Sophie—the police are coming to the house. Do you think they'll search? Should I get rid of the gun case?"

Sophie shook her head. "You've got nothing to hide. It may not be wise to lose track of a gun, but it's not a crime. And if you were seen throwing out the case, it could look like you're guilty of something."

Clara nodded. "You're right, of course."

"Besides, I think they'd need a search warrant. And there isn't any evidence against you."

"Except for that calling card."

The card had been weighing on Sophie's mind, too. "Why do you think she had it?"

"I haven't any idea. We hadn't been on speaking terms for years."

Sophie reached for a piece of bread from a plate on the table. "Go on."

Clara sighed. "I barely know where to begin." After a pause, she continued, "Lucy and I knew Hilda when we were all much younger. We weren't friends, but friendly acquaintances. It seemed like Hilda was one of us, you know. Part of the suffrage movement."

"Do you know what happened? How could she change her mind like that?"

"We never understood it. It was after her husband died. She just vanished from our circle. He had owned a small brewery. I heard that when he passed away, she found out he was in debt. I stopped seeing her around town, at club meetings and things. We all thought she was in mourning. Lucy and I called on her once. But then David passed, and we just lost touch."

"When did you find out she was anti-suffrage?"

"It happened gradually. A few years after her husband died, I remember seeing her talking with some of the anti-suffragists outside a shop, but I thought little of it. Then, let's see... it was 1909, I believe. She started speaking publicly. And you know what she's been like in the past year or two."

"Vehement is a word that comes to mind."

Clara nodded. "We should have tried harder to maintain the acquaintance. Perhaps she needed friends."

Sophie placed her hand on Clara's. "You can't blame yourself. She knew what she was doing. Did she try to get in touch with you?"

"No, I suppose she didn't."

"See? It goes both ways."

Clara bit her lip. "Sophie, do you think her murder could be somehow connected with her being an Anti? Or with her choice to switch sides?"

Sophie frowned. "I don't see how it could. Suffragists are passionate, but we wouldn't resort to murder. And Hilda's voice was only one among many, unfortunately."

"You must be right."

The front door opened. A quiet exchange followed that

Sophie couldn't make out. After a moment, Agnes Thompson breezed into the dining room.

"Hello there," she said. "Soup? Looks delicious."

Agnes had Clara's tall, slender frame, but the resemblance stopped there. Her thin brown hair was pulled into a severe knot that emphasized the wrinkles on her weathered face. She was only two years older, but her face showed evidence of a harder life. Her eyes were a pale, washed-out blue.

She dropped into the spot across from Sophie. "I'm starved."

Ellen set a hot bowl in front of Agnes, and steam wisped upward to her face. She looked almost cheerful, Sophie thought, which was a change from her usual surly demeanor.

"You're certainly lively," Clara said. "Have you been visiting someone?"

Agnes shrugged. "No, I just ran a few errands and walked home. It's a lovely night." She took a few hearty spoonfuls of soup, then reached for a chunk of bread. "What have you been up to?"

"I was at the police station, being questioned."

Agnes went still. She looked up at Clara, her eyes unreadable.

"What happened?" she asked.

"My calling card was found in Hilda Rock's pocket. They wanted to know why."

"Your calling card? What did you tell them?"

"That I had no idea, of course. As you know, I haven't spoken civilly to Hilda Rock in years."

Agnes nodded slowly.

"The odd thing was," Clara continued, "It was a very old calling card. One that I haven't used in some time."

Agnes furrowed her brow. "An old card? What do you mean? Your name hasn't changed."

Clara explained how she'd purchased new, colorful cards.

Sophie thought it was odd that Agnes hadn't noticed this, but she reasoned that Clara and Agnes rarely went about in society together. As far as Sophie could recall, the only times they were together were at home or at the suffrage office. Beyond that, they had separate friends and interests.

Agnes put down her spoon. "So you convinced them you had nothing to do with Hilda's death?"

"For the time being, I suppose. They don't have any real evidence. But they're coming here to question the household. They will want to speak with you as well."

"Me? I don't know anything about it."

"Well, I am sure they will ask you. I have been trying to remember what we were doing on Saturday night. That's when she was killed. I think I was in the library all night."

"Do you remember what you were doing, Miss Thompson?" Sophie asked, looking at Agnes.

Agnes's pale-blue eyes darted to Sophie. "I was in my room. I wasn't feeling well, so I went to bed early."

Sophie glanced at Clara, who was studying Agnes intently.

"Mrs. Elliot heard the front door at some point. Are you sure you didn't go out?" Sophie asked.

"Yes, I'm sure," Agnes said.

"There's something else," said Clara. "David's gun is missing."

Agnes jerked her head toward Clara. "Wh-what gun?"

"You must remember. He talked endlessly about how he inherited it from his father. He kept it in his dressing room."

"Well, I wouldn't know what was in David's dressing room."

"But you do remember him mentioning it."

Agnes stared at the table, as if trying to recall.

"I don't think so," she said. "And it was so long ago."

Clara nodded. "Eight years have already passed. Sometimes I can hardly believe it."

Agnes picked up her spoon again and stirred the soup listlessly. "Did the police say when they're coming?"

"Detective Zimmer didn't specify a time, did he, Sophie?"

Agnes looked at Sophie. "Were you questioned too?"

"Not today. I had already talked to them. Mrs. Elliot asked me to come to the police station, since I had met the detective before, when I found... Mrs. Rock."

They were silent for a few moments, and the only sound was the soft clinking of silver against ceramic bowls. Then Agnes stood.

"I think I'll go upstairs," she said. "I'm feeling unwell again. Like Saturday night."

"Shall I tell Ellen to bring you a hot water bottle?" Clara asked.

Agnes shook her head. "I'm sure I'll be fine. I'll just rest. Good night."

She swiftly left the room.

Clara took a few more spoonfuls of soup, then set down the spoon.

"I am certain Agnes heard David talking about that gun," she said. "He was quite proud of it. I believe a cousin had used it during the Civil War." She smiled ruefully. "Well, as Agnes said, it was a long time ago."

She reached out to squeeze Sophie's hand. "I cannot tell you how much I appreciate you coming today, Sophie. I was quite out of my element."

Sophie smiled. "Of course. I'm glad you sent for me. This whole thing is a holy mess. And that Detective Zimmer— well, I suppose it's his job to be unpleasant, but he's truly obnoxious."

～

THAT NIGHT, Sophie lay in bed, staring at the ceiling. No matter how hard she tried to put the day's events out of her head, sleep wouldn't come. After a restless hour, she got up and went to the window. She looked out at the starry sky, barely lit by a sliver of moonlight, and forced herself to breathe.

The gnawing anxiety in her chest reminded her of childhood, after her mother died. She'd walked on eggshells to avoid triggering an angry outburst from her father. He'd rarely paid attention to her except to give her odd jobs to do at his grocery store, but when his self-control snapped and his temper lashed out, it terrified her. Finally, when she was twelve, Aunt Lucy had visited on one of her trips for the traveling library and rescued her. She hadn't spoken to her father since her eighteenth birthday, four years ago.

Sophie hugged herself, rubbing her arms to fight off the chill in the air. The events of the past several days ran through her mind: the angry debate, the violence at Wolff Mansion, finding Mrs. Rock's body, meeting Clara at the police station, and the intimidating Detective Zimmer.

As she gazed at the shimmering moon, Sophie recognized the sickening sensation of feeling unsafe and powerless. There was a murderer out there somewhere. Mrs. Elliot had been threatened by the police. What if Detective Zimmer decided to question Aunt Lucy? Or what if he came after Sophie herself? Innocent people sometimes ended up in jail. Zimmer wanted her to stand aside and let the police handle everything.

But what if they didn't?

Policemen could be incompetent or corrupt; they might arrest the wrong person. She didn't know a thing about Zimmer or his character. Would the killer come back to hurt someone else—maybe someone she loved? Sophie remembered that horrible instant when she'd thought it was Aunt

Lucy crumpled against the door of the suffrage office. Tears stung her eyes, and she let them fall.

She rested her forehead against the cool glass of the window. After a moment, she wiped her tears with the sleeve of her nightgown, the torn lace flapping against her cheek. She'd be damned if she'd sit back and let a bunch of men determine her fate and that of the people who meant everything to her. The women journalists she idolized risked everything for justice. Nellie Bly got herself locked in an insane asylum, to publicize the inhumane conditions and make things better for other women.

Sophie could be just as brave. She'd put the clues together, make deductions, and then hand over her findings to the police. She would keep Aunt Lucy and Clara and herself safe.

She went to her bag and pulled out her notebook, sleep forgotten, and started writing a list of ideas to launch her investigation.

11

Sophie knocked on the door of Hilda Rock's modest bungalow, noting the peeling green paint. Never in her wildest dreams did she expect to be calling at the home of Milwaukee's most notorious anti-suffragist. There was no answer. She knocked again, more insistently. When no one came, she reached for the knob and turned.

"Hello?" she called, poking her head inside. "Hello? Is anyone home?"

A thud sounded from above. She froze, realizing that she had no idea what she was walking into. Did Mrs. Rock have relatives? Friends? Was she being robbed?

Just as she was about to close the door and leave, she heard footsteps descending a staircase. A slim, middle-aged woman in a simple gray dress emerged into the entryway, carrying a wooden crate.

"Hello, miss," she said. "Can I help you with something?"

"Hello. I'm Sophie Strong. I was sorry to learn about Mrs. Rock's passing." The woman cocked her head, and Sophie wondered if Mrs. Rock's household had perhaps not received many condolence calls. "Are you a relative?"

The woman tucked a strand of faded brown hair behind one ear. "I'm Millie Hanson. I'm her housekeeper—well, I was."

"I was wondering if I might speak with you for a few moments. I—I'm a friend of Agnes Thompson's. I believe you know each other?"

Millie wrinkled her forehead. "You're Agnes's friend, are you? Well, you'd be her first." She carefully placed the crate on the bottom step, then went to the door and opened it wider for Sophie to enter. "I guess I can talk for a spell."

Sophie stepped into the dim entryway and glanced around. A few photos dotted the papered walls, though there were large dark patches where other frames had once hung. A hall tree stood opposite the stairway, with a couple of cloaks on its hooks. Through a doorway at her right, she could see into the kitchen.

"We can go in the parlor," said Millie.

Sophie followed her down a short hallway and into a small room with two chairs covered in a well-worn floral print, a sofa, and a low wooden table. The mantle above the fireplace was empty of the usual candlesticks and other ornaments.

Millie gestured to the sofa, and Sophie took a seat, the cushion firm and unforgiving beneath her. Millie sat in an adjacent chair.

"Would you like some water? Or tea?" Millie asked. It sounded like a reluctant afterthought.

"No, thank you," said Sophie. "I'll only stay a few moments. You must be busy."

"I'm packing up. Mrs. Rock had no family, so it's left to me."

"I didn't know. How sad." She noticed that Millie didn't seem particularly troubled by her employer's demise. "Have you worked for Mrs. Rock long?"

"Let's see... It must be fifteen years, at least."

"Her death was such a shock." Sophie swallowed as the memory came back. "You see, I was the one who discovered her. On Sunday."

Millie's eyes widened. "Oh, my."

"I confess, it's made me quite curious about what may have led to her death."

"A thief, I should think," said Millie. "Bad luck."

"You may be right." Sophie paused, then asked, "Did she tell you what her plans were on Saturday?"

Millie shook her head. "She didn't tell me much. I was at the market that afternoon, and when I got back, she was gone."

Sophie waited. Mr. Barnaby always said that people will tell you just about anything if you keep quiet. Silence makes folks antsy, he said. But Millie offered nothing more.

"The odd thing was," Sophie said, "she was found outside the suffrage office. And she was fiercely opposed to suffrage, as I'm sure you are aware."

"Oh, yes. I'm aware."

"So it's puzzling what she was doing there. The place was deserted. I had stopped by to pick up some papers for Mrs. Elliot—that's Mrs. Thompson's sister." Millie listened with a blank expression on her face. "Do you know if she was meeting someone, late on Saturday?"

"I really don't know," Millie said. "As I said, she didn't tell me much."

There was another knock at the door. Millie jumped up. "My word, she's busier in death than she was in life. Excuse me."

Sophie heard a man's voice, but she couldn't make out what was said. After a quiet exchange, the door closed, and Millie came back into the sitting room, followed by a gentleman in a fine suit.

"Mr. Pitman!" Sophie blurted out, astonished to recognize the lawyer who worked down the hall from the suffrage office. He jerked his head toward her.

"Oh, I beg your pardon," Sophie went on. "I'm sorry if I startled you. I'm surprised to see you here."

"Miss Strong," stammered Pitman, stroking his wispy black mustache. "Hello. I'm surprised to see you as well."

Sophie opened her mouth to reply, but Millie cut her off. "I thought you were coming at five o'clock, sir," she said to Mr. Pitman. "The minister told me that's when Mrs. Rock's lawyer would be here."

"Oh! Um… I managed to get here early. Still, I'd better get started." He glanced at a door next to the fireplace. "Er… Did Mrs. Rock have a study? Or a desk?"

"Right through here, sir," said Millie. She led him across the room and opened the door.

Mr. Pitman paused before entering and looked back at Sophie. "Excuse me, Miss Strong. I have a great deal of work to do."

With another glance at Millie, he went inside and slammed the door.

Millie returned to her seat and smoothed her skirt, not meeting Sophie's eyes.

"Do you know Mr. Pitman well?" Sophie asked.

"Never met him before," said Millie. She finally looked up. "Are you sure you don't want some tea?"

"No, thank you, but I appreciate the offer. Mr. Pitman's office is in the same building as the suffrage office. We've met there from time to time. He is Mrs. Rock's lawyer?"

"I-I suppose so," said Millie. "She never mentioned him."

Sophie stayed silent, but to her irritation, Millie didn't continue.

"I know you must be terribly busy, Millie," said Sophie. "I

just have one more question. This might sound strange, but was Mrs. Rock acquainted with Ruben Wolff?"

An odd expression flashed across Millie's face, then disappeared.

"Mr. Wolff? You mean, from the brewery?"

"That's right. I attended an event at his home on the night Mrs. Rock died. Do you know if she had planned to attend the Wolffs' Spring Gala?"

Millie exhaled a rush of air that sounded more like a chuckle. "No, Mrs. Rock wasn't invited to any party at the Wolffs'." She shifted in her seat. "Miss Strong, is this an interview for your newspaper? I don't want to talk about Mrs. Rock's business behind her back, even if she is no longer with us. I'll need to find another job, and it won't do for me to be gossiping."

Sophie held up a reassuring hand. "Oh, no. As I said, I'm just curious. I wrote a brief account of the tragedy, and it appeared in the paper on Monday."

She thought she saw Millie's shoulders relax slightly. "I see. Well, I do have a lot of work to do."

Sophie stood. "Thank you for speaking with me. I appreciate your time." She reached into her bag for a calling card. "I wish you the best of luck in finding a new position. If I can be of any assistance, you can find me at the newspaper office."

Millie eyed the card with uncertainty. "Thank you." She tucked it into her pocket and started for the hallway.

On impulse, Sophie took two long strides across the room and opened the study door without knocking. Mr. Pitman sat at a large desk, frantically shuffling through documents strewn across its surface. The desk drawers were ajar, and strands of his slick black hair hung in his eyes.

"Mr. Pitman," Sophie said. His head popped up and his

mouth opened. "I just wanted to say goodbye. I hope to see you again soon."

He frowned. "Goodbye, Miss Strong."

A breeze from the open window behind him stirred some of the papers, and he slammed his hands on the desktop to hold them down, then piled them under a book. He cleared his throat, then resumed his work, this time moving at a more dignified pace.

Sophie turned and caught Millie giving her a cold stare, but it was quickly replaced with a smile. Millie gestured for Sophie to precede her into the hallway. As she passed the stairs, Sophie glanced at the crate, but its contents were just out of sight. Millie opened the front door.

She swept through the door, then turned. "Goodbye, Millie. Thank you again."

Millie nodded once, unsmiling, and closed the door.

Sophie slowly made her way down the stone walkway, sure she was still being watched from the window. Turning the conversation over in her head, she started along the sidewalk. A few doors down, a neighboring house looked quiet, as if the occupants were away. On impulse, Sophie darted through its front yard, then skirted the side of the house to the back. She dodged around the porch, heading toward Mrs. Rock's.

At the next house, she saw and heard a woman with her back to the open kitchen window as she worked at the stove, singing a bit off-key. Sophie ducked and jogged behind her house. When she was safely past the window, she paused and rested her back against the wall, eyeing the brick bungalow next door to Mrs. Rock's. Seeing no signs of life, she crossed the narrow strip of grass.

Just then, the back door of the brick house burst open and a hefty man in overalls appeared.

Sophie froze, certain he would spot her. But he turned his head and called to someone inside. Sophie flattened her back against the side of the house, her heart pounding.

The man bellowed, "Don't be late! I'll be there at six."

Boots clomped down the wooden steps, then rounded the house to the front.

Sophie stayed still, willing herself to breathe calmly. After a few long moments of silence, she peered around the corner. The yard was empty. She dashed across to Mrs. Rock's house. The small back porch in need of repair leaned forward at an awkward angle. She ducked around it, then pressed herself close to the back wall, resting her head against boards that needed fresh paint even more than the front door.

Her right arm barely touched the frame of the study's open window. She heard Mr. Pitman rummaging around inside. A drawer slammed shut, followed by the low rumble of angry muttering. Then she heard the study door open.

"Find anything?" The voice was Millie's, the deferential tone she'd used earlier now replaced by harsh urgency.

"No, damn it," growled Mr. Pitman.

A sharp voice called from farther inside, "Millie, look at this."

Sophie heard footsteps and guessed that a third person had entered the study. She wondered who it could be—she hadn't noticed any movement in the house when she'd been inside talking to Millie. "It's not exactly what we were looking for—"

Sophie caught her breath. She recognized that voice.

Cautiously, she moved her head to get a brief glimpse into the window. Agnes Thompson and Millie had their heads together, bent over something that Agnes was holding. She couldn't see what the object was or make out their words, but by their tone, they seemed to be disagreeing.

"What in the hell—" She heard Mr. Pitman's chair scrape back. Sophie ducked out of sight and heard his footsteps as he joined them.

Desperate to get a look at whatever had their interest, Sophie took a tiny step closer to the window. A twig snapped beneath her foot, and her heart leaped into her throat. She flattened herself against the house and held her breath, praying they hadn't heard her. But the conversation had stopped. Should she run off, even if she made a racket?

Her mind raced for a plausible story to explain her presence if she was caught, but she drew a blank. If someone put their head out of the window and looked around, she was sunk. Sweat prickled the back of her neck as the image of the bullet wound in Mrs. Rock's chest flashed in her memory. Any one of these three could be a murderer.

Someone tugged the window shut. Sophie allowed herself to breathe again, but she still wasn't safe. At any moment, someone could come out onto the porch or decide to look around the yard. It was three against one.

She stole one more glance again at the window, but the curtains had been drawn. She crept back around the porch the way she had come, placing each step precisely to avoid breaking more twigs.

On the other side of the brick house, Sophie saw the singing cook emerge onto her porch, still humming, shake out a damp dish towel, and drape it over the railing. Sophie straightened and tried to walk calmly along the side of Mrs. Rock's house, as if she had every right to be there. If the woman spotted her, she didn't make it known before going back inside.

Sophie figured her best bet was to make a break for the sidewalk and skedaddle. She was about to dash across the neighbor's front lawn when she heard new footsteps approaching Mrs. Rock's front door. She ducked back to the side of the house and peered around the corner.

A portly man in a brown suit and matching homburg hat, carrying a briefcase, walked up to the door and gave four sharp raps.

When it opened, he announced, "I am Mr. Sage, the attorney for Mrs. Rock's estate. You must be Mrs. Hanson?"

"Yes, sir," Millie answered.

"I was told you'd be expecting me."

"Yes, sir."

"Well, may I come in?" he sounded annoyed.

He entered, and the door closed once more.

Did Mrs. Rock have two lawyers? Then Sophie heard the back door open. She caught her breath again, willing whoever it was not to find her. A moment later, Mr. Pitman emerged from the opposite side of the house, holding a bulging satchel. He hurried down the sidewalk. She stared after him until he disappeared from view.

Why had he slipped out the back?

Sophie considered following him, but decided she'd pressed her luck quite far enough for one afternoon.

She scurried to the sidewalk and headed off in the direction opposite Mr. Pitman's route. This necessitated a circuitous journey back to the boarding house, but she had plenty to think about as she turned the day's events over in her head. Millie, Agnes, and Mr. Pitman were up to something—and they had lied about it. Could one of them be responsible for Mrs. Rock's death? And if so, why? Judging from the dilapidated house and its meager contents, the woman wasn't rich. What on Earth could they be searching for?

If Agnes Thompson was involved somehow, she could drag her sister Clara into it. And the police had already questioned her once.

Sophie needed to figure out what was going on. She was too fond of Clara to let the matter drop. Aunt Lucy might be swept right along with them. Sophie herself might even be a suspect. How could she untangle things and keep them all safe?

12

———

The clouds shimmered in a hue that seemed ominous as Sophie approached the Majestic Building late that afternoon. Aunt Lucy said that the police had finished investigating and removed all traces of the crime. Still, her stomach clenched as she walked up the stairs. It felt impossible that she'd glibly ascended the same steps just a few days ago, unaware of the appalling sight that awaited her.

A tuneful whistling floated down the hallway, and Sophie recognized a favorite melody from Mr. Watson, the janitor. She remembered the streaks of blood on the floor and realized he must have cleaned them. Had he been called in on Sunday for that purpose? Was he ever here alone? If so, that had to make him uneasy after the horrid events of Saturday night.

She followed the whistling and found him washing a window that looked out into the alley behind the building. She cleared her throat, not wanting to startle him.

He turned. "Miss Sophie, how are you?"

"I'm doing fine, Mr. Watson. I hope you're well."

"Not bad for an old man." His dark brown face creased

into a smile, but there was concern in his eyes. "Your aunt told me what happened—that you found Mrs. Rock. I'm sorry you had to see that. It must have been frightening."

She nodded, feeling the anxiety bubble up again.

"You'd best stay away from empty buildings when you're alone, if you don't mind my saying. You never know who could be waiting."

She smiled politely, wanting to end the conversation. She hadn't realized how strongly being in the building would affect her.

He shook his head. "Hard to believe what the world is coming to. Mrs. Rock was a pill, to be sure. But why would anyone take her life?"

"Did you know her?"

"No, not to speak of. I'd seen her go into Mr. Pitman's office once or twice."

"So he *was* her lawyer."

He nodded. "But usually she'd send another lady."

"Did you speak with her?"

"Oh, no. I couldn't help but overhear her sometimes, though. She raised her voice once, and it sounded like she was upset. I heard her mention Mrs. Rock's name."

"Do you remember what she looked like?"

Mr. Watson peered up at the ceiling as if trying to jog his memory, then shrugged. "You know, a white lady, maybe middle-aged."

Confusion gnawed at Sophie's mind. Had it been Millie who came to see Mr. Pitman? If so, why had she lied about knowing Mr. Pitman? And why would Mrs. Rock send her maid to handle a legal matter?

"She always came late in the evening or early in the morning, when there weren't many people around. I don't suppose she'll be back."

"I suppose not."

Mr. Watson looked at the rag in his hand and smiled sheepishly. "I'm sorry to keep chin wagging. This window won't wash itself, and you must want to see your aunt. You tell her and Mrs. Elliot to take care."

Sophie smiled and tried to sound cheerful. "It will take more than this to slow down their suffrage work."

"Well, there's no reason at all that ladies shouldn't vote, if you ask me. You and your aunt and Mrs. Elliot could do a better job than most men I know."

"Thank you, Mr. Watson. I heartily agree." She held up the newspapers she was carrying. "I should get these to Aunt Lucy. Nice to see you, Mr. Watson. You take care too."

"I always do, Miss Sophie."

The suffrage office was quiet when Sophie went in, and for a moment she thought she'd missed Aunt Lucy entirely. Then the familiar, smiling, dimpled face popped up from behind a low bookshelf.

"Aunt Lucy! Are you here alone?"

She held a bunch of pamphlets and newspapers. "Hello, Sophie. I sent Clara home about an hour ago. She seemed tired after her run-in with the police the other day. And I haven't seen Agnes today."

"You shouldn't be here on your own. Not after what happened to Mrs. Rock."

Aunt Lucy carried her burden to the desk and set it down with a sigh. "Oh, I'm not alone. Mr. Watson is around somewhere. And I knew you'd be along shortly."

"Still, it's not safe. Promise me you won't stay here alone. At least not until the police solve the case."

Aunt Lucy smiled and patted Sophie's cheek. "All right, dear. I don't want you to worry about me. But you're a fine one to talk, traipsing around the city at all hours."

"I'll try to be careful." She had no idea how to accomplish

that and still do her job, however, and she was sure Aunt Lucy guessed as much.

She set the newspapers she'd brought on the desk and gave her aunt a hug.

"Thank you for these, sweet thing," said Aunt Lucy. "It's always helpful to see what our sister suffragists are up to in other cities. You just put your feet up while I finish some filing. Then I'll repay you with a bite to eat."

"I can help," said Sophie. "Then we can eat sooner."

Aunt Lucy handed her a sheaf of papers and directed her to a filing cabinet.

After they'd worked in silence for a few minutes, Aunt Lucy said, "Thank you for helping Clara at the police station, Sophie."

"I don't know if I was much help, but I didn't mind going. I just hope that's the end of the trouble for her."

"Well, they can't arrest her for something she didn't do."

"I hope they won't. But innocent people do get arrested by mistake, Aunt Lucy."

"But a woman of her social standing—surely that protects her, whether it should or not."

"They'll have to check Mrs. Elliot's alibi. Something could go wrong." Sophie bit her lip. "I just have a funny feeling about the whole thing."

"It's mighty odd that Hilda Rock was in the building. What could she possibly have been doing? And who on Earth would shoot her?"

"Mr. Watson said it wasn't the first time she'd been there. She'd visited Mr. Pitman before."

"Really? She must have been very discreet. I'd never seen her."

"He said it was at unusual hours. And often she'd send someone on her behalf."

"Oh, yes. Probably Millie Hanson. Agnes had mentioned bumping into her in the hallway."

Sophie didn't mention that she'd questioned Millie. She didn't want her aunt to worry. "That Detective Zimmer is suspicious. He found out about the argument between Mrs. Elliot and Mrs. Rock at the suffrage debate."

"Clara is still bothered by that. She hates to lose her temper."

Aunt Lucy pushed her file drawer closed and slapped her hands down on her generous thighs. "Well, that's done. I'm starved. Let's go."

AT AUNT LUCY'S snug apartment, they opened tins of tomato soup and ate it with fresh bread from the bakery. After washing up, they carried teacups into the sitting room. Sophie took her favorite spot on the sofa, and Lucy plopped into her rocking chair. Her cat, Austen, was on her lap in an instant, purring with satisfaction.

They sat in companionable silence for a bit, but something tugged at the back of Sophie's mind.

"How long did you know Mrs. Rock, Aunt Lucy?"

"Hilda? Oh, my. It's hard to say. Many years."

"When I was at Wolff Mansion, I saw a framed copy of that paper you and Mrs. Elliot helped with—the women's charity edition. Mrs. Rock's name was there, and so was Mrs. Wolff's. You all must have worked on it together."

"Well, there was quite a group of us..." Aunt Lucy trailed off.

Sophie sensed there was more to the story.

"Why didn't you tell me you knew each other?"

"It was so long ago—" Loud knocking on the downstairs door cut her off. "Who in the world—"

Urgent pounding followed, as if someone were beating on the door with both fists.

"My goodness!" Aunt Lucy moved to push Austen off of her lap, but Sophie stopped her.

"I'll go," said Sophie.

Her senses were on alert. The pounding came again.

Sophie dashed down the stairs. "Who is it?" she called through the door.

"Miss Strong? It's Sam."

Sophie flung open the door.

"Sam!" He looked terrified. "Sam, what is it?"

"It's Harry—" He looked up at Sophie with wild eyes.

"Who? Who's Harry?"

He blinked, fighting back tears. "My brother. He's real sick. I don't know what to do." He grabbed her sleeve. "Please—I need help, miss."

"Of course I'll help you." She looked over his shoulder. "Is he with you?"

Sam shook his head fiercely. "No, I-I couldn't wake him up. Oh God, he can't be dead!"

She felt his fear in her bones, and for an instant she was six years old again, shaking the lifeless body of her mother, the person she loved most in the world. She enveloped Sam in a quick embrace.

"It'll be all right," she murmured.

She had no way of knowing if Harry was alive, but she desperately wanted to soothe the trembling boy.

Then she pulled away and held him firmly by both arms, looking into his eyes. "Where is he? At your place?"

He opened his mouth to speak, but then he snapped it shut and just nodded.

"Wait right here," she said. "I'll only be a moment."

She ran up the stairs to grab her coat and purse, but Aunt Lucy was already holding them, her key in hand.

"I heard. Let's go," she said.

They made an odd trio, running down the empty street. Sophie waved her hand as a hansom cab approached, but it raced along too fast for them to flag it. The driver didn't meet their eyes and appeared intent on passing them by. Sophie jumped into the horse's path, splashing through a puddle as she did so.

Startled, the driver yanked on the reins.

"You could have been killed!" he shouted at her. Then in a gruff tone he added, "I'm on my way home. It's dinner time."

"This is an emergency," Sophie said, wrenching open the door. She held out her hand to Aunt Lucy. The older woman lurched into the seat, followed by Sam. "Take us to..." Sophie looked at Sam, waiting for an address.

"The viaduct," Sam muttered. "Sixth and Grand."

Sophie instructed the driver. "Please hurry."

Their urgency must have convinced the man. The cab tore off through the night. All three were silent while houses slipped past the window. Tidy middle-class dwellings gave way to dilapidated apartment buildings and streets littered with refuse. When the vehicle pulled to a halt, Sophie opened the door and leaped out, with Sam right behind her.

"I'll keep the cab here," said Aunt Lucy. She fished in her bag for coins.

Sophie followed Sam, who ran across the sidewalk and under the stone arches of the viaduct. Barely visible in the dark, amid a cluster of bushes, was a makeshift tent of blankets propped up by wooden crates. Sam disappeared inside. Sophie swallowed hard and ducked in after him.

The stench was appalling. It was clear that the boy had been ill for some time. She smelled vomit and human waste. In a nest of blankets she saw a pale, still face, with Sam's pointed chin and matted sandy-brown hair.

Without stopping to think, Sophie slipped her arms under

the boy's neck and knees and scooped him up, her heart constricting as she lifted him too easily, like a sack of discarded chicken bones. She didn't stop to determine whether he was breathing, just carried him swiftly back to the cab as Sam ran along at her side. She wasn't sure if she was taking the child to be healed or buried.

13

Aunt Lucy helped Sophie nestle Harry's weak form on one seat of the cab. Sam jumped in and cradled his brother's head in his lap.

"We've got to get him to the hospital," Sophie said.

Sam shook his head, his eyes wide with fear. "No—please—we hate hospitals. When our Ma—" He swallowed. "Is there somewhere else?"

Aunt Lucy put her ear to Harry's chest. She opened a compact and placed its small mirror under the boy's nose. His almost imperceptible breaths misted the glass.

"I suppose we can go to my place," she said.

Sophie spoke to the driver, and the carriage raced back the way it had come. Several anxious minutes later, Sophie carried the frail boy up the stairs and tucked him into bed. His eyelids fluttered slightly as she arranged the blankets around him. Sophie wondered how long it had been since he'd rested on a mattress and pillow—if he ever had. She smoothed dirty strands of hair away from his forehead, feeling heat under the skin.

"He has a fever."

Aunt Lucy nodded and left the room, returning almost instantly with a basin of cold water and several clean cloths. With practiced hands, she placed a wet cloth across Harry's forehead. She dipped another cloth in the water and squeezed droplets onto his parched lips. She coaxed his mouth open with gentle fingers and dribbled more water onto his tongue.

"Keep changing the cloth as it gets warm," she told Sophie. "I'll make some broth. Maybe we can get something into him."

Sam's stomach rumbled.

"I'll bring you some soup too," Aunt Lucy said.

Sam nodded, keeping his eyes focused on his brother's face as she bustled out.

When the cloth on Harry's forehead warmed, Sophie replaced it, praying silently for his recovery. She looked at Sam, whose eyes were clouded with worry as he held his brother's frail, sweating hand.

"I'm glad you came, Sam," she said. "How did you know where to find me?"

Sam glanced at her, then shifted in his chair. "You musta told me where you live."

"Really? I don't remember that. And this is my aunt's place."

A silence stretched between them.

After a few moments, Sam said, "I walk with you sometimes. When it's late."

"You follow me?" She tried to meet his gaze, but he stared at his shoes.

"Just to see you get home safe."

"It's not safe for you either."

"I'm used to it, though," Sam insisted. "I know my way around."

Sophie didn't press the matter, but resolved to keep a

closer eye on her surroundings when she walked alone in the city. They sat quietly for a while, Sam stroking his brother's hand and Sophie bathing his forehead with cool cloths.

"Still holding on to your jacket, I see," she said, noticing the worn blue sleeves rolled up to reveal bony wrists.

He gave a half smile. "Told you I would."

Aunt Lucy brought in a tray and set it on the bedside table. She tucked a cloth under Harry's chin and began pushing tiny spoonfuls of broth between his parched lips. Most of the liquid dribbled onto his chin and was absorbed by the cloth, but some of it reached his tongue.

Sophie handed Sam a bowl of hearty soup and a piece of fresh bread. He tore off a huge bite of the bread.

"Slow down," said Sophie. "There's plenty more."

Sam didn't look up. She wondered if he'd eaten a decent meal since they met at Louie's a few days ago. He made short work of the soup, and Sophie fetched a second bowl. When that was empty, Sam sat back in the chair.

"Thank you, miss."

"You can call me Sophie, remember?"

Aunt Lucy set the remains of the broth back on the tray. "I think we can let Harry rest for a while," she said.

Sam's shoulders sagged with relief. "Thank you for helping us."

"Of course," said Aunt Lucy. She looked from Sam to Sophie and back again. "You two are friends, I take it?"

"I sell papers," Sam said shyly.

"We're friends," Sophie said. "Or at least, I hope we will be."

Aunt Lucy extended her hand to Sam. "I'm Lucy Strong," she said. "You can call me Miss Strong. Or Aunt Lucy, if you like."

Sam stretched out slim, dirty fingers and said, "Sam Goodwin."

Lucy grasped his hand. "Welcome to my home, Sam Goodwin."

Aunt Lucy met Sophie's eyes over Sam's head. Sophie knew they were both remembering a long-ago day when she was no older than Sam, and just as desperate.

"Sophie, maybe Sam would like to wash up. We can make a bed for him on the sofa."

"I want to stay with Harry," Sam said.

"I supposed we could put some blankets on the floor," said Aunt Lucy. "The sofa would be more comfortable, though."

Sam looked around the tidy room, its walls papered with a pattern of yellow roses. On the wall opposite the bed stood a bureau, its top adorned with two framed photos resting on a lace doily.

"This used to be Sophie's room," Aunt Lucy said.

"The floor's fine," Sam said.

Sophie thought of the sad tent made of blankets under the bridge, barely sheltered from the wind. How long had they lived like that? Had they ever had a home? Sophie had dozens of questions, but asking them would have to wait.

She reached out a hand and touched his narrow shoulder. "I'll show you the bathroom."

She led Sam to the door at the end of the hall and opened it. The bathroom was a bit old-fashioned, the water tank for the toilet mounted high on the wall, the flush chain hanging down from it. She saw Sam's eyes widen as he took in the deep bathtub, clean white hand towels arranged neatly on a rack, and the rag rug in warm autumn tones resting on the tile floor, inviting the step of bare feet.

"Would you like to take a bath?"

Sam looked at her uncertainly. Sophie took that for a yes. She grasped the handle of the hot water tap and gave it a firm twist, since it tended to stick. Water flowed into the tub.

When it ran hot, she stuffed the rubber plug into the drain and turned on the cold tap, holding her hand under the stream until the temperature felt right.

"I'll get you a towel," she said. She went to the hall closet, then returned with a towel and facecloth.

For the first time, she peered critically at the clothing Sam wore beneath the hard-won jacket. The thin shirt of tan cotton was torn at the bottom and had been haphazardly mended in a few other spots. The brown pants were in a similar state, held in place by a fraying belt that looked like it could fall apart at any moment.

"I'll find something clean for you to wear when you're done," she offered.

Sam frowned at her. "I'm not wearing girls' clothes."

"Don't worry, they're not girls' clothes," she said with a grin. She turned and left, pulling the door softly shut.

Sophie tiptoed into the bedroom where Harry slept. Aunt Lucy had nodded off in the chair next to him, one hand resting protectively on the bed. She eased open the bottom drawer of the bureau and rummaged around the pile of old shirtwaists and petticoats. Underneath them, she found what she was looking for: a blue shirt similar to Sam's, but in much better shape, despite its age. She pulled it out, along with a pair of gray pants, and ducked back into the hallway.

Sophie shook out the garments and inspected them. They brought back memories of summer days she'd spent with Aunt Lucy, exploring the woods after a picnic. This was one of her freedom outfits, as they'd called them—a costume she wore for outings in the countryside when she relished the sweet release of wearing pants. She remembered her heart soaring as she scrambled up a tree or ran along the lakeshore without a skirt twisting between her knees. Sophie could almost smell the rich aroma of pine needles and that earthy scent of a wooded path, strewn with fallen leaves, tree roots reaching up through the ground to form ancient ledges.

In a daze of nostalgia, she wandered to the bathroom door and knocked twice, then pushed it open just wide enough to insert the clothes and rest them on the side of the sink.

"Sam, I'll just—"

"Don't come in!" Sam's voice was high-pitched with panic. "Ooof!"

Sophie heard the squeak of a slipping foot, then the sickening thud of flesh and bone hitting porcelain.

"Owww!"

Without thinking, she turned to look at him. "Are you all ri—" Her eyes skidded over Sam's skinny frame, and Sophie let out a gasp. She locked eyes with Sam for an instant, then squeezed her eyes shut. "I'm sorry, I—"

"Get out!" Sam's frantic shout cut her off.

Sophie pulled the door shut and stood stock still. Had she seen what she thought she had? She heard a stifled sob from the other side of the door.

"I'm really sorry, Sam," she called. "I only meant to put the clothes on the sink. I hope you're okay."

After a long moment of silence, he said gruffly, "Just give a guy some privacy."

Sophie walked slowly back to the kitchen, thinking over their past encounters and considering young Sam in a whole new light.

14

———

Sophie sat at the kitchen table, sipping tea from her favorite plum-colored mug. She'd been using it since she was a little kid, drinking hot chocolate at this very table. Sam appeared in the doorway, brown hair damp from the bath, the ends curling slightly. The shirt fit perfectly, but the pants were a bit long, the cuffs rolled up, bare feet looking clean and vulnerable on the wood floor. It was almost like gazing into a mirror a decade earlier, Sophie thought, when she was just as scared, but trying not to show it.

"Do you want some tea?" she asked.

Sam nodded. "Thanks."

Sophie poured a cup from the pot on the table. Sam sat down across from her and took a slow sip.

"Sam," she began. "How long have you and Harry been on your own?"

"It's always just been the two of us."

"But your parents—"

Sam grimaced and cut her off. "Our Ma's dead. We were living with her man when she got sick. He took off after she was gone. Left the place one morning and didn't come back."

"How old were you?"

Sam shrugged. "Harry was about five. I'm a few years older."

"Didn't anyone help you? Surely you had neighbors."

"It wasn't a nice place. Everybody had their own trouble. The landlord came in one day and told us to get lost. There was a woman with him who had three kids and a baby. I guess they were moving in. She looked at us like she wanted to help, but her kids were in worse shape than us."

"What about an orphanage?" She'd never been inside, but she'd walked past the Milwaukee Orphan Asylum on Marshall Street, and she'd seen nuns shepherding children into similar buildings near various churches. The places looked grim, but at least there would be food and a bed.

"I figured we were better off on our own. Those places give me the creeps." Sam was quiet for a moment, then continued. "We had a friend for a while. Frannie. We stayed in an old empty building together. She sold papers. I helped out sometimes. Then she got sick, and I took over her job."

"And when she got better?" Sophie asked gently.

"She didn't get better, so..."

Sophie let a silence grow between them while they sipped their tea. She hoped Sam would bring it up, but that didn't happen.

"Sam, you can trust me, you know."

"Yeah? I've been told that before. Lots of times."

She reached out a hand to cover Sam's smaller one, resting on the table top, but he pulled it away before she could.

Sam was quiet, staring glumly into the mug. "I can't keep it up forever, I guess."

"Maybe not. I guess it depends on, well... how fast you... develop."

Sam frowned. "Yeah. Then I'm in for it. I hope Harry's

doing better by then." Sam looked at her with pleading eyes. "Please don't tell anyone, Sophie. If the paper finds out, they won't let me work. Girls have to be fourteen to sell papers, but boys can sell when they're ten."

Sophie wanted to scoop Sam into her arms and erase every worry from that young face. But she knew her embrace would make them both uncomfortable.

"I won't tell," she said. "May I ask—is your full name Samantha?"

Sam scowled. "No one calls me that."

"Did your mother?"

"Not much." Sam's face looked pained. "Sometimes."

"Well, I think Sam is a perfect name for you."

Sam smiled. "Thanks, Sophie. I owe ya one. I owe you a lot, actually."

Sophie stood up abruptly. "You owe me exactly nothing. You deserve to be taken care of, Sam." She opened the cupboard and pulled out a small plate, then reached for the cookie jar on the counter. "Do you like cookies?"

"Well, of course I like cookies." Sam's familiar blustery tone returned. "I'm not an animal."

Sophie laughed and filled the plate. "Chocolate chip," she announced, placing it on the table. "My favorite."

After the tea and cookies, Sophie convinced Sam to lie on the couch. She tugged one of Aunt Lucy's cozy afghans around her, and Sam's tired brown eyes began to droop. She blinked and forced them open.

"Try not to worry," Sophie said. "Aunt Lucy will take care of Harry. When I was a kid, she was always awake when I woke up, no matter what time it was. It's like a magic power."

"No such thing as magic," Sam mumbled. But she let her eyes close, and soon drifted off to sleep.

Sophie sat in Aunt Lucy's favorite chair, lost in thought.

Then she dozed off herself, tumbling into dreams where she was twelve years old again, snuggled on the same sofa, wondering what her future might hold.

SOPHIE WOKE as the first rays of dawn peeked through the window. She saw Sam blink her eyes open and give a start at the unfamiliar surroundings, her gaze darting around the room. But then the girl's tension eased, and she closed her eyes once more. Sophie's heart warmed at the thought that Sam might feel safe here.

She looked in on Harry and saw him still sleeping, the clean white bedspread rising and falling with his rhythmic breaths. Aunt Lucy, sitting at his side, gave Sophie a wink, and she felt reassured.

She went into the kitchen, filled the kettle for tea, and heated a large saucepan of milk for oatmeal. When it boiled, she pulled out the familiar jar from the cupboard and spooned almost all of the contents into the pan, then stirred it with a wooden spoon. She heard the tap of Sam's bare feet and turned.

"Good morning," Sophie said. "Breakfast will be ready in a few minutes. Harry's still sleeping."

Sam rubbed sleepy eyes. "Mmmm. Thanks." She padded off.

Sophie heard the door to the bedroom open, followed by quiet murmurs from Sam and Aunt Lucy. She looked out the window above the sink at the misty morning air, hovering over the tiny patch of grass in the back yard. Being in this kitchen and hearing the sounds of a household waking up filled an empty spot in her heart that she hadn't known was there. It was different from the sounds of the boarding house

—warmer somehow. She felt a surge of protectiveness toward Sam and Harry.

The thick oatmeal bubbled in the pan, and Sophie pulled three bowls from the cupboard, smiling as she noticed the chip in the base of one of them, the result of her own hasty dishwashing long ago. She divided the oatmeal into three hearty portions, then sprinkled it with cinnamon and spooned in brown sugar. She set two of the bowls on the table and got out spoons and the tin of raisins, wondering if Sam liked them.

Sam came in, her face looking freshly scrubbed, her short brown hair damp in spots and smoothed into place. The blue wool uniform coat was folded over her arm. She laid it on the table, then sat down and eagerly dug into the oatmeal.

"You still want that old thing?" Sam asked, nodding to the coat.

Sophie sat across from her and nodded. "I do. If it won't cause you too much trouble."

"Nothing I can't handle. Just give it back when you're done."

Sophie reached for the coat, glad for the chance to study it for the first time. The navy blue wool was thick, a higher quality than she'd realized. Even after being rescued from fire and worn by Sam around the city, the fabric felt durable as she rubbed it between her thumb and forefinger. The red cuffs were smudged with dirt. She looked closely at the arcing red lapels. A line of nearly invisible pick stitching ran along the edges, signaling hours of close, careful work with practiced hands. Silver stripes were set at angles, anchored with silver buttons. Only one button was missing, an impressive feat considering Sam's rough and tumble lifestyle. The bottom of the coat had been sheared off, probably with a pocket knife, judging from the uneven and fraying tears. As she studied it, she noticed small blackened and burned patches on the back and sleeves.

"So what are you gonna do with it? Look for the rest of the uniform? If you find it, I could sure use the sword it came with," Sam joked.

"Very funny." Sophie rested the coat on the table once more and reached for her spoon. "It's very well made," she told Sam. "Expensive. If I can find the tailor who made it, he might tell me who bought it."

Once the words were out, Sophie heard how unrealistic they sounded.

"Why do you want to know?"

Sophie hesitated. She wanted to shield Sam from the harsh puzzle she was wrestling with. But then she reasoned that Sam had already been exposed to much worse in her short life.

."There was a murder Saturday night. And I-I found the body. Just outside an office where Aunt Lucy works. And it was someone I knew, in a way."

Sam's eyes widened. "You found a dead body? Scary."

Sophie let out an unsteady breath. "It *was* scary."

She hadn't admitted to herself how shaken she was by it. Murder had been like an impossible abstraction until now. It was something vague that happened to others, and that anonymous police officers dealt with. Even though she and her colleagues wrote about such crimes, finding Mrs. Rock had made it vividly real. And much closer to her own life than she cared to think about.

"Sophie? You okay?" Sam asked.

When Sophie met her eyes, they looked older than Sam could possibly be.

"Sam, how old are you? The truth."

Sam hesitated. "It doesn't matter. I'm old enough."

"Please tell me. It matters to me."

Sam sighed. "Fine. If you must know, I'm twelve. Well, I will be. In September. Really and truly. My birthday is September ninth. Happy?"

Sophie remembered being eleven or twelve, and feeling like she was quite grown up.

She gave a small smile. "Thank you for telling me."

"Now you tell *me* something: what does a soldier's beat-up coat have to do with a murder?"

Sophie shrugged. "Maybe nothing. It's just a hunch. It seems odd to me that someone would have been burning this fine coat late at night, near where the murder happened. I was at a costume party that night, and I saw men wearing coats like this one."

"So you think one of the people from the party killed your friend? The soldier who wore this?"

Sophie hadn't put her suspicion into words yet, but there it was.

"Maybe. Maybe somebody at that party wanted Hilda Rock dead."

15

____

At her desk, Sophie rubbed the stiffness in her neck. She laced her fingers and stretched her arms out in front of her, feeling the muscles groan. She'd typed a healthy stack of recipes and social announcements for the women's page, and she still had an hour before the Women's Club meeting started. There was plenty of time to walk. She pinned on her hat and sailed out of the office.

Sophie walked down Kilbourn Avenue toward the Women's Club building. It amazed her that she'd been there for the suffrage debate just a week ago. It seemed as if a lifetime had passed. She shivered as she realized that had been the last time she'd seen Hilda Rock alive. The peaceful blue sky with its floating tufts of cottony clouds were terribly at odds with her thoughts of murder and its motivation.

She forced the case out of her mind and turned her attention to the meeting ahead. While she attended lots of dreary meetings, the Women's Club made good on its lofty goal of "advancing women's knowledge and elevating civilization." Sophie always learned something interesting. Today Mrs. Antoinette Peterson would speak about how the laws of

Wisconsin affected women who were wives and mothers. Sophie loved the lawyer's life story. She had owned a millinery shop on the south side of the city, somehow managing to save up enough money to go to law school by making and selling hats there.

Sophie admired the elegant, leaded glass windows as she strode into the building. She walked through the same parlor where Clara had lost her temper after the debate, and winced at the memory. The hallway was filled with richly attired ladies who had the means to spend an afternoon listening to a lecture. Mrs. Peterson was talking animatedly to a circle of rapt admirers. Sophie entered the meeting room, took a seat at the back, and pulled out her notebook and pencil. She jotted down a few names of ladies she'd seen and some details about flower-trimmed hats, shades of pastel poplin, and lacy wraps. She wondered if Mrs. Peterson assessed them with the same professional eye, honed from her days as a milliner.

She felt a sudden odd, prickly sensation on her scalp. She turned and scanned the room. From a small knot of chattering ladies in the corner, Mrs. Thelma Wolff stared at Sophie with a stiff posture and a stony expression.

Sophie blinked. Mrs. Wolff had been impatient with her when she'd summoned her to the mansion. But there'd been no mention of the fracas at the Spring Gala in the next day's paper, despite Sophie's best effort, so Mrs. Wolff couldn't be upset about the press coverage. Was she just distracted and staring without realizing it? Sophie gave the older woman a shaky smile, trying to convey friendly respect. Mrs. Wolff's mouth remained tight and pinched, then she swept toward the front row of chairs and took a seat, her back ramrod straight. Friends flanked her on both sides.

Sophie bit her lip. Had she offended Mrs. Wolff? If so, it certainly wouldn't help her journalism career. Mrs. Wolff had her hand in every major organization in the city, not to mention all the newspapers.

Sophie's thoughts were interrupted by the sound of a tinkling bell, calling the group to attention. She focused on the podium, where a stout, overdressed matron introduced the esteemed speaker. Sophie could only catch glimpses of Mrs. Peterson due to the towering hats of the women in front of her. As the lecture began, they continued to bring their heads together and exchange quiet whispers. Sophie suspected that their concern about the law was minimal at best.

She tried to focus on the speaker's words, but her mind kept drifting back to the murder case. What had Millie, Agnes, and Mr. Pitman been doing at Mrs. Rock's house? Why had Mrs. Wolff stared at her just now with so much hostility? Did the Spring Gala have anything to do with the death of Mrs. Rock? Instead of taking notes, she penciled question marks across the page.

Before she knew it, the hour had slipped by and the audience members were applauding and getting to their feet. Sophie joined in, trying to recall some of the speaker's points.

A snatch of conversation drifted from the gossiping pair in front of her. "You heard about Hilda Rock, of course."

Sophie leaned forward and turned her ear toward the ladies.

"Indeed. So appalling," came the reply. "I can't imagine what she was doing in that office building in the middle of the night."

"She had something of a past, you know. She and Ruben Wolff were sweethearts once upon a time."

Sophie froze, wondering if she'd heard correctly.

"You can't be serious," her listener said.

"Yes, when we were young," the first lady explained.

"Long before he was so wealthy, of course. He seemed devoted to Hilda. But then Thelma's family moved to town. She was rich, and Ruben was ambitious."

"Oh, my. I can't imagine him with Hilda. She's so—that is, she was—well, you know what she was like."

"Hilda always claimed he was going to propose to her," her companion went on. "But then we started seeing him at Thelma's family's parties. I was a newlywed then, and Hans and I were invited everywhere. Ruben worked at a small brewery—I forget the name. He wanted to buy it, and he needed an investor."

"So their money comes from Thelma, then?"

"Originally, yes. One day we read in the newspaper that Ruben and Thelma were engaged. That was the last we saw of Hilda for quite some time, I assure you. She went out east somewhere, I believe."

"She must have been humiliated, poor girl." The woman's tone suggested that she relished the thought.

"I'm sure she was. Thelma and Ruben had a magnificent wedding, and Thelma's father bought the brewery for them. Ruben hired his previous employer as his foreman." She paused for effect. "Otto Rock."

Her friend gasped. "Rock? You don't mean—"

"Yes! Hilda came back a few years later, and she married the foreman."

The voices faded away as the ladies moved into the aisle and joined the slow-moving stream of silk and organza.

Sophie's mind whirled. Mrs. Rock and Mr. Wolff? She found it hard to imagine a more unlikely pair. The quiet *harumph* of a lady clearing her throat startled Sophie from her reverie. She looked up to find that she was blocking the path of a gray-haired woman who stared down at her with a frown.

"I beg your pardon," Sophie apologized, jumping to her feet.

She moved to the aisle of the nearly empty room and then out to the hallway. Ladies had clustered near a long table and held teacups or plates of delicate petit fours in their gloved hands.

Sophie spotted Thelma Wolff from the back, and not wanting to encounter her threatening gaze again, she headed in the opposite direction. She heard a few murmurs as she moved along.

A thickset woman in a deep rose gown said, "What on Earth do we need the vote for? We can leave that mess to the men."

Her young companion bubbled, "Why shouldn't we vote, Aunt Bess? Not all men have the interests of women and children at heart like Uncle Michael does."

The older lady sniffed, unconcerned. She'd clearly never had to fret about how to feed her family while her husband drank away his week's wages.

On one of the gleaming sideboards along the wall, Sophie spotted a printed program she'd missed before. She picked it up, scanning the topics from Mrs. Peterson's speech about women's rights after a husband's death. Sophie folded the program and tucked it in her bag. At least she'd have some idea of the substance of the lecture for her article. She approached Mrs. Ness, the president of the Women's Club, who was supervising the assembled members with a proprietary air.

"Good afternoon, Mrs. Ness. It was an enlightening event, as always." Sophie hoped she wouldn't ask for particulars.

"Hello, Miss Strong. Indeed it was. I'm very happy with the attendance. I counted forty-seven." She looked pointedly at Sophie's notebook. Sophie wrote down the number.

"Thank you. That's so helpful."

"You'll find next month's topic posted on the notice board in the foyer," Mrs. Ness said, as she always did, not trusting Sophie to manage this basic research.

"I look forward to it."

The crowd was thinning. As Sophie walked out, she didn't turn her head to check if it really was Mrs. Wolff's eyes boring into her back.

ONLY BENJAMIN TURNER and two other reporters were at their desks. Sophie assumed the others were out on assignment or toasting each other at the pub. Sophie stopped at the office library and pulled out a thin file with a few lackluster articles about women's legal rights. As ever, it was in the bottom drawer. After leafing through it and finding herself none the wiser, she put it back. Her eyes caught another label: *Wolff, Thelma*. She tugged out the bulging file and rested it on top of the cabinet.

She flipped through old clippings about Thelma's garden parties, European vacations, and the death of her affluent parents. At the back of the file, she found a large account of the Wolff wedding in 1897. A drawing of the bride revealed a younger, radiant Thelma Wolff in an opulent white silk gown studded with long rows of pearls in floral patterns. A gossamer veil cascaded from the crown of tiny flowers atop her elaborate curls and spread at her feet in a swirl of lace. She looked like the queen of the world. Sophie wondered what the spurned Hilda Rock had endured, hearing about her former beau's rise to fabulous wealth. Had her own wedding to the brewery foreman even warranted a modest line or two in the paper?

Her thoughts were interrupted by the sound and vibration of a drawer at the end of the row being pulled open. Sophie slapped the Wolff file shut, but she wasn't fast enough to elude Benjamin Turner's gaze.

"Mooning over wedding gowns, Miss Strong? Is there some happy news of your own on the horizon, perhaps?"

Sophie glared at him, then crouched down and tucked the thick collection back into its spot.

"I have higher ambitions than to subject myself to the indignities of marriage, Mr. Turner."

His eyebrows arched. "Oh, indignity needn't be part of the equation, if you choose your spouse carefully."

She blushed for a reason she couldn't fathom, and kept her head bowed so he wouldn't see the red staining her cheeks. When her face cooled, she rose to her feet.

"Any news of our friends, the Wolffs?" he asked, not looking up from his perusal of the open drawer.

Sophie was about to dismiss him with a cutting remark, but she stopped herself. "Actually," she said, "I heard an interesting tidbit today."

Benjamin looked up, eyebrows raised. "Do tell."

"Did you know that Mr. Wolff was romantically involved with Hilda Rock in his youth?"

"Rock? Isn't that the lady who got shot?" Sophie nodded. His brow wrinkled. "I don't believe I'd heard that before. Though now that you mention it—" He shook his head. "Never mind. It's nothing."

"Do tell."

"Remember that ribbon cutting at Wolff Park, when they opened the new castle? I noticed a woman haranguing Mr. Wolff pretty thoroughly afterward. At the time, I thought it was one of the temperance ladies giving him an earful about the dangers of drink. It could have been Mrs. Rock, though. They seemed quite familiar with each other."

"Why do you say that?"

He rubbed his chin. "Oh, I don't know. Something about

the way they stood close to each other. And I think she called him 'Ruben'." He grinned. "Maybe it's *men's* intuition."

She rolled her eyes. "That's a fine thing. You'd think such intuition would inspire more chivalry."

"Ah, Miss Strong, if you wanted chivalry, the newsroom is not the place to seek it." His tone was mocking, but somehow gentler than usual.

"I assure you, that's not what I seek in the newsroom," she said airily.

She exited the library, his chuckle drifting after her.

16

––––––––––

The Majestic Building loomed large as Sophie trudged up the steps the next afternoon. She still felt uneasy as she entered, but not panicky. Aunt Lucy had asked her to check for mail at the suffrage office. She was waiting for responses about the summer boat excursions, but wanted to stay with Harry.

As Sophie passed Mr. Pitman's office, she was surprised to see light under the door. It was the first time she'd seen him there since the murder. She glanced at her watch. It was getting late, but she didn't want to pass up the opportunity to talk to him. She backtracked and raised her hand to knock. Then, on impulse, she grasped the knob instead and thrust the door open.

The office was empty. Sophie checked over her shoulder; the hallway was still deserted. She slipped inside, leaving the door ajar. The large wooden desk was neat and sparse, with a stack of papers and files at one side, a glass of water, and an electric lamp with a dark-green shade casting a small pool of light. A telephone sat in one corner, the handset silent in its cradle. One of the new self-filling fountain pens and an inkwell rested next to a letter that Mr. Pitman had apparently been composing.

She read the salutation "Dearest" followed by a single character—she couldn't tell if it was a J, T, or L. Then a shaky line of black ink veered off the page. Next to this was a creased piece of thick, cream-colored stationery that looked as if it had been crumpled into a ball and then smoothed out again. The handwriting was commanding, yet feminine. Spurred by insatiable curiosity, Sophie reached toward the wrinkled page.

"Miss Strong!" Pitman's voice erupted behind her, and Sophie jumped.

For an instant, she froze, her mouth open. Then she regained her composure and turned, pulling her hand back to rest it on her upper chest. Alonzo Pitman stood glaring at her, his eyes wide and red-rimmed, a soggy handkerchief crushed in one hand. Sophie's heart beat madly underneath her palm. "Oh, Mr. Pitman! You gave me a fright!" She willed her voice not to waver.

"What are you doing here?" he demanded. His eyes darted to his desktop, and he edged past her to stand behind the desk. With a sweep of his hand, he moved some papers to cover both letters.

Unable to answer his question, she diverted him with a question of her own.

Peering into his face with concern, she asked, "Is every-thing all right, Mr. Pitman? You haven't had bad news, I hope?"

"Pardon? Oh—" He glanced at the handkerchief and shoved it into his pocket with a sniff. "No, I'm fine. Just hay fever." He drummed his fingers on his papers as he eyed her warily. "You do have a way of barging in on one, don't you?"

"I'm so sorry we didn't get a chance to talk at Mrs. Rock's house the other day."

He coughed. "Err—yes. Do we have something to discuss?"

Drat! She should have thought of a cover story—she must get better at that.

Her mind raced. "I had no idea that Mrs. Rock was one of your clients. There must be so much to do with her estate."

"I—of course, I can't reveal a client's identity to anyone. I'm sure you understand."

Sophie switched tactics. "You know, I was the one w-who discovered her." Sophie bit her lip, hoping she looked meek and distressed.

"I beg your pardon?"

"When she was—you know—killed." Sophie broke off with a gasp and fluttered her lashes, as if blinking away tears. "It was so frightening."

"Yes, I'm sure it was."

"I thought you were here that morning. I saw a light on in your office, but when I knocked, looking for help, you didn't answer."

Pitman stared at Sophie, sweat glistening on his forehead. "I-I'm sorry I wasn't here to be of assistance. Now, if you'll excuse me, I really must get back to work."

As he took up his pen, he bumped the water glass, and it spilled over the desk. "Damn!"

He grabbed his wrinkled letter and some other papers and held them away from the liquid. He pulled out his soggy handkerchief with his other hand and dabbed ineffectually at the spill.

"Oh dear!" Without thinking, Sophie reached into her own pocket to for a handkerchief and began mopping up the water.

Mr. Pitman stared at the fabric she held and pointed. "Where—where did you get that?"

Sophie glanced at the handkerchief and realized it wasn't

her own. She looked at it blankly, but then the memory came flooding in. Her body flushed with heat as she was forced back to that moment, when she had walked innocently toward a crime scene.

"I—it was in the hallway," she said. "The day I found Mrs. Rock. I meant to put it on the lost and found table, but then… I forgot I had it."

The lawyer's face looked pale as he continued to stare at it.

"Why do you ask? Is it yours?" said Sophie.

"Mine? No, no, of course not." He jerked open a desk drawer and pulled out a stained cloth napkin and used it to wipe away the spill. Without looking up, he said, "If you'll forgive me, Miss Strong. I must get back to work."

"Oh, yes. How rude of me. I'll be going." Sophie turned, but something caught her eye. Hanging behind the door was a black tricorn hat. It reminded her of the soldiers she'd seen at the Spring Gala. She reached over and pulled it off the hook, aware that she was trying Mr. Pitman's patience.

"What an unusual hat," she exclaimed, keeping her eyes trained on Mr. Pitman's face. "Wherever did you get it?"

He blew out an aggravated breath and walked over to where she stood, turning the hat around in her hands. "Oh, that. I forgot it was there. Picked it up at a thrift sale somewhere. Just a lark. I used to have one like it as a boy."

"A thrift sale? It looks new."

He reached for the hat, but she didn't relinquish it. "You know, I attended the Wolffs' Spring Gala last weekend, for the paper. It was a masquerade party, of all things. Several gentlemen were dressed as soldiers, wearing hats just like this."

He stared at her again, then said, "I suppose that's a popular type of costume." He plucked the hat from her grip with one hand, and with the other, he opened the door wider.

"Good day, Miss Strong," he said firmly.

"Yes, I must be off. I just need to pick up some things for my aunt, and then I'll be on my way. Good day, Mr. Pitman."

She smiled brightly and headed down the hall. She expected to hear the door slam behind her, but the sound didn't come. Sophie felt tingling between her shoulder blades, and she was sure that Mr. Pitman was watching her as she walked toward the suffrage office. When she reached its door, she turned to wave at him, but she heard his door close softly, followed by the click of a key turning in the lock.

Sophie let herself into the office, which was empty. She rarely saw ladies there other than her aunt, Clara, and Agnes, but she knew at least a hundred members were on the rolls. How they contributed to the work, she wasn't sure.

She examined the damp handkerchief in her hand more closely, rubbing the ivory fabric between her fingers. It was of thick silk, embroidered with an intricate red-and-gold honeysuckle pattern, the white lace edging interwoven with more gold. A memory tugged at the back of her mind. Where had she seen that pattern before? The fabric was of such high quality that it may have cost more than the entire outfit she now wore.

She brought the handkerchief to her nose and inhaled the faint scent of roses. Suddenly she was back at Wolff Mansion, greeting a haughty Queen Elizabeth, who held a delicate piece of lace and silk in her bejeweled fingers. Could it possibly be Thelma Wolff's handkerchief? How had it ended up in the Majestic Building hallway?

She gasped. Could Mrs. Wolff have killed Hilda Rock? She recalled the coldness in her eyes at the Women's Club meeting. Yes, she believed Thelma capable of murder. But why and when? She couldn't have slipped away from her Spring Gala to commit murder and then returned to the party —could she?

Sophie collected the letters someone had stacked on the desk Aunt Lucy used, as she wondered what to do next. Take her suspicion to Detective Zimmer? She imagined his smug expression as he listened to her chatter on like a nervous schoolgirl. The handkerchief was evidence; she'd have to turn it over. If only she could add more facts to her theory before she did.

Frowning, she stuffed the stack of correspondence into a canvas bag she'd found in a drawer and headed to Aunt Lucy's.

She tried to enjoy the mild spring evening and put thoughts of Hilda Rock out of her mind. She was eager to see how Harry was faring. Soon she'd traversed the mile-long walk. She let herself in the outer door and took the stairs up to Aunt Lucy's apartment. As she reached for the doorknob, she heard a whoop of delight, followed by laughter. She found Sam and Harry on the rug in the front room, a deck of playing cards splayed out on the floor between them.

Sam fell over with a moan of defeat, holding one hand to her forehead in mock despair.

She looked up at Sophie. "He got me. I'm no match for Heartless Harry."

Harry laughed again. "I won, I won!" He lifted thin arms over his head in triumph. His brown eyes, identical to Sam's, turned a bit shy as he looked at Sophie.

"Well, hello there, Harry," she said. "I'm glad to see you're feeling better. I'm Sophie." She walked over and extended her hand. "May I shake the hand of the mighty victor?"

He grinned. "You may." He slipped his hand into hers, and she squeezed gently. His fingers felt fragile and cool.

Lucy looked up from her chair where she was reading a letter, a pile of opened envelopes stacked in her lap.

"Hello, Sophie," she said. "As you can see, our Harry is

making a beautiful recovery. You're just in time for supper. I have a chicken roasting in the oven." She gathered her work in one hand and stood. "You can help me set the table."

In the kitchen, Sophie took out four plates from the cupboard. "So he's doing well?"

Lucy was peering into the oven, her face flushed with its heat. She closed the oven door and straightened.

"He's much better. Still coughing a bit, but no fever." As if in response, Harry gave a raspy cough from the other room.

"They seem comfortable here," Sophie said.

"They do liven up the place," said Aunt Lucy. "They remind me of another sweet girl who lived here not too long ago. It seems like yesterday." She rubbed Sophie's arm.

For a moment, Sophie tumbled back in time, remembering evenings just like this one when she and Aunt Lucy would eat a simple meal together, after which Sophie would do homework at the kitchen table while Aunt Lucy read or wrote letters.

"Ten years ago already," Sophie said with a smile.

"And now look at you, a career woman, all grown up."

Sophie rested the plates on the counter and pulled her aunt into a fierce hug. "You saved my life."

Aunt Lucy returned the hug. "Oh, it went both ways, my dear."

When they released each other, Aunt Lucy looked thoughtful. "They can't go back to living under a bridge, Sophie. I couldn't stand it."

Sophie nodded. "I couldn't either."

"I'm not as young as I was ten years ago, though. I don't know if I can keep up with them."

"There has to be a way," Sophie said. "Sam is very self-reliant, as I'm sure you've noticed."

"That she is," Aunt Lucy chuckled. "I panicked when I woke up this morning and she was gone, but she was back before lunch. She has a job she can't afford to lose, she says." Lucy shook her head. "She's had to grow up much too fast."

"They need some time to just be kids. Maybe we can help with that."

～

AT THE SUPPER TABLE, Aunt Lucy said a blessing over their simple meal. Sam elbowed Harry, and he followed his sister's lead, bowing his head and squeezing his eyes shut. The chicken, mashed potatoes, string beans, and biscuits were just as delicious as Sophie remembered from her childhood. In recent years, Aunt Lucy had favored simpler meals, but having children in the house seemed to have reawakened her culinary ambitions.

Sam and Harry ate eagerly, and when Harry began licking the chicken grease from his fingers, Sam elbowed him again. Sophie smiled, noting that someone must have taught her table manners when she was small, and wondered if she was remembering long-ago suppers with her mother.

"Since Harry is doing so well, I wonder if you're all up to a little outing on Saturday," said Sophie.

"What kind of outing?" Sam asked.

"Have you ever been to Wolff Park?" she asked.

Harry's eyes grew wide. "You mean with the roller coasters, and the underground riverboat, and the Ferris wheel, and the water slide?"

Sophie laughed. "That's the one. You seem to know a lot about it."

"It costs money to get in, doesn't it?" asked Sam.

Sophie waved her hand. "Don't worry about that. I have free passes. I'm a newspaper woman, you know."

Sam relaxed and sat back as Harry babbled on about the wonders he'd heard of.

"What do you think, Aunt Lucy? Are you up for an adventure?" Sophie asked.

"I don't recommend a water slide, given Harry's health, but the rest of it could be fun, if we take it slowly."

Harry bounced in his chair, clapping his hands. "How many days till we can go?"

Sam nudged her brother. "Saturday. That's in two days, ya loon. Today is Thursday."

"As long as you're still feeling well, Harry," Aunt Lucy cautioned.

"I will be, don't worry." Harry took a huge bite of potatoes, followed by a swallow of milk. "See? I'm eating like a horse."

Sophie laughed. She had two passes from the newspaper, but paying the twenty cents for two more admissions would be well worth it to see the kids' excited faces. Sam laughed at her little brother, and the carefree sound swelled Sophie's heart.

"What time will we go?" asked Sam. "I have to sell the Saturday morning paper first."

Sophie met Aunt Lucy's eyes and knew what she was thinking. Sam should give up her job and go to school, along with Harry. But she also knew that Sam wouldn't surrender her hard-won independence lightly.

"How about ten o'clock?" suggested Sophie. "I have some work that morning, too. We can meet outside the *Herald* office."

Sam nodded in agreement, then focused on her plate, making short work of the meal.

When they finished, Aunt Lucy went to the kitchen and brought out a rich chocolate cake covered in thick frosting. "I hope you saved room for dessert."

Aunt Lucy cut each of them generous slabs of cake and refilled Sam and Harry's glasses of milk.

"I'll get us some tea," offered Sophie. When she returned a few minutes later, Sam was scooping up the crumbs with her fork, and Harry was starting on a second piece. Sophie was full from supper, but she couldn't resist Aunt Lucy's baking, and she'd eaten half of her slice before she knew it.

She pushed the plate with the other half over to Sam. "I'm stuffed."

"Me too, but it's so good," said Sam, plunging her fork into the remains of cake. "Thanks."

After dessert, Sam herded Harry into the bathroom to wash up for bed.

Sophie sipped her tea. "Thank you, Aunt Lucy," she said. "They look like new kids entirely."

"No need to thank me," said Aunt Lucy. "It's my absolute pleasure. Did you know that Harry can read?"

"Really? He hasn't been to school, has he?"

"I doubt it," said Aunt Lucy. "Sam must have taught him."

"You don't have any books for him, do you?" Sophie teased, gesturing to the overflowing bookshelves.

Aunt Lucy chuckled. "More than he could read in a lifetime. He's already started on the bookshelf in your old room."

"Wonderful. Did Sam sleep on the sofa again last night?"

"She did, but today I borrowed a cot from Mrs. Keller downstairs. That will do for now."

"Has Sam said anything about going back to... where they were living?"

Aunt Lucy shook her head. "They had at least a few belongings there, didn't they?"

"I couldn't see much when we were there. It was pitch dark. I suppose they must have some clothes or something. Or maybe there's not enough worth returning for. I guess we could ask Sam."

"Let's wait," said Aunt Lucy. "For now, let's just enjoy them."

She sat back with a smile, listening to the quiet rumble of the siblings' banter. Sophie closed her eyes and embraced the fatigue seeping into her bones. She wanted Sam and Harry to stay with Aunt Lucy, though she didn't know where the money to feed and clothe two growing kids would come from. But somehow these two had wriggled their way into her heart, and she was determined to figure it out.

She couldn't save all the starving kids on Milwaukee's streets, but Sam and Harry had appeared in her life as if by magic, and she would cling to them with all her might.

17

Stepping under the stone archway at the Wolff Park entrance felt like entering another world. Sam and Harry took it all in with saucer-wide eyes as they were swept along with Sophie and Aunt Lucy in a wave of eager couples and families. A whistle blew as a miniature train chugged by on its winding railway. The path forked, one side leading to a midway of carnival games, and the other steering guests to various rides. A third, shorter path ended a tall fence, its walls solid, blocking any view of what lay beyond. "Under Construction: Splash Ride Coming Soon!" promised a sign painted in the trademark forest green of the Wolff Lager label.

The enticing scents of buttery popcorn and candied pecans wafted through the air. Sophie heard a cacophony of children's laughter, tunes played by roving accordionists, and the lilting cadence of barkers as they lured visitors to their attractions. Amidst the hubbub stood huge striped tents where guests could enjoy plenty of ice-cold Wolff Lager.

Harry and Sam raced to the line snaking toward the massive Dazy Dazer roller coaster. Aunt Lucy bought a brown-paper sack of popcorn and planted herself on a bench nearby to wait for the young adventurers. Too restless to sit, Sophie strolled along the midway, passing a ring toss game. A teenage girl squealed with delight when her ring landed neatly on the neck of a milk bottle. Happy families seemed to be everywhere, the children's faces shining with wonder. As she passed a dart game, a lanky young man offered a plaster kewpie doll to his date, who blushed and looked up at him shyly. At the shooting gallery, men took aim at wooden ducks and rabbits.

The joyful hoots of two boys caught her attention. A man had rolled up his sleeves and was expertly pitching baseballs at pyramids of tin cans. The cans scattered with a racket that delighted the boys.

"We have a winner!" shouted the barker. He handed the man a paper bag of sweets.

The man reached in and took out a peppermint, which he popped into his mouth. The boys protested loudly, grabbing for the bag.

"Yo! Who was throwing those baseballs?" the man teased. "Use your manners." He shook his head in mock frustration.

A chorus of "please, please, please" answered his admonishment.

"Danny, are you going to share these fair and square with your brother?"

The taller boy nodded, and the man handed over the candy. The boy grabbed the sack and savored his first piece of candy, making sounds of delight that distressed his brother.

"Dan..." the man warned.

The boy grinned and held out the bag to his brother, who reached in for a sweet. The man tousled their hair, and they ran off gleefully. He turned, and Sophie was astonished to see Detective Jacob Zimmer. She hadn't considered that he might have children. With horror she realized that she'd stopped in her tracks to stare at him. She felt her face get warm. Just then, he looked up and caught her eye. An odd expression flitted across his features, then he raised his eyebrows.

"Well, if it isn't Miss Strong," he said. "What brings you to the park on this fine day?"

She was surprised to hear what almost sounded like friendliness in his voice. In their other interactions, he'd been stern and brusque.

She tried to match his tone. "Detective Zimmer, is that you? I would have thought you'd be at the shooting gallery. You must have extensive experience with firearms."

"I don't care much for guns," he said. "Stay away from them when I can."

She nodded in approval. "I don't want to keep you from your young companions," she said. "Surely their appetite for adventure hasn't been satisfied."

He chuckled. "Those scamps? They're probably off to Kiddie Land, to trade their candy for better prizes." He gestured to the baseball-throwing game. "Are you going to try your luck? Some ladies are fairly adept at baseball. You've heard of the Bloomer Girls?"

"That's the women's team that tours the country, is it not? I haven't had the pleasure of seeing them play. And I'm not particularly athletic myself."

"Your career keeps you quite occupied, no doubt."

"It does indeed."

"I'm surprised you were able to get away from your desk on a Saturday. The *Herald* has a Sunday edition now, doesn't it?"

Sophie nodded. "It does. I finished my articles this morning. I'm here with my aunt. Speaking of which, I should get back." She turned to retrace her steps and find Aunt Lucy.

"I'll walk with you, if you don't mind," said Zimmer. "I'm heading that way myself."

She wondered why he didn't seem concerned about his sons' whereabouts, but it was none of her business. They passed a tent promising glimpses of the World's Tallest Man and the Incredible Strong Woman. As Sophie gazed at the attractions, her foot hit a dip in the ground, and she stumbled.

Zimmer took her upper arm helpfully. "Steady there, Miss Strong."

His grip on her arm eased slightly, and Sophie noted the firm, reassuring presence his hand provided. Then he paused and tilted his head to the side, squinting down at the shrubs that edged the pathway. He bent down and picked up a man's leather wallet.

"Someone will be missing this," he said, showing it to Sophie.

"Oh, my." She looked around. "How would one find its owner in this crowd?"

"Shouldn't be too hard. A man can't go very far in this place without needing to reach for his billfold."

They resumed their walk, scanning the crowd as they passed games, food stands, and a roped-off oasis dotted with small tables and chairs. They noticed a commotion ahead at the line for the carousel.

"I had it right here," sputtered a man's voice, as complaints went up from the others waiting behind him. The school-aged girl and her mother standing near him looked mortified by the unwanted attention.

Zimmer craned his neck, peering over the heads in front of them. "That's our man," he said to Sophie. He pushed through the disgruntled throng, and she followed in his wake.

The man patted his pockets frantically, as the ticket seller urged him to step aside and let other riders take his spot.

"Sir?" called Zimmer. "Did you lose something?"

"My billfold is missing."

"Can you describe it?"

The man looked up hopefully. "Did you find it? Dark-brown leather, with my initials tooled on it: H.B."

Zimmer glanced at the wallet in his hand, and seeing it met the description, held it out. Relief broke out on Mr. H.B.'s face.

He jogged toward Zimmer, one hand outstretched. "Thank you, yes, that's my billfold," he said. "I don't know what could have happened."

Zimmer and Sophie turned to go, but the man put a hand on Zimmer's shoulder.

"I appreciate your honesty," he said, opening the wallet and taking out a dollar. "Allow me to buy some lemonade for you and your lady friend."

"There's no need," Zimmer began. "We're not—"

Sophie felt the heat rise to her face at the assumption they were a couple. She opened her mouth to join him in protest, but the man cut them off.

"I insist," he said. "And thank you." He pressed Zimmer's hand, then turned back to the line for the carousel, which had begun to move, its cheerful music playing.

Zimmer shrugged at Sophie. "Well? It's free lemonade."

Sophie started to demur, then realized that she actually was thirsty and refreshment would be welcome. She might even learn something about the case from a quiet conversation with the detective.

She gave Zimmer a winning smile. "Why not?"

They strolled to a grassy area they'd passed, and Zimmer led her to a small wooden table nestled under the shade of a maple tree. He held her chair as she seated herself.

"Lemonade, then?" he asked her.

"Yes, thank you," said Sophie. She wondered if he would

buy Wolff Lager for himself. It was apparently his day off, after all.

Zimmer strode to the refreshments stall at the side of the garden, its wide window open to receive customers. She noticed that he politely gestured to an older gentleman with a cane, inviting him to take the spot in front of him. His height enabled him to scan the crowd, and she saw him taking the measure of the place. She wondered if he envisioned potential criminal activity simmering below the surface everywhere he went. Was it exhausting to be constantly suspicious?

He returned with two glasses of lemonade and set them down. Then he moved the free chair around the side of the table, closer to Sophie, where he had a clear view of the garden and its patrons, and settled in. Sophie picked up her glass and took a long, cool drink; the tart liquid soothed her parched throat.

"I hope your aunt won't be concerned about you, Miss Strong," he said.

Sophie glanced toward the midway. She felt a stab of regret that she couldn't watch Sam and Harry experience their first roller coaster ride.

He seemed to sense her discomfort.

"We needn't stay, if you'd rather find her," he said, leaning forward as if ready to rise and escort her out of the garden.

Sophie shook her head. "She won't worry. She has her hands full, I'm sure."

He raised his eyebrows. "How's that?"

"We brought two boys with us today. They've been staying with Aunt Lucy. One of them—well, it's a long story."

"You've got my interest."

She found herself telling him about Sam's frantic late-night visit to the apartment, the squalid makeshift tent he had lived in, and Harry's illness. She remembered to refer to Sam by name, so she wouldn't slip up and use the pronoun "she." Sam guarded her secret carefully, and Sophie felt bound to do the same. She was pleased to have been taken into Sam's confidence, even though it had been motivated by an awkward accident.

Finally, Sophie fell silent and picked up her glass again.

"So your aunt is now the caretaker of two young lads," said Zimmer. "Is she a lady of independent means that she can take on such a responsibility?"

Sophie thought of Aunt Lucy's modest home and her work with the traveling library service. She surely couldn't put it off forever if she was to keep a roof over her head.

"No, she has to work," Sophie answered. "But she's managing. And Sam plans to continue selling papers. Though we'd much rather see Sam in school."

"Those newsies are a scrappy bunch," said Zimmer. "They like their independence."

A silence gaped between them. "Have there been any more developments in the Rock case?" she asked him.

"You know I can't discuss it with you—or with anyone," he said. "Especially not a member of the press."

"I'm just asking as a concerned citizen," she insisted. "Not as a reporter."

He gave a suspicious smirk. "Well, I can tell you that we're investigating several suspects," he said. "We haven't located the murder weapon. It could be anywhere in the city, of course." For a moment his eyes looked bleak, but then he appeared to renew his resolve. "It's early days, though. We'll sort it out."

"How long do such cases usually take?" she asked. She'd never paid attention to the time that passed between the report of a crime and an arrest, but now she realized there might be a time-consuming, painstaking inquiry.

He shrugged. "It varies. Some are never solved. But this one—there's something about it. Where it happened and the way she was left at the suffrage office. The killer was making a statement. Almost as if he—or she—wants to be found."

Sophie swallowed nervously, recalling that Clara Elliot most likely remained on his list of suspects. They were interrupted suddenly by a jumble of exclamations as a red balloon bobbed near their heads. Sophie turned to find Sam jabbering about the roller coaster ride, Harry grinning but looking a bit green. Sam appeared youthful and relaxed in a way that Sophie hadn't seen yet.

Aunt Lucy caught up with them. "Boys, we mustn't interrupt Sophie."

Zimmer stood as Lucy reached the table. "Please, take my seat."

Sophie's eyes were on Harry, who vibrated with energy. "The roller coaster was amazing! Then Sam won the ring toss, and got me this balloon," Harry babbled. His bright eyes caught her half-full glass. "Is that lemonade?"

Sam jabbed him in the ribs with an elbow as Sophie reached for her purse. But Zimmer held up a hand.

"Please, allow me," he said. "I'm Jacob Zimmer, an acquaintance of Miss Strong. We happened to... bump into each other."

Sophie blushed. She had been so surprised to see the trio that she hadn't bothered to introduce them. "I'm sorry. This is my aunt, Miss Lucy Strong. And these two ruffians are Sam and Harry."

Zimmer nodded respectfully at Aunt Lucy. "I'll be back in a wink," he said, and headed to the refreshment stand.

Aunt Lucy eyed Sophie. "So you've found a friend, I see."

"He's—we're working together..." She was reluctant to bring up the sordid details of their meeting.

"He's a copper," Sam put in.

Sophie glanced up, startled. "How did you know?"

"They've got a way about 'em," Sam said.

"He is a detective," Sophie admitted. "But he's here on his day off."

Zimmer returned with three glasses of lemonade, two of them balanced in one large palm, and set them on the table. Harry nestled close to Aunt Lucy, resting against her ample thigh, and reached for one of the glasses. Lucy nudged him before he could gulp it down.

"Thank you," he said quickly, glancing in Zimmer's direction.

"Thank you, Mr. Zimmer," Sam said, lifting her glass.

"You're welcome."

Aunt Lucy gave Zimmer a warm smile. "It's very kind of you," she said, then took a drink. "Oh, my, that's good."

The tiny table was crowded with five people around it, even though two of them were skinny kids.

Zimmer pulled out the pocket watch that Sophie remembered from their first meeting and glanced at it. "Now, if you'll pardon me, I'm afraid I must be off. I need to meet a couple of youngsters and get them home before supper."

Sophie felt an odd prick of disappointment, but she reasoned it was because she hadn't learned anything new about the case.

Zimmer said his goodbyes to the others, then gave Sophie a smile. "Miss Strong, meeting you is always a memorable experience. I hope you enjoy the rest of your afternoon."

The heat rose in her cheeks again, though she couldn't imagine why.

"And you as well, Detective Zimmer," she said. "Good day."

He lifted his hat slightly, then turned away. She watched him walk off, her gaze on his broad, proud shoulders as he exited the garden and blended with the crowd.

18

Sophie strolled down Grand Avenue after attending a fashion show at Gimbels, the warm spring air deepening her reluctance to return to the office. She had a story to write, but her mind kept returning to the puzzle of Hilda Rock. It was clear that Mr. Pitman knew Mrs. Rock, and he appeared to have worked for her. What had he been doing at her home, rifling through her papers? Surely if he had a legitimate reason to be there, he wouldn't have been so uneasy. What were he and Agnes and Millie looking for?

Then there was the soldier's coat, which still hung on a hook in her room at the boarding house. Was it related to the murder in some way? Sam had said that a wealthy man was burning it—could he have been a guest from the Spring Gala? People did odd things under the influence of liquor.

The commanding form of Detective Jacob Zimmer swam into her mind. Despite his kindness at Wolff Park, she recalled the persistent way he'd interrogated Clara Elliot. What was to stop him from arresting Mrs. Elliot or Aunt Lucy, and blaming them for the crime? She'd read about the underhanded machinations of officers in New York and

Chicago. If enough money was offered, some policemen could be enticed to turn a blind eye to injustice.

She quickened her step, passing two more blocks of shops. The cross street was Broadway, and with a decisive nod to herself, she made her way north to police headquarters. As a citizen of this city and a member of the press, she had every right to know about the investigation into Mrs. Rock's murder. Maybe Detective Zimmer would be more amenable to discussion, now that they knew each other a little better. This time she wouldn't let him brush her aside.

The tall, brick building loomed into view. Taking a deep breath, she opened the door to the main entrance. The entryway was a jumble of bodies. Two officers she didn't recognize held both arms of a rough-looking man in handcuffs. An angry young woman with vivid makeup and brassy red hair pleaded with one of the grim-faced officers behind the elevated front desk, her voice rising to a dramatic wail as she gestured toward another man. Sophie surmised she was a lady of the night, though it was still afternoon.

No one had noticed Sophie yet. She was tempted to lurk in the background and watch events unfold, in case it was something interesting she could write about for the paper. Instead, she inched her way along, then peered into the large office space beyond the desk. Near the back of the room, she caught sight of a familiar bent head of light-brown hair. A younger officer approached him and the man looked up, confirming her guess that it was Detective Zimmer.

She heard the peal of a telephone, and one of the officers at the front desk turned to pick up the instrument. Sophie took her chance while his back was turned and slipped past him.

"May I help you, miss—" A beefy officer sitting near the front of the room called to her. She shook her head, walking with determined steps toward Zimmer's desk. "Miss, wait!" he called. "You can't—"

The commotion caught Zimmer's attention, and he looked up, his startled expression turning to resignation when he saw her. Sophie heard footsteps behind her and wondered if she'd be thrown out before she had a chance to speak to him. Then Zimmer stood up, and she was struck by the formidable bulk of his chest and upper arms.

He glanced past her and held up a hand. "It's all right, Rudolph. I'll take care of this."

She reached his desk and gazed up at him. He was taller than she remembered, and he looked annoyed at her intrusion.

"Miss Strong." His voice was guarded.

She swallowed, then cleared her throat and forced herself to speak. "Hello, Detective Zimmer. I trust you are well." Her eyes strayed to the surface of his desk, but whatever he had been working on was carefully tucked away.

"To what do I owe the honor?" He gestured to the empty chair next to the desk and waited while she sat down. Then he eased himself into his own chair and looked at her expectantly.

"I came for the costume," Sophie said on impulse.

"I beg your pardon?"

"Mrs. Elliot's costume. The one I was carrying when we met last Sunday. Surely you no longer need it, since you found no reason to suspect Mrs. Elliot."

He smiled wryly. "I had no reason to detain her, you mean. I don't believe we discussed my suspicions."

"You *can't* still think she was involved in the murder," Sophie insisted.

"Miss Strong, as I've said, I can't discuss an open case with you. No matter how curious you may be."

"That's a shame," she said. "There are a few things I wanted to mention."

"Really. And what might those be?" His lips twitched slightly, and she wondered if it was because he was trying not to smile or holding back a frustrated diatribe.

She tried to look nonchalant, but when she glanced at her hands in her lap, she realized she was twisting her fingers nervously. She laced them together and forced her hands to be still. She pursed her lips and wrinkled her brow, as if uncertain whether to continue her tale.

"If you have information about a case, it's your duty to share it, Miss Strong. It is the law, in fact," he said sharply.

"Well, sometimes things slip my mind, you see. But talking with you might jog my memory." Her attempt at feminine persuasion sounded feeble, even to her own ears.

Zimmer exhaled forcefully, but he kept his voice low. "Don't play games with me, Miss Strong. If you have information, tell me. Otherwise, I have work to do."

His friendliness from their encounter at Wolff Park had disappeared.

Sophie worried she might be testing his patience, but she went on. "I came across a few details—in the process of doing my job as a reporter, you understand. I have no idea if they're relevant. As I was nearby, I thought I'd have a chat with you. Where *is* the costume, anyway?" She looked around the room, as if expecting to see the delicate gown hanging from one of the dingy walls.

"It's locked up, and it will be returned to Mrs. Elliot when the case is closed. It's too early for me to release potential evidence."

"Evidence of what? That Mrs. Elliot has a nice wardrobe?"

"If you just came to bait me, you can be on your way. As I said, I have work to do."

Giving up her attempt to use feminine wiles, Sophie reverted to her customary direct approach.

"Have you spoken to Mr. Pitman, the lawyer in the Majestic Building?"

"Not yet. Why do you ask?"

"I don't know anything definite, but he's connected to Mrs. Rock somehow."

"And on what do you base this claim?" He studied her face, and she felt her cheeks grow warm.

"He was at her house, searching through her papers."

His brows furrowed. "You saw him doing this?" Sophie nodded. "What were you doing at Hilda Rock's house, may I ask?"

"Paying a condolence call," she said.

He cocked his head to one side. "Mrs. Rock had no family. Who did you think required your condolences?"

Sophie coughed. "Her maid, Mrs. Hanson, is—" she couldn't say "friend," even in her wildest embellishment of the relationship "—an acquaintance of my family."

Zimmer nodded, unconvinced. He pulled a notebook out from under a pile of papers on his desk and picked up a pen. "What exactly did you see?"

She felt the eyes of officers from nearby desks on her, and her face flushed again. "Would it be possible to speak somewhere a little more private?" she asked quietly.

He studied her, as if still unsure whether he should take her seriously.

Then he stood. "I believe you're familiar with the interrogation rooms from your last visit."

She got to her feet, and he gestured toward the hallway. She walked in front of him, oddly self-conscious as she tried to ignore the smirks of Zimmer's colleagues. Honestly, did respectable women never enter this establishment? Probably not.

She reached into her bag and pulled out her notebook and pencil, feeling more secure with the tools of her trade in her hands.

"Rudolph, I'll be in two," Zimmer told the young officer near the front of the room.

Sophie walked at Zimmer's side down a hallway that was just as grim as she remembered from her visit with Mrs. Elliot. Her head only came up to his shoulder, she noticed. He opened a door, and they entered a room that looked identical to the one that she and Mrs. Elliot had occupied the previous week.

He pulled out a battered wooden chair for her in a gesture of unexpected chivalry. She smoothed her skirt underneath her and sat. Zimmer took the chair at the head of the table. In the close setting of the interrogation room, he seemed even more intimidating.

"All right, Miss Strong," he began. "You said you visited Hilda Rock's home, to pay a condolence call on her maid, Mrs. Hanson. When was this?"

"It was Tuesday afternoon."

His blue eyes met hers steadily. "Start at the beginning, and tell me what happened."

She related her visit to Mrs. Rock's, her conversation with Millie Hanson, and the sudden appearance of Mr. Pitman.

"So you're saying this Mr. Pitman is Mrs. Rock's lawyer, and he came to the house. What did you find suspicious about that?"

"It wasn't that he was there, but his demeanor—he seemed very nervous. He was in Mrs. Rock's study, and before I left, I went in to say goodbye. He was rifling through her papers, as if he was frantically searching for something."

Zimmer shrugged. "Perhaps Mrs. Rock's desk wasn't as organized as he would have hoped."

"But then, when I left, I went around to the back of the house. That's when it got really odd."

He drew his brows together. "What were you doing at the back of the house?"

She bit her lip. "I just—I had a feeling that something wasn't right."

He kept his face impassive, waiting for her to continue.

"I heard them talking. They were searching for something."

"They? You mean Pitman and Mrs. Hanson?"

She nodded, opened her mouth, then closed it again. Now that she was relating the story, she wondered if she could leave Agnes Thompson out of it. She was Mrs. Elliot's sister, after all. Sophie didn't want to cast more suspicion in that direction.

He watched her intently. "Was there anyone else with them?"

"Well..." She met his eyes and found it impossible to prevaricate. "Yes. Miss Agnes Thompson was there."

"Miss Thompson... That's Mrs. Elliot's sister, is it not?"

"Yes, but—" She struggled to put her suspicions into words. "The thing is, they all seemed to know each other well. But earlier, when I had asked Mrs. Hanson about Mr. Pitman, she said she'd never met him before."

"That's odd, but not a crime, Miss Strong." He tapped his pencil on the table impatiently.

"Mrs. Hanson had been seen going to Mr. Pitman's office several times, on errands for Mrs. Rock. Why would she lie to me about knowing him?"

He gazed at her with an unflappable expression.

"They *must* be hiding something," she insisted. "And then there's the handkerchief..."

"Handkerchief?"

She reached into her pocket to pull it out. "I found this in the hallway, right before I discovered Mrs. Rock."

He examined the fabric, his fingers pinching only a corner of the lace border. Then he looked at her. "Withholding evidence from the police is a serious offense, Miss Strong."

Sophie's heart beat faster. She swallowed. "I didn't withhold evidence—"

"The murder took place nearly a week ago, and this is the first I've heard of this handkerchief. It's been in your possession all that time, has it not?"

"Yes, but—I didn't *intentionally* withhold it. I forgot I had it. I was upset after finding Mrs. Rock that day."

He considered her excuse. "Are there any other details you haven't shared with me?"

She shook her head. "But that handkerchief... It could be the one that I saw Mrs. Wolff holding at the Spring Gala."

He gave her a dismissive smile. She didn't appreciate it. "So if I understand correctly, your theory is that Mrs. Wolff left her annual Spring Gala, which she considers the social event of the year. She shot Mrs. Rock, dropping her handkerchief in the process, and then returned to the party."

It sounded crazy when he said it like that, but she refused to back down.

"It's one theory," she said. "It's worth investigating."

"Miss Strong, I understand that you're curious about this case, but as I've said before, murder investigations are dangerous. Someone *killed* Mrs. Rock in cold blood."

"Yes, I know that, Detective. I did find her, after all."

He let out a long, slow breath, as if trying to hold his temper in check. "But you don't seem to grasp the *gravity* of this situation." She saw his left hand was clenched into a fist. "It isn't a game, Miss Strong. It's dangerous. If you snoop in the wrong direction, you could get hurt."

His patronizing tone set her teeth on edge. "I'm not *snooping*. I'm a journalist. I'm doing my *job*."

"This is a police investigation," he said, raising his voice slightly. "We don't need your help. Trained officers—*armed* officers—are working on it. By sticking your nose in, you could raise the killer's suspicions and make things harder." He ran a hand through his hair. "Damn it, you could end up dead yourself!"

He nearly shouted the last sentence. Sophie stared at him, her blood boiling. Angry words leaped to her lips, none of them suitable, and she bit her tongue to avoid snapping at him. She knew he was right about the danger. But at the same time, she wanted to grab him by the lapels of his coat and shake him. It was infuriating to feel so powerless.

After a moment, Zimmer continued in a more controlled tone of voice, meeting her eyes. "I apologize, Miss Strong. I should not have raised my voice or used that language."

She leaned forward. "Mr. Pitman is hiding something, and you haven't even talked to him."

He lifted his brows. "Are you telling me how to do my job, Miss Strong?"

"I'm doing *my* job. This is a newspaper story as well as a police investigation." She didn't add that she was terrified for her aunt and Mrs. Elliot.

"You can report the story when the crime has been solved," he said. "Until then, leave the investigating to the police."

"Did you know that Ruben Wolff and Hilda Rock had a romance in their youth?"

"I beg your pardon?"

"They were courting when they were young."

He sighed and pinched the bridge of his nose. "Why is this relevant?"

"What if they were *still* romantically involved?"

"Are you accusing Mr. Wolff of infidelity?"

"I'm just thinking aloud, Detective. If he was unfaithful, wouldn't that give Mrs. Wolff a motive for killing Mrs. Rock?"

"Miss Strong. You have to be careful about throwing around rumors. You could find yourself in a lot of trouble."

She ignored this. "The jacket is another possible clue."

"What jacket?"

"A man was seen burning a navy-blue jacket in the alley near the Majestic Building."

"When was this?"

"The night Mrs. Rock was shot. What if it was the killer, covering his tracks? What if the jacket was part of a costume?"

He steepled his fingers and closed his eyes briefly, then met hers again. "You're thinking of the Spring Gala. The one the labor protesters crashed. I was told they set fire to the ballroom."

She nodded. "You see? Too many things went wrong about that night. They *have* to be connected somehow."

"Actually, they don't," he told her. "The solution to a crime is almost always the simplest one."

Sophie swallowed, hoping the simple solution didn't involve pinning the blame on Clara Elliot.

"*Almost,*" she said, "is not the same as always."

"Correct. Not always. But in this case, we have other important angles to consider before we start on hunches and overheard conversations from girl reporters."

She pressed her lips together hard, holding back a furious retort.

"I haven't heard anything from you that warrants my immediate attention," he said. "Rest assured that the police know what we're doing."

She shook her head in disgust and jammed her notebook

into her purse. She pushed out her chair forcefully, nearly knocking it over, and rose to her feet.

"If you don't solve this crime, someone else will," she said, hoping he didn't notice the quiver of emotion in her voice.

His jaw clenched, but she didn't wait for a reply. Instead, she swept over to the door.

Her hand was on the knob when he spoke again, in a low voice that was almost in a growl. "Stay out of this, Miss Strong. It is *dangerous*."

Not looking back, she squared her shoulders and left the room, pulling the door shut behind her. She made her way down the hallway, staring straight ahead and willing tears not to spill over. She should have known he wouldn't listen to her. Coming here was a waste of time.

Without glancing at the officers at the front desk, she strode out the door. The prostitute she'd seen earlier was resting her back against the building's brick façade, smoking a cigarette. The woman glanced over when Sophie came outside, then blew a cloud of smoke upward. Sophie brushed aside the tears that blurred her vision. She shook her head, impatient with herself.

The woman smiled wryly. "No use cryin' over men, sweetheart. They just ain't worth it." She took another long drag of her cigarette. Sophie met her heavily made-up eyes, seeing deep weariness mingled with compassion.

On her way back to the office, Sophie replayed the conversation with Zimmer in her head. Did he even *want* to solve the crime? Sometimes police officers didn't bother investigating without a hefty bribe. Other times, they were paid off by the criminals. Could she trust Jacob Zimmer? Or was he just another obstacle standing between her and the truth?

Sophie emerged from the *Herald* office on Friday evening to find Clara Elliot's familiar Cadillac parked in front of the building. Dante opened the door for her, and Sophie slid into the backseat where Clara was waiting.

"What did I do to earn a ride home in style?" she asked.

Dante pulled away from the curb without needing instructions. Sophie sobered when she saw the expression on Clara's face.

"What's happened?" she asked.

"Detective Zimmer came to the house today with some of his men, and they questioned everyone. Well—almost everyone. They couldn't question Agnes, because she's missing."

"Missing? What do you mean?"

"We haven't seen her since yesterday afternoon. She didn't come home last night. We've been driving around, hoping to catch sight of her somewhere. I don't understand where she could have gone. She doesn't have many friends."

Sophie frowned. "Did you ask Millie Hanson?"

"That was the first place we went. Millie hasn't seen her."

Sophie squeezed Clara's hand. "I'm sure she'll come home soon."

Clara clenched a damp handkerchief. "I'm just so worried. There's a murderer on the loose. What if Agnes was his next victim? Or worse—" Her voice cracked.

"Clara—"

"She's been acting so odd of late. I'm not sure what she's been doing."

Sophie didn't know what to say. If Clara wasn't sure about her sister, how could she offer reassurance? She patted Clara's hand as the older woman fought to control her emotions.

After a moment, Clara blew her nose and gave Sophie a small smile. "I am sorry. I don't mean to be so emotional."

"You have a lot on your mind."

"Detective Zimmer was suspicious when Agnes couldn't be located. He said I should send her to police headquarters to make a statement. If she doesn't go, he will probably come looking for her again. And then—" She broke off again.

Sophie saw real fear in Clara's eyes. "What is it?"

"When Agnes didn't return home, I went into her room. I searched for a letter or an appointment book that would give me a clue as to where she might be."

"Did you find anything?"

Clara let out a shaky sigh. "Oh, yes. I got curious, so I looked around. Under her mattress..."

"Yes?"

"I found David's gun."

Sophie gasped. "But she told us she didn't remember it."

"I know. She lied right to our faces. What if—" She shook her head. "I can't believe she'd really hurt someone. Not even Hilda Rock."

Sophie was silent for a moment. "If you think she's innocent, we'll just have to prove it. We have to find the murderer. I've been doing some investigating."

"Investigating? That sounds dangerous, Sophie."

Sophie jutted her chin upward. "We've both read plenty of detective stories. We'll be like Lady Molly of Scotland Yard."

"You do realize that Lady Molly is fictional."

"Okay, we'll be like Mary Holland. She's a real detective in Chicago who's an expert on fingerprinting. She testified in the Thomas Jennings trial a couple of years ago."

"I didn't know that," said Clara. "Maybe we could hire *her* to investigate instead."

"I'm sure *you* could do that. But it wouldn't be as interesting," said Sophie, trying to lighten the mood. Clara managed a slight smile.

Clara asked Dante to drive through the city for the next hour. She and Sophie gazed steadily out the windows, looking for any sign of Agnes. Sophie thought chances were slim that they'd catch sight of her, but she wanted to support Clara.

Finally Clara muttered, "This is useless." Sophie saw lines of worry etched around her eyes.

"If Agnes doesn't want to be found for some reason, she can probably find a way to stay hidden."

"What could she be thinking?"

Sophie had no idea, but the mysterious disappearance did cast suspicion on Agnes. Could she possibly have murdered Hilda Rock?

Clara rubbed her fingers across her forehead.

"My head is pounding," she said.

"You should go home and get some rest," said Sophie. "Maybe Agnes will be there when you arrive."

Clara nodded, but didn't look optimistic. "Would you like to come for dinner? It was kind of you to ride around with me for so long."

Sophie looked at her watch. "Mrs. O'Day will just be cleaning up the kitchen. I can get something at home."

Clara told Dante to take Sophie home, and soon he braked in front of the boarding house. He jumped out to hold Sophie's door open.

Sophie wanted to comfort Clara and tell her not to worry, but the situation did seem dire.

"Send word if you have news. I'll talk to you soon," she said. Clara gave her a tired smile, and Sophie went inside.

Vivian Bell was in the hallway, flipping through the few envelopes stacked in the mail tray. She looked up as Sophie entered.

"Hello, Sophie," she said with an air of nonchalance. "You're certainly riding home in style. Was that a chauffeur I saw with you?"

"Oh, yes, that was Dante," Sophie said casually.

She started up the stairs, feeling Vivian's curious eyes follow her.

THE NEXT AFTERNOON, Sophie decided to continue her own investigation. She headed for the theater district, the scorched blue jacket tucked into a small satchel. The dressmakers in the area seemed to do a steady business, from what she could discern. As she visited shop after shop, she encountered wealthy women seeking original additions to their wardrobe, as well as individuals she mentally labeled as "theater types." She wasn't familiar with a theater's personnel, but she surmised that the harried men and women in eccentric color combinations and unusual hats must be actors, costumers, or managers of some kind.

She presented the tattered wool jacket to several tailors and their assistants. Most welcomed her warmly as she entered, but when they learned that she had come for information and not to place an order, their manner grew brusque. Most gave the jacket no more than a cursory glance before sending her off with a flap of their hand, their glinting scissors and needles veering dangerously close to her skin.

Sophie rarely wished for a fine wardrobe, but seeing the bolts of rich velvet and silk in jewel tones of turquoise, ruby, and sapphire sparked a new pulse of longing. Women placing their orders for expensive gowns and coats swept past her as they departed, holding their fashionable skirts above the floor with an elegantly gloved hand and chatting with their companions about this or that special occasion. Some nodded politely in her direction, but most ignored her after a quick, assessing glance.

She consulted the list in her notebook and checked off yet another fruitless visit. Despite the number she'd been to, several unvisited shops remained on her list. Who could have guessed that the city had such a crying need for custom-made clothing?

It was becoming clearer that her entire venture might be hopeless. The jacket could be entirely unrelated to the costumes she saw at the gala, or to Hilda Rock's murder. It could have been ordered from another city altogether.

She sighed. The mystery novels she read often glossed over this tedious aspect of the sleuthing process.

Her feet and head ached in equal measures, and evening was approaching. She decided to visit one more shop and then quit for the day. The door was painted a lively shade of blue, and a cheerful bell rang as she opened it. The man who peered at her over the tops of his spectacles gave her a warm smile, and she smiled back.

"Hello, sir, I'm Sophie Strong of the *Milwaukee Herald*."

"Well, Miss Strong of the *Herald*, what can I do for you

today? Don't tell me one of my humble products merits a mention in your fashion column?"

She looked around the shop, noticing the ornate medieval costumes on display, in addition to a few more customary coats and gowns. "I'd love to interview you about your business another time, Mr...."

"Jeremiah Jarvis, at your service, miss." He bowed his head solemnly.

"Mr. Jarvis, I'm afraid my errand is much simpler today. I came across this jacket while covering an important story, and I'd like to learn more about it. Is it by chance one of your creations?"

She held out the blue coat, keeping its burns and holes folded neatly away from view. He stretched out a hand and took it, peering at the high-quality fabric, now smudged with dirt from Sam's adventures. He tilted his head to one side and looked at the stitching on the red lapels, running an expert finger along the nearly invisible line of tiny, even stitches. Then he turned back a red cuff and rubbed the heavy silk lining inside the sleeve with a fond smile.

A glimmer of hope sparked in Sophie's chest. Maybe she'd found the right tailor at last.

"It's not mine, miss," he said.

Her heart sank, and she reached out to take it back from him.

"That stitching does look familiar, though. Few tailors do that kind of work."

"Do you know who made it?"

"I can't be certain," he said. "But have you asked Mrs. Cooper?"

"I'm not sure." Sophie consulted her list. "I've talked to so many people today."

"Her shop is at the end of the alley down this street, between the milliner and Darcy's Pub." He indicated the direction with one hand. "It's not one you'd come across by chance. You'd have to know it's there."

She felt a flicker of hope. "In that case, no, I haven't been there."

"You might want to ask her about it."

She asked him to explain again where to find the shop, then she slipped out the door and headed south.

The alley, when she located it, was dark and strewn with litter. This couldn't possibly be the right place, she thought. Who would have a shop in such a location? She turned to go, but then her eye caught a glint of light at the end of the alley. Maybe it was the reflection of a gaslight in a window. She squinted and peered into the darkness, checking the corners for any lurking miscreants. It appeared to be deserted. Taking a deep breath, she picked her way forward over the cobblestones.

When she opened the door to the shop, she was pleasantly surprised. It was neat and clean, the wooden floor faded but carefully swept. A single gas lamp sat on the wide counter. Behind it, almost hidden among bolts of colorful fabric, sat a slim woman with gray-black hair, her head bent over the piece she was stitching in the meager light.

"Hello," said Sophie.

The woman glanced up. Her eyes traveled down Sophie's form, taking in her crumpled dress, the unruly brown curls escaping from their knot, and black shoes that bore the scuffs of a long day spent traipsing around the city.

"Yes?" she asked, showing little energy or interest.

Sophie cleared her throat. "I'm Sophie Strong of the *Milwaukee Herald*."

The woman's eyebrows rose, then she was overtaken by a fit of harsh coughing.

"Virginia Cooper," she finally said. Her eyes caught the

tattered jacket in Sophie's hand. "What's that? If it's mending, I don't have the time."

"No, it's not mending." She held up the jacket. "I found this, and I want to find out where it came from."

Virginia reached out one hand and rubbed the smudged, dark-blue fabric between her thumb and forefinger.

She traced along the charred edge of the sleeve. "Looks like it's been in a fire."

"Yes, it was rescued from one."

Virginia's mouth tightened. "That fabric's not cheap. It's good wool."

"Have you seen this before? Did you make it?"

Virginia looked into Sophie's face, as if taking her measure. Then she nodded once. Her eyes returned to the jacket. She picked up the sleeve and rolled it back to reveal the inner lining.

"See that? Real silk." Her finger ran along a line of neat stitches.

"It's beautiful work," Sophie said.

"Shame to destroy it like that." Virginia shook her head. "Some people have more money than is good for 'em."

"Do you remember who ordered this coat?"

"Oh, yes. I won't be likely to forget *him* any time soon."

"What can you tell me about him?"

A wary look crossed the woman's face. "Why do you want to know?"

Sophie wasn't sure how to answer. "It's just a hunch. I think the person who burned it was hiding something. They may have killed someone."

She bit her lip, unsure if it was wise to share her theory so openly.

Virginia raised up a hand, as if to hold Sophie at bay. "I don't need trouble with the cops. Had enough of that in my time."

"I'm not with the police."

Virginia snorted. "You said something about a paper, didn't you? Well, the cops usually turn up when folks start poking around in things. And they don't much care if they get it all right, as long as somebody goes to jail—or worse."

Sophie wondered what injustices Virginia Cooper had seen in her time. She suspected the woman hadn't always been a seamstress in a quiet side street.

"Can you just tell me... was this part of a costume? Ordered recently?"

After a pause, the seamstress nodded. "A Revolutionary War soldier. From the American side. It was a fine costume." There was pride in her gravelly voice.

"And the gentleman who ordered it?" Sophie pressed on in a soft voice. "Who was he?"

Virginia was overtaken by coughing again. She reached under the counter and pulled out a small, brown glass bottle. She tugged out the cork and took a swig of liquid, then wiped her mouth with the back of her hand.

"He was dressed nice. But he wasn't rich. I could tell. He maybe worked for somebody rich. He was nasty, too. Told me I'd be sorry if I didn't get it done in time."

"In time for what?"

She barked a laugh. "I didn't ask questions. I just sewed." She took another drink, then tucked away the bottle under the counter.

"But it was recent? Maybe in the past month?"

Virginia shrugged. "The days kinda blend together after a while, you know? I just sit here and work."

She gazed at the shop window with a far-off look in her eyes, and Sophie wondered if the substance in the bottle had addled her thinking.

Then Virginia shook her head again. "I've got work to do.

You'd better get home before it's dark. You don't want to be walking around here alone at night."

"What about you? Don't you have to go home?"

"I *am* home, honey." She jerked her head at a doorway behind her. Between two panels of a patchwork curtain that covered it, Sophie could see the end of a neatly made cot.

Virginia tucked her sewing needle into a fold of the fabric she was working on and rested the bundle on top of the counter. Then she eased off her stool, grimacing as if her joints felt stiff.

"Come on now," she said firmly. "Time for me to lock up."

Sophie reached into her bag for her tin case of calling cards. She held one out to Virginia. "If you think of anything else you can tell me, this is where to find me. It could be important."

The woman took the card, glanced at it, and stuffed it into her pocket. She walked to the door with halting, awkward steps, then pulled it open and looked at Sophie expectantly.

Sophie folded up the jacket and returned it to her satchel. At the doorway, she paused.

"Thank you, Mrs. Cooper." She touched the woman's arm lightly. "I appreciate your time."

Mrs. Cooper was quiet, and Sophie stepped out into the alley. As she began to walk away, the woman's voice followed her, and it sounded just a tiny bit warmer than before.

"You take care, Miss Sophie Strong."

Sophie didn't tarry in the dark alley, and she was relieved to emerge onto Wells Street, where cars and horse-drawn wagons jockeyed for position. She glanced at her watch. She was supposed to be at Aunt Lucy's for dinner in half an hour, and her feet were too sore to make the long walk. Though she couldn't afford it, she pulled a nickel out of her coin purse and went to board an approaching streetcar.

20

———

Sophie left the boarding house early the next morning and took a circuitous route that led past the Majestic Building. She chided herself. A clue to the case wasn't likely to flutter out of a window and into her path. Still, she couldn't resist stopping for a moment to look up at the fourteen stories of white-glazed terracotta and brick. Most of the offices were dark. What secrets lurked behind those dozens of windows that faced Grand Avenue like solemn, unblinking eyes?

Suddenly, Sophie saw a faint glimmer of light in a second-floor window. She blinked, and it had disappeared just as quickly. Could Mr. Watson be working up there? Why wouldn't he turn on a brighter light? Her breath caught in her throat as she recalled her terrible discovery of Mrs. Rock. Could the murderer be lurking upstairs?

Immediately, Detective Zimmer's face flashed into her mind. Should she go to the police? But if she did, whoever was in the building might run off before they arrived.

She heard a familiar, melodic whistling coming up the street, gradually growing louder. Looking down the sidewalk, she saw the janitor Mr. Watson approaching, swinging a lunch pail. When he caught sight of her, the whistling stopped.

"Miss Sophie? Is that you?"

"Good morning, Mr. Watson."

"Good Lord, you gave me a start. It's mighty early to be out here."

"I couldn't sleep, so I decided to take the long way to work."

"And your feet took you here, did they?" He cocked his head.

She nodded. "It looks deserted, but I thought you might have been working on the second floor. I saw a light flicker in the window."

He jingled the keys out of his pocket and inserted one into the lock. "Lots of empty offices up there."

"You don't sound surprised."

"There's not a whole lot that slips by old Ezekiel Watson."

She'd never heard his first name before, and decided it suited him.

"Is someone up there? Someone who shouldn't be?"

His warm brown eyes met hers. "If there is anyone up there, they haven't done a thing to alarm me."

Sophie felt somewhat reassured, but curiosity rippled through her mind. She followed Mr. Watson into the building and up to the second floor. But instead of turning left down the hall to the suffrage office, she took a right and headed for the source of the light she'd seen earlier. There were several offices with windows facing the street. She crept along the hallway, listening for any sign of life. All was still.

One by one, she soundlessly tried each doorknob. None of them budged. She inched along the hallway. When a doorknob at the end of the row turned easily in her hand, she gave a small gasp. She should have brought a weapon of some kind—even Mr. Watson's broom could be useful—but it was too late now.

She took a deep breath and flattened herself against the wall so she wouldn't be in view of anyone inside. Then she flung open the door.

"Who's there?" she called out in a low tone that she hoped sounded threatening.

"Don't shoot!" pleaded a trembling female voice.

A jolt shot through Sophie's chest. She hadn't expected a response. "Who is it? I'm not going to hurt you. I just want to talk to you."

She heard a shaky sigh from within. "Sophie? Is that you?"

The voice was hoarse and rough, but Sophie thought she recognized it. "Is that Miss Thompson?"

The flashlight snapped on, and in its beam Sophie saw the drawn and frightened face of Agnes Thompson. Her limp, brown hair hung around her face, and her eyes had dark smudges under them. She huddled on the floor against the wall, wrapped in a grimy blanket and looking as if she hadn't slept in days.

"What are you doing here?" Sophie asked, stepping into the room. "Clara is worried sick about you."

The sharp stench of urine pinched Sophie's nostrils, along with the stale odor of Agnes's unwashed body. Sophie realized she must be using a chamber pot of some sort.

"I can't go home, can I? The police are after me."

"They only want to talk to you, Miss Thompson," said Sophie.

Agnes barked a laugh. "And throw me in jail."

"Why do you think that? Is it because of the gun Clara found in your room?"

Agnes drew a sharp breath. "Did she tell the police?

"No, she didn't. But she might, if she doesn't find out what's become of you."

Agnes nodded miserably. "I didn't kill Hilda Rock, Sophie. But who would believe me?"

Sophie understood her concern. Her churlish personality, the presence of the gun, and now her disappearance did cast suspicion in her direction.

"Clara will believe you, if you're truly innocent."

"See? Even you don't believe me." Agnes chewed her lip miserably.

Sophie took in their surroundings. Her eyes had adjusted to the darkness, and she could see the abandoned desks and chairs against one wall. A few forgotten papers, now covered in dust, littered the floor. A wastebasket had been over-turned, and the few scraps inside looked like they'd been gnawed by rodents.

She moved closer to Agnes and lowered herself to the floor. The older woman didn't look up. Sophie noticed a thermos and a small bundle of supplies at her side.

"Why don't you explain it to me? If you didn't kill Mrs. Rock, why did you have the gun?"

Agnes gave a shuddering sigh. "You don't know what it's like, having a sister like Clara."

Sophie's eyes widened. "You wanted to shoot Clara?"

"No!" she cried. "I didn't want to shoot anyone. But it made me feel safer, having the gun with me. You see—oh, it's a long story."

"I know you were at Hilda Rock's house the other day. Looking for something."

Agnes looked surprised, but then she closed her eyes and nodded. "Hilda was a complicated person."

Sophie stayed silent, hoping Agnes would continue.

After a moment Agnes spoke, her voice low and weary.

"Did Clara ever tell you about when we were kids? About our parents?"

"Not much. Wasn't your father a professor?"

She gave a rueful laugh. "Not *my* father. Our parents were bakers. They made the most delicious Danish pastries. Our father used some of his mother's recipes from Denmark. He loved baking. He would whistle or sing most of the day, while Mother talked to customers and ran the shop."

Sophie had never heard this story. She wondered if Agnes could be imagining it, since it was so different from the bits and pieces Clara had mentioned over the years.

Agnes continued. "When I was about eight, something went wrong with the big oven. Mother and Dad saved for a new one, and they almost had enough. My father was too proud to ask for a loan. Then early one morning, as he was kneading the first batch of bread, the oven started a fire somehow. Mother pulled me and Clara out of our beds—we lived over the bakery, of course. She got us outside." Agnes paused, and then continued in almost a whisper, "But she went back. She and Dad died trying to save that place."

"Oh, my," said Sophie. She felt a wave of empathy. She knew what it was like to have your childhood shattered by the loss of a parent. "You were so young. I'm sorry."

She heard the grief in Agnes's voice. "We don't talk about it. Clara barely remembers our parents. She was only six when they died. We didn't have family in the States, and our parents had been so busy with the bakery, they didn't make many friends. So Clara was taken in by a distant cousin—the history professor and his wife. They were older and had never had children. But they said they couldn't manage both of us. So I went to live with another cousin, in Iowa."

"You were separated? I had no idea."

Agnes's eyes took on a vacant look. "The Hansens adored

Clara. They gave her the best education, parties, clothes… They weren't rich, but they did well enough."

"What about you?"

"Me? I was an unpaid farmhand. We just scraped along. I barely had a chance to go to school. And the family I lived with—they were unkind. The older boys—well, never mind. It made me bitter, I'll admit," said Agnes.

Sophie couldn't imagine what it was like to have a sibling, let alone one who had been taken away and coddled while you eked out an existence with strangers.

"But then you came to Milwaukee?"

"Those people… they wanted me to marry a boy from the farm down the road. I was twenty-one, and they didn't need me anymore. Their sons had married, and there were plenty of hands to do the work. I was just another mouth to feed. The boy who courted me—if you could call it that—was an oaf. And a heavy drinker. Marrying him would have meant more long years of backbreaking farm work. And babies."

After a long moment, Agnes continued, her voice like acid. "Meanwhile, Clara married David Elliot, the handsome lawyer. They weren't living in the mansion we're in now, but their first house was quite nice."

"She must have married young."

Agnes nodded. "He was quite a bit older, but they were crazy about each other. I remember the night I finally wrote to her from Iowa. I hated to do it. We didn't really know each other. And I couldn't spell. But she sent money for the fare to Milwaukee. She asked me to come for a good long visit. I knew I'd never go back."

Her mouth pursed, and she stared at the floor, as if seeing the scene unfold. "When I stepped off the train that day, I recognized her right away. She was bright-eyed and smiling, wearing a rosy-pink gown, standing next to her tall, dignified husband. I could tell she was shocked when she saw me. I saw it on her face before she could hide it. All those years of being outside at all hours, in all weathers… I looked old and used up. Still do."

Sophie didn't bother to contradict her.

Agnes clenched her fists in her lap. "Clara was *so* kind. So happy. She welcomed me with open arms. But it ate me up inside, thinking about her life, and all those years I worked on the stupid farm. Sometimes I wanted to push her down the stairs. But of course I never did. I got used to being invisible. The poor relation."

Like jigsaw puzzle pieces snapping in place, a picture of Agnes's past began to appear. It was clear why she'd become sour and angry.

"I'm sorry to hear all this," Sophie said quietly. When Agnes didn't continue, she added, "Where does Mrs. Rock come in?"

"I wanted to be out on my own. I couldn't stand living on Clara's charity. But I needed money. And I had no skills but farming. I couldn't earn my way."

Sophie thought of the many young women who worked in factories or shops, but she didn't mention them. "Did you think about school?"

Agnes gave her a disgusted look. "It would have been hopeless. But… people have a lot of secrets."

"Secrets?"

Agnes nodded, and Sophie saw an odd kind of pride on her face, warring with shame.

"Things they want to keep hidden. That they'll pay to keep hidden."

"So you…"

"I kept quiet and listened, mostly," Agnes said. "People can't keep their mouths shut."

It occurred to Sophie that what she described wasn't much different from her own job as a reporter.

Agnes went on, "I've been getting money from these rich, lying fools for years. I almost have enough to say goodbye to Clara and her handouts."

More of the puzzle became clear. Agnes's comings and goings at odd times of night. Her swinging moods. The sneaky silences.

"Blackmail," Sophie whispered.

Agnes nodded.

"And Mrs. Rock?"

She looked up at Sophie, her bloodshot brown eyes glittering with malice.

"Hilda Rock had some of the biggest secrets of all. And she was desperate to keep them quiet." She paused, as if remembering her twisted triumph. Then she continued, "But I didn't kill her. Why would I? I needed her money."

"But you had the gun?"

"People act funny sometimes. Some of them wanted to stop paying me. But I wasn't having it. They shut up when you pull out a gun." Sophie heard that flinty pride in her voice again. "I never shot anyone," she claimed. "But I fired it a few times. I made threats."

It didn't look good for Agnes, Sophie admitted to herself.

She tried to keep her tone upbeat. "Well you can't stay here and wait to get arrested."

"I don't know what else to do."

"We can go to the police," Sophie said. "You said Hilda had secrets. Maybe there's a clue in one of them. Maybe you weren't the only one who was threatening her."

She couldn't have been the only one if Agnes wasn't the killer. But she still wasn't sure if Agnes was telling the truth.

"They can just blame me and forget about it. You know how they are. All they want is an easy arrest. It doesn't matter what really happened."

"Detective Zimmer isn't like that," Sophie said. It was a gut feeling, but she hoped it was true.

"I thought they might put Clara in jail when they found her card."

Sophie frowned. "You knew about the card? The one in Hilda's pocket?"

Agnes bit her lip, not meeting Sophie's eyes. "I-I put it there."

"What? How is that possible?"

"I was here that morning. I found Hilda. Before you did."

Sophie gasped. "You found a corpse and put your sister's card in her pocket?" She couldn't keep the skepticism out of her voice. "You didn't call the police?"

"I was afraid. I thought they'd suspect me. I could have been seen meeting with Hilda those other times. Someone could have seen me go into the building that Sunday. I had just come from meeting one of my... contacts. I panicked. I always carried one of her cards, in case—in case anything happened to me. So I thought Clara would get questioned, and that would keep me safe."

Sophie's stomach churned. "Your own sister?"

"I didn't think anything would happen to her—maybe a day or two in jail. She's rich, and she has powerful friends. People like that never pay for their crimes." Agnes's eyes filled with tears, and they spilled down her cheeks.

"But Clara's committed no crime."

Sophie considered leaving Agnes to fend for herself. She could tell Zimmer what Agnes had said and let him sort it out. But then she remembered that he'd already questioned Clara once. He might think Clara and Agnes were in on it together. What if they *were*? The thought popped into Sophie's head before she could stop it. What if Clara was putting on an act, and she wasn't innocent at all?

No, it couldn't be. She was Aunt Lucy's oldest friend.

She'd always been so kind. And she was truly worried about her sister.

Agnes was weeping, her face in her hands. Sophie realized she wouldn't get any more of the story just then. And the police could very well return to the building at any moment. It was the scene of the crime, after all, and Zimmer had said he would question Mr. Pitman.

Sophie pulled herself to her feet. "Let's get you out of here," she said.

Agnes looked up at her, not bothering to wipe away the tears or the mucus that dripped from her nose. Her expression was that of a frightened, fragile child. "And go where?"

Sophie knew she should drag Agnes down to the police station and force her to tell Zimmer everything. But despite her reassuring words about Detective Zimmer, she still wasn't sure who to trust. And if Agnes and Clara were blamed for the murder, Aunt Lucy could get pulled in right along with them. They were a team, bonded over suffrage, always seen together.

"We'll go to Clara's house," Sophie said. "We'll talk to her and figure out what to do next."

She held out a hand to help Agnes up, but Agnes ignored it.

Agnes wiped away the tears and mucus with her sleeve. She gave a defeated sigh and squeezed her eyes shut. Sophie wondered which of her demons she was battling in her mind.

"Fine," Agnes muttered. She stood, and the blanket fell from her shoulders. "Let's go."

"What about your things?"

"I don't want them. The janitor can throw them out."

Of course you expect someone else to clean up your mess, Sophie thought. She scanned the room and caught sight of an old jar pushed under a desk, telltale yellow liquid inside.

"You're not leaving *that* for him to deal with," she said, nodding to the makeshift chamber pot.

Agnes grimaced. She went over to the window and tugged it open with effort, then picked up the jar and poured the contents to the grass below. She looked at the jar as if contemplating tossing it as well. But then she shrugged, set it on the floor, and shut the window again. Sophie contemplated picking up the dirty blankets herself, but she wasn't sure what she'd do with them, and she didn't want to touch them.

She walked to the door. "Come on. Let's go. You can tell me *and* your sister about these secrets you were holding over Hilda Rock."

21

When Ellen let them into the house, her eyes grew wide at the sight of Agnes, who didn't meet her gaze.

"Where is Mrs. Elliot?" Sophie asked as they entered the marble-tiled foyer.

"She's in the library with Miss Lucy. Shall I announce you?"

Sophie waved her off. "It's all right, Ellen. She knows me well enough by now."

Ellen looked relieved as she retreated into the recesses of the house. Agnes moved toward the grand central staircase as if to escape to her bedroom, but Sophie grabbed her arm and pulled her to the library door.

"First we talk," Sophie insisted.

Sophie heard the buzz of friendly conversation on the other side of the door. But when she opened it, Clara and Lucy fell silent and snapped their heads in her direction. The long table was covered with envelopes, letters, and newspapers with headlines like "Will Wisconsin Women Vote?"

Sophie assumed Clara and Lucy had moved their office duties here to avoid spending time at the crime scene.

When Clara saw Agnes, her face went white. Then her cheeks flushed red and her mouth became a hard, tight line. After a quick glance at her sister, Agnes trained her eyes on the floor. Clara pushed her chair back and marched over to Agnes, breathing hard. She took in Agnes's disheveled appearance, her limp hair hanging in greasy strands around her face, and the defeated sag of her shoulders. Then Clara opened her arms wide and pulled her sister into a tight embrace.

"Oh, Agnes," her voice trembled.

Agnes let herself be hugged, but stood woodenly, not lifting her arms to return the embrace. Clara released Agnes and swiped at her own tears.

"I was worried to death, you foolish woman. Sit down." She steered her sister to a chair at the head of the table. "Tell me *precisely* what is going on. Leave *nothing* out."

Clara returned to her seat across from Aunt Lucy, and Sophie sat at Lucy's side. Aunt Lucy gave Sophie's forearm an affectionate squeeze under the table.

Agnes chewed her lip, as if uncertain where to start. Her eyes were fearful when she lifted them to Clara's.

"You're going to hate me," she whispered.

"Tell me," Clara ordered.

"I-I've been hiding in the Majestic Building. In one of the empty offices."

"Oh, for heaven's sake, *why?*"

"Let me tell it my way," Agnes said. "Just listen."

She related her sorry tale of eavesdropping and blackmail over the course of several years. It had begun with a young maid she'd caught looking in Clara's jewelry box soon after arriving from Iowa. Clara looked thoughtful, and Sophie wondered if Agnes's odd comings and goings were making a warped kind of sense to her. Agnes left out the part about being consumed with jealousy of Clara. Instead, she mentioned wanting to be on her own and live independently. Sophie longed to point out that an existence funded by the suffering and guilt of others was hardly independent, but she kept quiet.

As Agnes recounted her story, she grew more animated, as if she was proud of her own ingenuity. Sophie recognized some of the names of her blackmail victims. A butcher who had once sold tainted meat that resulted in a customer's serious illness. A prominent member of the Women's Club had committed her mother to an asylum in order to take over the family home and fortune. A doctor's wife was in love with her husband's young assistant. The list went on and on. No crime was too petty, no secret too sordid for Agnes to sniff it out and press her advantage. It sounded to Sophie like Agnes could have accumulated many thousands of dollars by now. Why wasn't she already living on her own?

Sophie saw revulsion on Clara's face as Agnes spoke. Aunt Lucy watched both women with compassionate eyes.

"I took David's gun about a year ago," Agnes admitted. "I used to carry it when I was out late at night. People liked to meet me at odd hours, in places where we wouldn't be seen. The gun made me feel a little safer." She swallowed. "Once or twice, it helped me persuade someone who wanted to stop paying. I only shot it a couple of times—just to scare people. I didn't hurt anyone."

Sophie could believe that Agnes hadn't caused any bullet wounds, but she'd certainly inflicted pain on many scared and regretful acquaintances.

"I *didn't* kill Hilda Rock," Agnes insisted. "I-I wouldn't."

Sophie studied Agnes's face, trying to judge the truth of her words.

"I had no reason to kill Hilda. She was paying me quite a

lot. And she said she would have more money soon. A lot of it. She wanted to make one big payment and be done with me. I agreed."

Sophie was sure that agreement would have been temporary.

"Where was Mrs. Rock going to get this money?" she asked.

"She wouldn't say. She just said it would be soon."

Sophie's mind raced. Had Hilda been planning to steal it? Or had *she* tried to extort money from someone else and been killed in the process? Perhaps she'd just had the bad luck to lose her life before she could implement her money-making scheme, whatever it was.

"I've heard enough," Clara spit out.

"No," Sophie said. "We haven't." Clara raised her eyebrows. "We have to know what Mrs. Rock was hiding. It could help solve her murder."

"But the police—" Clara broke off.

"She's right, Clara," Aunt Lucy put in. "We don't know what the police are doing about this. Any one of us—or all of us—could be blamed."

"I don't want to visit you three in jail," Sophie said. "And I certainly don't want to end up there myself."

"Oh, you won't—" Aunt Lucy began, but then said more quietly, "Oh."

"Yes. I found the body. We've all spent hours at the suffrage office where Mrs. Rock was found. You three are notorious for hating her. And, I might add, you have a past relationship that you've been hiding from everyone, though I have no idea why."

Clara and Lucy exchanged glances, and Sophie could only guess what they silently communicated. They seemed much more like sisters than Clara and Agnes would ever be.

Clara sighed. "All right. Continue, Agnes."

Agnes licked her dry lips. She must have been thirsty from all of the talking, but Clara didn't offer her refreshment.

"Well, you know that Hilda thought she was going to marry Ruben Wolff, until Thelma came along. And when Ruben and Thelma got engaged, Hilda left town."

"Yes, we remember," said Clara.

Agnes looked around the table with an air of grim satisfaction. "While she was gone, she had a baby."

All three of her listeners gasped, and Agnes lifted her chin, triumphant.

"She has a child?" Clara asked.

"No. She gave up the child."

"And the father..." Clara said slowly.

"Ruben Wolff."

There was a beat of silence as this revelation sunk in.

Sophie asked, "So she paid you to keep that secret?"

Agnes nodded. "That, and the fact that they continued their affair, from time to time. I saw them together one night, and I overheard her threatening him. 'You can't do this. We had a *child*,' I heard her say. That was all I needed to hear."

"So they were *both* deceiving their spouses," said Aunt Lucy.

Agnes nodded. "Of course, neither one wanted the secret to get out. And they didn't want anyone to know about the child. Wolff wants to keep his reputation as an upstanding citizen. The scandal could ruin his business. And Hilda was terrified that her husband would find out. Something went wrong while she was giving birth, so she wasn't able to have more children. But she didn't tell Otto that when she married him."

"So many lies," Sophie said.

They were all quiet for a moment. Then Agnes said, "There's more."

"*More?* What more could there possibly be?" Clara's eyes were wide.

"When Otto died, Hilda ended up with nothing. But then Wolff started paying her. In exchange for—"

"Never mind, we can guess what he got out of it," muttered Lucy.

"—for speaking against women's suffrage," Agnes finished.

Her eyes glittered as the mouths of the others dropped open.

"Why that—of all the devious, underhanded—" Clara clenched her hand into a fist.

"So when she changed her mind, when she became an Anti…" Lucy began.

"She was paid to do it," said Agnes.

"Those greedy, devious brewers," said Clara. "They're so sure women will vote for Prohibition and take money out of their pockets."

"It could destroy their businesses," Lucy said.

"Oh, surely not. They'd think of something."

"It wouldn't look good for Wolff if it came out that he was paying for anti-suffrage propaganda," said Sophie.

"That's right," said Agnes. "He paid Hilda to speak, and not to tell a soul about his part in it."

"How did you find out about this?" Clara asked.

"Hilda let a few things slip. In front of her housekeeper."

"Millie Hanson," said Sophie. "She told you about it?"

Agnes nodded. "Millie had secrets of her own."

Clara held up her hand. "Stop. We don't need to hear those."

"So when I saw you and Millie and Mr. Pitman at Mrs. Rock's house…" Sophie said.

Clara and Lucy turned to Sophie. "When was this?" Lucy asked.

Sophie shook her head. "It doesn't matter now." Leaning toward Agnes, she said, "What were you looking for? Money?"

"And evidence."

"Evidence? Of what?" Lucy asked.

"Her relationship with Wolff. His payments. Their child. Whatever we could find."

"So all this time, you didn't have any proof?" Sophie asked.

"Just what I'd overheard," said Agnes.

"But if she was dead, why were you—" Clara stopped and looked at Agnes incredulously. "You were going to blackmail *Ruben Wolff*?"

Agnes didn't respond.

"Agnes, he's one of the most powerful men in the city— maybe the whole country. Who knows what he might do to stop you!"

Agnes's expression was sour. "Well, we didn't find anything. Yet."

"Oh, no. Your blackmailing career is over, as of this moment," said Clara.

Agnes shrugged. "Millie won't go after Wolff. She's too scared of him. But Pitman might."

"How did Mr. Pitman get involved?" Sophie asked.

"He gave Wolff's payments to Hilda. Millie picked them up sometimes."

"Alonzo Pitman is Wolff's lawyer?" Sophie asked. "In that tiny office? How is that possible? Wolff can afford the best lawyers money can buy."

"I'm certain he employs a whole cadre of lawyers," Clara said.

"Pitman does his dirty work. At least some of it," Agnes said.

Sophie tried to sort through the ugly, twisting threads of deception. "What a mess."

Agnes stifled a yawn. "Clara, I need some sleep."

She got to her feet, and Sophie saw that her skirt was crumpled and stained from sleeping on the floor. Her face looked pinched.

Clara eyed her sister with both pity and exasperation. "We'll talk more later."

Wordlessly, Agnes shuffled from the room.

Sophie frowned. "Could Millie or Mr. Pitman have killed Mrs. Rock?"

"I think anyone could have," said Clara. "You know what she was like. I'm sure she wasn't easy to work for."

"But that would put Millie out of a job," said Aunt Lucy.

"How about Mr. Pitman? Maybe he and Mrs. Rock argued when she picked up one of her payments," Sophie said. "She told Agnes she was going to come into some money. Perhaps she thought Mr. Pitman would have a big payment for her."

"So she got angry with Mr. Pitman? That's possible," said Clara. "She did have a terrible temper when we were younger."

"Perhaps Mrs. Rock threatened Mr. Pitman with a gun," Sophie theorized. "He had to wrestle it away from her, and he ended up shooting her. He's been especially nervous the past few times I've seen him. Maybe it's his guilty conscience."

"That sounds like a detective novel," said Clara. "There's another obvious suspect. The woman scorned."

"Thelma Wolff?" asked Aunt Lucy.

Sophie said, "I've thought of that too. Detective Zimmer says it's ridiculous. Mrs. Wolff has an alibi, since she was hosting the Spring Gala that night."

"You've been seeing Detective Zimmer?" asked Aunt Lucy, raising her eyebrows.

Sophie felt her face grow hot. "No, I'm not *seeing* him. I just stopped by the police station to ask for an update."

"And did he provide one?" asked Clara.

"He said they were looking into suspects. Then he basically told me to mind my own business. But he *would* say that."

Aunt Lucy rested a warm hand on Sophie's. "That's probably for the best, Sophie. The police may be questioning people we've never heard of. We aren't detectives, after all."

"Even if we do like to read about them," said Clara.

"I know, I know. It's just that after I found her body… well, that's how detective novels usually start out. And if I solved the crime, I'd have an amazing story for the paper."

"You know what would be a great story?" asked Aunt Lucy, reaching for a stack of letters and envelopes. "Women winning the vote in Wisconsin."

Sophie looked at her watch and jumped to her feet. "Speaking of stories, I'd better get to the office and write some." Clara pushed back her chair. "You don't have to get up."

But Clara ignored this, walked over, and gave Sophie a warm hug.

"Thank you for returning my wayward sister. You've solved *that* mystery, and it's not even lunchtime yet."

22

Sophie was returning to the *Herald* office after a quick bowl of soup at Louie's when she caught sight of a tall figure in a black trench coat lingering near the door. Her heart sped up.

"Detective Zimmer? I'm astonished to see you here."

"Hello, Miss Strong. I hoped I'd catch you."

"Indeed. Do you have news to report?"

He nodded grimly. "May I buy you a cup of coffee?"

"I suppose that would be all right."

She gestured to the cafe she'd just left. "We can go to Louie's."

They walked to the cafe, and for some reason Sophie was relieved to see none of her fellow reporters. Customers, bent over tall sandwiches or bowls of soup, didn't look up when they entered. Sophie led him to a booth at the back. He took the seat facing the door, and she wondered if that was a policeman's habit.

Louie's wife, Nellie, came over to their table, looking unsurprised to see Sophie back again so soon. "What'll it be?"

"Just coffee for me," Sophie said.

"I'll have coffee," said Detective Zimmer. "And maybe something sweet to go with it, if you have it."

She nodded and bustled off.

"Do you have a sweet tooth, Detective Zimmer?"

He looked abashed. "You can't beat these German places for homemade pastries."

Nellie plunked two well-used mugs on the table, followed by a small ceramic pitcher of cream and some spoons. Zimmer poured a generous dollop of cream in his cup and stirred. Balancing a tray expertly on one palm, Nellie set a small plate topped with a flaky rolled pastry in front of him.

"Franzbrotchen," she announced. "Enjoy."

She bustled back to her spot behind the counter.

Zimmer picked it up and took a bite, closing his eyes as he savored the sweet, cinnamon-laden treat.

Sophie's mouth watered a bit, but she just sipped her own coffee, not bothering with cream. "Has there been a development in the case?"

He nodded, resuming his professional air. "Possibly. You had mentioned something about a costume, so I wanted you to know about this. We got an anonymous call last night to the theater district. The windows at a tailor's shop got smashed, and the place was ransacked. It didn't look like the kind of place that would have a lot of cash, but what was there had been grabbed."

"What did the owner say?"

Zimmer shook his head. "We didn't find any sign of the owner. She must have decided to beat it."

"She? Who was it?"

He nodded. "Virginia Cooper. Do you know her?"

Sophie smiled ruefully. "I talked to her. I spoke to every tailor I could find, actually. She was the one who made the costume I told you about. The one that someone was burning the night Hilda Rock was killed."

"You said it was a soldier's uniform, I believe."

"That's right."

"Mrs. Cooper kept records about her orders, but they're a mess. A disorganized pile of notes, really. Do you think you might recognize the description if you saw it?"

She raised her eyebrows. "I thought you wanted me to mind my own business."

"And are you?"

"Our opinions about what *is* my business may differ."

He frowned and took another bite of his pastry. "The records are at the station. The problem is I don't have many men I can assign to go through them. And they don't really know what to look for. It would help if you could come down to the station and take a look."

Sophie bit back a triumphant smile and said, "I don't have any urgent deadlines this afternoon."

"Your help would be appreciated," he said. "And perfectly safe, I might add, unlike your previous efforts. You'll be surrounded by police officers."

She gave him a grimace and continued sipping her coffee.

"What did you think of Mrs. Cooper when you met her?" asked Zimmer.

Sophie blinked, trying to recall. "Her store was neat and clean. Her fingers seemed to fly as she sewed. I think she's very good."

"Anything else? Did any customers come by while you were there?"

"No. It was in the early evening, and she was about ready to close. I did wonder why her shop would be tucked away in an alley."

"Rent must be cheap."

"She had a bad cough," Sophie remembered. "When she

started coughing, she took a drink of something in a dark bottle."

"Alcohol, probably."

"At one point, she said she didn't want any trouble with the cops. Said she'd had enough of that in her time. She didn't say what it was about, though."

"Maybe that's why she was nowhere to be found when we arrived."

"I hope she's all right," said Sophie.

He'd almost finished his pastry. He broke off a piece and pushed the plate with the remaining untouched bit in her direction.

She picked it up, unable to resist. "Thanks."

He dunked the last piece into his coffee, then popped it in his mouth. He pulled two quarters out of his pocket and set them on the table. Sophie took a last swig of coffee and set down her empty mug.

They stood, and he gestured toward the door. "After you."

AT THE POLICE STATION, an interrogation room had been set aside, and several boxes of papers were stacked on the table. A young officer squinted at a small slip of paper with spidery handwriting, his brow furrowed in concentration. Sophie recognized him as Officer Rudolph, who she'd seen before.

He stood when she entered, and she gave him a friendly nod.

"Carry on, Rudolph," Zimmer said. He pulled out a chair for Sophie, and she seated herself across from Rudolph.

"As I said, the place had been ransacked. And the record-keeping system is rudimentary at best." Zimmer reached into one box to retrieve a slip of white paper and held it out to

Sophie. The penciled lines were faded, and the wrinkled paper had several tiny holes at the top.

Sophie could make out a few scrawled words. "Berger—that's probably the customer's name." The next words looked like *blu org gn*, followed by *W7*. "That could be—let's see—maybe blue organza gown. I don't know about W7. It's too small for a waist measurement."

"Could it be for a wrist?" Zimmer asked.

"I suppose, but I'd be surprised if such a thing was necessary." She moved her finger along the figures. "That looks like a twelve—the price, I expect." She studied the slip.

"Could it be—" Zimmer began.

"What about a date?" Sophie said at the same time. She caught his eyes and blushed, thinking of a completely different meaning for the question.

"Wednesday the seventh?" Zimmer finished.

Sophie nodded. "That makes sense. Are these pin holes?" she asked, pointing. "Maybe she pinned the slips to the fabric."

Rudolph stared at her, dumbfounded.

Zimmer gave her a smile. "None of us are seamstresses, so you're already doing much better than we did. We found these papers scattered all over the floor. Whoever was searching the place might have been interrupted. Or maybe he just got frustrated."

Rudolph looked up and indicated the box on his left. "These are ones that don't sound like soldier costumes—dresses, monsters, animals, that sort. These—" he pushed a second box in her direction "—are the rest."

"The possibilities, then." She picked up the few slips Rudolph had singled out, shaking her head as she deciphered them. "This uniform was navy blue—a very fine wool. Lined with cream silk. And the trousers would have been light-colored as well. Oh, and there was red at the lapels." She reached into the overflowing box of unexamined notes and pulled out a handful of them.

"We appreciate your help, Miss Strong," Detective Zimmer said.

Sophie nodded absently, already absorbed in her decoding task.

THE SKY outside the barred window had turned dark when Detective Zimmer returned later.

"You've earned a break," he said. "It's nearly eight o'clock."

Sophie squeezed the bridge of her nose. She hadn't noticed Officer Rudolph leave or the hours pass by, but now fatigue had caught up with her.

"Thanks," she said, sitting back with a sigh.

"Find anything?" he asked.

Sophie pointed to about a dozen slips that she'd put aside. "These mention clothing and fabric that could be the coat Sam found. They have names scrawled on them, and some have addresses. She must have sent some of her work to her patrons." She gestured to the box she'd been working through. "I have more to examine, though."

"You've been an enormous help already."

She reached into the box and handed him a handful of slips. "I'm not a quitter, Detective Zimmer," she said with a smile. "And I *am* expecting an exclusive out of this."

He returned her smile and sat down across the table from her.

"I'll give you the ones that I think are possibilities," he said. "We're looking for blue wool then?"

"Yes. And cream silk. I've been putting aside anything that mentions a soldier, too, just to be safe."

Another hour slipped by as they worked together, but they added only a couple of slips to her small pile of likely options. Zimmer stifled a yawn.

Then she spotted something.

"Look at this," Sophie said. She pushed a paper in his direction and pointed to the notes. "This could be navy merino wool, red trim, cream silk lining. That would fit."

He squinted at the scrawled notes. "Hmph. That looks kind of familiar."

He rifled through a small pile he'd set aside, then pulled one out.

"Here." He walked over to her side of the table and placed it next to hers. "Is this the same?"

She examined the two pages side by side.

"They look almost identical. And here it says thirty. They're the same price."

She held the two slips next to each other. He leaned closer to see. She could smell his shaving soap.

"Is that an address?"

"There's a name, too," she said, peering at the paper. "Ritson? Pernan? Or is that a B at the start? It's a good thing she was more careful with her stitches than her handwriting."

Zimmer tapped the second slip. "No address here. This one looks like it was picked up by—err—Dottie? Darin? But why would she make two identical costumes? I thought these people prided themselves on their originality."

"They do," Sophie said. "Maybe it was easier to just duplicate a pattern. If the costumes were for different events, the customers might not notice."

"Do you remember which men dressed as soldiers at the Wolff party?"

"Some of them. I have a few notes in my notebook."

"But both of these costumes wouldn't have been at the

same party, would they?" he asked. "Even I know that much."

"No, that would be an embarrassment for both."

"How did they know what other people planned to wear?"

"Gossip, I suppose," said Sophie. "The servants all know each other, too." She snapped her fingers. "Mrs. Wolff gave me a copy of the guest list. She wanted me to memorize it, if you can believe that."

"Do you still have it?"

Sophie nodded. "I thought I might need to refer to it."

Zimmer looked out the window at the dark night. "We'd better quit for tonight. Could you bring the list in tomorrow? Or make me a copy?"

"All right. I'll be looking at it tonight, though. I'm sure I won't be able to sleep with these endless slips of paper dancing in my head."

He smiled. "May I give you a ride home? My car is just outside."

"Oh, I can get a trolley—" She looked at her watch.

"It's no trouble. It's the least I can do, since you've been so helpful." His blue eyes looked earnest.

"Well, if you're sure it's no trouble."

"I'll just get my coat and hat," he said, and left the room.

Sophie opened her notebook and wrote down the details on the two matching slips, including several options for names that could plausibly be interpreted as the ones Mrs. Cooper had scrawled. Detective Zimmer returned, wearing his black trench coat and homburg hat. She pulled on her cloak.

"We'll go out the back," Zimmer said. "It's closer to the car."

He guided her down the hallway. Through one open doorway, she saw a small kitchen area with a sink, coffee pot, and a couple of tables. The scent of beef gravy and fried potatoes hung in the air.

"I take most of my gourmet meals in there," he said with a grin. "Some of the restaurants will even deliver."

"You must work a lot of late hours," she said.

"It feels like I live here sometimes."

"Do you… live nearby? If you don't mind my asking."

"It's not far. My mother's there too. It's the house I grew up in."

"And your father?"

Tension flickered across his face. "He passed away when I was young."

"Oh, I'm sorry," she said. "Your mother must appreciate having you at home, then."

"She relies on me quite a bit," he said, holding the outside door open for her.

"I hope she and your wife get along. I've heard tales of some tense households."

He was preoccupied with locking the door behind them and didn't respond.

"It's just over here," he said.

He led her to a black roadster. She was glad to see that it had a top and a windscreen, instead of being open to the elements like some automobiles. The night air had grown a bit chilly. He opened the passenger door for her and held out a hand to help her inside. She rested her gloved fingers on his palm and stepped up onto the running board, then eased into the seat. The gray upholstery had an elegant striped pattern. Zimmer went to the front of the car and turned the crank several times to start the engine, which sputtered to life.

He got in behind the steering wheel and looked at her expectantly. "Where to?"

"It's not far. 107 Franklin Street. A boarding house."

He nodded and pulled out into the street. "Been there long?"

"I lived with my aunt through college. I've been rooming with my friend Ruth for about a year now."

"It's good to have some family nearby," he said.

"My father lives up north. My mother died when I was small." She didn't usually mention her parents to people she didn't know well. But it struck her that she and Zimmer had this in common: the loss of a parent at an early age.

He glanced at her, empathy in his dark blue eyes.

"I'm sorry," he said. "I know how difficult that is."

She nodded.

They didn't speak again until he drew close to the boarding house. She pointed it out. "It's right there—the yellow one with the big front porch."

He pulled up in front of it. She reached for the door, but he cut the engine and leaped out.

"Oh, you don't have to—" she began. But he was already opening her door. He helped her out of the car and walked with her up to the porch. A gaslight flickered in the window, and she saw Mrs. O'Day sitting next to the fireplace, her knitting needles flying.

"Thank you for the ride, Detective Zimmer," she said.

"It's my pleasure, Miss Strong. Thank you again for your help."

She walked up the steps and paused at the front door, sensing that he watched her from the sidewalk.

Then she turned. "You know, if you'd like to see the guest list tonight, you could come into the parlor. My landlady, Mrs. O'Day, will be there." She didn't want to suggest she was inviting him to spend time alone with her.

"Are you sure? It's getting a bit late."

"I won't be able to resist at least looking it over," she said. "But I'm sure you'd like to get home—"

He shook his head. "I'd love to take a look at the list, if you really don't mind."

He came up the stairs and stood by the door as she fished out her key and unlocked it. She was conscious of his closeness and the warmth of his body.

Inside, she took off her cloak and greeted Mrs. O'Day, who looked at Sophie's guest with curiosity.

"This is—" Sophie began.

"Jacob Zimmer," he inserted. She noticed he didn't mention his title.

He removed his hat and walked over to shake Mrs. O'Day's hand. "I'm sorry for the intrusion, ma'am. Miss Strong and I are working together. I won't stay long. I know it's getting late."

Mrs. O'Day discouraged her boarders from entertaining gentlemen callers on weeknights, especially at such a late hour. Sophie had never brought a gentleman to the house, but she'd heard Mrs. O'Day reminding the other girls. She could tell by Mrs. O'Day's smile that she approved of Zimmer's courtesy, though.

Her eyes were bright as she gestured to a chair. "Please have a seat, Mr. Zimmer."

"I'll get that list," said Sophie.

Zimmer removed his coat and folded it over the back of a chair. Sophie hurried up the stairs as he exchanged pleasantries with Mrs. O'Day.

Ruth was in bed, but still sitting up, reading a huge medical tome by candlelight. Her expression was intent as her lips moved silently, and Sophie surmised she was memorizing one of the endless lists in her course of study. Sophie fluttered her fingers in a wave and grabbed Mrs. Wolff's guest list from the desk, then went back downstairs.

When she entered the sitting room, Mrs. O'Day was chuckling appreciatively. Sophie slipped into the chair next to

Zimmer, which was far enough away from Mrs. O'Day that they could speak quietly without being overheard.

The older woman set aside her knitting and got to her feet. "I was just about to make some cocoa before bed. Would you both like some?"

Sophie gave Zimmer a smile. "Mrs. O'Day makes the best cocoa," she told him. "I'd love some, thank you," she said to her landlady.

"Mr. Zimmer?"

"I don't want to put you out," he said.

"It's no trouble at all. I'm making two cups already."

"Well, if it's the best, I'd love to try some," he said. "I haven't had cocoa in ages."

Mrs. O'Day bustled out, and Sophie unfolded her list. She took out the notebook with the details she'd copied from Mrs. Cooper's records.

"Let's try to find a name that starts with an R first. That slip was the most complete."

"Or it could be a P or B." He reached into his pocket and pulled out the two slips of paper they'd been studying earlier.

She raised her eyebrows. "Isn't the evidence supposed to stay at the police station?"

"Must have accidentally slipped it into my pocket," he said with a grin.

He leaned in next to her as her finger inched down the row of names on her list. "Robinson? Bowman?" she read.

"Hmmm." He frowned. "Robinson might be too long. It's not Berry." He indicated another name.

"It doesn't look like Pfister," said Sophie.

"Is that Pfister, like the hotel?"

She nodded. She flipped over the list and looked at the back. "Schultz, Stanley, Wagner, Frank—" She gasped, her finger halting at one of the last names.

"What is it?"

"A. Pitman," she said.

"Is that the one—"

"Could it be Mr. Pitman, a lawyer in the Majestic Building? His first name is Alonzo. It's on the door of his office."

"Do you know if he's a friend of the Wolffs?"

She shook her head. "He does some work for Mr. Wolff. But I would have thought he was quite beneath their notice, socially."

"You didn't see him there?"

"I didn't recognize many people, since everyone was in costume. I hadn't noticed his name before. I didn't study the list thoroughly, to be honest."

"Could this Pitman even afford this getup?"

Sophie pondered. "He wears very fine clothes. I've wondered how he manages. I don't see many clients come to his office."

Mrs. O'Day returned with a tray of cocoa and a plate of her delicious oatmeal cookies.

"Here you go, nice and hot," she said, holding out a mug.

Zimmer rested the slips of paper on a small table between the two chairs, and took it from her. She set the cookies on the table.

Sophie took her mug with a smile and sipped the sweet, creamy cocoa.

"Delicious, Mrs. O'Day. Thank you."

Zimmer tasted his cocoa and murmured appreciatively. "Just like my mother used to make. Very kind of you."

Mrs. O'Day took her own mug back to her chair near the fireplace.

Sophie put down her cup and picked up the slips of paper from Mrs. Cooper. The scrawled name at the top looked more like "Pitman" the longer she studied it, but she wondered if that was the power of suggestion.

She tapped her finger on the numbers below it. "See these

numbers? Could that be 221 Grand Avenue? That's the Majestic Building."

"I think it's time I paid a visit to Mr. Pitman."

Sophie restrained herself from pointing out that she'd suggested that days ago. "You know, I saw a tricorn hat in his office," she said. "He claimed he'd bought it on a whim. But what if it was part of this costume?"

Zimmer frowned and reached for the slips of paper. His fingers brushed against hers in the process, and Sophie felt a jolt of energy, as if she'd been shocked by a new-fangled light switch.

Flustered, he pulled his hand away. "I-I apologize," he stammered. He held his palm open, keeping it close to his side. "If I could just have those papers, please?"

Sophie kept them in a tight grip. "What are you going to do?"

"I'll do my job," he said. At her raised eyebrows, he went on, "I will be interrogating Mr. Pitman. I thank you for your help."

"I'm coming with you."

"You'll do no such thing. This is a police investigation, Miss Strong." He kept his voice low, apparently not wanting to alarm Mrs. O'Day.

"An investigation that would be at a standstill without my help."

She saw a quiver in his jaw, as if he was clenching his teeth together in an effort not to snap at her.

"Fine. You may accompany me to the Majestic Building tomorrow morning. Eight o'clock?"

She gave him a half smile. "I will meet you there."

He beckoned with his fingers. "Now I'll take those notes."

Sophie smiled sweetly and slipped them into her bodice, then patted the fabric, holding her hand against her chest. "I've got them, safe and sound."

Zimmer's mouth dropped open as he blinked at her hand. Then his face flushed red.

"That's police evidence," he growled.

"If you were so worried about it, you shouldn't have handed it over to a reporter." She jumped to her feet. "I declare, Mrs. O'Day. It's time Mr. Zimmer said good night, wouldn't you say?"

Mrs. O'Day's head jerked up, and Sophie guessed she'd dozed off in her cozy chair near the fire.

"Oh, yes indeed. I'm all in," she clucked. "You take care on your way home, Mr. Zimmer."

"I-I... that is—" Zimmer stuttered.

His eyes slid from Sophie to Mrs. O'Day, then back again. She could tell he wanted to avoid the embarrassment of explaining to Mrs. O'Day what Sophie had done with the evidence, and then forcing Sophie to relinquish the papers, or even threatening arrest.

He sighed. "Good night, Mrs. O'Day." His smile for the landlady was kind, despite his consternation. "Thank you again for the cocoa and the cookies."

"You're most welcome. I hope we see you again sometime."

Her eyes danced as she looked at Sophie, and Sophie knew that her motherly brain was spinning romantic fairy tales.

"Oh, you will, I am sure," Zimmer said. He glared at Sophie and smashed his hat onto his head. "I'll see *you* in the morning," he said in a low, serious voice.

Sophie felt a shiver zip up her spine at his tone, but she just nodded and walked him to the door. Her gaze lingered on his broad back as he returned to the automobile. He was maddening in some ways, but in a tiny corner of her mind, she admitted to herself that she was looking forward to untangling this crime with Detective Jacob Zimmer.

23

———

At seven the next morning, Sophie pulled on her coat in the front hallway. If she could get to the Majestic before Detective Zimmer, she might snag a few private moments to question Mr. Pitman on her own. As she reached for the doorknob, the enticing aroma of bacon wafted from the kitchen. Knowing how difficult it could be to stop for a meal during the day, she spun on her heel and walked toward the scent.

"Good morning, Mrs. O'Day," she called.

The landlady turned from her station at the stove, where bacon sizzled in a cast iron frying pan.

"Good morning, Sophie. I hope you slept well."

She gave Sophie a wink that made her blush. She was sure they were both thinking of the previous evening's visit, since she'd never had a gentleman caller before.

"As always," Sophie said, hoping to curtail further questioning. "I'm sorry, I can't stay for breakfast. Early appointment. I'll just grab a piece of toast."

She reached for a buttery slice from the plate on the counter.

Mrs. O'Day's forehead wrinkled. "You need a good breakfast, Sophie. Don't let them run you into the ground like they did to poor Miss Ferber."

Edna Ferber's name was often mentioned as yet another reason why young women shouldn't work in a man's world. She'd been a reporter at the *Milwaukee Journal* for a few years, then collapsed of exhaustion and returned home to Appleton. Last year, she'd published a novel called *Dawn O'Hara* that was loosely based on her experiences. Sophie had read it three times, focusing on the narrator's journalistic adventures, and skipping the more romantic sections where Edna got swept off her feet by an older physician.

"Don't worry, Mrs. O," said Sophie. "I'll stop for lunch." She hoped she could fulfill that promise.

Sophie emerged into the sharp morning air and took in the sounds and scents of the neighborhood. The soothing aroma of fireplace smoke and the fresh scent of dewy grass mingled with the occasional whiff of manure from the horses that had traversed Franklin Street in the early hours. Silver racks of milk bottles stood on neighbors' porches, attesting to the milk wagon's deliveries. A misty lemon sun peeked out from behind the clouds. She caught sight of a few schoolboys chasing each other down the street, their books tied with leather straps that flapped at their sides. A cluster of girls walked at a more dignified pace, studiously ignoring them.

Sophie descended the porch steps and turned toward downtown. A figure emerged from the side of the house, causing her to gasp and stop short.

"Good morning, Miss Strong. You're out bright and early," Zimmer drawled.

His voice had a knowing tone that rankled—somehow he'd guessed her plan to slip over to the Majestic Building ahead of him.

Collecting herself, Sophie pressed one gloved hand to her throat, as if to slow the terrified beating of her heart.

"Detective Zimmer! You scared me half to death. I couldn't sleep this morning, so I decided I might as well head out. No sense tossing and turning."

She realized too late she'd conjured an image for Zimmer of herself in bed, and her cheeks flushed.

"Oh, certainly," he said in apparent disbelief.

She frowned. "Oh, *fine*. I wanted to leave without you. That's why you're lurking here, waiting for me, isn't it?"

"Me?" His eyes widened. "Just out for a morning stroll."

He grinned and fell into step beside her.

"I keep turning the facts around in my head," she said. "Why would Mr. Pitman have been at the gala?"

"No idea. We can only keep our eyes open, and try not to form any theories until we have more evidence."

It gratified Sophie that he used the word "we," signaling that he saw her as a capable associate.

As if reading her mind, he added, "If you *insist* on trailing along."

"Just doing my job, same as you."

They came to the crossroad at Roy Street and paused for a grocer's wagon to trundle past before stepping into the road. Zimmer grasped her elbow protectively, which she assumed was his instinct when walking with a lady. Her impulse was to jerk her arm away, but she found the warm pressure oddly comforting. He released her when they reached the opposite side.

A familiar tension churned in Sophie's stomach as they approached the door of the Majestic Building. She felt Zimmer's eyes on her as she fumbled with the key.

"Here, let me," he said, his fingers brushing hers as he took the key. He deftly turned it in the lock and swung open the door. "You wait here while I check things out."

"I'm fine. I was here just the other day." Her voice was fainter than she would have liked.

"It's normal to have powerful memories. You had a terrible experience here," he said.

His voice held more compassion than she expected.

"Pish," she said. "I'm not the one who got shot."

She pushed past him and jogged up the steps.

As they reached the top, they heard the bang of drawers being slammed shut. They hurried toward Mr. Pitman's office.

"I'll do the talking," Zimmer warned. Sophie pretended not to hear him.

Through the half-open door, they saw Alonzo Pitman frantically tossing file folders into a paperboard box. Some of his filing cabinet drawers stood open, their contents jumbled. He was in his shirt sleeves, his suit coat hung over the back of his chair. Books, folders, and papers littered the floor, some pages wrinkled and torn.

Zimmer gave the door two sharp raps.

Pitman yelped and dropped the file he was holding. The papers scattered, some slipping to the floor. Pitman glared at them and bent down to sweep up the pages into an untidy stack.

Then he stood and said, "The office isn't open yet."

"Mr. Pitman? I am Detective Jacob Zimmer."

Pitman stared at him, uncomprehending.

"I need to ask you some questions about the murder of Hilda Rock," Zimmer explained.

Pitman's eyes grew wide. "I-I don't know anything about her murder." He looked at Sophie. "What did you accuse me of?"

Sophie put up her hands in defense. "I didn't accuse you of anything."

"Then what are you doing here? Are you a policewoman now?" Pitman sneered.

Before Sophie could reply, Zimmer said, "Miss Strong is assisting me with part of my investigation. Let's sit down, Mr. Pitman." He gestured to Sophie to take a chair opposite the messy desk. Then he looked pointedly at Mr. Pitman.

Pitman sighed. "I supposed I have a few minutes. I'm expecting a client soon."

Zimmer said, "You look like you're in quite a hurry. Is your office always this disorganized?"

"I don't believe that concerns you."

"Actually, everything about you concerns me. You're a potential suspect in a murder investigation."

"Suspect? Me? I wasn't even here that day." He glared at Sophie.

"So you've said. But you did work for Mrs. Rock."

"My clients' identities are confidential," said Pitman, though his face glistened with sweat.

Zimmer's lips tightened. He leaned forward, placing one hand on Pitman's desk, and eyed him steadily. "Mr. Pitman, I am investigating a murder. If you don't wish to cooperate here in your office, we can continue this conversation at the police station."

Pitman swallowed. "I-I had some dealings with Mrs. Rock."

"In what respect?"

"She—that is—I handled some financial paperwork for her. Routine matters."

"When did you last see Mrs. Rock?"

Pitman gazed up at the ceiling, his brows furrowed. "It had been quite some time. Maybe early last month."

Sophie reached into her bag and pulled out the slips of paper that she and Zimmer had been studying the night before. Zimmer took them from her with a meaningful glance. He held out the top one for Mr. Pitman to see, while keeping it firmly between his fingers.

"Is this your name, Mr. Pitman?"

Pitman squinted at the paper. "It could be, I suppose. I don't know. It's not my handwriting."

"We found this in the shop of a seamstress named Virginia Cooper. The place had been ransacked."

Mr. Pitman's face was blank. He shrugged. "That's a shame, but I've never heard of her."

"And yet, your name and address are on this paper. An order for a soldier's costume."

Zimmer couldn't be sure about that, but Sophie guessed he was trying to see what Mr. Pitman would admit to.

Remembering something, Sophie stood abruptly. She turned to the door and was glad to find the tricorn hat still hanging on its hook. She picked it up.

"You wore this at the Wolffs' Spring Gala, didn't you, Mr. Pitman? I'm sure I saw you there," she bluffed.

She tossed the hat onto his desk, and he pulled away from it, as if disgusted.

"Why are you lying about the costume, Pitman?" Zimmer pressed.

Pitman made a guttural noise and swiped at the hat with one shaking hand, knocking it to the floor.

"Yes, I was at the damn party," he said. "But I don't know why. Someone sent me the costume and invitation. I don't know if this Cooper person made it or not."

"Who sent you the costume?"

Pitman stared at his desktop. "I don't know that either."

Sophie clicked her tongue in disbelief.

Pitman glanced at her, then back to Zimmer. "I know, it's crazy. There was a note telling me to go to the party. I thought I knew who sent it, but I was wrong."

"Who did you think it was?"

"I can't tell you that."

"Can't? Or won't?" Zimmer leaned in. "Didn't this whole situation strike you as odd? Or even dangerous?"

"Of course it was damned odd. But I thought something might come of it. Maybe a new client. I'm not going to turn down a chance to rub elbows with rich businessmen."

"Did you have any business with the Wolffs prior to that night?"

Pitman swallowed. He opened his mouth, as if to protest about his clients' confidentiality, then closed it again as Zimmer's eyes bored into him.

"I do a little work for Mr. Wolff now and then. Small things."

"Go on," said Zimmer.

Pitman's eyes darted from him to Sophie and back. "When I got to the party, nobody said anything to me about why I'd been invited. I didn't even see Mr. Wolff—he must have been surrounded by his rich friends. So I had a few drinks. I listened to the music. The band was good. The Wolffs spent a fortune that night."

Zimmer was silent, and Pitman's voice was quieter when he continued. "When I finally did spot Wolff, he was wearing the exact same costume as me."

Sophie felt a surge of triumph. The costumes *were* identical, just as they'd guessed.

"How did you know it was him, if everyone was in costume?" Zimmer asked.

Mr. Pitman smirked. "There's no missing Ruben Wolff. He has a certain swagger. He walks like a millionaire. And talks like one."

"Did *he* send you the costume?" Sophie blurted. "Why would he want you to wear the same one as him?" She ignored Zimmer's warning glance.

"I have no idea. He didn't say a word to me all night. Then those thugs barged in and started fires—"

"They talked like unionizers," said Sophie.

"When the fires started, I took off. I wanted to get as far away from those crazies as possible."

Zimmer leaned forward, peering into Pitman's face. "Where did you go after that, Mr. Pitman?"

"I went home." He pulled at his collar with a shaky finger.

"Did you? Or did you come *here* and murder Hilda Rock?"

"No! I didn't kill her. Why would I?"

"That's what I want to know," Zimmer said.

"I didn't do it! I went home."

"Did anyone see you?" Zimmer asked.

Pitman shook his head. "I live alone. And then today—" He broke off.

"Yes?"

He bit his lip, looking reluctant to go on, but Zimmer stared at him.

"Someone broke in and searched my office," Pitman said. "I don't know what they were looking for. But I'm not waiting around to find out."

Zimmer looked around the office, taking in the disarray.

"It may be a good idea to lie low for a while," he said. "But don't leave town. I may need to speak to you again."

"I'm not under arrest, am I?" said Pitman. "I can go where I like."

"The police would appreciate your cooperation," Zimmer asserted. "And you'll look guilty if you run."

Pitman met his stare but didn't reply. He took a deep breath and glanced at his watch. "Is that all, Detective? I *am* waiting for someone."

"Do you want to file a complaint about the break-in?"

"No," Pitman said quietly.

Zimmer pushed back his chair and stood, then held the

door open for Sophie. "Thank you for your time, Mr. Pitman. I'll be in touch."

Pitman didn't answer, but he ran a hand through his thin dark hair and let out another shaky sigh. Sophie glanced at Zimmer as she walked out. He was staring at Pitman, his blue eyes cold, his mouth a tight line of suspicion.

They were silent as they left the building. Sophie paused on the front walkway and looked up at Zimmer.

"He seems scared," she said.

"That doesn't mean he's not guilty."

"Do you really think he could have murdered Hilda Rock? He doesn't look like he has it in him."

"You can't always tell a killer by his looks."

"Well, now we know he was at the Spring Gala."

"That is unusual. Still, it may have nothing at all to do with this murder."

Sophie felt a surge of frustration. "But it *must*, don't you think? Those two events were on the same night, and we're finding these strange connections. Why did Mr. Pitman have a duplicate costume? And who sent it? Ruben Wolff? Or someone else?"

Zimmer rubbed a hand across his forehead. "It's possible they're connected. But I can't go ask Wolff about it," he said.

"Why not? You're a detective, and this is a murder."

"There are limits, even for detectives. I'd need some hard evidence to question someone as powerful as Ruben Wolff. The rich don't take kindly to the police poking around in their business. Even your friend Clara had some pull with the chief, remember?"

Sophie wanted to put Clara out of his mind.

"Maybe I could talk to Wolff," she said. "I could write a story about him for the paper."

"What makes you think he would see you?"

"Well, I was invited to cover the Spring Gala. I can say I'm following up with another story."

Zimmer frowned. "Stay away from him, Miss Strong. Your assignment about the Spring Gala is over. Go to a school board meeting or something."

She narrowed her eyes at him.

He cleared his throat. "I didn't put that very well. I'd just rather see you cover less-threatening subjects."

She relaxed a bit at this awkward attempt at kindness. "Don't worry about me, Detective Zimmer. I'm a trained journalist."

He met her gaze, his blue eyes full of concern. "That's what I'm afraid of."

24

———————

At her desk later that morning, Sophie replayed in her head the conversation with Detective Zimmer. She was sure the Spring Gala held a clue. Pushing aside the gardening tips that clamored for her attention, she flipped to a blank page in her notebook.

Who could have sent the costume to Mr. Pitman?

Thelma Wolff was one possibility. She hadn't wanted Ruben to wear the soldier costume, after all. But what could have been her motive? Sophie tapped her pencil and stared into space. Maybe it was a secret enemy of Pitman's who wanted to—what? Or perhaps Ruben Wolff had sent it? But she couldn't imagine him noticing what another man wore. Perhaps Mr. Pitman was lying. That seemed most likely. But why? Every thought only led to more unanswerable questions. Frustrated, Sophie scratched some harsh lines on the paper, then threw down the pencil.

Walking past her desk, Benjamin Turner raised his eyebrows with a smirk. She felt her face flush. She was acting like an emotional female, which wouldn't do at the office.

If she had an opportunity to question the Wolffs, she

233

might be able to figure this out. She certainly wouldn't be admitted to the mansion again. Mrs. Wolff had expressed hostility at the Women's Club. But Mr. Wolff had always been pleasant. She pushed back her chair, walked over to Mr. Barnaby's door, and knocked twice.

He looked up. "Strong? What is it?"

"I have an idea. I want to interview Ruben Wolff."

"Wolff? For the women's page? I don't see the connection. Now, Mrs. Wolff is another story. You can talk to her about fashion, parties—what have you." He waved his hand, indicating the mysterious realm of women's concerns.

Sophie grimaced at the thought of encountering the disapproving Thelma Wolff again.

She said, "Women readers are interested in Milwaukee businesses and their owners. They buy Wolff's products. Lots of women and girls work in his bottling plant. And others are trying to make ends meet on what their husbands earn there. Working hours, worker safety, and wages affect the whole family, Chief."

He rubbed his chin. "Even if I give you the okay, what makes you think he'd see you?"

"It's worth a try."

"Well, you can ask. If you get in, we'll try to do something with it."

"Which means we'll run the story and you'll give me a byline?"

He looked at her over the top of his glasses. "It depends what's *in* the story, Strong."

Sophie's chest fluttered with anticipation as she walked back to her desk, imagining her name on the front page. Maybe she'd stumble upon a scandal and uncover a smuggling ring or a group of spies.

Then reality drenched her fantasy. How would she get an interview with the mighty Ruben Wolff? She wouldn't get anywhere by barging into his office. If she sent a note with her request, would it even reach him?

The telephone would be much faster.

She eyed the three phone booths along the wall, then looked around the room. At half of the desks, men stabbed the keys of their typewriters with awkward index fingers or scribbled in notebooks. Two of the booths were occupied, but the middle one was open. It was right next to Mr. Turner's desk, so he'd overhear every word. But she refused to be deterred by any snide comments he might make.

She took a deep breath and strode over to the telephone, keeping her eyes focused straight ahead. Was it her imagination, or did Benjamin's gaze follow her? She didn't look his way. She slid into the seat and picked up the handset with a sweating hand.

"Operator? Wolff Brewery, please."

"One moment." The woman's voice sounded weary.

Sophie heard a few clicks on the line, then a man's voice. "Good day, this is Wolff Brewery. May I help you?"

Sophie swallowed, her heart thumping.

"Hello?" the man asked again.

"Hello. Um—this is Sophie Strong from the *Milwaukee Herald*. I'd like to make an appointment to speak with Mr. Wolff."

There was a silence on the other end of the phone. "And what is your business with Mr. Wolff?"

"I would like to interview him for a story about his inspiring career."

"Mr. Wolff does not give interviews upon request, miss."

Sophie's heart plummeted. "Um, may I speak with his secretary, please?"

"As I said, Mr. Wolff does not give interviews. Good day, miss."

"But I covered—" The line went dead.

"Why, you—" she began, then fell silent. The dismissal stung more than she'd expected, and she felt tears prick at her eyes. She blinked them back with a heavy sigh and replaced the handset on its hook. Well, she'd try writing a note. It had a chance of reaching Mr. Wolff. The man who answered the telephone might be mistaken.

She stood up and smoothed her skirt, then turned to go back to her desk, ignoring Benjamin and hoping he'd mind his own business.

"Trouble with a lead, Miss Strong?" he asked as she walked by.

"Nothing I can't handle, Mr. Turner." She didn't pause her step.

"What if I got you in to see Wolff?"

That caught her attention. She stopped and looked back. He met her eyes with a challenging smile.

"You? Why would you help me?"

He smiled in what she was sure he considered a debonair manner. "I'm a generous person."

She gave a dubious huff, but he'd aroused her curiosity. "How could you manage it?"

"I know some people. At the Wolff office."

"What people?"

"Just people. Never mind. If you don't want my help, that's fine. Knock on his office door and see what happens."

Sophie knew that effort would be hopeless. "What would you do?"

"I'm heading over there in about an hour. Why don't you come along?"

She eyed him suspiciously. "Today? With no introduction?"

"Not to talk to Wolff today. But you can get your foot in the door."

Sophie bit her lip. She didn't trust him, and she doubted

he could help, but she didn't have any better ideas. "All right."

"I'll meet you out front at one-thirty," he said.

Sophie nodded, glad he had the sense not to suggest they leave the office together. If they did, their colleagues would be sure to harass them mercilessly.

ON THE STREETCAR THAT AFTERNOON, she challenged Benjamin. "You haven't explained how you know people at Wolff Brewery."

"True." Benjamin didn't offer any additional details, and Sophie was too proud to pry.

When they reached the office, its size and complexity awed her. Previous experiences with Wolff Mansion had given her an idea of the massive fortune behind the enterprise, but it was still impressive. Benjamin circumvented the ornate front entrance, leading Sophie to a side door that he opened for her. She looked at him quizzically, then entered.

Inside, he led her down the hallway and into a cramped room with bins of correspondence and packages stacked on a central wooden table. A couple of tired-looking men glanced up when they walked in, and one nodded. Sophie got the impression that Benjamin was expected.

"Do you *work* here?" she whispered to Benjamin.

"Sort of." He picked up a flat-topped hat from a hook on the wall. "You can leave your coat and hat here," he said, pointing to an empty hook.

As she took off her coat, he grabbed a wheeled cart holding a bin of correspondence sorted into organized stacks. He pushed the cart out the door, jerking his head in her direction to indicate that she should follow. She was surprised that the other employees didn't question her presence, but she chalked it up to their apparent familiarity with Benjamin Turner.

For the next quarter of an hour, they stopped at various offices where Benjamin dropped off mail, introducing Sophie as a new employee to the few people who noticed her. Most seemed too absorbed by their own responsibilities to take notice of one delivery man and his protégé.

Benjamin led Sophie to a service elevator, and they rode up to the fourth floor. They exited into a plush foyer, its silence reverent. Benjamin gestured toward an open doorway leading to a large anteroom, where a young man sat at a desk with his head bent over a stack of papers.

Benjamin whispered to her, "Okay, when you get my signal, pretend to faint."

"Faint? What are you talking about? I've never fainted in my life," Sophie hissed.

"Do you want to talk to Wolff or not?"

"Of course. But why in the world—"

The secretary glanced up and frowned in their direction. "That's the plan. Take it or leave it." Benjamin wheeled his cart forward.

Sophie hesitated for an instant, then followed.

They entered the vestibule, and Sophie noticed a massive wooden door behind the young man, blazoned with "Ruben Wolff, President" in gold letters.

Benjamin pushed the cart close to the secretary's desk. "Hello Mr. Ness," he said. "Beautiful day." The man grunted but didn't look up. "New employee today," Benjamin said, with a nod in Sophie's direction. Mr. Ness barely glanced at her.

Benjamin placed a tall stack of mail on the desk, where it towered over the ledger that Mr. Ness was writing in. Benjamin gave Sophie an exaggerated wink.

She took a deep breath, envisioning other ladies she'd seen succumb to the vapors.

"Oh!" she cried, resting the back of one hand against her forehead. "Oh, I-I feel faint."

Her voice sounded ridiculous to her own ears, but Mr. Ness looked up, opening his mouth as if to order her out of the room. Benjamin gave Sophie an urgent nod. Hoping for the best, she collapsed to the floor, praying her skirt didn't ride up too far, revealing her calves. She kept her eyes closed.

"Dear heavens." Mr. Ness rushed to Sophie's side. "Miss? Are you all right?"

Benjamin didn't immediately join him in assisting Sophie, but instead coughed violently into his handkerchief. Mr. Ness gingerly picked up Sophie's limp hand and tapped it.

"Miss? Can you hear me?"

"Get over here, man!" Ness snapped at Benjamin. Sophie felt Benjamin's presence on her other side and caught a whiff of his tangy spearmint gum.

"Miss—er—Smith? Are you all right?" Benjamin asked. His finger poked her arm in a silent signal.

Sophie let her eyelids flutter open, and a weak moan escaped from her lips. She hoped she wasn't overplaying her role.

"Can you sit up?" said Benjamin.

"Oh my. I am so sorry." She sat up unsteadily.

"Take it easy," said Benjamin. He looked at Mr. Ness. "Do you have any water, sir? I don't want her to faint again."

Ness sighed, looking impatient now that the crisis had passed. He went to a sideboard, poured a glass of water from a pitcher, and brought it to Sophie. She took a grateful sip, then fluttered her lashes in his direction. "Thank you, sir," she said.

The man cleared his throat. "Well, it's nothing," he insisted, heading back to his desk.

"Come on, Miss Smith," said Benjamin. "Let's get you back to the mail room." Sophie looked at him, a question in her eyes, then glanced at the closed door to Mr. Wolff's office.

"Here we go," said Benjamin, helping her to her feet. He walked solicitously at her side, pushing the cart in front of them, and they exited the anteroom.

When they were out of earshot, she turned on him and muttered, "I don't know what you're up to, Benjamin Turner. How was a fainting spell supposed to get me an appointment with Ruben Wolff?"

"Well, while you were fainting, I scheduled you in Wolff's diary," said Benjamin.

"You did? How did you manage it with Mr. Ness right there?"

"Ness couldn't see me behind that stack of mail, and your performance kept his attention. You could always try a life on the stage if journalism doesn't suit you."

She frowned and playfully punched his arm, but she didn't hold back a grateful smile.

"He'll be expecting you at three o'clock tomorrow afternoon," said Benjamin.

"Won't that be obvious?" she asked. "Mr. Ness will know he didn't write in that appointment himself."

"I've seen other managers put things in Wolff's diary," said Benjamin. "If you're lucky, he'll just think it's one of those."

"And if I'm unlucky?"

"They'll toss you out for trespassing. I said I'd get you an appointment, Miss Strong. I didn't say it was foolproof."

"Well, thank you, Mr. Turner," she said. "I'll do my best not to get tossed out."

They returned to the mail room, and she retrieved her hat and coat.

"I'll be on my way" she said. "Are you leaving?"

"I have to work the rest of my shift here," said Benjamin.

She shook her head in confusion, but she was sure he wouldn't explain.

"All right. Don't work too hard." She slipped out the employee door.

As she pulled it shut, she caught him watching her before he turned back to delivering mail.

25

———————

On Friday afternoon, Sophie stepped off the streetcar a few stops away from Wolff Brewery. She wanted to walk for a bit and prepare herself for the task ahead. The earthy scent of yeast and malt hung in the air. Some people complained about it, and some called it the smell of money. Sophie found it appealing.

The office building stood across the street from the complex of structures that made up the brewery itself. Bypassing the side door she'd used with Benjamin, Sophie looked up at the steep, gabled roof, mirrored by a similar covering over the entrance pavilion. Two tall chimneys decorated with molded bricks ornamented each side of the building. A majestic archway crowned the entrance, with the words *Wolff Brewing Company est. 1884* carved into the stone.

A uniformed doorman opened the door for her, and she stepped into a magnificent lobby with marble floors and gleaming dark paneling. A young man in a gray suit with thin, mouse-brown hair sat at a desk in one corner, a tense expression on his face.

"May I help you?" he asked.

"I'm Sophie Strong from the *Milwaukee Herald*. I have an appointment with Mr. Wolff."

The man squinted at his clipboard, as if a host of female reporters were expected and he needed to check Sophie off of the list. "This way, please."

She followed him up a sweeping staircase framed by elegantly carved posts and a shining banister. Large oil paintings depicting quaint Bavarian villages and mountain landscapes hung on the walls. Sophie recalled that Ruben had emigrated from Germany in his youth. The assistant led her to the vestibule where she'd fainted the day before.

"Miss Sophie Strong from the *Milwaukee Herald*," the young man announced.

Mr. Ness looked up from his work and gave a terse nod to his colleague, who spun on his heel and retreated downstairs. Ness eyed Sophie with a suspicious gaze that made her pulse quicken with alarm, but he didn't seem to recognize her as the hapless young lady who'd collapsed in this spot. He stood and gestured for Sophie to join him at Mr. Wolff's door. He knocked twice and waited for the gruff response before turning the filigree brass doorknob.

Ruben Wolff sat behind an enormous desk of the same dark of wood that adorned the rest of the building. The pungent scent from his cigar drifted toward Sophie. He slapped shut a ledger on his desktop and rested the cigar in a marble ashtray. Her head held high, she walked toward him, extending her hand to shake his. He heaved himself to standing and squeezed her fingers briefly. Sophie noticed that the jovial expression he'd worn when she met him previously was now replaced with a more serious demeanor. Hard lines framed his eyes and mouth, and his hair was thinner than she had realized.

"Good afternoon, Miss Strong," he said, indicating a leather chair that sat opposite his desk.

When they were both seated, Sophie found she was forced to look up at him, the chair's short legs putting her in a position of inferiority that she assumed was intentional.

"Remind me of the purpose of your visit," he said. "I believe one of my managers must have made the appointment."

She gave him her warmest smile. "I appreciate any time you can spare," she said, willing her voice not to waver. "As you know, I write for the women's page. Our readers have expressed interest in learning more about the business leaders of Milwaukee."

He flashed his familiar smile and launched into a spiel that sounded rehearsed. "Well now, we started out in 1884, and I built the business to what it is today. We brew 800,000 barrels of beer every year."

He paused for effect, and Sophie tried to look impressed, though in truth she had no idea how many barrels the other breweries put out.

"That makes us the top brewer in the city," Wolff said, as if answering her thought. "I employ 750 men."

"And how many women?" Sophie asked.

"Beg pardon?"

"You employ a number of women as well, do you not?"

He chuckled. "You know, that's true, I do. I'd say we have about fifty girls in the bottling house. We made the first bottled beer in the city. My brewery and bottling house are spotlessly clean, and the beer is one hundred percent pure, making it safe and healthy for men *and* ladies. Beer is a food, you know."

Sophie had no doubt that many people considered it a staple of their diets.

"You mentioned starting out," she said. "You took over Otto Rock's brewery, correct? And then he worked for you as a foreman?"

Wolff rubbed his chin and grimaced. "Oh, yes, that's right. It was years ago."

Sophie took a shot in the dark. "My condolences at the loss of your friend Hilda Rock," said Sophie.

His eyebrows knit together as if trying to place the name. "I beg your pardon?"

"Otto Rock's widow. The poor lady was killed a couple of weeks ago. The same night as your Spring Gala, as a matter of fact."

An expression Sophie couldn't interpret flashed across Ruben's face, but it vanished just as quickly.

"Killed, you say? I hadn't heard about that." He picked up his cigar, then put it down again without taking a puff. "Well, let's not discuss such somber topics. I'm sure your lady readers aren't interested in something so dismal."

"It's quite the mystery," she said. "The police are investigating the murder, of course."

"Indeed," he said in a clipped tone, clearly uninterested in pursuing the subject.

Sophie cleared her throat. "What are your plans for the future of the brewery?" she asked, hoping to draw him into further discussion.

He launched into a monologue about the three hundred taverns he owned across the country and his intention to build a Wolff Hotel in New York City. Meanwhile, Sophie's mind raced as she sought a reasonable way to introduce something more about the case into the exchange.

"I always say, if you're not moving forward, you're going backward. There's no standing still in business," Wolff proclaimed.

"Wolff Park is quite an impressive venture as well. I went there with my aunt recently."

"Oh, yes indeed. It's on fifteen acres, and we see three thousand guests every summer."

"I was just saying to my friend Alonzo Pitman the other day—you know Mr. Pitman, I believe?"

Wolff was silent for a beat, then he looked up at the ceiling. "Hmmm, Pitman? I don't know anyone by that name. But then, you and I surely run in different circles, Miss Strong." He chuckled.

She wrinkled her brow and tilted her head to one side. "Oh, I thought he was your attorney."

Wolff's jaw tightened. "Miss Strong, your research leaves quite a bit to be desired. My team of attorneys doesn't include a Mr. Pitman. But I fail to see how my legal counsel is any of your concern." He stood and looked at her expectantly.

Racking her brain for something to say, she slowly got to her feet. "I want to thank you again for the invitation to the Spring Gala. Before the… unfortunate incident, it was a beautiful event."

"You're most welcome, Miss Strong," he said. "You may be assured that I'll be hiring additional security for future gatherings."

"There were so many guests that night. I know Mrs. Wolff wanted to avoid duplicate costumes. I did see another Revolutionary War soldier costume, though. Just like yours." She focused on his face, watching for any flicker of emotion. He met her eyes, then looked down and casually straightened some papers on his desk.

"Is that so? I suppose that's bound to happen."

"Just one more thing, Mr. Wolff. Are your employees part of a union? I recall the intruders at the Spring Gala shouted something about wages." She wondered if he'd dodge the question, as he had when they first met at Wolff Mansion.

He gazed at her with hardness in his eyes. "Naturally, ruffians like that would say such things. They had to know that many employers were in attendance. But there is no need for a union here, Miss Strong. I pay my workers fairly, and they only work eight-hour days. As far as the intruders at the Spring Gala, I assure you they were in no way associated with Wolff Brewery. I am certain they have been brought to justice by now."

"Really? I didn't hear about that."

He ignored her prompt, pulled a watch from his vest pocket, and glanced at it.

"Well, Miss Strong, I believe you have plenty of material for your article." He gestured to the door as he came around his desk.

Sophie took a few reluctant steps toward the exit. "I *was* hoping for a tour of the brewery," she said.

He looked down at her. "I'm sorry, that will not be possible. As I mentioned, we have the highest standards of sanitation, and that precludes allowing the public entrance into the brewery itself."

"But—"

"I do have another appointment," he said, gesturing again to the door. "If you have any other questions, you are welcome to phone my secretary, Mr. Ness. I am sure he has more than enough information to meet your needs. Will your story be in tomorrow's paper?"

"Umm... probably in Monday's paper. I could stop by with a copy—"

"Oh, no need, no need. I read the *Herald* religiously." He opened the office door, and Mr. Ness jumped to his feet. A datebook lay open on his desk, and he flipped it shut with one hand.

"Ness, show Miss Strong out."

Sophie bit her lip. She couldn't think of any other pretense to prolong her stay. She wasn't going to pretend to faint again—that would jog Mr. Ness's mind about her identity, and besides, it was embarrassing.

She turned to Mr. Wolff with a gracious smile. "Thank

you so much for your time, Mr. Wolff. I greatly appreciate it, and so will my readers."

She held out her hand, and he squeezed her fingers slightly, giving her a quick nod.

"Good day, Miss Strong." He retreated into his office and closed the door.

Sophie flashed a bright smile at Mr. Ness. He looked at her with his head cocked to one side, brows furrowed.

"Hello, Mr. Ness. I appreciate your help. Have you worked for Mr. Wolff long?" she asked.

"Two years," he answered curtly. "This way, please, Miss Strong." He gestured toward the door of the anteroom, blocking his desk from her view, and she had no choice but to move in that direction.

"I suppose you make all of his appointments," she said. "He must be very busy."

He nodded distractedly, but didn't answer.

When they emerged into the hallway, Sophie was startled to see Benjamin Turner pushing his mail cart toward them, his flat-topped cap pushed low over his forehead. Sophie's expression must have given away her surprise, because Mr. Ness looked at Benjamin, then back at Sophie, his eyes narrowed. He pointed at Benjamin and opened his mouth to speak.

"Ness!" Mr. Wolff bellowed from his office.

Mr. Ness turned toward the sound, then looked back at Sophie uncertainly.

"I'll see myself out," she said quickly. "Please don't let me keep you."

She headed for the staircase.

"Ness!" called Mr. Wolff again.

Ness gave Sophie a wary look, but she grasped the ornate banister and prepared to descend. When Ness had retreated, Benjamin continued moving toward Sophie. She stood on the first step of the staircase, waiting for him to make eye contact, but he kept his gaze trained on the cart in front of him. Then just as he turned to enter Wolff's anteroom, he quickly glanced her way and winked. Sophie smiled and descended the stairs, then emerged into the late afternoon sunlight.

At the corner, Sophie caught a streetcar to return to the *Herald* office. It was four o'clock, and the car was crowded with women and a few men heading home for the evening. She found a seat at the back and squeezed in, replaying the conversation with Mr. Wolff in her mind as the streetcar rambled along its electric rails and the proud buildings slipped past the windows.

26

———

When Sophie exited the *Herald* building, the street was quiet. The sky had eased into the lavender tones of early evening. She walked toward the boarding house at a brisk pace.

Sophie recalled a notice she'd seen for a women's self-defense class. At the time, she'd only glanced at it as she rushed past to meet a deadline at the paper. Would she have more confidence on these late-night walks if she knew she could put up a fight against a man? At the very least, attending such a class would make a good feature article.

She began to tick through her wish list of dream stories she'd like to cover and people she wanted to interview. A survivor of a great disaster like the *Titanic*, perhaps—would readers ever tire of that story? She'd love to interview President Taft, the First Lady Mrs. Helen Taft, King George and Queen Mary of England, Harry Houdini—he was from Ripon, Wisconsin, after all, just 100 miles to the north. She imagined herself speaking with famous suffragists—Emmeline Pankhurst from England and Belle Case LaFollette, the governor's wife.

At long intervals, she spotted another pedestrian on the opposite side of the street. Periodically a wagon passed by, the tired horses clomping down the empty pavement.

Heavy footsteps sounded behind her. Sophie's heart sped up in her chest. The steps came closer. She looked over her shoulder and saw a tall figure in a black trench coat some ways back, his head bent down. No other details were visible in the gathering dusk. Sophie quickened her step, her pulse pounding in her ears. From now on, she'd pay attention when the reporters' room emptied, and she'd leave with a colleague. Her work could wait until early the next morning.

The footsteps sped up, forcing Sophie to walk faster. But they were gaining on her. Her hands bunched into fists, and she held her breath. A bulking figure barged into her peripheral vision: a big man with a black hat atop his bald head. Sophie squeezed her eyes shut, but he swept past her without a word or even a glance her way.

Sophie let out her breath and chided herself for her timidity. Her heartbeat slowed to its normal pace, and she wondered if she should stop reading the police reports so carefully each morning. They were activating her imagination needlessly.

She returned to her mental list of longed-for interviews. Amelia Earhart. 'Abdu'l-Bahá, the Persian religious leader who was touring the country. Nelly Bly, her brave sister-journalist. She turned onto Division Street and could see the boarding house in the distance, only six blocks ahead. Her shoulders relaxed, and her thoughts drifted to the hot dinner that awaited her.

Sudden pain shot through Sophie's right arm. She nearly lost her balance as she was jerked sideways into a dark, narrow alley between two brick buildings. Someone slammed her against the wall, and her head smacked into the bricks, making her vision swim. She opened her mouth to yell for help, but brutal blows smashed into her stomach and ribs, knocking the wind from her lungs. Panicked and gasping for air, she tried to identify her assailant's face, but a bandanna obscured his nose and mouth. The brim of a knit cap shadowed his eyes.

He pulled back one muscular arm, the front of her shirtwaist twisted tightly in his other fist. A heavy blow landed on her face, sending her head back into the bricks again. Her teeth cut into the tender flesh of her mouth, and she tasted blood. Through a haze of terror, she dimly sensed the gloved hand raise again. Pain seared through her face a second time, like fire. Then the world went black.

SOPHIE BLINKED HER EYES OPEN; her face and body screamed in anguish. She felt the hard, wet paving stones beneath her. The stench of rotting food, urine, and decaying animal flesh stung her nostrils. In the darkness, she could make out a pock-marked brick wall and some trash strewn about the ground. She lifted her head and eased herself up on one elbow, but a wave of nausea enveloped her, and she stopped.

She closed her eyes, willing the horrifying dream to disappear. But when she opened them, her disastrous reality remained in view. She gritted her teeth. Every muscle protested as she pushed herself onto her knees, then struggled to stand up. Her hands braced against the wall for balance. Bile burned the back of her throat and she heaved several times, but her stomach was empty. She pulled the torn front of her shirtwaist to cover her chest as best she could and staggered onto the sidewalk.

As she took step after shaky step, the six blocks to the

boarding house felt like sixty miles. She didn't let herself think; instead, she focused on resolutely putting one foot in front of the other. When the house was just steps away and she saw its warm lamplight glowing in the window, tears sprang to her eyes. If she had only left the office an hour or two earlier, she could be resting comfortably in that safe haven. Angrily, she brushed away the tears and willed herself forward, then up the porch steps to the front door.

Somehow, her purse string was still wrapped around her wrist. With great effort, she found her key, relieved that she wouldn't have to summon Mrs. O'Day and submit to unanswerable questions. Thankfully, the parlor was empty when she entered. She dragged her feet up the staircase, gripping the banister with shaking fingers, silently begging the house's inhabitants not to stir. The thought of Ruth kept her going. Ruth would know what to do, with her medical training and her calm efficiency. Finally, Sophie reached their room and used another key to let herself in. She breathed a sigh of relief as she closed the door and rested her back against it.

Raw disappointment swept over her. The room was cold and empty. She dimly recalled Ruth mentioning plans for the weekend—visiting some relative of either hers or Oliver's, somewhere. That morning, Sophie had let the conversation float past her. She never dreamed she might ache for her friend's gentle ministrations now.

Not bothering to undress or even take off her shoes, Sophie collapsed onto her bed and sobbed.

A MISTY DAWN light was beginning to glimmer in her window by the time Sophie awoke. The pain in her head, face, and torso assaulted her again. She steeled herself and sat up, gasping with the effort. Then she stumbled down the hall to the bathroom that she and Ruth shared with the three other girls. She turned on the hot tap, soaked a cloth, and dabbed at her face, wincing as she dislodged tiny pebbles from a scrape on her cheek. When her wounds were as clean as she could manage, she rinsed the cloth, checking the sink and wiping away any traces of blood.

Back in her room, she found Ruth's satchel of first aid supplies. She opened a glass jar of Vaseline, looked in the bureau mirror, and dabbed it on the worst cuts and scrapes on her face. The wounds and red splotches would soon turn into ugly bruises. Sophie tugged off her ruined clothes, rolled them into a bundle, and kicked it to a corner of the closet. She'd replace them somehow, because she never wanted to see them again.

She pulled on her cotton nightdress, then went to the mirror and stared at the stranger in the glass. Her hair was matted and tangled, but she didn't have the energy to lift a comb. She looked deeply into her brown eyes and saw steel in them. There was no doubt in her mind that the attack had been a warning. The man could have easily killed her. Instead, he'd left her bloody and battered, still carrying her purse. His only aim had been to cause pain and fear.

Whose hands had pummeled her? Or who had sent him? The faces of Alonzo Pitman, Thelma and Ruben Wolff, and Agnes Thompson flashed in her mind. Or was there some other unknown villain that she had unwittingly disturbed, like a scorpion in its nest? For the briefest instant, she considered trying to forget the limp and lifeless body of Hilda Rock and the troubled eyes of Clara Elliot and Aunt Lucy. From deep in her memory, her father's cold, angry face swam into view, towering above her as she trembled.

Should she call the police? She imagined facing Detective

Zimmer and explaining what had happened. She hadn't seen her attacker's face, and she hadn't talked to anyone on the street. There would be no chance of finding out who it was, unless he'd conveniently dropped a clue in the alley. Zimmer would be even more insistent that she stay away from the case. Now that she thought of it, Ruth would probably have said the same thing. Maybe it was a blessing that she wasn't home. She would have urged Sophie to give up on the case and focus on reporting.

No. She refused to surrender. She could not give up. Her battered face was a signal that she was inching closer to the murderer. Whoever it was, their greed or hatred or anger had ruthlessly led to taking a woman's life. The roots of this crime might snake into the wealthiest institutions of the city. Whatever was fueling the injustice, she would find it and stop it. She would make sure the monster paid the price.

She stumbled back to bed and fell into a deep sleep once more.

AT SUPPER TIME, Sophie heard a light tapping on the door. "Sophie? Are you all right? It's Margaret."

Sophie faked a cough, hoping it sounded convincing to her fellow boarder. "I'm okay, Margaret. I just came down with a bad cold."

"Poor thing. Shall I bring you some soup?"

"That would be great, thanks. Leave it outside the door, would you please?"

"Sure. I'll be back in a wink."

Sophie stared up at the ceiling, her stomach growling at the thought of food.

A short time later, Margaret knocked softly again. "Here's your soup, Sophie. Do you want me to bring it in?"

"No thank you, Margaret. I look a fright."

"Oh, that doesn't matter among us girls."

"I'll be fine. But thanks again."

"All right, if you're sure. You take care." Her voice sounded doubtful, but she didn't argue further.

Sophie waited until she heard Margaret's steps recede down the hall and her door click shut. Then she limped over to the door, turned the lock, and peeked out. The hallway was deserted. A soothing chicken broth scent wafted up from the tray at her feet. Two thick slices of Mrs. O'Day's homemade bread swathed with butter made her mouth water. Sophie bent down gingerly and tugged the tray inside, then secured the lock once more.

O SATUR AY A SU AY, Sophie barely left her room, sneaking out to use the bathroom and get cups of water from the sink when the hallway was quiet. She had almost no appetite, so she nibbled on the snacks that she and Ruth had tucked away: a couple of boxes of Cracker Jack, a tin of Hydrox biscuits, and a few apples. She took aspirin from the bottle in her nightstand drawer and tried to put the pain out of her mind.

When she wasn't sleeping, Sophie mused about the case. Her most recent conversation with Mr. Wolff had grown foggy in her memory. She remembered that she'd mentioned Hilda Rock. At that moment, how had Mr. Wolff reacted? Had he looked like he knew the identity of her killer? Or was *he* the murderer himself? What emotions might a guilty man's face reveal when he thought about his crime, and how would that look to an observer? She grudgingly admitted that Detective Zimmer's job was harder than it looked. Wolff hadn't blurted out the true story, as suspects often did in plays and radio shows.

He hadn't admitted to knowing Alonzo Pitman, either, though Pitman had claimed to work for Wolff. Why would he hide such a connection? Or perhaps these unknown tasks were assigned to Pitman by Wolff's legal team, and Wolff truly didn't know the man.

And what about the two identical costumes? Did they have anything to do with the murder? Maybe Hilda's death was unrelated to the Wolffs or to Pitman. But their stories intersected in so many places that she was sure there must be a connection.

Ruth returned to their room late on Sunday, and Sophie pretended to be asleep so she wouldn't have to explain her appearance. There would be plenty of time for that uncomfortable conversation later.

That night, she dreamed she was back at the Spring Gala. The dance floor was empty except for two Revolutionary War soldiers. They circled each other menacingly, bodies tense and alert, hands ready to fight. Then they both drew their wooden guns, aimed—and somehow the fake weapons fired. The two men shot each other again and again, bloody wounds blooming in their chests, but they remained standing, as if oblivious to pain. Then they tossed the weapons aside and charged each other, wrestling to the floor, punching wildly, smashing flesh and bone. Several more soldiers dressed the same way rushed forward to join the melee, until all Sophie could see was a pile of blue-cloaked, bleeding, heaving bodies.

Sophie jerked awake and sat up straight in bed. Her nightdress clung to her sweating skin. Two soldiers. Two soldiers. The words ran through her mind. Was Pitman telling the truth about leaving the party? Did he go to his office and shoot Hilda Rock? Or did the costumes have nothing to do with the murder? With a pounding head she slipped out of bed, got a cup of water from the bathroom, and took more aspirin. She lay down again and puzzled over the case for hour after restless hour, until sleep finally came.

~

"Sophie? Are you awake?" Ruth shook her shoulder gently. "It's Monday morning. Don't you need to get up?"

Sophie kept her eyes closed, shifting the edge of her quilt to better hide her face. She coughed, and her voice sounded hoarse after barely speaking for two days. "I'm not feeling well. I think it's a bad cold. I'll telephone the office in a bit."

"Oh, you poor dear. Do you have a fever?"

"I don't think so. I'll be okay. I just want to sleep."

"All right, if you're sure. I'll get you more water, though. You need plenty of liquids."

"Thanks." Sophie breathed deeply and evenly, feigning sleep as she heard Ruth take the glass from her bedside table, leave the room to fill it, and return. She gave Sophie's shoulder a compassionate pat, then picked up her books and left.

When the house had grown quiet, Sophie heaved herself out of bed and braved another look in the mirror. There was a purplish black bruise on her right cheekbone, and a matching one on her left jawbone. Her bottom lip was swollen, though the split skin was starting to heal. There was a nasty scrape on her chin. But at least she didn't have black eyes.

She pulled a fresh chemise and drawers out of the bureau, then grabbed a pink cotton day dress from the closet. Picking up her towel and toiletries, she opened the door a crack and peeked out. As expected, the hallway was empty. Sophie slipped out and ducked into the bathroom. Lathering Pear's soap in her scraped palms, she cleaned her body, avoiding the tender purple and blue bruises. She dressed quickly, then spent several minutes tugging at her tangled brown curls with a comb. When her hair was tame enough, she twisted it into a simple bun, which she secured with hairpins.

She looked at her reflection. There was no denying she was injured. What would her story be? She tripped and fell on her way home from work? That was believable. She picked up her things and opened the bathroom door.

Vivian Bell stood in the doorway, her fist raised to knock.

"It's about ti—" She broke off, taking in Sophie's bruised face.

Sophie's free hand flew to cover her cheek, though she knew it was useless.

"I—um—fell—" she stammered.

For the first time, she saw empathy in Vivian's eyes.

Vivian grabbed her hand. "Come with me," she said, pulling a stunned Sophie down the hall to her room.

Vivian's room was even smaller than Sophie and Ruth's, with one bed, a desk, a bedside table, and a bureau. Sophie was surprised to find that it was tidy—for some reason she'd always imagined Vivian living in a sloppy nest, with delicious dresses, stockings, and wraps strewn everywhere. A fountain pen and half-finished letter were on the desk, with an open dictionary nearby. Another book rested on the tiny table, but Sophie couldn't make out the title. A wooden hat stand at the corner of the desk held a lovely peach and yellow hat trimmed with delicate flowers.

Vivian pushed Sophie onto the bed. "Sit. I can help."

"Vivian, I—" Sophie began.

"You don't have to explain."

Vivian pulled open a drawer in her bureau and took out three tins, a handkerchief, and a powder puff. She opened the first tin and dipped the handkerchief into the peach-colored cream, then dabbed it on Sophie's bruised face. She followed this with a lighter colored cream. Then she opened the third tin and used the powder puff to cover the creams with a layer of rose-scented powder. Standing back, she surveyed her work with a practiced eye.

"There," she said. "Take a look."

Sophie stood and peeked in the bureau mirror. To her surprise, the bruises were invisible at first glance. Her skin almost looked natural if you didn't study it too closely.

Her mouth dropped open. "How did you do that? Thank you."

"It's nothing. I've done it for myself in the past."

She didn't explain the circumstances, and Sophie didn't inquire.

Vivian tugged open her drawer again and pulled out a drawstring bag. She dropped the makeup inside. "You can borrow these for as long as you need them."

Sophie took the bag and glanced again in the mirror.

"Thank you so much," she said. "I didn't know how I was going to explain."

Vivian nodded. "I had a friend who was a stage actress. She taught me a few tricks." She smiled ruefully. It occurred to Sophie that Vivian looked almost sweet when she wasn't delivering haughty insults. She felt an impulse to hug her, but she brushed it aside.

"Must run, though, or I'll be late for work," said Vivian.

"Of course, sure." Sophie gathered the things she'd brought from the bathroom and went to the door. She turned to Vivian, who was rummaging about in her top drawer. "Thanks again, Vivian."

"Don't mention it." Vivian didn't look up.

Sophie walked down the hallway in a daze. She put her things away, tucking the bag of makeup at the back of a drawer. Her stomach growled. Mrs. O'Day would be busy cleaning something or she may be out shopping. She wouldn't mind if Sophie made herself some toast, since she'd barely eaten all weekend. If they did meet, Sophie could attribute the flat pallor on her cheeks to her feigned illness.

She pulled a shawl over her shoulders, then took hesitant steps down to the kitchen.

27

Fortified by three slabs of toasted bread with Mrs. O'Day's strawberry jam, Sophie went to the telephone on the hall table. Keeping her voice low and gravelly, she left a message for Mr. Barnaby, claiming a severe cold. She returned to her room, dropped back onto the bed, and closed her eyes.

When she opened her eyes, a pale-gray sky glowed through the window. Unsure of the time, Sophie reached for her watch. A rugged scrape from her attack now marred the watch face, but she was thankful it hadn't broken. The hands stood at seven-thirty. Sophie blinked in confusion, before realizing she'd forgotten to wind it. With no sun in sight, the time was a mystery.

Sophie suddenly felt restless, aware that she'd seen almost nothing beyond her four walls since Friday. She went to the mirror and dabbed on more of Vivian's makeup, then pinned on her hat, wincing at the pain as she lifted her arms. She tucked the watch into her skirt pocket, donned her spring coat, and eased herself down the stairs, feeling sharp jabs with each step.

On Franklin Street, the air was pleasantly mild, a light breeze ruffling the tree leaves. It felt surprisingly pleasant to be outdoors. With a fierce effort, she put Friday night's experience out of her mind. Taking slow steps, she focused on appreciating nature and the fact that she was still alive. The typical sounds of a Milwaukee afternoon rose around her: shouting school children released for the day, streetcars rolling on their tracks, horses clopping down the street with wagons and cabs rattling along behind them. Periodically, an automobile chugged past or bleated its horn.

She found herself just a few blocks from Aunt Lucy's apartment when her energy began to lag. Longing for friendly faces, she turned in that direction and made her way to the familiar door at the top of the steps. She knocked three times, then opened it.

"Hello? Anyone home?"

"Sophie!"

Something hit the floor with a *thunk*, followed by the sound of running footsteps. She braced herself for Harry's exuberant hug just before he flung himself at her. As he squeezed her bruised middle, she managed not to cry out, and instead ruffled his hair affectionately.

"Hello there, Sir Harry. You're certainly energetic."

"Harry, my goodness," chided Aunt Lucy, coming into view with what looked like a schoolbook. "You can't go tearing around a schoolroom like that, you know."

Harry pulled Sophie farther inside. "Aunt Lucy is teaching me math and reading."

"You're getting ready for school?"

"I guess so. Aunt Lucy says I can go in the fall. But I'd rather play checkers with you."

Sophie laughed and met Aunt Lucy's eyes. Her aunt's round cheeks glowed as she watched Harry's scampering dance into the front parlor.

"I suppose you've earned a break," Aunt Lucy told him.

Lucy's perceptive gaze landed on Sophie's face, and she paused, drawing her brows together. "Are you all right, Sophie? We rarely see you at this time of day."

"I'm fine," Sophie said, turning to join Harry. "I just got a rare day off."

"I'll make some tea. You look as if you could use it."

Harry chatted excitedly about the stories he and Lucy and had been reading and how quickly he was learning his multiplication tables. As he set up the checkerboard, she quizzed him on the three's, which had always been her favorite.

Aunt Lucy handed Sophie her mug; the hot liquid soothed her throat. Lucy dropped into her chair and picked up a newspaper, but within minutes her head drooped. Having the two young kids around must exhaust her, Sophie thought.

Harry won the first game easily and was leading in the second when Sam breezed in, hanging her empty canvas bag and her cap on a hook by the door.

"Hi, Sophie!" she called, before ducking into the bathroom.

Aunt Lucy opened her eyes and stifled a yawn. "Oh, heavens, did I drift off?"

"Just for a minute," Sophie said.

"I'll get some supper going," Lucy said, pulling herself to her feet. "Can you stay, dear?"

Sophie glanced out the window. Sunset was approaching, and she felt a flicker of anxiety at the prospect of walking home alone. But she pushed her fears aside.

"That would be lovely," she told her aunt. "I'd love to catch up with Sam, too."

~

HARRY AND SAM eagerly dug into the supper of roast beef and potato salad, talking over each other as they updated Sophie on their new lives. They seemed to be settling in, and Sophie wondered if Sam had agreed to stay permanently. She could tell by the protective look in Aunt Lucy's eyes that she wouldn't let them go without a fight.

"I suggested that Sam go to school this fall when Harry does, but I'm getting some resistance," Lucy said.

Sam waved her fork, scoffing at the idea. "I don't need school. I've got a job. And I'm too old anyways."

"It's the law for children to attend school for twelve weeks a year until they're fourteen," Sophie said. "You're in that category, I believe."

"I can pass for fifteen," said Sam. "And I want to pay our way. We're not here for a handout." Her back was straight, her expression serious.

"Sam's earnings from the paper help with expenses," Aunt Lucy told Sophie. "Still, we'd manage for a while."

Their eyes met briefly, and Sophie read her aunt's concern in them. Education would better prepare Sam for some kind of indoor employment and a secure future.

"How is your library work?" Sophie asked her aunt.

"I'm keeping my hand in. We found a new young man to make deliveries, so it's mostly correspondence. I can do that from here."

A hearty bark sounded outside, and Harry and Sam looked up.

"It's Buster!" cried Harry, leaping to his feet.

"May we be excused?" Sam asked politely, tugging on Harry's sleeve to hold him back.

"Yes, you may be excused," said Aunt Lucy.

Sam carried their plates through the swinging kitchen door as Harry ran to the window to peer into the backyard.

"Mrs. Keller's nephew has a new dog he brings over," Aunt Lucy told Sophie. "They're fascinated."

"Sam, look how big he's getting," called Harry. Sam dashed over to join her brother at the window.

"Why don't you help me clean up, Sophie, if you have the time?"

"Of course." They gathered plates, dishes, and cutlery from the table and took them to the kitchen. Aunt Lucy turned on the tap to fill the sink. She eyed Sophie with a frown. "What happened?" Her voice was covered by the sound of running water.

Sophie's fingers flew to her cheek as if to check that her injuries were still camouflaged. Aunt Lucy grasped her hand gently.

"You look all right," she told Sophie. "But I can tell something's wrong."

The warm pressure of Lucy's hand on hers and the soothing tenderness of her voice brought tears to Sophie's eyes. She opened her mouth to make an excuse, but the words caught in her throat.

Aunt Lucy's eyes searched hers, absorbing the story with motherly intuition. "Are you hurt? Did someone—"

Sophie bit her lip and looked over her shoulder, checking that the kitchen door was still shut. Knowing Aunt Lucy would imagine the worst if she tried to hide the truth, Sophie nodded.

"But it could be worse," she said.

"Tell me," Lucy said, her voice clipped.

"It was Friday night," Sophie began. The story spilled out in a torrent, mixed with conjecture about who the culprit might have been and whether it was connected to Hilda's murder.

Aunt Lucy listened, her expression growing more troubled as Sophie continued. When the sink had filled, Lucy shut off the tap but left the dishes untouched.

Finally, Sophie fell silent. She heard a shuffling sound behind her and turned to see Sam standing in the doorway, her face unreadable. How much had she heard?

"Sam, hi," Sophie said. "We've just been chatting. How's the dog?"

"They went inside," Sam said guardedly. "Harry's getting tired. We're going to get ready for bed."

"I'll just say goodnight then," said Sophie. She walked to the doorway and gave Sam a quick hug. Instead of simply allowing it, Sam surprised her by returning the embrace with a fierce squeeze. Then Sam turned and headed down the hall toward the bedroom.

Sophie followed and found Harry at the hall window, peering up at the darkening sky.

"I like to wish on the stars," he said.

She squeezed his shoulders, and he rested his head comfortably against her.

"The first one you see, do you mean?" asked Sophie.

"All of them," said Harry.

AN HOUR LATER, Aunt Lucy insisted on going to Mrs. Keller's apartment downstairs to use her telephone and call a cab for Sophie. Though Sophie protested that the expense was unnecessary, she was relieved to settle into the cab and close her eyes, lulled by the clopping hooves of the horse.

Sophie's head and body still ached when she entered the boarding house. The staircase looked like a mountain to be scaled. Instead of starting the climb, she went to the hall table and idly flipped through the letters in the tray, finding nothing for herself, as expected. Mrs. O'Day slouched in her chair next to the fire, dozing with an open book in her lap.

Sophie smiled, taking in the cozy scene, with the crackling flames and the sharp scent of wood smoke. The frozen hands of the mantel clock jogged her memory. She reached into her pocket and pulled out her stopped watch. She'd forgotten to set and wind it while she was at Aunt Lucy's.

With a sigh, Sophie trudged up the stairs. She tapped Ruth's mezuzah and entered their room. Her roommate's slow, rhythmic breathing signaled that she was already asleep, and Sophie felt a stab of disappointment. She'd been hoping to hear a cheerful account of Ruth's latest challenges at medical school. She yearned for reassurance that some parts of life were undisturbed by the recent bizarre events.

Sophie placed her watch on her bedside table so she'd remember it in the morning. As quietly as possible, she slipped into her nightgown, then padded down the hall to brush her teeth, though she left the makeup in place.

When she returned to the room, Sophie eased herself into bed and pulled the quilt around her. She picked up her watch, its hands still locked. The scraped watch face was rough under her finger. She hated knowing her timepiece would be forever flawed because of the ordeal she'd endured. She shuddered, remembering the shattered glass of Hilda Rock's smashed timepiece. What if the man attacking Sophie had carried a gun? Would she have been found in that alley, her stilled watch the only clue?

She glanced at Ruth's watch on her side of the table to get the accurate time: nine-twenty. She pulled out the tiny crown of her own watch and moved the hands into place. Then she pushed it back in and began winding the crown forward. Timepieces danced through her mind: her watch, Ruth's watch, the broken clock downstairs, stately clock towers, the shattered glass of Hilda Rock's timepiece. She continued winding, wishing she could close her eyes and drop through time to her previous life, when murder had been an abstract concept. Did Mrs. O'Day have a similar urge whenever she saw her late husband's clock on the mantel? Was ten after ten a significant moment, or just when the hands happened to stop?

Sophie gasped, and her fingers froze. She stared at her watch, which had started its rhythmic ticking, like a tiny heartbeat. Hilda Rock's watch had been smashed at exactly eleven-oh-five. *Or had it?* A broken clock doesn't always tell the time it stopped at, she thought—the hands could have been moved.

Could the killer have pulled the fob from Hilda's lifeless chest and coolly set the hands backward or forward, knowing it would throw off the police? Suppose the murder had happened at midnight, or at ten? Why might he or she have chosen eleven-oh-five instead?

Sophie threw off the covers and jumped to her feet, barely feeling the nagging aches. She opened her purse and pulled out the little notebook. Standing at the window, she flipped through the pages with shaking fingers, squinting to read the words by moonlight.

There it was: *supper at eleven.* The night of the Spring Gala, Thelma Wolff would have expected hundreds of guests to vouch for her presence at the buffet. It was a perfect alibi. But Sophie recalled the richly arrayed table, its silver platters of sandwiches and tarts nearly untouched after the shocking intrusion.

She flipped the notebook pages, her eyes scanning the lines of scrawled pencil. What time had the protesters invaded? Surely she'd written it down. She forced her eager fingers to slow and went through the pages again, taking in every word. Nothing. She'd probably assumed she wouldn't forget the sequence of events, the terrible chaos. But that was before her head had been knocked against a brick wall and her brains jangled with punches.

Disgusted, she crawled back into bed and tossed the note-book on the bedside table. Ruth started at the sound, made a sleepy moan, and rolled over. Sophie longed to shake her awake, but stopped herself. She couldn't infringe on her friend's few hours of rest.

Sophie dropped onto the pillow, nerves tense as she stared at the ceiling. Her temples throbbed as she tried to pull facts from the gloomy swamp of memory. As the hours crawled by, she drifted in and out of restless sleep. Images of the party flashed behind her eyes: Thelma's ornate crown and haughty laugh, Sophie's single dance with the mysterious Spaniard, roses spilled across the dance floor, and orange-red flames licking linen tablecloths.

28

On Tuesday morning, Sophie feigned sleep until she heard Ruth leave the room. Then she eased out of bed and looked in the mirror to assess the damage to her face. The bruises appeared less angry, but still clearly visible. With soft dabs of her fingertips, she reapplied Vivian's makeup, then got dressed. Though she'd managed to walk to Aunt Lucy's the day before, her battered torso ached, and she had a nasty bruise on her hip. Unable to deal with the ten-block walk to the office, she got out a nickel for the streetcar. The crowded ride was uncomfortable, but she endured.

Sophie spent most of the day at her desk, typing up society notes and recipes. A helpful nurse had sent a long-hand article entitled "Hand Washing to Prevent Disease," and Sophie typed that, too. In between tasks, she tried to focus on the details of the Spring Gala. Had she seen Mrs. Wolff at eleven? What about ten? Her struggle to pull the memories into consciousness gave her a headache.

Throughout the day, Sophie's colleagues kept their distance, and Mr. Barnaby seemed absorbed in editing articles, occasionally calling out for a copy boy or one of the other reporters. Benjamin Turner tossed no barbed comments her way. She saw him glance at her quizzically once or twice, but she ignored him. She was sure he'd noticed that she was pale and drawn, but hopefully he and the others attributed it to her fictitious illness.

Ruth was absent from dinner at the boarding house that night, and Sophie assumed she was studying late at the library. After a quiet meal with the other girls where she picked at her food, Sophie went straight to bed, exhausted by the effort of getting through the day.

After Ruth left the next morning, Sophie felt a little more energized. She was pleased to see that her bruises were fading to greenish yellow. Again she covered them with makeup. She'd have to replenish Vivian's supply.

After lunch, she attended a meeting of the Service Club of Milwaukee. On her way back to the office, she considered seeking out Detective Zimmer to demand an update on the investigation. But she was afraid he'd be able to guess she'd been attacked—her appearance or demeanor might give something away. Perhaps in his line of work, he had seen makeup-covered bruises too many times to be fooled. He'd be furious with her for not reporting the crime and tell her once again to leave the detecting to the police. He'd tell her she was putting herself in danger by continuing to ask questions—or snoop, as he liked to call it.

She typed up the story about the club's upcoming rummage sale and dropped it into Mr. Barnaby's box, thankful that he seemed too busy to look up from his work. Her thoughts returned to the Spring Gala as she tried to recall the exact timing of the night's events. How much had she related to Aunt Lucy? Maybe she would remember something that could help. As the office began to empty for the evening, she pinned on her hat, grabbed her purse, and headed out the door.

Walking down Aunt Lucy's street, she breathed in the lilac-scented air and appreciated the refreshing breeze on her face. Her muscles moved with a little less pain than the day before.

When she entered the apartment, she was surprised to find Clara Elliot sitting at the dining table with her aunt, both of them whispering over their teacups. Harry sat on the floor of the living room, engrossed in the machinations of a battalion of small wooden soldiers.

"Hello, Sophie," said Aunt Lucy, her mouth pinched in a tight line. "Would you like a cup of tea?" She didn't wait for a response, but rose to get a third teacup from the kitchen.

Sophie sat down next to Clara.

"What's going on?" she asked. "It feels like something's up."

Clara's eyes darted toward Harry. "I'll let your aunt tell you," she said quietly.

Aunt Lucy returned and handed Sophie the cup, but didn't bother picking up the teapot to pour.

"What is it?" Sophie asked.

"Sam didn't come home last night," Aunt Lucy said, keeping her voice low.

"What? Sam was out all night?"

Aunt Lucy nodded. "She's been late before, but this is the first time she didn't come home at all. I thought she'd be back tonight, but—"

Sophie noticed Aunt Lucy used the correct pronoun for Sam's gender. Either Sam had confided in Aunt Lucy, or in her anxiety Aunt Lucy simply forgot to keep up the pretense that Sam was a boy.

"What did Harry say?" Sophie asked.

"I just told him Sam was late last night. And then this morning, I said Sam wasn't here, and he didn't question it. She leaves early sometimes. I don't want him to worry."

"Do you think Sam is okay? Could she have stayed with a friend?" Sophie envisioned the pathetic little tent Sam and Harry had once lived in.

"I just don't know, Sophie." Aunt Lucy's eyes swam with fear. "Maybe she felt too restrained living here. What if she wanted to be free and live on her own? I shouldn't have pushed her about school."

Clara reached over and grasped Aunt Lucy's hand. "Don't blame yourself, Lucy. Of course you want her to go to school. You only want the best for her."

Sophie turned Aunt Lucy's words over in her mind. It suddenly came home to her how little they really knew about Sam. "I don't think she'd just leave Harry like that."

"I hope not." Their eyes met, and Sophie felt a sick roiling in her stomach. She thought of her attack on Friday night. What if her assailant had somehow found Sam? She imagined the girl's slim shoulders and fragile limbs, so easily broken. She imagined bones crushed, or a frail, unconscious body dropped into the Milwaukee River.

"It could be nothing," Clara said. "We don't know her habits, after all."

Harry had apparently tired of the wooden soldiers, because he came running up to the table, putting an end to their conjecture.

"Sophie! Can we play checkers now?"

Sophie's eyes met Aunt Lucy's. *What can we do?* she mouthed, as Harry tugged at her hand.

Aunt Lucy shrugged helplessly.

"Well, Dante is outside with the car," said Clara. "I'm going out to loo—" She glanced at Harry. "To drive around."

"I'll go with you," said Sophie. "One second."

"Soooo-phie!" complained Harry.

She let him pull her into the living room, where the checkerboard already perched on the coffee table, the red and black disks carefully positioned. She pulled Harry into a fierce hug.

"I'm sorry, buddy," she said. "I'm just not feeling very well. I've been a little bit sick."

As she released him, his face sobered. He looked up at her with a frown, rubbing her arm gently. "Do you have a fever? You don't have spots, do you?"

The words stabbed at Sophie's heart, as she remembered that his mother and at least one friend had died from illness. Maybe measles, since he was worried about spots.

"Don't worry about me," said Sophie. "It's only a cold, but I don't want you to catch it. I just came to say a quick hello, and Mrs. Elliot is going to give me a ride home."

Harry wagged a small, admonishing finger at her. "All right, but get better soon. Have some soup when you get home, and go straight to bed."

She smiled. "I will. I'll be back to beat you at checkers before you know it." She ruffled his mop of sandy brown hair.

"Beat *me*? Ha!" His bravado sounded just like Sam's.

She had to be found, thought Sophie, as she turned toward the door. She had to be all right. Sophie chased away the horrible scenarios that sprang, unbidden, into her mind.

"Ready, Sophie?" Clara stood with one gloved hand on the knob.

Aunt Lucy bustled into the living room. "I'll play checkers with you, Harry. I'll show you a few tricks I know."

"Okay, but no cheating," said Harry.

Aunt Lucy chuckled. "No cheating, I promise. And we want to read another chapter of *Treasure Island* before bed, right?"

"Yes! It's the best story ever."

"Now, you go first, because you're red, and fire comes

before smoke," Sophie heard Aunt Lucy say, as she slipped out the door and followed Clara to the waiting Cadillac.

AS DANTE MANEUVERED the car around the downtown area and nearby neighborhoods, Sophie and Clara each kept watch out of opposite windows. It occurred to Sophie that they'd done the same thing when Agnes had been missing. As they drove along, every newsie or street kid Sophie saw made her heart speed up. But none of them was Sam.

"Why don't we go to the *Herald* office?" Sophie asked. "She might be there. Or maybe someone has seen her."

"Good idea." Clara gave the instructions to Dante.

"Go around back," suggested Sophie.

Dante turned the corner and pulled up to the familiar alley where Sophie had seen Sam and the other newsies before.

"I'll be right back," said Sophie.

She entered the alley, squinting to see the faces of the few boys loitering there. No sign of Sam. The boys eyed her suspiciously as she approached.

"We're all outa papers, lady," drawled the one who looked oldest. He slouched against the building's brick wall, smoking a cigarette.

"I'm Sophie," she said, trying to sound friendly. Her eyes moved hopefully to each face, but they just gazed back silently.

She settled on the oldest.

"Are you Archer?" she asked, glad she could remember the name Sam had mentioned a few times.

He dragged on the cigarette, then blew the smoke upward. "Could be."

"Sam's little brother Harry is asking about he—him. Have you seen him around?"

The boy gave an amused grunt. "Lots of guys hang around here."

Sophie heard footsteps and turned to see Clara approaching. Dante kept a few paces behind her, looking around warily.

"Young man, if you and your friends help us find Sam, I'll pay you a dollar each." She waved a fan of several bills with one hand.

The boy straightened. "You really want to find him. He in trouble or somethin'?"

"Nothing like that," said Sophie. "Like I said, his little brother is worried about him." She tried not to sound too desperate, resisting the urge to shout.

"If he's so worried, why ain't this brother with ya?" piped up another boy.

"He's been sick," said Sophie. "Have you seen Sam or not?"

The eldest boy shook his head. "Sorry, lady. You seem nice and all. But we don't rat on other guys."

"Arch, that's a lotta money," one of the younger boys began, but Archer glared at him and he fell silent.

"Are you certain?" Clara asked.

Archer didn't hesitate. "Yep, we're sure. If he wanted ya to know where he is, he'd tell ya."

The glimmer of hope in Sophie's chest flickered out as fat raindrops began to fall. The boys drifted toward the other end of the alley. Sophie wondered where they went for shelter and hoped it was somewhere safe. She met Clara's disappointed gaze, and they turned to go back to the car.

"Sam'll be okay, lady," Archer's voice carried down the empty alley. "He can take care of himself."

Sophie linked her arm in Clara's and hoped that was true.

"He's right, you know," said Clara as they rode back to the boarding house. "Sam knows how to take care of herself. She did it for a long time."

"I'm sure you're right."

"She has a way of wiggling into a person's heart, doesn't she?"

Sophie nodded. She glanced at her watch, then looked at it thoughtfully, tracing her finger in a circle around the scraped face.

"What is it, Sophie?" Clara asked.

"I thought of something last night," she said. "It might help with Mrs. Rock's murder."

"Did you tell Detective Zimmer?"

"No, not yet. It's just a vague theory. I'm having trouble piecing it all together, though." She told Clara about Hilda Rock's timepiece and how it may not reveal the actual time she was killed.

"I wish I could ask someone who was at the party. But Mrs. Wolff made it clear she didn't want to talk to me again. I doubt I'd even get in the door of Wolff Mansion."

"What about the guests?"

"I can't really question them without casting suspicion on Mrs. Wolff, and if I'm wrong..."

"Oh, yes," said Clara. "You don't want to start those rumors."

Sophie listened to the soft patter of raindrops on the roof of the automobile until Dante pulled to a stop in front of the boarding house.

He turned around in his seat. "I'm sorry for overhearing," he said. "But if you don't mind my saying, the servants would know about folks' comings and goings that night."

"Good point, Dante," said Clara. "Do you think any of them would talk to you, Sophie?"

"There were so many of them," Sophie said. "I wouldn't

know who—" She stopped, frowning with concentration. "Wait a minute. There was someone… Bridget? No, Brigid. That's right. I met her in the garden. She was fighting off one of the male servants. I forget which one."

"That could be important," said Clara. "Perhaps more will come back to you."

"Maybe."

"For now, we'll try not to worry. You heard Harry—soup and straight to bed!"

Sophie smiled faintly. "That's good advice."

Dante jumped out of the driver's seat and jogged over to Sophie's door. He opened an umbrella and held it up as she stepped out.

"Thank you, Clara," Sophie said, looking back.

"Don't mention it, my dear."

"And thank you, Dante," she said, as he walked her to the front door. "I appreciate your help."

"Glad I could be of service, Miss Strong."

She pulled her key from her purse and he took it, unlocked the door, and opened it for her. Sophie stepped inside.

"Good night, Dante."

"Good night, Miss Strong."

The hall and parlor were empty, the fireplace cold and dark. Sophie sighed and made her weary way up the stairs.

29

———

Sophie emerged from the office library holding a generous file of clippings about Decoration Day to find Benjamin Turner hanging up the phone at the booth along the wall.

He let out a long whistle. "That Majestic Building is an unlucky spot for sure."

Her skin prickled with alarm. "What do you mean? What happened?"

"My buddy was at the Walker Beer Garden next door when he saw the cops go in. It's another body. That Rock lady was killed there last week, wasn't she?"

Sophie swallowed. "W-who was it this time?"

"I don't know, Miss Strong. But I'm going down there to find out."

Her heart raced. It couldn't be Aunt Lucy or Clara, could it? Or what if Sam... She pushed aside the thought. She wouldn't be able to sit still until she knew for sure. Mr. Barnaby's office door was ajar, and she could see his head bent over a stack of copy. He'd told her to stay glued to her desk for the week, but would he notice if she slipped out?

"I'm coming too," she said.

Benjamin held up a placating hand. "No need, Miss Strong. I've got it covered. Don't you have recipes to sort through?"

"I'm going, Mr. Turner, whether you like it or not."

He raised his eyebrows and grinned. He glanced at Barnaby's office, then back at Sophie.

"All right, if you must," he said. "We can share a cab if you hurry."

She tossed the files on her desk, grabbed her purse and hat, and slipped into the hallway before Mr. Barnaby could spot her. Then she followed Benjamin as he raced down the stairs. She hadn't yet pinned her hat when they emerged onto Grand Avenue.

With a shrill whistle and a wave of his arm, he hailed a hansom cab, then gave urgent instructions to the driver. Sophie climbed inside, grateful for the ride. She wouldn't have been able to walk the two blocks at a dignified pace with her raging anxiety, and running through the street would be conspicuous. Benjamin leaned forward on the seat, clutching the top of the waist-high cab door in a fierce grip. For the first time, Sophie noticed his muscular arms and determined jawline. The vehicle swayed. She braced herself against the side of the carriage as the driver steered the horse around slower-moving wagons and automobiles.

The instant the cab slowed at the towering Majestic Building, Benjamin jumped down and offered a hand to Sophie. Her fingers brushed his palm as she stepped into the street. Benjamin thrust some coins at the driver, and they dashed through the front door. Her heart thumped hard in her chest as she ran up the stairs to the second floor, then rushed down the hall, images of Hilda Rock's corpse flashing through her mind. She wheeled around the corner, past businessmen arguing with two harried policemen who seemed to be pushing them back.

"Hey!" one officer called to her. "Miss!"

She didn't stop, zeroing in on the suffrage office door. Spots swam into her vision as she tried to make sense of what she saw.

The door was shut tight, the surrounding hallway empty. Sophie halted, touching one hand to the wall to steady herself as relief washed over her. *Thank God.* She closed her eyes and took shaky breaths, suddenly aware of the sweat on her back and the bite of her corset around her ribs.

The rumble of voices tugged her attention to the scene, and she blinked her eyes open. Two more uniformed officers stood at Mr. Pitman's door, gazing in with grim expressions. She took two steps in that direction, then stopped as Detective Jacob Zimmer emerged from the office. Their gazes locked.

"What are you doing here?" he demanded.

She straightened. "I'm doing my job as a reporter. Is it—" She craned her neck to get a view inside, but he blocked the doorway.

"Miss Strong, are you—" Benjamin's question trailed off as he jogged around the corner and came to her side. "There you are." She felt the light pressure of his hand against the small of her back, and she didn't pull away.

Zimmer's gaze flicked to Benjamin and then to Sophie, his mouth tight. "This is a crime scene."

Sophie brushed past him and moved closer to Mr. Pitman's doorway. On the floor, polished black-and-white shoes pointed upward at inelegant angles from terribly still legs.

"Oh!" She knew it had to be Mr. Pitman, but her fingers still flew to her lips.

She took another step closer to the office and captured the

scene with camera eyes. A dark blood stain across his chest marred the usually impeccable suit coat. His arms lay open at his sides, as if ready for a final embrace, the palms limp. His mouth was slack, his eyelids half-closed over a blank stare. One of the wooden chairs had been knocked over, and the green-shaded lamp shade had shattered on the floor. Papers and files were strewn about.

"Another gunshot wound," Zimmer said, moving to stand next to her.

"Did anyone see anything?"

He shook his head. "This corner of the building was empty. The janitor called the station. He was just starting to clean this area when he found the body."

Sophie felt a pang of empathy for Mr. Watson and wondered where he was now. Surely he hadn't returned to his duties after talking to the police? She kept her eyes on the disordered room, though Mr. Pitman's corpse loomed at the periphery of her vision.

"It had to be the same person who shot Hilda Rock," she said.

He pursed his lips. "That's our guess, but nothing is certain."

"I think it was Thelma Wolff."

He frowned. "Mrs. Wolff? How would she even know someone like Alonzo Pitman?" He gestured toward the small office, so crude compared to the Wolff finery.

"Maybe he knew something. Maybe he was here when she shot Hilda Rock."

"We don't know she did *anything* to Hilda Rock," Zimmer said. "In fact, your suffrage friend looks a lot guiltier than Thelma Wolff, who was busy hosting an enormous party when Mrs. Rock was killed. Clara Elliot doesn't have the strongest alibi, remember?"

"Thelma Wolff could have—"

Zimmer held up a hand. "Please. Leave the deductions to the police. You can report that Alonzo Pitman was killed sometime last night by a gunshot wound to the chest."

Benjamin had been listening attentively at Sophie's side.

"You knew him?" he asked her. She nodded.

"You a reporter too?" Zimmer asked him.

"Yes, sir. Is this linked to the earlier murder? Mrs. Hilda Rock?" Benjamin pulled a notebook from his jacket pocket.

"As I said, nothing is certain. We've only begun to investigate."

"Detective Zimmer, this is Benjamin Turner of the *Herald*," Sophie said.

Benjamin stuck out his hand to shake, but Zimmer ignored it.

"We have no more details for the press at this time," he told them. He nodded to Sophie. "Good day, Miss Strong, Mr. Turner."

Zimmer turned on his heel and went back into Pitman's office. She heard him speak harshly to someone inside, and two officers appeared at the doorway, blocking it entirely.

"You'll have to move on, folks," one of them said.

"We just have a few questions—" Benjamin began.

The other officer shook his head. "No comment."

Benjamin nudged Sophie. "Come on, let's talk to some of the other people on this floor."

Sophie cast one more glance at the scene before she turned and followed Benjamin back the way they had come.

SOPHIE AND BENJAMIN split up to visit the twenty-four occupied offices on the second floor. The suffrage office was closed, of course, along with a few others that had presumably been shut to avoid the commotion. Half a dozen offices appeared to be empty and available to rent. No one had seen or heard anything of note, having arrived that morning to find the police already on the scene. A few curious souls nosed around the corridors, but most had gone back to their work. Sophie didn't see Mr. Watson, and a quick scan of the third floor revealed he wasn't there, either. She wondered if he'd gone home for the day to recover from the shock.

Several other male reporters arrived, recognizable by their notebooks and observant gazes, and a few of them retraced Benjamin's and Sophie's paths. She noticed Benjamin chatting amiably with one of them.

Sophie's feet ached and her bruises throbbed after a steady hour of walking around the second floor, knocking on doors and making inquiries. She caught Benjamin glancing at her curiously a couple of times and hoped Vivian's makeup hadn't worn off. When she slipped into the ladies' lounge on the first floor to freshen up, she was relieved to see that her face still looked composed. She pulled Vivian's compact out of her bag and dabbed on some powder, then tucked it away when another lady entered the lounge.

She found Benjamin near the front entrance of the building.

"Any luck, Miss Strong?"

She shook her head. "Nobody saw or heard a thing. That means it must have happened late last night."

"Or very early this morning."

"I suppose so."

"How well did you know him?"

"Not terribly well. I spoke to him in passing." She decided he didn't need to know about her previous questioning of Mr. Pitman.

"Shall we head back to the office? Or do you want to slip away to a fashion show?" He grinned.

She rolled her eyes. "The office is fine." She hoped he wouldn't suggest walking.

"I'll get another cab," he offered, holding the door for her as she gave him a thankful smile.

SOPHIE WALKED into the newsroom to discover Mr. Barnaby standing at her desk, looking over the tops of his glasses at the copy stacked neatly in one corner.

"Miss Strong," he said, glancing up. "I was surprised I didn't see your copy on my desk, so I came in search of it. I had expected, of course, to find you here as well."

"Mr. Barnaby," she said, reaching up to unpin her hat. "I was following a lead."

He crossed his arms. "A lead? I wasn't aware you had any new assignments."

"There was another killing at the Majestic Building."

"Not your assignment, Miss Strong."

Benjamin breezed in before Sophie could answer.

"Thanks for your help with that concert ticket, Miss Strong," he said.

Sophie blinked, unsure how to respond. "Um—you're welcome."

He turned to Barnaby. "The Wolffs are attending a charity concert tomorrow night, and I want to be there for my other story. Miss Strong helped me wrangle a ticket."

"What does that have to do with this new murder?" asked Mr. Barnaby.

"Miss Strong's contact was in the Majestic Building, so I asked her to go with me. We thought our access would be cut off if we didn't act fast."

Mr. Barnaby sighed. "Write it up, Turner. We've got a paper to get out." He headed back to his office. "And get the rest of your copy in, Miss Strong," he called over his shoulder.

Sophie looked at Benjamin. "I don't need you to cover for me, Mr. Turner."

He smiled. "But it can't hurt, right?"

"I'd heard about that concert. Are you sure the Wolffs will attend?"

"I have my sources."

"Well, I don't have a ticket. Are you really going?"

"I am. I only have one, though. You'll have to find another date."

She rolled her eyes at his insinuation that she was interested in his companionship. Another reporter chose that unfortunate moment to walk past them.

"Oh ho!" he exclaimed. "Miss Strong is consenting to step out with our own Mr. Turner?"

"I'm not stepping out with anyone," Sophie said, wishing her cheeks weren't flushing with embarrassment.

The idea, however, caused her to frown thoughtfully. All the movers and shakers in Milwaukee society would be gathered in one place. If she could go, she might have a chance to speak to Thelma or Ruben Wolff, or to someone else who could fill in some of the blanks in the case.

"I've seen that look, Miss Strong," said Benjamin. "Relax, it's one concert. I've got it covered."

"Wouldn't you rather be at a baseball game or something?

"Sure." He shrugged. "But I've got to keep my eye on these beer barons too. You're not the only one following a lead."

OVER A DELICIOUS DINNER of glazed ham at Clara's house, Sophie lamented missing the upcoming concert.

"Thelma and Ruben Wolff will be there for *hours* on Friday night, away from the mansion. It could give me an excellent chance to question them."

"*If* they would talk to you," put in Aunt Lucy. "At least they couldn't throw you out of a public concert, like they can their own home."

"Or I could eavesdrop." Sophie sighed. "I just have this nagging feeling I'm missing an opportunity."

"It's too bad you can't attend," said Clara. "But I can't think of anyone who would have an extra ticket."

Sophie stared at the velvety slab of devil's food cake that Ellen, the housekeeper, had just placed in front of her.

"They won't be home," she said slowly, as a thought hit her.

"Yes," said Aunt Lucy. "We've established that."

Sophie sat up straight, her eyes wide. "*That's* the opportunity. I'll go to the mansion." She sank her fork into the rich layers, then savored the sweetness as the cake melted on her tongue.

"What good will that do?" asked Clara. "Surely the servants would turn you away."

"Maybe not," said Sophie. "There's one person who might talk to me."

30

S ophie dressed in her oldest frock and pulled a drooping straw hat low over her face. She'd borrowed a marketing basket from Mrs. O'Day. Thankful that Vivian wasn't around to comment on her shabby appearance, she slipped out the door and headed for Wolff Mansion. As it loomed into view, she slowed her usual speedy steps. The sheer beauty of the towering structure again impressed her. How could someone live among so much grandeur and still have Thelma Wolff's stony heart?

Sophie slowed her walk down Grand Avenue, then turned onto Sixteenth Street. She kept her head down, but from the corner of her eye she caught several servants exiting the house. With a pang of worry, she prayed Brigid wouldn't be among them. It hadn't occurred to her that the Wolffs might dismiss their staff for the evening. She paused at the street corner, looked up thoughtfully for a moment, then gave a decisive nod as if she'd forgotten something, and retraced her steps. She wasn't sure who she was performing this melodrama for, but hoped she appeared inconspicuous doing it.

Sophie walked leisurely past the side of the mansion, then

turned back onto Grand Avenue. At the end of the long block, she rounded the corner, took a few more steps north, then turned and headed back to the house once more. This time as she passed, the Wolffs' chauffeur looked up from polishing the silver-plated woman in billowing robes that ornamented the hood of the Rolls Royce. Sophie kept her head bowed, focusing on her feet.

When she reached the corner, her resolve wavered. How many times could she traipse back and forth before someone reported her to the police? She imagined the humiliation of facing Jacob Zimmer and explaining what she was up to. She'd begun to consider giving up when she heard a motor and peered hopefully at the mansion. Were the Wolffs leaving for the concert at last? Her heart sank when a delivery truck emerged from the back of the house. What if they'd decided not to go after all?

Just then, the gleaming black automobile rolled out of the driveway. Sophie ducked behind a large shrub that almost hid her completely. The chauffeur glanced in her direction, but Sophie didn't think he noticed her. She glimpsed two figures in the back seat before the car turned onto Grand Avenue and disappeared. Two more servants emerged from the kitchen door, chatting animatedly. She crouched among the leaves, trying to make herself even smaller. She recognized the cook and housekeeper, but they walked by, oblivious to her.

It was now or never. She ran up driveway to the kitchen door, hoping Brigid was still inside.

Sophie was debating whether to knock or just enter when the door opened to reveal Brigid, pinning her straw hat in place. She let out a yelp when she saw Sophie.

"Miss Sophie? What are you doing here?"

"I need to talk to you."

"Me? Why?"

"I'm investigating a murder."

Brigid's eyes grew wide. Then she frowned. "You'll have to come back when the Wolffs are here. I can't be seen talking to you. Mrs. Harding warned us."

"Please, Brigid. I can't come when the Wolffs are here."

Brigid gazed at her, unmoved. Sophie realized she must convey the seriousness of the situation in order to convince her.

"I think Mrs. Wolff is a killer."

Brigid went pale. Sophie heard the buzz of conversation approaching, and Brigid bit her lip.

"Go over there," she whispered to Sophie, waving her toward a potting shed. "Don't let them see you."

"Coming, Bridge?" someone said. Two girls who looked to be about Brigid's age appeared in the doorway.

"We've got a whole five hours," one of them said. "We could see a show *and* shop at Gimbels."

Brigid hesitated. "I-I left something upstairs. You girls go ahead. I'll meet you there."

"Are you sure? We can wait."

"No, you go on. I'll be right behind you."

When they were gone, Brigid waved Sophie back over. "Now, what's this about Mrs. Wolff?" she whispered.

"I think she killed Hilda Rock. Did you hear about her? She got shot in the Majestic Building."

"Of course I heard, but—how can you say such a thing about Mrs. Wolff?"

Sophie didn't want to reveal any more than necessary. "They have an old rivalry. Please, just give me a few minutes."

Brigid frowned more deeply, then tugged Sophie inside and led her to the servants' hall. The room was empty, so they sat at the long wooden table.

Sophie pulled out the notebook she'd stashed in her basket and flipped it open.

"It happened the night of the Spring Gala," she said. "I think she planned it that way, so she'd have an alibi."

"A what?"

"An excuse, to prove she couldn't have done it. She can say she was hosting this huge party."

"That's the truth."

"I think she slipped away for a while, though. Now, when you and I met in the garden, do you remember what time it was?" Brigid's face flushed, probably at the memory of her attack. "I'm sorry to mention it, but this is important."

The girl knit her brows, as if recalling the altercation with Mr. Davis. "Well, the supper was to be at eleven. I had just helped put out the food when—when he took me out to the garden. It would have been... maybe a quarter of eleven?"

"And what about when you were setting up? Did you see Mrs. Wolff anywhere?"

"We were run off our feet that night," she said. "But I think I saw Mrs. Wolff talking to Mrs. Harding in the doorway. Mrs. Wolff had that beautiful crown on. I remember noticing it."

"Okay, so she was here then. What about before that? You were serving trays of appetizers to the guests. Did you see her then? Maybe between nine-thirty and ten-thirty?"

Brigid gnawed on a fingernail. "There were so many people. And all of those costumes. Let me think." She paused, then recalled, "I was assigned to the side of the ballroom closest to the entrance. I made a few trips back to the kitchen for fresh trays. But I don't remember seeing her then."

Sophie felt a prickle of hope in her chest. "Mrs. Wolff could have snuck away to the Majestic Building, shot Hilda Rock, and returned in time to be seen in the supper room."

Brigid's eyes were wide. "You really think she'd do that? How would she have gotten there?"

"It's close enough to walk."

"In that gown?"

Sophie grimaced. "No, she'd have had to take it off, put on something else, then get back into it."

"She couldn't do that without help."

"But would her maid have helped her? Without asking questions?"

Brigid considered this for a moment, then nodded. "Ida would do anything for Mrs. Wolff. And she never tells tales. But there were so many people here. Just because I didn't see Mrs. Wolff doesn't mean she left."

Sophie had to admit this was true. It had been too much to hope for that Brigid might have seen something suspicious enough to carry any weight with the police—like Thelma Wolff creeping off into the night, holding a pistol.

She smacked her hand down on the table. "Damn it! She can't get away with this, just because she's richer than Croesus."

"Who's that now?"

"Never mind."

Sophie slouched, sinking into gloomy silence. There had to be a way to convince Detective Zimmer to investigate the Wolffs.

"There must be some kind of evidence," Sophie mused. "A letter someone wrote, or notes in a diary, or even an appointment book. If I had something like that, the police would have to believe me."

"But how would you get it?"

Sophie let a silence stretch out.

Then Brigid shook her head decisively. "No. You can't go snooping around. I'd lose my job."

Sophie grasped her hand. "Please, Brigid. No one will know it was you. Mr. and Mrs. Wolff are both gone. I saw them leave. And it looks like most of the staff is out, too."

Brigid shook her head again.

Sophie tightened her grip on Brigid's hand and leaned closer. "If you're working for a murderer, don't you want to know?"

The girl searched Sophie's face uncertainly. As the seconds ticked by, Sophie prayed she would bend.

"You have to be quick," Brigid finally said. "The girls will wonder where I am."

"You go ahead. I'll slip into Mrs. Wolff's room and right back out again. I'll lock the kitchen door behind me. No one will ever know."

Brigid blinked rapidly, and Sophie feared she might be wavering.

"I'll only be here about fifteen minutes," Sophie insisted. "Go join your friends."

Brigid finally gave a small, hesitant nod.

"May I borrow a cap and apron? Just in case there's someone around to see me."

Her eyes looked fearful, but Brigid only said, "On the hook by the door." Then she stood. "Be sure to lock up when you go."

"I will. I promise."

With another wary glance over her shoulder, Brigid scurried off.

Sophie let out a sigh of relief and stepped into the kitchen. She found the cap and apron where Brigid said they'd be. Leaving her hat and coat on the hook in their place, she tied on the apron and rested the white mob cap on her head. It felt like a costume, though eons removed from the ensemble she'd worn a couple of weeks ago.

Her heart pounded as she crept up the stairs. At the top, she put her ear to the green baize door, but heard nothing. She paused. She could still slip out of the house and leave the investigating to the police. But then she remembered the punches and kicks in the alley. She was onto something. She had to see it through.

Sophie started in Mrs. Wolff's sitting room, where they had met the day before the party. She flipped through the books on the side table—history and poetry. Not surprising that a confidential diary hadn't been left lying around. She reached under the cushions of the chairs and love seat. Nothing. She tiptoed out into the hall and looked up the stairs. Did she dare search for Mrs. Wolff's bedroom? It could be behind any of twenty or thirty doors.

This whole thing was a fool's errand, she thought. How would she possibly locate a tiny piece of evidence in such a vast mansion?

She glanced down the hallway. What about the library? It seemed to be Mr. Wolff's domain, but she remembered seeing a few feminine touches when she had wandered in on a previous visit. She ventured down the hall, hoping she wouldn't get lost this time.

She passed a few closed doors and began to wonder if she was heading in the wrong direction. Then she saw a sitting room with a semi-circle of leather chairs and a broad window facing the back garden. That looked familiar. Next to it, an open door revealed tall bookshelves filled with leather volumes.

She entered and scanned the perimeter. Heavy damask curtains were drawn, shrouding the tall windows and giving the room a stifling gloom. She quickly fanned the pages of the books resting on tables. She felt under the cushions of chairs. No luck. She trailed her hand along rows of volumes, looking for anything unusual. Everything seemed in perfect order. She remembered the framed silk ladies' edition of the newspaper, went over to it, and pulled the frame off of the wall to see if anything was secured to the back. Nothing. She replaced it and looked around.

If only she could find something incriminating that connected Thelma and Hilda—a threatening note, or maybe a suspicious journal entry—Zimmer would have to question Mrs. Wolff. Surely he only needed a nudge in the right direction. Then she'd happily relinquish the detective work and let him ferret out the truth. He seemed too smart to let Thelma Wolff slip through his fingers.

She went to the fireplace and felt along the marble mantle, hoping for a hidden latch that would reveal a secret compartment or a door to a mysterious passage, while chiding herself for reading too many detective stories.

Then in the corner, she noticed that the last bookshelf in the row didn't meet the back wall. Tucked behind it was a nook she hadn't perceived before, facing the curtained window. She hurried over and peered around the corner to find a large mahogany desk with a tall leather chair. Papers, letters, and ledgers stood neatly stacked on its gleaming surface.

Her heart beating wildly, Sophie rapidly flipped through the papers, careful to return everything to its proper place after she'd scanned it. She found dull business correspondence, invoices, and reports—this looked like Mr. Wolff's domain. She opened a skin-bound volume that had a date at the top of each page, terse notes scrawled below it. As she squinted at the abbreviations, she realized that *Wo Cl* could stand for the Women's Club. *T-Harp* might refer to a tea party at the Harper home. This book could be Thelma's. But what was it doing on Mr. Wolff's desk? Had he borrowed it for some reason?

She turned to Saturday, May 4, the day of the Spring Gala. The page had notes suggesting deliveries, but those weren't suspicious. She fanned through the rest of the pages and spied nothing of interest.

The unmistakable sound of a door opening in the distance

jolted Sophie to the core. Her stomach roiled as the strident voice of Thelma Wolff carried down the empty hall. "I can't believe you forgot them."

"You didn't remind me," her husband snapped.

Footsteps headed in her direction, and Sophie froze. Her eyes darted frantically around the room. She spotted a door on the opposite wall, its knob placed high, surrounded by elegant carving. Could she get there in time?

The footsteps drew closer. She had to move fast. Crouch under the desk? Too easy to get caught. She heard the click of the library doorknob turning. She dashed behind one of the long curtains, arranging its folds to cover her shoes and praying she was well concealed.

31

———

Sophie heard heavy footsteps enter the library, then move toward the alcove, where she hid behind the curtain. She smelled cigar smoke, hair pomade, and a cloying men's cologne. Ruben Wolff muttered under his breath. Sophie didn't dare peek out, but she sensed him entering the alcove, so close that she tried not to breathe. She heard the rustling of papers on the desk's surface and the scrape of drawers being opened, followed by impatient rummaging. He uttered a curse.

"Did you find it?" Thelma's strident voice cut in. Ruben didn't answer. "Ruben, did you hear me?" He grumbled, and she sniffed in annoyance.

Thelma's footsteps came into the alcove. Sophie heard her annoyed sigh and smelled her sandalwood perfume. The woman's presence on the other side of the curtain was palpable. Sophie willed them to find what they were looking for and leave.

Suddenly, the curtain jerked aside. Sophie gasped, horrified, as she met Thelma Wolff's icy glare. A chill crawled up her spine.

"What the hell?" Ruben said. Sophie was too paralyzed to look in his direction.

"What are you doing here?" Thelma hissed. "Stealing?" Her blue eyes were hateful slits.

Sophie's voice stuck in her throat.

"Well? Speak up!"

"No, ma'am. I-I—" She kicked herself for not thinking up a cover story. It was a basic rule of detective work. "I wanted to look at-at the charity edition of the *Herald*." She gestured toward the framed front page near the door with a shaking hand. "I didn't think you'd let me in."

"You are correct about that. You stupid girl."

Sophie's heart thumped hard in her chest, and sweat broke out on her back. Only Brigid knew where she was. She had no idea if anyone else was in the house. And she was face-to-face with a cold-blooded killer.

"Is that... the newspaper girl?" Ruben asked.

"Miss Sophie Strong," said Thelma. "A nosy little tramp. I should never have let you enter our home."

Thelma grabbed her arm and yanked her away from the window, her nails digging painfully into Sophie's skin.

"Miss Strong is leaving," she said.

A tiny flicker of hope stirred in Sophie's chest. Was it possible they might let her go?

"What is she doing here?" Ruben demanded.

"I-I was just—" Sophie stammered.

Thelma's gaze raked down Sophie's front, taking in the shabby dress and white apron. "She apparently visited one of the maids and decided to inspect our library. I'll fire whoever it was first thing in the morning."

"No, I—no one helped me."

Thelma smirked. "We'll see about that."

Thelma's nails dug in deeper as she turned to Ruben. "We

won't call the police. Rumors are still flying about the Spring Gala, and we don't need any more scandal."

"Certainly not."

Sophie swallowed. "Please, I didn't do any harm. I'll just go—"

"I'll deal with her," said Thelma to her husband. She glared at Sophie, then pulled her to the library door and out into the hall.

Sophie stumbled, her feet numb. Did Thelma have a gun in her beaded handbag? Would she shoot Sophie, as she had done to Hilda Rock and Alonzo Pitman? As Thelma hurried her down the hall, Sophie tried to pull her arm free, but Thelma pinched it tightly.

To Sophie's relief, Ruben followed them. Surely Thelma wouldn't murder her in front of her husband.

"Did you find what you needed?" Thelma snapped at Ruben.

"Actually, no."

Thelma halted. "What? Why aren't you searching for it?"

"You've been looking forward to this concert, and I don't want you to miss it. Have Davis take you. I need to go through some files."

Thelma looked at her husband with pure hatred. She looked back at Sophie, her eyes traveling up and down her slim form, lingering at her bosom. Her mouth turned downward in a bitter grimace.

Then she shoved Sophie hard in Ruben's direction. "I bet you do," she spat out, as Sophie staggered toward him. "You beast."

Sophie understood Thelma's implication, but her shoulders relaxed when Ruben caught her elbow. He had been unfailingly considerate toward her. She watched Thelma flounce toward the foyer. The front door opened and slammed shut.

Sophie swallowed and turned to look up at Mr. Wolff. "I'm so sorry, Mr. Wolff," she said, pulling her arm out of his grip. "I've been unprofessional."

"Oh, never mind that now," he said good-naturedly.

Sophie heard the automobile drive away.

"Thank you for understanding," she said. "I promise, I won't bother you again." She headed for the front door.

Sudden pain shot through her right arm as Ruben Wolff yanked it behind her back and twisted upward. She cried out, and tears sprang to her eyes. Her mind raced in a panicked jumble. What was happening? Ruben kept her arm pinned behind her and pushed her against the wall with his left hand. She looked into his face. His eyes were dark with fury, his mouth a cold, bloodless line.

"You don't know when to quit, do you?"

"What? I-I don't know what you mean." She winced as his left hand slid up to her throat and squeezed hard.

"I tried to warn you off. I sent Davis to persuade you a few nights ago. But here you are, nosing around again."

Sophie blinked. Davis? The chauffeur? She stared at Ruben, her mind working through the possibilities.

He laughed mirthlessly. "You look confused. Do you *really* not know what you've gotten yourself into? I almost feel sorry for you."

Her mouth went dry. "*You* killed Hilda Rock."

"And you won't live to tell a soul," he said. He leered at her chest. "Maybe I'll have a little fun while I wait for Davis to come back and finish you off."

Sophie went cold. She tried to pull herself out of his grip, but he held her fast. She kicked out, but he dodged the blow. He jerked her away from the wall and pushed her in front of him, keeping her right arm pinned behind her. It throbbed terribly.

"You wanted to inspect the library. Here's your chance."

She dragged her feet, trying to slow their progress down the marble-tiled hallway, but he overpowered her, pushing her forward easily.

"Help! Help me!" she cried.

"You're wasting your breath. There's no one here."

He shoved her through the library door, and she tumbled to the floor. She tried to scramble to her feet, but before she was fully upright, new pain seared across her scalp. Ruben grabbed her by the hair and shoved her backward onto the sofa, his left hand gripping her throat.

Sophie squeezed her eyes shut. She was going to die. She wished he'd just shoot her.

The loud rap of the knocker hitting the front door echoed down the hallway. Wolff glanced up.

"Now what?" he muttered.

The moment he turned his head, Sophie wrenched her left arm upward and clawed at his face, aiming for the eyes. Her fingernails tore into his flesh.

"Bitch!" He slapped her face, and pain exploded across her jaw, still sore from her vicious encounter with the thug she now knew had been Mr. Davis. Tears streamed down her cheeks. The knocking sounded again.

"I should kill you now," he growled, squeezing her throat.

Her vision blurred, but she could make out three red lines down the side of his cheek, glistening with blood.

The knocker sounded a third time, followed by rapping knuckles.

"Mr. Wolff? Mrs. Wolff?" a male voice called.

"Help!" she cried. "Help me!"

He swore and slapped her again. She felt her lip split and tasted blood. Then he reached into his pocket and pulled out a handkerchief. He stuffed it into her mouth, making her gag.

Ruben jerked Sophie to her feet and pulled both arms behind her back. The right one throbbed. Over her shoulder she saw him tug off his necktie. He wrapped the silk fabric around her wrists and knotted it tightly. She whimpered as pain seared through her arm.

He pushed her toward the far wall. Sophie's mind raced. What was he going to do? How could she get away? She tried to twist out of his grip, but he was too strong. He wrenched open the door with the high knob that she'd seen earlier. It was a narrow, dark closet, with crates of books pushed against the back wall. He shoved her inside, and she fell to the floor, landing painfully on her right arm. The door slammed, and the little remaining light disappeared.

The insistent knocking sounded again. "I'm coming!" Ruben called. Sophie heard his departing footsteps.

The walls of the tiny closet seemed to close in on Sophie. She tugged at the bonds around her wrists, but they only tightened. She had to get out. Whoever had knocked at the door was her only hope.

Through the wall, she heard Ruben Wolff's voice carry down the hallway. "Right this way, Detective Zimmer," he said.

Zimmer? Sophie felt a glimmer of hope. He was here. He would save her. Was Wolff bringing him into the library? Though there was barely room to maneuver, she rolled onto her good arm until her back was against the side wall. By pulling her legs up to her chest, she was able to brace her feet against the other side of the closet and sit up. She thumped the soles of her shoes on the floor three times. Then she did it again. He had to hear her. He *had* to.

The voices didn't come any closer. They must be in the sitting room next to the library, she thought. She heard Jacob Zimmer's voice, and a flush of a warmth bubbled inside her. The sound was muffled, but she heard him say "Pitman."

She smacked her feet against the floor again. And again.

Tears of frustration sprang to her eyes. It was hopeless.

With the mansion's thick walls, there was no way he'd hear her, even though he was right in the next room. She squeezed her knees underneath her again, then lurched forward and rocked to her feet, trying to ignore the shooting pain in her arm. It *must* be broken.

She forced the thought from her mind.

Sophie put her back to the door. She pushed her weight against it, hoping it somehow hadn't latched properly. But it held fast. She fought a wave of despair. She tried to grasp the doorknob, but it was positioned too high. Her broken arm was in misery. She got on her tiptoes and stretched her fingers upward behind her. They managed to just touch the doorknob, then slid off, her hands slick with sweat. She swore and tried again.

She heard the calm tones of the men's voices, as if they were exchanging pleasantries. The sounds grew fainter and farther away.

No! She screamed silently. *Jacob, don't go! Help!*

With a frantic thrust she reached upward, grabbed the doorknob, and twisted, throwing her weight against the door. It opened! She staggered out of the closet and fell to her knees.

There was silence in the hallway. Had they heard her? She tried to yell, but with the gag in her mouth, she could only muster a pathetic groan. She heard the front door slam shut. Anguish engulfed her, and new tears fell. She pulled herself to her feet and prayed Zimmer would inspect the perimeter of the house and see her through the window.

The library door burst open. Ruben looked down at her with an ugly grimace. This time he pointed a gun at her.

"Well, what have we here?" he sneered. "I was just talking to that nice police officer. Apparently another unlucky sap got himself killed. But I don't know a thing about that. I have an alibi. I always have an alibi, Sophie Strong. You can bet on that."

He looked her up and down. "You're not much to look at, are you?" he said. "Davis!" he yelled over his shoulder.

The chauffeur came into the room. He was the same man who had attacked Brigid in the garden on that long-ago evening.

"Help me get this tramp in the car," Ruben said. "We're going for a ride. I'll just make sure she doesn't cause any trouble on the way."

He raised one arm, and Sophie saw the solid grip of his weapon moving toward her temple before she lost consciousness.

32

———

Sophie saw only black through the car window. Her head and arms throbbed. She was sprawled across the rear seat, her wrists bound tighter than ever. A surge of panic rushed through her. She tugged at the bonds, but they didn't budge. No longer choking on a handkerchief, she tasted dirt and what felt like a thick rope cutting into the sides of her mouth. Her brain raced through scenarios for escape. At least her feet were free. She closed her eyes and lay still, waiting.

The car slowed, took several sharp turns, then came to a halt. The engine died, and the door at her feet opened. Barely lifting her lids, she made out Davis through her lashes. He reached for her and she kicked out fiercely, aiming for his face.

"Oof!"

She connected with the underside of his chin, and he stumbled backward. Sophie lurched her body upright, scooted out of the car, and felt relief when her feet hit solid ground. But she wasn't fast enough. Davis found his balance and gripped her right arm tightly in one gloved hand.

"Bitch," he spit out. He smacked her face, and Sophie's

head jerked back. Davis tugged her throbbing arm and forced her to stumble ahead of him.

"Easy, Davis," said Ruben. "She's not going anywhere. Ever."

A fresh wave of fear ripped through her. She was going to die at the hands of these monsters. Wolff had shot Hilda Rock and Alonzo Pitman. How many other lives had he snuffed out?

In the darkness, she peered at her surroundings, trying to orient herself. She smelled the rich scent of overturned earth and saw a gigantic pit stretching out in front of them, about four feet deep. Next to a shed stood an abandoned wheelbarrow with a few shovels resting inside. A tall fence loomed in the distance.

They were in Wolff Park, now eerily deserted. This must be the area under construction, Sophie thought. She remembered the cheerful sign promising a future "Splash Ride."

Davis pushed her, and she stumbled toward the pit, nearly falling over the edge. Then her head jerked back painfully as he caught a handful of her hair, which had long since tumbled from its knot.

"Not so fast," said Wolff. "I want to enjoy this."

Sophie's stomach recoiled at the oily malice in his voice. His jolly persona as the benevolent ruler of his kingdom had been a facade. He was even more ruthless than Zimmer had predicted.

He jerked her around to face him, eyes glowing with hostility.

"I tried to warn you," he said. "But you kept snooping where you don't belong. Now you've learned your lesson, but it's too late." He shook his head in mock sorrow. "You won't have time to put your hard-won wisdom into practice. You'll be cold and dead in the ground."

She glared at him. He reached forward to pull down the

rope that gagged her. The instant her mouth was free, she sank her teeth into his hand.

"Ouch!" he said. Then he chuckled. "You're a feisty little piece, aren't you?"

"Why did you do it?" Sophie's voice was hoarse with exhaustion and dread. If this was the end of her life, at least she wanted answers.

"Get rid of Hilda Rock, you mean? She got greedy and demanded more money. She threatened to go to the papers with her story about how I cheated her husband out of his brewery. I can't afford for the public to hear about that. I've worked too hard to let a cheap piece of trash ruin my business."

"She jeopardized your empire, and you took her life?"

He shrugged. "The business world isn't always pretty."

"And Mr. Pitman? You shot him, too?"

"That weasel… I paid him a good salary, but it wasn't enough. Greed gets people into trouble." He seemed oblivious of the fact that his own lust for money and power was ugliest of all.

"And you." He jabbed a finger in her face. "You could have done all right. A few years writing your little stories, then marry a nice boy and have a few brats. The business world is no place for a girl."

Sophie heard a scrape on the gravel behind her. Was someone else here? Someone who could save her? A raccoon skittered by, racing toward a trash barrel. Her heart fell. The faces of Aunt Lucy, Clara, Sam, and Harry flashed into her mind as she envisioned them learning of her demise. Somehow, she felt the worst for Sam. Sam needed her most. Maybe if Sophie had tried harder to find Sam and spent less time digging into Wolff's crimes, she wouldn't be facing her death. Would Zimmer try to solve the case and bring Wolff to justice? Or would pursuing the powerful man only endanger his career?

Ruben Wolff smacked his hands together with the air of someone eager to start a new project. "Well, enough talk. Good-bye, Sophie Strong. Davis, you know what to do." Wolff stepped back, as if to watch a pleasant display unfold before him.

Davis released her briefly and came at her head with a rough burlap sack. She panicked and backed away, but he advanced with a wicked grin.

Thunk! A rock thudded into his temple. Davis cried out in pain, one hand reaching for a spot already glistening with blood. Sophie took advantage of his confusion. She ducked her head and rammed into his torso with all her might. He stumbled backward, his arms flailing as he lost his balance and fell into the pit.

Wolff reached for his gun just as a good-sized rock smacked into his forehead. His head jerked as he let out a curse. A second rock flew into his eye, eliciting another cry of pain.

Sophie saw Davis struggle to his feet in the freshly dug pit. He moved toward the edge, glaring up at her. As soon as he was in range, Sophie lifted her leg and drove her foot into the side of his face with all the force she could muster. He fell backward again.

Suddenly a short figure ran into view, heading straight for Wolff.

"Sam! No!" Sophie cried. Wolff's head was down, his hands at his bleeding face, but he still had a gun.

Sam ignored her. With a primal yell, she plowed into Wolff. He was twice her weight, but the force of her motion and his preoccupation with his injury caught him off guard. He fell to the ground on his side, with an astonished cry. Sam sent a flurry of fierce kicks into the man's throat, then drove her booted foot right into his face. Sophie heard a crunch of breaking bone, and Wolff screamed. Sam gave a powerful kick to the soft flesh at his groin. He gurgled in misery.

Sam ran to Sophie. "Are you okay?" she cried. "Can you run?"

"Untie me!" Sophie said, turning to show her the bonds at her wrists. Davis was staggering to his feet in the pit.

Sam pulled out her pocket knife and sawed at the rope with shaking hands, nicking Sophie's wrist with the blade. Sophie could hear Davis moving toward them. When Sam had cut enough rope to loosen the knots, Sophie wrenched her hands free.

"Come on!" she yelled.

As they ran past the parked car, Sophie cursed herself for not having learned to drive. They tore across the grass toward the giant fence, and Sophie frantically searched for a way to get past it. She risked a look over her shoulder and saw Davis, limping and covered with dirt, but advancing rapidly. As they neared the fence, Sophie spotted a gate that was still ajar.

"This way!" she called to Sam.

She dodged through the opening and ran across the grass, glancing back to make sure Sam was following. The area was littered with wagons, crates, and other detritus, a few tents pitched here and there. She navigated the obstacles, hoping Davis would lose sight of them or trip and fall.

Sophie heard a scream behind her. She turned to see Sam squirming to free herself, with Davis's arm hooked around her neck.

"Sophie, run!" Sam cried. Her face twisted in pain as Davis tightened his hold.

But Sophie slowed and stopped, her breath coming in painful gasps, her corset a vice around her ribs. She caught the flash of a knife blade in Davis's hand.

"I'll kill him!" Davis yelled.

Sophie prayed he wouldn't discern Sam's true identity in the softness of her chest. That would only make her more vulnerable. Seeing Sam so helpless twisted Sophie's heart.

"Let h-him go!" she called. "I surrender!"

Sophie yelped as Wolff emerged from behind a tent and strode over to her, his face streaked with his own blood, his gun aimed in her direction.

"Little bitch," he growled. "We'll kill you both." He pressed the cold, hard steel into in her side.

"You won't get away with it," Sophie said. "Here at your own park? The police will be after you in a flash."

He laughed. "The police can't touch me. But they won't find your body. It'll be like you vanished into thin air."

She swallowed, not letting herself imagine what he had planned.

"Let the boy go," she pleaded. "He's innocent. He's just a kid."

Wolff leered at her. "Like him, do you?" He stroked Sophie's cheek with one hand, and her stomach clenched. "Perhaps I could be persuaded to go easy on him."

"Let... him... go," Sophie said through gritted teeth.

She heard scuffling as Sam struggled with Davis, then the smack of a fist hitting flesh. Sam made a choking sound, and Davis punched again. Sam went silent.

Wolff pushed Sophie against the side of a wagon, holding her wrists in one hand. In her terror, she was no longer conscious of the pain in her arms. He stuffed the gun into the back waistband of his trousers, then snatched the fabric at her throat and ripped downward, exposing her nearly transparent chemise. He grinned as her chest heaved with fright.

"Police! Drop your weapons!"

A startled Wolff looked in the direction of the shout.

Relief coursed through Sophie as Jacob Zimmer came into view in the moonlight, his gun aimed at Wolff.

"You're under arrest!" Zimmer shouted. "We've got you surrounded, Wolff."

"Do you now?" Wolff said. "Funny, I only see one of you. It's Detective Zimmer, isn't it? I sent you away once already tonight."

"I didn't believe a word you said, you lying piece of filth." Zimmer's voice was cold with fury. His eyes flickered to Sophie's and then back to Wolff.

Wolff reached back to retrieve his gun, his eyes on Zimmer. In the instant that his grip loosened slightly, Sophie pulled one knee up hard between his legs. He made a grunt of pain but didn't release her. He aimed the revolver at Zimmer.

Sophie marshaled all the fury and horror coursing through her veins. She dug her feet into the ground, and with a savage cry, she twisted her body fiercely. A loud crack came from her forearm, but she didn't pause. She drove her head into Wolff's throat, and he stumbled off balance. His gun went off.

Jacob Zimmer fell.

"No!" Sophie cried.

She threw her body into Wolff's, knocking him to the ground and tumbling down at his side. The gun flew out of his hand. Sophie scrambled to her feet. She felt him grab for her ankle, but she brought her foot down hard on his wrist, and he howled in pain. She kicked him in the neck, then in the soft underside of his jaw, her mind a red ball of fury as she connected with his flesh.

"Enough!" cried Davis. Sophie looked up to see him aiming Wolff's gun at her, one finger poised to pull the trigger. "You're dead, you little—"

The report of a gunshot cut off his words, and Davis

crumpled to the ground, eyes wide, as blood oozed from his upper chest. Zimmer staggered toward them, dragging one injured leg. Sophie scrambled to grab the gun Davis had dropped. Zimmer trained his weapon on Wolff. Sophie heard the sound of running feet.

"Police!"

"It's over, Wolff," Zimmer said. "No matter how rich you are, we've got you now."

Ruben Wolff looked up at Zimmer, his eyes black pools of loathing.

Officers rushed toward them. Two descended on Wolff, wrenching his wrists into handcuffs as he shouted obscenities. Two others hoisted Davis's lifeless body.

Sophie began to shake, cold overtaking her.

Zimmer limped over to her. "Sophie? Are you all right?"

She nodded, suddenly embarrassed, as she realized her chemise was still visible. She grabbed the torn remains of her dress and tried to cover herself, crossing her arms in front of her. Her teeth chattered and her breath came in shaky rasps. A desperate gulp escaped her lips.

Zimmer tugged off his jacket, wincing as he moved closer. He draped it around her, one muscular arm gently encircling her shoulders. "It's okay. You're okay now."

She allowed herself to relax into his embrace for a moment. Then he gave a sharp intake of breath.

She stepped back, recalling the bloodied tear in the thigh of his trousers. "You're hurt," she said. "He shot you."

"I'll be all right," he said.

"What about Sam?" She pulled away from Jacob. "Sam?" she called out. "Are you all right?"

An officer came into view, Sam's limp body cradled in his arms. Sophie's heart thumped. "Is sh-he—"

"He's just unconscious," said the officer. "He'll be fine."

Sophie breathed a sigh. Her right arm began to pulse with

pain, and she couldn't quite remember why. She looked at the officers rushing around, their flashlight beams lighting up the deserted park grounds, checking for more intruders. Two men carrying a stretcher rushed over, and the officer laid Sam across it.

Another officer came up to Jacob. "We only saw the two men, Detective Zimmer." Zimmer nodded.

The officer glanced at Zimmer's bleeding leg. "Medical!" he shouted over his shoulder.

"Just my leg," Zimmer muttered, but Sophie heard the strain in his voice.

"Miss?" the officer turned to her. "Are you hurt?"

"M-my arm," she said, the pain reasserting itself. The officer gently guided her, and they took a few steps toward the waiting police cars.

Two more men rushed forward, carrying a stretcher between them. Over Zimmer's protests, they coaxed him onto the stretcher. Sophie turned to see him lying flat, his blue eyes staring up into hers. She gave him a tremulous smile, then let herself be led away.

33

———————

Sophie stepped through the French doors of Clara's conservatory and into her sunny backyard. A long table covered with an apple-green cloth nestled under the trees, its platters heaped with sandwiches, fruit, and butter cookies. Ellen stood at one end, pouring fresh lemonade into sparkling glasses. A breeze fluttered through the air, ruffling the lavender crepe skirt of Sophie's new dress—a thank-you gift from Clara. A wide lavender ribbon encircled her straw hat, enhanced with sprigs of violets. The only thing that marred the picture of early summer serenity was her plaster-encased right arm, held in place with a white cotton sling.

"Sophie! Lovely to see you, my dear." Clara welcomed her with a gentle hug, careful not to jostle her arm. "I hope you're giving yourself plenty of time to recover."

"I am taking some time off of work, thanks. Just to catch my breath."

Clara gestured to some wicker chairs arranged under a broad, shady tree. "Take a seat next to your aunt, and Ellen will bring you some food. I'll be right back." She went into the house.

Sophie settled into a floral-cushioned chair next to Aunt Lucy.

"You're a heroine, Sophie," said Aunt Lucy, biting into a curried egg sandwich.

"I'm so glad it's over," said Sophie. "It got a little too close for comfort. How is Sam doing?"

"My goodness. She hasn't stopped talking about it, and Harry never tires of hearing the tale. It gets more embroidered with each telling. She had a nasty bruise on her cheek where that monster hit her, but she's bouncing back. Nothing broken, thank heavens." Aunt Lucy's concerned gaze lingered on Sophie's arm, but she didn't mention it.

Sophie looked toward the end of the rolling lawn, where Sam played catch with Dante. It warmed her heart to see Sam acting like an ordinary kid, instead of being run off her feet selling newspapers. Sam still sold them in the evenings for pocket money, but the tension was fading from her eyes, and her cheeks had gotten plumper on Aunt Lucy's cooking. Harry sat on the grass nearby, patiently teaching Agnes to play cat's cradle with a length of string.

Sophie didn't realize how hungry she was until Ellen offered her a generous plate of food. She took it with her left hand and placed it in her lap, then bit into her sandwich. Ellen put a glass of lemonade within easy reach.

"You've been through such an ordeal, Sophie," said Aunt Lucy. "I still can't get over Ruben sneaking away from the Spring Gala to kill Hilda, and then going right back to the party."

"It was cold-blooded indeed," said Sophie with a shiver. "He'd sent that duplicate costume to Mr. Pitman to cover his absence. He was terrified Hilda would reveal to the public how he had cheated her husband out of his brewery."

Sophie took a sip of her lemonade and continued, "He

must have gotten blood on his coat and decided to burn it in an old barrel behind the building. But he didn't have time to wait around for it to burn completely, and that's when Sam found it. She's a heroine too."

Aunt Lucy shook her head. "And then he cast suspicion on Clara by dragging Hilda's body to the suffrage office. Thank goodness you and Detective Zimmer got to the bottom of things."

"The woman who made the costumes, Mrs. Cooper, hasn't turned up yet," said Sophie.

"I expect Detective Zimmer will track her down soon."

Aunt Lucy's gaze traveled to the house, and Sophie looked up to see Clara strolling toward them, her arm linked with that of Jacob Zimmer. He appeared striking in a dark-gray suit with a royal-blue tie, with only a slight limp from his injury. He carried a pie, and Clara led him to the table to deposit it with the rest of the feast and fill a plate with food.

Sophie's heart beat a little faster as they approached. Seeing him must bring back memories of the terrible night at Wolff Park, she surmised.

"Look who I found," Clara said, steering him to the chair next to Sophie. "Detective Zimmer was thoughtful enough to personally return Sophie's costume to me, since he didn't require it for evidence."

Sophie couldn't resist a smug glance in Jacob's direction. Hadn't she told him as much?

"It was kind of you to invite me this afternoon," Jacob said to Clara. "I hope you like apple pie."

"It looks delicious. Please give my thanks to Mrs. Zimmer," said Clara. "Your *mother*." She gave Sophie a quick wink as she said the last, and Sophie felt her cheeks grow hot. "It's so good of you to take care of her. So many bachelors live on their own these days."

"Ah, she keeps me well fed," he said.

"Hello, Detective Zimmer," Sophie said. "I didn't realize you lived with your mother. When I saw you at Wolff Park, I thought you were with your sons."

Jacob chuckled. "No, they're not mine. Mother takes in stray kids around the neighborhood. She loves to feed them and find odd jobs for them. Somehow she roped me into taking them to the park."

Sophie blushed more deeply and took another sip of lemonade.

"How are you feeling, Miss Strong?" he asked her. "Mending all right?"

"The doctor says I'm doing fine," she answered. "I'll have this cast for about six weeks, though. And you? Your—err—injury?" She didn't look at his leg. It wasn't strictly proper for a young lady to mention something as intimate as a man's limb.

"Good as new before long." He cleared his throat. "I have some sobering news to share, though," he said. "Ruben Wolff is dead."

Sophie gasped. "Dead? I thought he was in jail."

"It seems he hanged himself in his cell. Late last night, it must have been."

The ladies were quiet, taking in the announcement.

"How sad," said Aunt Lucy. "His whole life, I mean. With all that money, he could have done so much good, instead of becoming a criminal."

"It is tragic. But Thelma's well rid of him," said Clara. "I wonder what she'll do now that he's gone."

"That would make an interesting story," said Sophie. "Especially if she puts some of her fortune to charitable uses."

"Sophie!" called Sam, running up to her with a wide

smile. "Look, I got my very own baseball mitt. Dante gave it to me."

"You seem to be having fun," said Sophie. "Can you catch?"

"Of course! Well, most of the time." Sam glanced at Zimmer. "Hey, you're the copper."

"Detective Jacob Zimmer," he said, holding out a hand for Sam to shake. "You were quite heroic the other night at Wolff Park."

Sam shrugged.

"It's true, Sam. If you hadn't sent your friend for the police…" Sophie's voice trailed off.

"How did you know to go to the park?" Zimmer asked Sam.

"I saw them take Sophie," Sam said. "So I jumped on the back of the car and rode along."

"Very dangerous," said Zimmer. "But I'm glad you did it, just that one time."

"Apparently Sam had been looking out for me, instead of staying safe and sound at Aunt Lucy's," said Sophie in a chiding tone.

"You needed me. I felt bad for not being there when you got beat up walking home alone," said Sam.

Zimmer gave Sophie a sharp look. "Beat up? What's this?"

Sophie cleared her throat. "Detective Zimmer, why don't you play catch with Sam? If I recall from your performance the *first* time I saw you at Wolff Park, you have a talent for baseball."

Sam looked hopefully at Zimmer. "You can use Dante's mitt."

"I have a hard time saying no to baseball," said Jacob, standing up. As Sam ran ahead, he turned and pointed a warning finger at Sophie. "I have more questions for *you* later."

He tousled Sam's hair as they walked away.

WHEN SOPHIE RETURNED to the *Herald* office, her arm healed, a copy of the paper from two months earlier waited on her desktop, next to a bright bouquet of yellow roses. "Terror at Wolff Park," read the headline. Below it shone the coveted words: "By Sophie Strong." She hadn't been able to type the story with a broken arm, but Ruth had been happy to type for her as she dictated the harrowing events.

"Well, Miss Strong, you did it," said Benjamin Turner. "A front-page story."

She looked up. "Not an easy one to get."

"There will be more, I'm sure. I hope the process is less dangerous next time."

"What about you?" she asked. "How did your undercover mission turn out?"

He smiled enigmatically. "It's not over yet. I just have to shift my plan of attack, now that Wolff is out of the picture."

Questions leaped to Sophie's lips, but she knew better than to ask.

"Good luck," she simply said with a smile.

He nodded and walked jauntily back to his desk. Sophie bent down to smell the flowers, then took her seat. She looked around for a card or note that had accompanied the bouquet, but found nothing. She'd take them home for the boarding house dinner table that night.

Sophie tucked her purse into her drawer and turned to the generous stack of correspondence that awaited her. In her absence, the women's page had featured articles from papers in other cities, along with some half-hearted pieces by her male colleagues. She wondered if they'd appreciate her presence now that she was taking over once more.

She doubted it.

"Strong!" P.J. Barnaby called from his office.

Surprisingly, the familiar bellow warmed her heart. She opened a drawer and pulled out her pencil and notebook. With her head held high, Sophie walked to her editor's office to learn about her next assignment.

HISTORICAL NOTES

Sophie Strong and her world, though fictional, were inspired by the compelling history of early Milwaukee. A long-time fan of historical mystery novels, my goal was to stay as close as possible to historical accuracy without becoming completely absorbed by research (it could go on forever, as any history buff with a laptop well knows). I spent many hours combing through books, articles, and websites on topics ranging from streetcars to restaurant menus to ladies' undergarments. In many cases, once I had absorbed the overall historical tone, I filled in the gaps with my imagination.

After living in or near Milwaukee for twenty-five years, I loved being able to call to mind its striking architecture and landscape while Sophie moved through its streets as an amateur sleuth. Helpful resources for refreshing my memory included *The Making of Milwaukee*, by John Gurda, and the fabulous websites of the Milwaukee County Historical Society and the Wisconsin Historical Society.

Milwaukee is, of course, famous for its breweries, though Wolff Brewery and Wolff Lager are my own creations. I dabbled in the vast amounts of material available on the originators of brews such as Pabst, Blatz, and Schlitz to create the Wolffs and their milieu. When I learned that some breweries established amusement parks around Milwaukee that featured roller coasters, fun houses, and riverboat rides, I knew I wanted to pay homage to them with Wolff Park. Other Milwaukee amusement parks, including one called Wonderland, were modeled after New York's Coney Island, but lacked its endurance. The accounts and photographs in *Entertainment in Early Milwaukee,* by Larry Widen, brought these vintage wonders to life for me.

Sophie begins her adventures in 1912 because I have some familiarity with that period, having written a nonfiction book set in that year. As I noted in *Voyage of Love: 'Abdu'l-Baha in North America,* many issues we grapple with today, including women's rights, racial justice, and immigration, were also hot topics at the start of the last century.

As a feminist, I was fascinated to learn that some women actually opposed the basic human right of suffrage for women before it became a federal law in 1920—a stance that seems unthinkable today. They argued, as does Hilda Rock in my novel, that politics are the province of men, while women are suited to family responsibilities. The debate in chapter one of the novel is adapted from real arguments, some of them advanced by the visionary lawyer and feminist, Belle Case La Follette. She and many other activists worked diligently to promote the 1912 Wisconsin suffrage referendum eagerly awaited by Sophie and her companions. Sources that enlightened me about the women's suffrage movement include *On Wisconsin Women: Working for Their Rights from Settlement to Suffrage,* by Genevieve G. McBride, and *Women Against Equality: A History of the Anti-Suffrage Movement in the United States from 1895 to 1920,* by Anne Myra Benjamin.

Sophie is the sole woman reporter at the fictional

Milwaukee Herald, but a number of female journalists worked at Milwaukee's many newspapers (at one point the city had nine dailies and dozens of weekly papers). For example, Ida Mae Jackson was hired by the *Milwaukee Journal* in 1890—a full twenty-two years before *Strong Suspicions* takes place. Edna Ferber, mentioned in chapter twenty-three, reported for the *Journal* before Sophie's time and went on to become a Pulitzer Prize-winning novelist. Her novel *Dawn O'Hara: The Girl Who Laughed* gave me a glimpse of her professional life, as did her autobiography, *A Peculiar Treasure.* And Edna Dunlop, hired by the *Journal* in 1910, gained fame as the first and only female member of the Milwaukee Press Club until the ridiculously recent date of 1971.

Speaking of newspapers, the women's charity edition, described in the book as engaging the efforts of Aunt Lucy, Clara Elliot, and other characters, is based on fact. A cadre of women took over the *Journal* offices and published a successful newspaper on February 22, 1895. Milwaukee wasn't unique in this regard; charity editions were created by progressive women in over one hundred cities and towns around the country in the 1890s.

Aunt Lucy was inspired by library champion and author Lutie Stearns, who almost single-handedly pioneered a system of 1,400 portable libraries throughout Wisconsin while energetically supporting suffrage. For nearly twenty years, she set up traveling libraries in post offices and general stores around the state and delivered rotating collections of thirty to one hundred books to far-flung Wisconsin communities. Though I don't describe Aunt Lucy's career in depth, it's modeled after that of Ms. Stearns.

Another interesting historical figure is Phoebe Couzins, whose story sparked the creation of Hilda Rock. Couzins was one of the first female lawyers in the U.S. and a public speaker in support of women's rights. However, in 1897, she changed her position on women's suffrage and was employed by the United States Brewers Association to speak *against* suffrage and Prohibition, causes that were often linked. In *Last Call: The Rise and Fall of Prohibition*, Daniel Okrent reports that brewery owner Adolphus Busch personally promised Couzins a lifetime annuity and stated to a colleague, "if ever should it become known that she is in the pay of the brewers...all of her work would be in vain." That intriguing twist of events got my creative juices flowing.

These are just a handful of the resources and that helped me to envision the life of Sophie Strong. Though I did purchase a larger bookshelf, I could only buy a limited number of titles, so I'm indebted to the wonderful librarians at the L.E. Phillips Memorial Public Library for their kind responses to innumerable requests, as well as to friendly professionals at the McIntyre Library.

This research piqued my interest in envisioning Milwaukee of the early 1900s and the rich opportunities it provides for mystery and mayhem. I'm currently at work on the second book in the Sophie Strong series. For updates or to connect with me, sign up for my newsletter at amyrenshawauthor.com. Thanks for reading!

If you enjoyed *Strong Suspicions*, sign up for my newsletter at amyrenshawauthor.com to get the latest updates on the Sophie Strong Mystery Series.

And if you have a moment to spare, please share a short review on the page where you bought the book, to help spread the word. Reviews help new readers to find the series.

To connect, visit @amyrenshawauthor.com on Facebook, or email me at amy@amyrenshawauthor.com.

ACKNOWLEDGMENTS

Writing a novel has been a goal since I discovered Nancy Drew books in first grade. At long last, I'm elated to have done it, with the generous support and encouragement from my friends and family. Many thanks to the Chippewa Valley Writers' Guild and the Kindred Spirits writers' group, especially Yia Lor, Katie Venit, and Anna Loritz. Thank you to the Creme de la Crime writers' group, who welcomed me into the fold and helped me buckle down and finish the manuscript. Since I couldn't buy every title that called to me, I'm indebted to the wonderful librarians at the L.E. Phillips Memorial Public Library for their kind responses to innumerable requests, as well as to friendly professionals at the McIntyre Library.

Deep appreciation goes out to my earliest readers of the complete manuscript: Sarah Edstrom, Susan Engle, Kitty Maddocks, and Donna Price. To Amy Hahn, who encouraged me and reminded me that the practice of any art is akin to worship in the Bahá'í Faith. To my *Brilliant Star* family, who cheered me on and provide a shining example of creativity and service. To Christine Alexander, Sue and Jim Renshaw, and Katie Stoecker for your continuous support. My eternal love and gratitude to my husband, James Neeb, and our young adults, Nora and Lindsey, for your constant encouragement and understanding. And thank you to the many wonderful friends and family members who aren't specifically mentioned here. I'm truly blessed.

ABOUT THE AUTHOR

Amy Renshaw loves writing, reading, and sleuthing about history. She's the Senior Editor at *Brilliant Star Magazine* and *Brilliant Star Online*, award-winning publications by the Bahá'ís of the U.S. Amy lives in Wisconsin, where she hikes in the woods, adores chocolate, and writes novels. She's also the author of the nonfiction historical work, *Voyage of Love: 'Abdu'l-Bahá in North America*, published by Bellwood Press.

www.ingramcontent.com/pod-product-compliance
Lightning Source LLC
Chambersburg PA
CBHW051216190726
48288CB00006B/1977